A Troll Walks into a Bar

This is a work of fiction. Names, characters, organizations, places, events, and incidents are either products of the author's imagination or are used fictitiously. Any resemblance to actual persons, living or dead, or actual events is purely coincidental. With one exception. One of the events in this book, although used fictitiously, is loosely based on an actual historical event. I'll leave it to the reader to discover which one.

Copyright © 2019 Douglas Lumsden
All rights reserved.
ISBN-13: 9781708740801

No part of this book may be reproduced, or stored in a retrieval system, or transmitted in any form or by any means, electronic, mechanical, photocopying, recording, or otherwise, without express written permission of the publisher.

Cover design and art by Arash Jahani (www.arashjahani.com)

A Troll Walks into a Bar

By

Douglas Lumsden

To Rita, for her love, constant support, and enthusiasm

Table of Contents

Chapter One 1
Chapter Two 9
Chapter Three 26
Chapter Four 40
Chapter Five 52
Chapter Six 69
Chapter Seven 80
Chapter Eight 91
Chapter Nine 102
Chapter Ten 114
Chapter Eleven 124
Chapter Twelve 135
Chapter Thirteen 153
Chapter Fourteen 165
Chapter Fifteen 182
Chapter Sixteen 194
Chapter Seventeen 204
Chapter Eighteen 217
Chapter Nineteen 227
Chapter Twenty 237
Chapter Twenty-One 248
Chapter Twenty-Two 259
Chapter Twenty-Three 269
Chapter Twenty-Four 280

Chapter Twenty-Five 295
Epilogue 309

Chapter One

If I had failed to notice that he was packing a quarter of a ton of rock-hard muscle into his seven-and-a-half foot frame, or if I hadn't observed the loose grayish skin that made his face look as if it were made of wet clay, the large close-set ears that rose to a point next to his hairless skull, his blood-red sunken eyes glowing like half-hidden warning lights beneath a stony brow ridge, his predator teeth behind oversized dark ruddy lips, and his large knobby hands with clawed fingers that extended like eight thorny tendrils, I wouldn't have known that he was a troll. Chalk it up to my keen powers of observation.

Everyone in the crowded, noisy Black Minotaur Lounge gawked at him as soon as he entered, and more than a few began to calculate how close they would have to pass by the giant on their way to the exit. I took another sip of cold beer from a still-frozen glass mug and leaned back into the cushioned booth.

The troll stood just inside the front door, puffing on a cigar, and began appraising the room as if he owned the joint. He wore an elegant custom-fitted dark blue pinstriped suit that must have been a size eighty-five. I wondered if he thought that the stripes were slimming. His imperial red tie perfectly complemented his glowing eyes, which pierced through the smoky haze in the dimly lit bar. When those eyes met mine, he gave me a slight nod and walked in my direction. I put my beer down and waited.

It didn't take him long to reach me. No one barred his way.

"Mr. Southerland?" he asked in a deep growling baritone that boomed from the depths of his massive chest.

I didn't answer. He obviously knew who I was.

The troll grunted, looked to his right, and grabbed the back of an empty chair from a nearby table. He pulled it to my booth and sat down with care, testing to see if the chair would hold his weight. I was surprised that it did. Whether he had planned it or not, I was now trapped in the booth. I'm not a small man by any means, a shade over six-foot one and a solid two-ten, but even while seated the troll loomed over me as if I were a child. Leaning toward me, he reached inside his suitcoat and pulled out a troll-sized leather badge holder. He opened it with his thick cable-like fingers, revealing a police detective's badge and an ID. "I'm Detective Stonehammer, YCPD. I need a quick word with you."

I leaned forward and read the ID, making sure to take more time than I needed: Octavian Stonehammer, Detective, Yerba City Police Department, Badge Number 68559. It appeared to be legit. After a few seconds, I sat back and took a sip of brew. Then I looked up and gave the troll a slight nod.

"You don't talk a fuckin' lot, do you," said Detective Stonehammer. I didn't answer, which proved his point, I suppose. He shook his head and sighed, apparently disappointed in my lack of social skills. "That's fine," he growled. "I didn't come here to bump gums anyway, so let's get to it." He paused to make sure he had my attention. He did. "An adaro woman is going to come by your office tomorrow. She will call herself Cora Seafoam. That's not her real name, but it's the one she's going to give you. Blue hair, big tits. Good lookin' dame, like all of those water nymphs. Fuckin' sluts! Anyway, this one's gonna want you to find a missing person."

He blew some cigar smoke into the air, waiting from me to respond. I didn't have anything to say. After a couple of beats, Detective Stonehammer told me, "You're going to turn her down."

I thought about that for a second or two. "How much is she offering?" I asked.

"Doesn't fuckin' matter," said the large detective, "because you ain't taking the job."

"I see," I said, keeping my face blank.

"Do you? Then we're good, right?" Stonehammer's expression told me that he was unconvinced.

I took another swig of beer and placed the mug on the table. I wiped my mouth with a napkin. "I could use a job," I said. "Business is slow. Rent's coming up, and, to be perfectly honest with you, I'm a little tight right now."

"Then maybe you shouldn't be wasting your dough on beer," Stonehammer advised me. His subterranean voice made my teeth rattle. "You've been given fair warning. Are you a smart man? Then you'll take my warning seriously."

"Is this 'warning' coming from you personally, or from the department?" I made air quotes around the word, "warning." To be honest, I was being rude. Generally speaking, pissing off a troll is a terrible idea. It occurred to me that maybe I shouldn't have ordered that third beer. The brew at the Minotaur was famously robust, which was why I liked coming here. But it did have a way of loosening healthy inhibitions at the worst possible times.

Stonehammer's eyes narrowed and burned like smoldering coals. "Maybe you aren't so fuckin' smart after all." He looked me up and down slowly, as if deciding whether there was enough of me for an evening meal. The decision made, he curled his lips into a snarl and growled at me, "Alexander fuckin' Southerland. Fuckin' tough guy. Human." His lips parted, and he showed me his pointed carnivore teeth. I hoped that I didn't look as unnerved as I felt. Stonehammer was a troll and a cop. If he bit off my head on the spot, no one in the place would bat an eye. I, on the other hand, was hard as nails, ruggedly handsome in dim lighting, and impossible to intimidate, or so I kept repeating to myself in my mind while I studied the troll's remarkable teeth.

"Call me Alex," I said, managing to keep my voice from breaking. "All my friends do." I didn't think the troll was going to be my friend.

But after a few long seconds, Stonehammer relaxed and eased back into his chair, which strained under his weight. He took a puff of his cigar and began looking around the room, eyeing the clientele with casual interest. It was an interesting crowd. Mostly human, of course, but a nice variety. A lot of business professionals smoking cigarettes and sipping cocktails after a hard day of, well, business. A dozen or so college-aged men and women passing around joints and dispersing enough pheromones throughout the room to make a eunuch punch a hole through a concrete wall. Some middle-aged working folks sizing each other up for possible later entertainment in quieter venues. A few non-humans, too: three well-dressed gnomes sitting in a corner at the far end of the room, toking hashish from water pipes, their fat ruby rings, polished pearl belt buckles, and grandiose diamond stickpins attesting to their obvious prosperity; two lovely and ageless water sprites wearing next to nothing and attracting the attention of a fortyish family man in the throes of a midlife crisis; and, at the end of the bar tossing back thick brown ales, two hulking gentlemen who I'd bet anything spent at least a couple nights a month running on all fours and howling at the moon. In other words, a typical weekday evening at the Black Minotaur.

"Nice place," said Stonehammer. "First time here. It's got a nice atmosphere. A nice--what do you call it? A nice ambience."

"Yeah," I said. "The beer's cold, too."

He looked back at me, his body relaxed, just two good ol' boys getting to know each other at the friendly neighborhood watering hole. He puffed on his cigar and blew smoke into the air above my head. "You did your mandatory stint for the state, didn't you?"

"Yeah," I confirmed. "Three years in the service of the Realm of Tolanica, just like every good citizen."

"Two years fighting Lord Ketz-Alkwat's war in the Borderland against the Qusco-backed insurgents and one year as a military cop at a base back home, that right?"

"Close enough."

"Earned some hardware, too, I hear."

I shrugged.

"Yeah, you're a decorated soldier, honorably discharged. Then you land here in Yerba City, get yourself an investigator's license, and start operating as a private snoop."

I guess he'd done his homework.

He leaned toward me again, biting down on his cigar. Through clenched teeth, he said, "So why didn't you become a cop? You know, a real one. Hell, the department always has room for a former army grunt, especially an M.P."

"What can I tell you, Detective Stonehammer," I said. "That I prefer a moderate degree of freedom to floundering helplessly through a miasma of officious bureaucracy and corruption?"

Stonehammer sat up a bit, removed his cigar from his mouth, and breathed smoke toward my face. "Lord's balls, man! 'A miasma of...what? Th'fuck you comin' off with that crap! You trying to impress the silly troll with your... erudition? You like that word? 'Erudition'? Didn't think I could drop such a fancy fuck-ass word like that on you, didja!" He snorted, a chilling sound that could have preceded an attack from a wild boar. "You humans. You can't help thinking of trolls as a bunch of Hell-spawned ignoramuses. Nothing but dumb-ass monsters."

"Not you, sir." I said. "You're an articulate gentleman."

"Fuckin'-A," he responded. "Make a good living, too. Enough to live in style. Fuckin' custom-made suits and sweet rides. You should see what I've got parked outside." He leaned in again, plopping a pair of gargantuan arms on the table. "So how 'bout you? What are you now, about thirty?"

"Thereabouts."

He shook his head. "You can't be making much jack in private investigation. Full grown adult, slaving away for chump change. In today's Tolanica, if you don't have money, you're nobody. A loser. A chump. The department takes good care of me, and an ambitious cop who knows the ropes can make a lot of extra scratch. I'm somebody in this city. You? You're what I scrape off my shoe."

The big troll was on a roll now, and he wasn't about to stop. "Private snoop," he scoffed. "Crummy, filthy work. Most of it is divorce shit, am I right? You peep through a lot of windows? Catch 'em in the act? Snap a lot of pics? Keep a lot of copies for yourself, I'll bet. Perks of the job, right?" He licked his lips and leered at me around his cigar. You've never lived until a troll has leered at you. Makes you wish you were big enough to punch him in the mouth.

I kept my eyes on his, keeping my emotions in check and hoping that he wouldn't notice the subtle way that while he'd been busting my chops for no good reason I'd been pushing condensation off my beer glass and slowly tracing out lines on the table-top—seemingly at random—but actually in a pattern that was familiar to someone like me.

"I get it," I said to him. "You're a big deal."

"And you're a fuckin' sap." His face lit up with a satisfied smirk. "Yeah, you've got it all right. I've got dough, and plenty of it. I'm welcome in all the best places in this city. And poor scum like you do what I tell them to do."

"So what you're telling me," I said, "is that when an adaro calling herself Cora Seafoam comes to me with a job offer, I should turn it down."

Streams of smoke from around the room began to gather over our heads, and the haze above us began to thicken. I hoped that the troll hadn't noticed.

"What I'm telling you," Stonehammer said, spacing out his words to make sure that I understood each of them, "is that when the nymph offers you a job, you *will* gracefully decline. And if, out of a plethora of stubborn resolve, you decide to take the job, despite my fair and friendly warning...." He paused for a full second. "You will quickly come to understand that my fair and friendly warning was fuckin' serious." The underlying threat in his message was unmistakable.

I nodded. "I think we're on the same page here."

The troll's face brightened. "Good," he said, climbing to his feet. I imagined that I could hear his chair breathe a sigh of relief. Stonehammer tossed the stub of his cigar to the floor, reached inside his suit coat, and pulled out a card. "Glad we had this talk. Don't hesitate to call me if you have any questions." He flipped the card in my direction. I picked it off the tabletop and put it in my shirt pocket.

Suddenly, Stonehammer reached across the table and grabbed my beer mug, which disappeared into his vast hand. He drew it to his mouth and drained the brew like it was a shot of whiskey. "Lord's balls!" he grunted, staring at the mug. "Not much to this carbonated piss-water, is there. Humans don't know shit about beer. You should try some of the brew that *my* people make. You couldn't handle it, but at least you'd fuckin' die happy." He placed the mug squarely on top of the sigil that I had traced on the tabletop. Then he slid the mug back and forth across the sigil, obliterating it. He glanced up and watched the smoke above our heads dissipate, as if disturbed by a sudden gust of wind.

The detective gave me a trollish sneer. "Nice try," he said, and placed a gigantic paw on my shoulder. His claws sliced through my shirt and undershirt and pierced the surface of the skin beneath. He flashed me a knowing smile and shook his head. Then he released my shoulder, leaving four tiny bloodstains on my shirt, and turned to go. "Have a nice fuckin' evening," he rumbled. Straightening his tie, he ambled across the room like a boss, large and in charge. He favored the sprites with a broad smile as he passed them, pushed open the front door, and, ducking under the doorway, disappeared into the street.

***

Detective Stonehammer was a clever troll, but he wasn't quick enough. He had seen right through my surreptitious attempt to summon an elemental, and by erasing the sigil I had traced on the tabletop he thought he had succeeded in thwarting my spell. But his desire to show me what a big shot he was compared to me, a mere self-employed human without enough sense to strive for money and style, had caused him to wait a few seconds too long before acting. Air elementals are difficult to see in the best of conditions, and the one I had summoned was small and practically invisible in the haze that floated above the crowd in the Minotaur. As the front door closed behind Detective Stonehammer, the elemental floated down from the shadowy rafters of the ceiling and hovered in the air a few inches above my tabletop.

The air spirit manifested itself as a tiny slow-moving whirlwind, maybe two inches tall. Elementals like this one were intelligent to a point. They understood simple instructions from their summoners and would follow them without question as long as they didn't feel threatened or inconvenienced.

"You saw the big fellow?" I asked.

"Yes. Troll," the elemental affirmed in a trembling whisper.

"Follow him. Stay out of sight. Tell me if he meets anyone or talks to anyone. Listen in and remember any conversations. Find me at dawn and tell me what you remember. Go. Hurry!"

The elemental grew taller and thinner, bent toward the door, and whisked itself away, disappearing from view in an instant. I didn't know if I would get anything useful from the little air spirit, but it didn't hurt to try.

A waitress came by, picked up my empty mug, and asked if I wanted another. I told her to bring me a cola, instead. I had a lot to think about, and some caramel-flavored cocaine-laced carbonated sugar-water was just what I needed to jolt my brain into gear.

Chapter Two

I woke up in my own bed at the crack of dawn with a searing headache, a queasy gut, and a two-inch whirlwind floating over my chest. Not all of my days start this well.

The little elemental was anxious to finish its job so that it could go do whatever shit elementals do when they are not rudely yanked away by two-bit summoners like me, but I wasn't quite ready to engage my brain. The little guy could wait a bit. I was the master and it was the servant, right? So I told it to chill, and headed to the bathroom.

Summoning is a skill that only a chosen few can learn. You have to be born with the gift, though the gift seems to choose when to show itself. Sometimes it takes its own sweet time, arriving so late in a person's life that it's nothing but a frustration. Like any skill, the technique for summoning and controlling nature spirits takes time and attention to develop, and if you've lived most of your life without the skill then there isn't much you can do with it once it comes to you. In my case, however, I don't remember a time when I wasn't sending off little swirling winds to annoy my family and friends. After a few slaps across the chops from my father, some whacks to the head with a hairbrush from my mother, and some memorable ass whoopings from my friends, I learned the value of restraint. The gift can be a son of a bitch if you let it. School taught me how to communicate with air elementals well enough to make the gift useful. Maybe I could have done more with my gift if I had been a better student, but, according to my teachers, I "lacked focus." I prefer to think that I simply didn't respond to their teaching methods. Maybe some people are motivated to achieve by beatings, electric shock, and waterboarding, but that sort of thing just tends to piss me off. Fuck 'em. I learned what I felt I needed to learn and then went on with my life.

School also revealed my limitations with elementals. I can easily control the small-fry. The medium sized require more of my strength, and dealing with them is often a challenging battle of wills. The greater forces, however, ignore me with impunity. They don't tend to take it well if I poke at them, either, so I can forget about summoning significant wind storms, much less tornados. Sky-related phenomena like lightning or atmospheric composition are likewise safe from my manipulations. Also, I can meddle with the air, but earth, fire, and water elementals are outside my skillset. Some people are gifted with the ability to control more than one type of elemental, or with truly powerful spirits. Some are gifted with some degree of power over all four classifications of elementals. The seven Dragon Lords who rule the seven realms of the world are said to be able to control all of the spirits of nature, large and small, regardless of type, though I don't know for sure if that's true. Hopefully, I'll never have to find out. I'm far beneath their notice and plan to keep it that way. Like I said, I learned my limitations in school, and most of the time I'm content to live within them.

Besides, if you are a human who depends too much on summonings, or magic of any kind, you'll never develop your *true* gift: your ability to think. My experience has taught me that humans have this gift in greater abundance than any of the world's other intelligent species, including elves, though I have to admit that everything I know about elves comes from history books, fantasy novels, bedtime stories, and rumors. Elves were supposed to be the oldest, wisest, cleverest species of intelligent creatures on earth. They are depicted in official histories as devious masters of ancient magical knowledge. But the way I see it, if the elves had been so fucking smart, they would never have launched the Great Rebellion against the Dragon Lords back in early days of history. Humans had more sense. They knew a lost cause when they saw one. Human leaders took a good look at the Dragon Lords—immortal unkillable hundred-foot flying fire-breathing masters of magic who supposedly emerged from a mythical underworld realm called Hell—and agreed to fight for them against the armies of elf insurgents. Smart move. The Dragon Lords won, humans still thrive, more or less, under Dragon Lord rule, and the elves were slaughtered. Today, they are all but extinct. Tough break, but they brought it on themselves.

I emerged from the bathroom in better shape than I had entered it. The elemental was waiting for me as patiently as it could, whirling near the ceiling above my bed. Anxious to deliver its report, it lowered itself to my shoulder and, without further prompting, began speaking to me in a quick breezy whisper.

"This one followed troll to metal box that moves. Troll opened door and went in. This one went in, too, and hid from troll on floor behind troll's chair. It was dark. This one could hear troll, but this one couldn't see troll. Troll talked. Here's what troll said: 'Hi, it's me.... Yeah, I found him and warned him off. I don't know if it took, though.... Yeah, well, he seems like a real asshole, so who knows.... Yeah.... Sounds about right.... Yeah.... Okay, Captain. See you in the morning.'"

"Captain," I said.

"That's what troll said."

"All right—what else?"

"Metal box began to move away. Troll didn't talk anymore. This one stayed in darkness. After long time, metal box stopped moving. Troll walked out door and this one followed. This one was in place where this one had never been. Troll entered wooden building and closed door. This one stayed outside building and watched troll through glass square. Troll ate food, drank liquid, and slept. This one floated in air currents with others like this one until dawn. This one followed bond that links this one to master and found master in this place."

"Was there anyone with the troll?" I asked.

"No," the elemental whispered. "Troll was alone."

"Could you find that wooden building again?" I asked.

"Yes."

"Can you tell me where it is?"

The elemental's whirling motion slowed, but it didn't speak at first. Then it said, "This one doesn't know how to tell master. This one could go there and master could follow."

"Hmm," I said. "Not now." I reached into a drawer in a table near my bed and pulled out a notepad and a pen. I sketched a sigil on the pad. "I'm going to name you in case I need to summon you again. Do you remember the crowded place where I found you last night?"

"Yes. That is where this one is when this one is not called to be elsewhere."

Interesting, I thought. The little nature spirit must have some sort of connection with the smoke-filled haze inside the Black Minotaur. "I'm naming you Smokey," I said, and I drew his new name into my sigil. Assigning a name was a convenient way to tag a specific elemental that I had previously worked with. I could then summon that same elemental again and tell it to repeat a complex task that I had given it before, rather than having to start from scratch with an "untrained" spirit. By drawing a name into my sigil, I could now use the sigil to summon this particular air elemental—Smokey—the next time I needed it to find and observe Stonehammer, or to lead me to Stonehammer's house.

"Smokey," the elemental whispered slowly, embracing the new name. A tiny spark flashed inside the whirling wind for just an instant, and the elemental stretched itself upwards so that for a moment it was a little taller and a little thinner. Then it returned to normal. It was tagged now, and as long as it was in range, I had easy access to this tiny elemental.

I considered Smokey's report, such as it was. All in all, I was lucky. On the previous night, I had only had the time and the focus for a quick generic summoning spell designed to attract the nearest air elemental in the vicinity. Not all elementals are as reliable or articulate as Smokey had proved itself to be. The little spirit hadn't given me much, but it had revealed a couple of pieces of information that were potentially useful. Stonehammer had clearly been talking on his phone to a "captain," and this captain was the one giving the troll his instructions. Yerba City is a good sized metropolis. There are twenty-seven captains in the YCPD, but Detective Stonehammer had most likely called his own captain, and it wouldn't be hard to identify him or her, what with me being an experienced investigator and all. Stonehammer had essentially been an errand boy, sent by his captain to intimidate me and keep me from interfering with... something. I could work with this info.

"Okay, Smokey, you did good. I release you from your service to me until I call again. And stop calling me master. From now on call me Alex."

"Alll-eksss," the elemental breathed, as if testing the name. Then the newly dubbed Smokey stretched itself upward and curled toward my half-open bedroom window before streaking through it and vanishing into the morning.

***

Today was Tuesday. If what Stonehammer had told me was true, I was going to receive a visitor to my office today, a visitor who wanted to hire me to find a missing person. Would I accept the job? Stonehammer had pretty much ordered me to turn it down, but, like he told his captain, I can be an asshole. Was I willing to defy a five-hundred-pound troll, especially one running interference for a YCPD captain? Being an asshole is one thing, but being a dead asshole didn't sound like a good career move. No, someone else would have to find the adaro's missing person.

Suddenly, a slight fluttering began to tickle the inside of the back of my neck. It was a familiar, soft, niggling sensation that I knew all too well and hated with a passion. I knew that it was going to land me in a world of shit. I'd felt it all my life, this tiny prickling that constantly got me into trouble, sometimes big trouble. It provoked me. It goaded me. It nagged at me with annoying questions: "Why...," and "How...," and "What's around that corner...," and "How bad would it be if I...," and "What would happen if I...." This time the feeling solidified into "Why does a police captain want to scare me away from this adaro?"

"Stop it!" I shouted out loud. "Go away!" I vigorously rubbed the back of my neck, as if that would drive the tingling away. It didn't. It never does.

Okay, I thought to myself. I'll at least listen to the lady. I never said that I wouldn't at least listen. Listening won't hurt anything. Right?

Right.

***

I showered, shaved, and dressed for business. For me, that means a clean, cheap navy blue suit, a white shirt, and a plain dark tie, dark socks, and a pair of real leather shoes. Unlike most men, I don't wear a hat. What's the point? Hats are an unnecessary expense, easily misplaced or lost, and my head, topped by a thick layer of well-behaved brown hair, is fine without one. When it comes to professional attire, my only concerns are that potential clients find me somewhat presentable, and that I don't stand out in a crowd. I never own more than one suit at a time, and when it is inevitably damaged, or wears out, I always buy its replacement at a second-hand shop down the street. Shoes are the exception. I never skimp on shoes. My footwear has to be light, comfortable, and durable.

I didn't feel like eating anything that morning, and I decided to head down to my office. It wouldn't take me long to get there. It was just down the stairs.

I live and work in an innocuous two-story stand-alone rental a couple of blocks away from the fashionable sections of downtown Yerba City. My apartment, mathematically large enough for one human male to eat, sleep, and take care of his personal hygiene, is upstairs. It consists of a bedroom with an attached bath-slash-shower room, a small living room, and an even smaller kitchen area. My business office is downstairs. The office has just enough room for a desk, a faux-leather desk chair, some metal filing cabinets, a small office safe, and a water cooler with a heavy five-gallon glass tank that you have to flip over so that the water drains through a narrow bottleneck into a dispenser. A couple of reasonably clean cloth-covered chairs suitable for clients sit on the guest side of the desk. No houseplants. I don't have an assistant, either. I'm capable of answering my own phone, keeping my own books, and typing on my own computer. Besides, there isn't room for anyone else. My private investigator's license hangs on one wall, and that's the extent of my decorating.

A door that I rarely use leads out of one side of my office, through a short hallway, and then through another door that opens into an alleyway behind my humble quarters. I like having a back way out in case of an emergency or an unwanted guest. Anyone coming to see me can enter through the front door, which leads directly into my office. Attached to the outside of this door is a small professionally printed sign that says, "Alex Southerland, Private Investigator." No logo. Below this sign is a rectangular card hanging on a string. On one side, it says, "Closed." The other side says "Enter." Welcome to my command center.

I like to think of myself as a useful resource. I have picked up some valuable skills and the tenacity (or maybe just plain stubbornness) to carry a job through to the end, even when faced with formidable obstacles. People hire me to find things, or to find other people. Businesses give me freelance contracts to do deeper background checks than most human resource departments are willing to do. I do legwork for a couple of lawyers, and, every once in a while, I do some undercover work for clients who need to know what's happening in places they can't go. I've discovered scammers and embezzlers, revealed swindles, cons, and frauds, and I once tracked down a prowling incubus. Some of my clients operate outside the law, but most of them have clean respectable jobs, even if they don't always behave like honest citizens. My work offers variety, and though it can be tedious, I find it fulfilling and meaningful most of the time. Detective Stonehammer's accusations aside, I don't do divorce work. Well, unless the state of my finances compels me to, but that's not often, and I stop short of snooping outside of windows. I've been in business for seven years, and, while not every case results in a desirable outcome, I get by all right.

Lately, though, business had been slow. In fact, I hadn't worked a case in weeks, which was unusual for me, but not unheard of. Sometimes it's like that. Problem was, my rent was coming due in a few days. I had a good working relationship with my landlady—Mrs. Colby—and I wanted to keep it that way. Mrs. Colby had lived on this earth for seventy-five years, and she gave the impression that she was tough enough to stick around for another seventy-five. Her face might be wrinkled, but she had a trim figure and perfect posture, and her brain was sharp enough to slice through a floating silk scarf. I met her grandson, Clint, in the army, and we became friends. Once, when we both had a three-day leave, Clint took me to his grandmother's home in the central Great Plains for what he promised would be a meal I'd never forget. He'd been right. Mrs. Colby's culinary skills were out of this world. She did things with noodles, tomatoes, garlic, onions, pork, cheese, honey, and some herbs she refused to identify that would make a five-star chef leap out of a ninth-floor window in shame. And Mrs. Colby herself was a delight. She could enthrall the most world-weary government clerk with her genteel manners and sweet, sweet smiles, and she could reduce a stonehearted loan shark to a puddle of cold sweat with her ferocious obscenity-laden tongue-lashings. Clint didn't make it back from the Borderland, and I made sure to call on Mrs. Colby after I was discharged.

That's when I learned that Mrs. Colby owned rental properties in scattered parts of the country, including one in Yerba City that happened to be vacant. She told me that she would rent the place to me at less than market value if I would help her with a problem she was having. She said that a man named Crawford had applied to rent one of her other Yerba City properties, a place in the Placid Point district, and turn it into a second-hand jewelry and novelty shop. He seemed like a nice, ordinary middle-aged man, she said, but, while he appeared to be solid enough on the surface, her instincts told her that he was hiding something. She asked me to do some investigative work and see what I could dig up. She even offered to give me some expense money up front. I had returned to the country with no firm plans, so, under the circumstances, it was too good a deal to pass up. In fact, it sounded like fun. I rented some computer time in a library, did a little traveling, looked up the right people, asked a few questions, and I uncovered Crawford's secret. Crawford was a were-rat. He appeared to be a normal human, but when he wanted to, he could transform himself into a swarm of rats. That turned out to be the beginning of my career as a private investigator.

 I told Mrs. Colby what I had discovered about Crawford, and she surprised me by renting him the property anyway. She later said that he was the quietest tenant she ever had, and that he never failed to pay his rent on time. After I formally established my business in Yerba City, I made a point of looking Crawford up and having lunch with him. He turned out to be a decent guy, if a bit twitchy. I was a little envious of his special ability, which would be pretty handy in my line of work. Rats can go just about anywhere, and they see everything. The ability comes with a cost, though. Too many people have a knee-jerk prejudice against were-rats, and it says a lot about Mrs. Colby that, after finding out his secret, she rented property to him without thinking any more about it. I might not be as quiet as Crawford, who spends all day in his modest little shop and patters through alleys a few nights every month, but I didn't want to be any less diligent about paying my rent.

 I descended into my office at 7:58 in the morning, unlocked and opened the front door, and turned the card to Enter. Four minutes later, the door handle turned, and a lady walked in. Showtime.

Stonehammer had described Cora Seafoam as a "good looker." The adaro in my office met that description and then some. The type of man who falls helplessly in love with every gorgeous female he runs across might have been momentarily dumbfounded by the way her silk ankle-length sky-blue dress clung to her enticing body and emphasized all the traditional female features that most men find attractive. Such a man would have found himself wanting to reach up and caress the smooth skin of her flawless face, the color of coffee and cream, enhanced by a small dark brown freckle just to the right of her delicate nose. A man lacking in willpower might have found himself drowning in the mysterious depths of her stunning blue eyes, eyes that held secrets begging to be discovered. He might have felt obligated to release her shimmering dark royal blue hair from the loose bun that kept it from falling freely past her neck and shoulders. He would certainly have been drawn to her full, vulnerable lips, dark brown and craving to be kissed. He might have found himself unable to resist the unspoken invitation to run his hands slowly down the soft curves of her—

"Mr. Southerland?"

As a trained professional, I, of course, was immune to such thoughts. Uh-huh. Adaros, often impolitely referred to as "nymphs," are seductive by nature. It's a survival trait. That's my excuse for gaping open-mouthed at my visitor like a teenaged boy with raging hormones. I stood, hoping that my legs wouldn't fail me, and indicated a chair. "Please." I said, "Have a seat."

She did so.

"Can I get you coffee?" I asked. She shook her head, and I sat as well, earning thanks from my trembling knees.

My name is Cora Seafoam," the adaro said in a low pleasant voice that reminded me somehow of gentle swells in the middle of the ocean. "I'd like you to find my sister."

Miss Seafoam sat facing me in my client's chair. She held an expensive-looking silver purse in her lap, gripping it with her two gloved hands as if the purse might jump away at any moment and race around the room. She regarded me with wide eyes and tried to radiate a relaxed confidence that I didn't believe she felt. For my part, I'm pretty sure that I only glanced for the briefest moment at the swell of her breasts exposed by her dress's low-cut cleavage before raising my eyes to her own, which were beseeching, moist, and lovely.

I nodded. "Go on, Miss Seafoam."

"Please, Mr. Southerland, call me Cora. My sister's name is Mila, and I think she's in trouble." Cora sucked at her plump bottom lip in a way that was probably unconscious. Pretty effective, though. I nodded at her to continue.

"I know where she is going to be tonight, and I'd like you to find her and bring her back to me. Can you do it?" She parted her lips in a way that no doubt caused most of the men in her life to fall on their backs, curl up their arms and legs, and show their bellies.

I regarded her luscious lips and the tiny pointed teeth behind them a little longer than I should have, but, as I said, business had been quiet lately and I didn't have anything else demanding my attention at the moment.

"Let's slow down a little, Miss Seafoam," I said, steadying my breathing.

"Cora, please," she corrected me.

"Okay, Cora, why don't you tell me how you came to me. I don't advertise, and almost all of my new business comes to me by word of mouth. Did someone refer you to me?"

"I... yes..., but if you don't mind I'd rather not say who it was. Let's just say that you were highly recommended as a man who could get things done."

I frowned at this. There were reasons why she might want to keep my advocate's name secret, but I couldn't think of any that I liked.

"All right," I said. "Let's put that aside for now. Now you say that your sister—Mila—is missing. When did you last see her?"

"About a week ago," she said.

"Does she live with you?" I asked.

"No," the adaro answered. "Our circumstances are quite different. She's a bit... wild, but the two of us are close and keep in close touch. It's not uncommon for her to disappear for a day or two, but we usually find a way to stay in contact. Lately, though, she's been associating with a rough group of... acquaintances, and I think that they are dragging her into something dangerous. In fact, I'm sure of it."

I grunted, just to be making a noise. "Can you be a little more specific?"

"These people she's been hanging out with are criminals. Humans. I... I think that they are dealers in black-market drugs." The adaro looked up and fixed me with her mesmerizing eyes. "I don't want to judge my sister too harshly. I don't want to interfere in her life if she's happy. You don't know what it's like for people like us in the city. She lives in the adaro settlement. Our natural home is the open ocean, but, as you know, it's been a long time since we could live there peacefully. We try to get by as best we can, but the crowded streets of a big city are no place for water folk. I'm afraid that my sister has had to engage in some unseemly behavior in order to survive."

I nodded. The fate of the adaros was a well-known story. The adaros formed thriving civilizations in the oceans long before humans climbed down from the trees, and they blossomed and prospered through several ages of earth's history. After the Great Rebellion, the Dragon Lords turned humans loose on the oceans. In time, the oceans were mapped, partitioned, and exploited in the name of progress and wealth. The adaros, along with other saltwater folk, were in the way.

At first glance, an adaro appears to be human. A more intimate look reveals otherwise. Miss Seafoam wore a slivery blue scarf around her neck, and I knew that if she removed that scarf she would expose two feathery gills on either side of the base of her neck. Adaros are amphibious, and they can live indefinitely under the surface of the oceans. Adaros differ from humans in other ways, too. Only about one out of ten adaros are male, and, in the water, they are terrifying! For centuries, sailors feared the ferocious adaro men more than they feared any living creature. A single adaro man could bring down a wooden sailing ship and send its crew to a watery grave. The steel ships of the twentieth century, however, proved to be too much for the adaros, and in the past fifty years modern armored warships have systematically hunted out and destroyed all of the known adaro strongholds. Only a fraction of the adaro people survived the destruction of their homes.

Naval officials from all seven realms herded the female adaro survivors into settlements in coastal cities and declared them to be a "protected species," which means that they live without the benefits of citizenship. The remaining adaro men retreated to remote sanctuaries hidden in the depths of the oceans. They sneak ashore every once in a while in order to visit their female population, but they mostly stay out of sight. I've heard that if an adaro man spends too much time out of water he weakens and dies, but I don't know if that's true. What I *do* know is that the adaro women have had a difficult time adapting to life on land. Freshwater nature spirits, such as the naiads, have adjusted to the changing world well enough. Many of them live good lives in the cities, as long as they are within easy reach of fresh water. But most of the adaro women live in poverty. The lucky ones find employment as house servants or in respectable hospitality work. More of them, however, are forced into the sex trades. Far too many simply waste away in the slum housing of the adaro settlements, unnoticed and disregarded.

A few adaro women have risen above the life of servitude and destitution. I regarded the attractive woman sitting across from me, dressed in more money than I made in an average month. Maybe she was a successful entrepreneur. Maybe she was a doctor, or a lawyer, or a CEO. But I didn't think so. I guessed that she was most likely either employed in the high end of the sex trade, or that she was attached in some way to a wealthy sponsor. Yeah, I was stereotyping. I call it playing the odds. And I knew that tattooed across her left wrist underneath her expensive pearl-colored glove was a string of numbers, and that a government official with access to an interrealm data base could use that number to open a file containing Miss Seafoam's real name, along with other identifying information, including her police record if she had one. Miss Seafoam might be living a life of luxury, but she was still an unfree refugee.

With these thoughts in mind, I shrugged at Cora. "Why not go to the police?" I asked.

"The police," Cora scoffed with what sounded like genuine malice. "How much time and effort do you think they would expend to find a missing adaro?" She dropped her eyes and then raised them to meet mine again. "Please, Mr. Southerland. Mila is in real danger, I know it. The police won't help me. Won't you? Money isn't an issue. I assure you that I can cover your fees and all of your expenses. There may be some danger involved, and I can add whatever bonus you think is appropriate."

I could feel my stone heart threatening to melt, but I kept my voice neutral. "Let's not worry about fees right now. You said that you know where she is going to be tonight?"

"Yes," she said. "Tonight at midnight. She's going to be with her friends at the old Placid Point Pier. That's the one they haven't used since they built the new Placid Point Pier further down the peninsula. I... I think they are going to do some kind of deal with one of the gangs in that area, a gang called the Claymore Cartel. I don't know much, but the last time I talked to Mila I got the impression that her...friends...had somehow acquired a large amount of drugs, and they were going to trade them to the Claymore Cartel for weapons." Cora reached up and gently wiped the corner of her mouth with a delicate gloved finger. "I'm worried, Mr. Southerland. I don't know what Mila is getting into, and I don't think she does, either. I don't mean to imply that all humans are untrustworthy, or that they are worse than other creatures, but Mila is young, and she doesn't understand humans like I do. My people have a saying: 'too far from the shore.' I think that Mila is a long way from the shore, and I'm scared for her."

When she stopped speaking, I remained silent for a while, gazing off into nothing. The story she was giving me was plausible, but it left me feeling vaguely unsettled. "What exactly do you want me to do?" I asked finally.

"I want you to find Mila and get her away from there. I want you to bring her back to me."

"You want me to kidnap her," I stated.

"I'd prefer it if you could talk her into coming with you willingly. Tell her how foolishly she is acting. Tell her I'm worried about her."

I smiled at her. "Really? You think that would do it? A man she's never met comes to her at midnight while she's engaged in criminal activity with her friends, asks her nicely to please come with him, and she'll shrug her shoulders and accompany him without making a fuss?"

"Then take her by force if you have to!" Cora gripped her purse so hard that her knuckles threatened to pop through her gloves, and a tear began to trickle from one eye.

"Hmm," I said. "While surrounded by her friends and in front of a bunch of gangstas. Drugs and weapons all around."

"Please, Mr. Southerland," Cora wiped her tear away. "I know it won't be easy, but that's the kind of thing you do, isn't it? I'm told you're a clever man. Can't you figure out a way?"

I resumed staring off into an imaginary distance while she fidgeted.

"Do you have a picture of Mila?" I asked her after a long pause.

"I have one on my phone," she said. "I can send it to you."

I gave her my number, and a few seconds later I was looking at the face of a pretty adaro girl on my screen. She looked to me like a younger, less troubled, and considerably more unkempt version of Cora. I laid my phone on my desk and sat back in my chair, thinking.

After several long moments I said, "See, here's the thing. You come to me out of nowhere. You won't say who referred you to me. You entice me with the promise of a lot of money. You give me a story that sounds like a setup for a cheesy movie. Drugs, gangs, weapons? A midnight meeting at the 'old pier'? You want me to kidnap your sister, which, last I checked, is a major crime."

"No!" Cora interrupted, shaking her head. "That's not what I'm saying. I just want you…"

"Okay, right," I interrupted. "We'll do it your way. You heard that I was a knight in shining armor, and you want me to heroically whisk an innocent damsel in distress from the midst of danger. And then you give me a picture of someone who looks an awful lot like you about five years ago. Do you even have a sister? Is she real, or are you pulling me into something you're not willing to tell me about."

Cora seemed to shrink. She opened her mouth to speak, but I waved my hand in the air dismissively. "And even if you are on the up-and-up, I don't know what you were told about me, or what you may think you know about private investigators in general, but I'm sorry. I'm no hero. I'm not a guy who willingly walks into danger with as little as you've offered me."

"I'll double your usual fee," Cora implored, misunderstanding my meaning. "I'll pay whatever it takes, Mr. Southerland. Please…."

"It's not a matter of money, Miss Seafoam." I shook my head. "I'm sorry. I'm afraid I won't be able to help you. I'll see you out."

I stood and moved for the door. When I got halfway, I stopped and waited for her. She hesitated for a moment, her face a mask of confusion, and then stood abruptly. She swept past me, giving me a look meant to ignite my blood and send it shooting out my eyes and ears. She reached the doorway, stopped, and turned. She regarded me with sad, defeated eyes, her shoulders sagging. "I made a mistake coming to you, Mr. Southerland. You are not at all the man I hoped you would be. You've been rude and dismissive, and I still need help. I hope you are pleased with yourself."

She opened the door, stepped through, and closed it gently behind her.

I didn't feel particularly noble about giving the bum's rush to the lovely Cora Seafoam. It wasn't just that her story didn't add up. It was more that Miss Seafoam was being less than honest with me, and I'm not fool enough to take dangerous cases when I'm being fed a bunch of hooey. I also felt manipulated. It's not that I'm prejudiced against adaros, but, as I said, they are naturally seductive, probably an evolutionary development having to do with the extreme discrepancy in numbers between males and females. The adaro females needed some powerful natural tools to attract the few males in their communities. These tools worked on human men, too, as I could now personally attest. Dealing with an adaro woman requires a firm grip on one's emotions and an extra-heavy dose of skepticism.

And let's not forget that Detective Stonehammer had most assuredly threatened me with harm—serious bodily harm at the very least—if I pursued this case. Not that I was afraid of that mountainous bastard. Not me. That wasn't it. No one tells Alex Southerland when to stand up and when to lay down, not even a troll with a badge. The case was bullshit, and that's all there was to it. Fuck Stonehammer and fuck the rest of Yerba City's finest!

So why didn't I feel better about walking away from this case? Why was I feeling like I had screwed up?

Chapter Three

I decided that I needed to get away for a while and clear my head. I walked out of my office and into the morning fog that had swept in off the Nihhonese Ocean during the night. I kept a nine-year-old plum-colored four-door sedan parked in a small pay lot just up the street. Nothing fancy, but it got me where I wanted to go. I walked to the lot, got into my car, and drove it for about an hour or so, turning corners at random, and running the wipers from time to time to scrape the accumulated mist off my windshield. As I maneuvered through the city traffic, I brooded over my meetings with Stonehammer and Seafoam. I was on the edge of something, and I didn't know what it was. The best thing I could have done about it was nothing, but I was having a hard time with that. Part of it was that nagging tickle in my neck, which wouldn't go away. Part of it was that I didn't like being told to take a hike by some big bruno without knowing the reason. And then there was that look of profound disappointment in Miss Seafoam's face as she was leaving my office. Had I been wrong about her? What if her hokey story was legit? Maybe she really was worried about a younger sister who was getting herself caught up in a bad life. And if she had been lying to me, why? To what end? And why were the police trying to push me away from her? The questions pummeled my punch-drunk brain as I fought the heavy downtown traffic.

Why hadn't I talked more with Seafoam, maybe given her a chance to explain herself? Maybe I could have gotten to the bottom of whatever was really going on. Why was I so anxious to rush her out of my office? Was it Stonehammer and his threats? I didn't want to think about that, because I might be forced to admit that maybe I wasn't the tough sonuvabitch that I thought

I was. But there it was: the elephant in the room. Or in this case, the troll in my face.

Fuck it! It was time to stop burning daylight, or, given the current weather conditions, sucking up fog. I had work to do, and I wasn't going to get it done by questioning my own manhood.

I decided to drive out to the old Placid Point Pier. I didn't know exactly what I was going to do when I got there, but I wanted to take a look around the place while the day was still young and get the lay of the land. Maybe I just didn't have anything better to do. Whatever the reason, I made a left turn and headed north.

***

It was after ten when I reached the parking lot in front of the abandoned wooden pier. I parked my car at the edge of the lot and got out. I walked to the front of the car, sidled up against the hood, and breathed in the dank air, which smelled of soggy wood and dead fish. A light breeze caused the morning fog to swirl. It was a typical late summer on the Yerba Peninsula. The wind would pick up in the afternoon and clear the air, and by two o'clock the sun would be beaming down from a partly cloudy sky. At dusk, the sun would shine through the low-lying clouds, creating a spectacular light show that would inspire art and romance, and by eight o'clock the city lights would chase the darkness into back alleys and abandoned lots. At midnight, something might or might not go down at this old pier. I needed to know about it, one way or the other, if for no other reason than my own peace of mind.

The old Placid Point Pier extended out from a disused parking lot and into the ocean from just west of the northernmost point of the Yerba Peninsula, the area known as Placid Point. The pier had long marked the entrance into Yerba Bay. Built more than two centuries ago, it had been the oldest operating wharf on the city's waterfront until about twenty-five years ago, when it was replaced by the larger, modernized, and much more consumer-friendly concrete quay and popular tourist site that opened about two miles down the southwest side of the Placid Point coast. The shipping and commercial fishers all relocated to the new Placid Point Pier. The city built a museum on the old site, and a few restaurants opened nearby hoping to capitalize on some sense of history or nostalgia, but the public showed little interest. The museum struggled to stay alive for a few years before closing for good, and none of the restaurants stayed in business for long.

The last restaurant to stay open was Fujita's Boarding House, a family style eatery with a boarding house motif that had served some pretty decent Nihhonese cuisine, including a nice dolphin steak. It mysteriously caught fire one night six years ago. The owner of the restaurant made an insurance claim, and the insurance company had hired me to be part of an investigative team. We found plenty of evidence for arson, but we couldn't pin it directly on the owner, who wound up collecting a pile of insurance money. The company hadn't been happy. A few months later the restaurant owner was found floating face down a mile offshore. A police investigation showed a great deal of money had mysteriously vanished from his bank account. I hadn't been involved in his death, but I hadn't been surprised by it, either.

After that, the whole area quickly deteriorated. No one comes to the old pier in the daytime anymore except a few fishermen. It's a much more interesting place at night, however. In recent years the morning sun has frequently revealed the grisly aftermath of the various illicit activities that take place after dark in this neglected and discarded scrap of the city.

I leaned against my car and let my eyes wander slowly across the parking lot and along the dilapidated pier. The asphalt in the lot was too cracked and broken to be used for parking anymore. The windows of the closed museum were broken, and someone had hacked a gaping hole through the door. Graffiti covered the walls of the museum, along with the walls of the abandoned restaurants and souvenir shops that ringed the parking lot. If Miss Seafoam had been straight with me, which I still doubted, some kids would be here trading drugs to a street gang for weapons later that night.

I crossed the parking lot to get a closer look at the graffiti. They were mostly gang tags, and they told a story. It seemed that the Northsiders and the Claymore Cartel were fighting over control of the pier, and that the Northsiders currently held the turf. The spray-painted "NS" insignias that covered the "CC" tags looked to be about a week old. Interesting, if Miss Seafoam's story was on the level.

I looked out onto the old wooden wharf. One lone fisherman was standing out near the end of the decaying structure with a bucket by his feet and his line in the water. I watched him through the gently swirling mists for about ten minutes, letting my thoughts drift. The fisherman wasn't catching anything, and my thoughts were leading me nowhere. I began walking toward him. I was feeling sociable.

The fisherman didn't move as I approached. I saw that he was tall, but somewhat stooped. He wore a stained hooded raincoat of some dark indeterminate color and a pair of leather boots that appeared well worn, but sturdy. His pole was leaning undisturbed against the railing with the line dangling into the water. If a fish took the line, the fisherman would have to grab his pole in a hurry to prevent it from being dragged out to sea. I reached the fisherman, who was staring out onto the horizon. Waves splashed languidly on the pilings of the pier and gulls cried out through the mist. The breeze out on the wharf was stronger and cooler than in the parking lot. It reddened my cheeks and threatened to numb my ears. I wished that I had brought along a flask of whiskey; a nip would have helped fend off the cold.

I leaned on the railing next to the fisherman, and, noting his empty bucket, said, "No luck, huh?"

Without turning his head, the fisherman said, "It would be a poor world if it held no luck at all, good or bad."

I was immediately transfixed by his voice, a melodious full-throated tenor that filled the space between us and silenced the crying gulls. His words were round, full-bodied, and clear, like fat crystal globes. Each one cut through the fog-soaked air like lasers, yet fell on my ears like silk. My breath caught in my throat, and I was momentarily unable to speak.

The fisherman turned toward me. His face was buried deep within his hood, but I could see that it was wrinkled and weatherworn, as if he had spent a long life outdoors. His eyes were larger than human, almond-shaped, the color of the inside of a lime, and remarkably bright. Thick gray eyebrows arched over his eyes, matching the strands of steely hair that hung over his forehead. He was clean-shaven without a trace of stubble. In the depths of his hood, I could just make out the outline of a pair of large pointed ears.

I took a step back, and the fisherman's ruddy lips broke into a sad smile. "Don't be afraid," he said, and I was immediately calmed by the sound of his uncanny voice. "Well, let's take a look at you."

My feet rooted themselves to the wharf's wooden deck as the fisherman examined me up and down with his alien eyes. Seemingly satisfied, he turned his gaze back to the sea. "When you said 'no luck,' I assume that you meant no *good* luck," he said, "and you came to that conclusion because I had no fish in my bucket. But luck comes in many forms: good, bad, and in between. It's possible," he continued, turning back to me, "that meeting you here today was good luck. What do you think?"

I stared back at him like a slack-jawed idiot. His voice consumed all my attention and made it difficult to think. "Um...," I tried.

The fisherman nodded as if I had made a good point. "Indeed!" he said brightly, looking back to sea. "Or," he continued, "maybe our meeting is *un*lucky, meaning characterized by *bad* luck, rather than devoid of luck entirely. Do you think this is the case?"

"I... I have no idea," I managed. "I hope not."

"Oh," he replied. "You have *hope*! Well that's very good. Very good indeed. There's too little of that in the world these days. Or maybe it's there, but we can't see it. I'd like to think so, although I can't be sure. I've been around for so long, and I've seen so little evidence of it. Still, if there's no hope, then why go on? No, no, no, that won't do. You have to believe that there's hope, even if there isn't. Because," he said, turning and focusing on me intently, "if there *is* hope, and you aren't looking for it, you'll never find it! You see?"

A spell seemed to roll off me at that moment, and I found that I could speak freely. I took a breath and nodded at him in a noncommittal way. "Whatever you say, old timer. I don't know about luck or hope. I just try to do my job and get by."

The fisherman flashed a brief smile. "Indeed, indeed. What else can one really do, eh? But, still, that's something. And maybe that's enough for one man. Maybe so, maybe so."

"Hey, can I ask you something?" I started, but the fisherman ignored my question.

"Why are you here?" he asked. "Go ahead. Tell me everything."

Although the fisherman's voice was no less compelling, I no longer felt rooted to the spot, nor did I feel spellbound to answer. I knew nothing about this strange, inhuman creature, though I had my suspicions. I had no good reason to trust him. Nonetheless, I answered his question. I'm not sure why, but I laid it all out for him, my encounter with Detective Stonehammer, my meeting with Miss Seafoam, my own feelings of uneasiness and self-doubt after rejecting Seafoam's case, and my subsequent resolve to get myself involved despite the risks. The fisherman listened intently without interruption.

He nodded to himself when I finished. "I thought it might be something like that," he said, a response that I found strange and unsettling. "This is no small matter, although you don't know it yet, and you may never know the full tale. Still, I think you have a part to play, perhaps a significant part. Yes, yes. And you may even be equipped to play it. You'll need help, though. Hmm...."

He looked off in the distance, thinking and nodding to himself. After a time, he seemed to make a decision. "Hold still," he commanded, and my feet once again rooted themselves to the wharf.

"Hey!" I protested.

The fisherman pulled his hand from his pocket. He was holding a small red gemstone about the size of a kernel of corn. He examined it briefly and then thrust it toward my forehead, pushing it into my skin right between the corners of my eyebrows. I experienced a flash of piercing pain, and then nothing.

"There!" the fisherman declared before I could react. "That should do it."

"What the fuck!" I said brightly.

"Well," he said, "it was nice to meet you. Yes indeed, a fine meeting all around. Good for you, and, I hope—there's that word again, eh?—good for me, too. Indeed. Well, goodbye!" He slapped me on the back, took up his fishing pole, and began to reel in his line.

"Wait a minute!" I exclaimed. "What just happened?"

But the old fisherman had already finished with me. He picked up his bucket, and, the next thing I knew, he was stepping off the wharf and into the parking lot. He disappeared into the fog before I could even think about trying to catch up with him.

***

The morning was wearing away, and I hadn't even had my morning coffee, much less any breakfast. I drove away from the pier and pulled into the first diner that I could find. Over a platter of greasy eggs and even greasier home fries, I thought about the strange fisherman. What *was* he? He had ears like a troll's, but he was too small, and he didn't have the sunken glowing red eyes that all trolls have. He was too tall to be a gnome, and, anyway, although gnomes have large ears, they're rounded, not pointed. Besides, he wasn't put together like a gnome. Gnomes are gangly creatures, with spindly limbs and big round paunches. This fisherman looked more like a tall, stooped human, except for the pointed ears and the bright lime-green eyes. I guess that he could have been some sort of sea creature, or earth spirit, but I knew that I was fooling myself. Deep down in my gut I knew that the old fisherman could be nothing other than an elf.

    Not that anyone would ever believe me if I told them. No one ever sees an elf. A lot of people think that they are extinct. Parents scare their kids with stories of crafty elves who steal babies out of their cribs and replace them with changelings, or who lure children into cars with candy and then take them home and eat them for lunch. In novels, elves are depicted as mysterious loremasters who scheme and plot in the shadows. According to some popular legends, they only come out at night to drink the blood and eat the flesh of unsuspecting living creatures that they happen upon. They don't walk the city streets in the light of day or stand around on abandoned wharfs waiting to hook a fish.

    According to the official government-authorized histories, the elves launched a treacherous rebellion, the so-called Great Rebellion, against the benevolent Dragon Lords and were defeated thanks in large part to the loyal human armies. I have my own thoughts about versions of history written by the winners, but, because I know what's good for me, I keep them to myself. After their victory, the seven Dragon Lords formed the seven realms with a Lord establishing a government over each one. Lord Ketz-Alkwat founded the city of Aztlan and made it the capital of the new Realm of Tolanica, and, being immortal, he's still in charge. Some six thousand years later, I emerged into the world under his stable rule. All hail Tolanica and the gracious Lord Ketz. Hurray for our side. Anyway, it seems that the Lords have been at each other's throats ever since the founding of the realms, but they all agreed that the elves were a bad influence on everyone else, and that they shouldn't be allowed to survive their uprising. In the genocide after the rebellion, the elves were eliminated as a species.

Officially, that is. But throughout the centuries, stories of elf sightings have persisted. Legends and rumors have spread throughout each of the seven realms, always discouraged by authorities, but never going away. And now I had my own story. Not that I could tell it to anyone. I mean, I didn't understand it myself. What was all that gibberish about luck and hope, small matters and larger tales? And what had he been doing there, anyway? I had the odd sense that the old elf had been waiting for me, or, if not that, then for something important to happen at that particular place and time. It was all over my head. And what had he done to me? Had he really jammed a red gem of some sort into my head, or was that just some sort of hallucination? I reached up to rub my forehead, but I couldn't feel anything, not a bump or a scar. I shook my head. All I had were questions without answers. And it wasn't even noon! I should have stayed in bed.

My stomach satisfied, or at least filled, and my mind a mess, I drove back to my own neighborhood with no further incidents. As I drove past my building on the way to the pay lot, I saw a figure in my doorway. A large figure. About the size of a troll. Terrific.

After I parked my car, I spotted the manager of the lot standing behind the wooden closet-sized booth that served as his office. He waved me over and reminded me that the monthly rental for my parking space was overdue. As if I didn't have enough on my mind. Breakfast had about emptied my wallet, and I didn't want to think about the hollow pit that was my bank account. The lot manager was a perpetually angry dwarf of indeterminate age with an unpronounceable dwarfish name. For the benefit of his customers, he went by Mac. Mac was about four-feet tall and nearly as wide. His permanently disheveled red hair spilled out of his size nine and seven-eighths fedora and hung down his back like ropes. A thick red beard streaked with gray covered most of his face, the hairs around his mouth stained yellow as a result of his constant chain-smoking. His heavily muscled right arm was covered in tattoos, the dominant one depicting the bearded face of a dwarf who was probably his mother. In contrast, he had only two tattoos on his left arm. A drawing of a snow-capped mountain with a lightning bolt striking the peak covered most of his upper arm. Printed on the mountain were the words, "Fighting 43rd." This tattoo was the emblem of the 43rd dwarf battalion of the Tolanican army, and it indicated that the dwarf had done some fighting in the Borderland. Beneath this tattoo was another one illustrating an old-fashioned black spherical bomb with a lit fuse, signifying that Mac had been a member of his battalion's bomb disposal unit. I told Mac that I'd have his dough in a day or two, and he glowered up at me with bloodshot eyes nearly buried under his bushy brows.

"Hey," I said. "I've got a new client. I just need to collect."

"You've got until noon tomorrow," scowled the dwarf. "And don't forget my policy: cash only, no checks and no credit cards." He plucked his cigarette from his lips and blew smoke in my direction.

"Come on, Mac," I said. "I've been late before, but you know I always pay."

"Noon tomorrow," repeated Mac. "I've got to make payroll."

"What payroll? You don't have any employees."

"I've got to pay myself, don't I?" Mac grumbled and popped his cigarette back in his lips.

I gave him my hardest stare.

Mac glared right back at me. "You don't like it? Find another lot. Lots of drivers would like your spot. Drivers who pay on time."

I held my stare. I doubted that I'd be able to find another pay lot with an available space within five miles of this one. Parking in the city was at a premium, and Mac's rates were actually pretty reasonable.

"Fine," I said at last. "I'll have your money by tomorrow."

"Noon!" Mac reminded me, and he turned and stomped into his booth.

***

I walked out of the lot, wondering how I was going to get my hands on enough scratch to pay Mac by noon tomorrow. As I approached my office, I saw Detective Stonehammer leaning against the front door, his arms folded across his massive chest. He was wearing a different suit than the one he had been wearing at the Minotaur—dark brown instead of dark blue—but still pinstriped. I guess he liked pinstripes. As I drew closer, he unfolded his arms and began cracking his knuckles. The sharp popping noises sounded like a small animal being slowly crushed to death.

"Mr. Southerland," the troll said with a broad smile. He clasped a big paw on my shoulder, the same one he had clawed the previous night. "We need to talk."

"Do you have an appointment?" I asked.

"Do I have--?" Stonehammer's smile widened even further. "That's a good one! Alkwat's balls, you're a funny guy."

I unlocked my door, but left the sign turned to "Closed." Stonehammer kept his hand on my shoulder and followed me into my office. When we were inside, Stonehammer closed the door behind him, but tightened his grip on me. He spun me around and backhanded me sharply across the face. He didn't put anything close to his full strength into the slap, but I went flying across the room and landed in a heap against a filing cabinet. A metal tray of papers came crashing down on my head.

Stonehammer crossed the room, placed a hand on either side of my shoulders and picked me up into the air so that my face was inches from his. "Where've you been, motherfucker?" He growled.

"Out," I said.

"I can see that. Where out?" he said.

"Just out, you big oaf! What's the matter with you?" I shouted.

Stonehammer carried me over to my desk and plopped my butt down on a corner. "Oh, there's nothing wrong with me," he said. "Is there something wrong with you? Did you forget what I told you last night?"

I checked myself over to see if anything was bleeding or broken. Other than being a little banged up and feeling like a mouse trapped by an overgrown alley cat, I guessed that I was all right.

"I didn't forget," I said. "You told me to turn down the case, and I did."

Stonehammer stared at me hard with his burning red eyes. "Did you? Well, shit. I was hoping that I could rough you up a bit. But if you really turned the case down, well...." He made a show of releasing me and straightening my coat.

"Now," he drawled pleasantly, "just tell me where you went after the skirt left your office this morning, and, if I like your answer, I'll be on my way."

"What do you care," I replied a little testily. "I didn't take the case. Anything else I did is none of your business."

"Let me be the judge of that, shithead. See, here's the thing," Stonehammer explained. "I'm not sure I believe you. You might have been out getting some coffee, or a late breakfast, or you might have been following up on the nymph's story. You might have even driven out to the old pier for some reason. But you wouldn't have done that, would you? I mean, what possible reason could you have for driving out to the old pier, if, like you say, you didn't take the little slut's case?"

I didn't respond. This wasn't going well.

"What? Nothing to say?" The troll grasped my shoulder. Again.

"What'd you do, have me followed?" I said. "Guess I should have seen that coming. That's what I get for being careless. Won't happen again."

"Alex, Alex, Alex," said Stonehammer, shaking his head. "Maybe I get to rough you up after all."

"Okay," I sighed. "I drove out to the pier. I admit, I was curious. But I didn't take the case. I turned her down. Find Miss Seafoam and ask her yourself if you don't believe me."

Stonehammer's grip tightened on my shoulder. "Don't worry about the nymph. She won't be needing your services."

"What are you talking about?" I asked. The troll's grip threatened to crush my shoulder joint.

"You don't need to know," growled the troll. "All you need to do is to forget the whole fuckin' thing and get on with your so-called life. So you were curious, huh? Well, maybe we'll have to put a little damper on that curiosity of yours."

I raised my arm to stop what was coming, but it didn't help. Stonehammer rapped the side of my head with his club-like forearm, and I tumbled off the desk to the floor. He picked me up threw me back down again. I groaned and tried to get my feet under me. Stonehammer kicked at me and I felt a rib on my left side break. I curled up into a ball to protect the rib and tried to make myself as small as possible. Stonehammer picked me up again and tossed me across the room. I crashed into my water cooler. The heavy glass tank toppled from the dispenser, and I fell to the floor on top of it. The tank exploded into big shards under the weight of my body, and I felt glass slice through my skin. Water tinged with blood flooded away from me.

Stonehammer stomped across the room toward me. I grabbed a thick pointed glass shard with both hands and brought it down with all my weight into the top of the troll's expensive dress shoe. It penetrated the soft thin leather and sunk deep into his foot. Stonehammer bellowed like a slaughtered bull. He yanked his foot away from me and tumbled to the floor, propelled by his own weight. I spotted a larger shard, about a foot-and-a-half long and maybe three inches wide. On one end of the shard was the tank's narrow bottleneck, still intact. I grabbed the shard by the thick cylindrical bottleneck, which provided me with an excellent grip, and, swinging with everything I had, I slashed the edge of the thick shard across Stonehammer's left eye.

"Motherfuck!" Stonehammer roared. Blood covered the left side of his face. I felt like I'd been run over by a bus, and my left side was on fire, but I managed to find my feet. I didn't press my luck. I knew that Stonehammer had been toying with me up till now, and I had no illusions about my chances against an enraged troll, no matter how scratched up he was. With no further thought, I made for the emergency door. Stonehammer tried to stumble to his feet but fell to his knees when he put his weight on his injured foot. I dashed through the door before he could recover. I ran down the hall to the back door and scrambled to unlock it. Stonehammer crashed through the first door without bothering to open it. I hurried outside and sprinted down the alley. I was battered, broken, and bleeding, but I was certain that I could outrun the lumbering troll even if I hadn't put a hole in his foot. My only question was where was I going to run to?

It didn't take me long to lose the troll, and once I did, I took out my phone. I found the picture of her sister that Miss Seafoam had sent to me, and tapped the reply box with my thumb. "Call me," I texted. And then I went searching for a quiet place to hide.

Chapter Four

A half hour passed without a call from Miss Seafoam. I wondered what Stonehammer meant when he said that she wouldn't be needing my services anymore. Was she in trouble? Probably, but it was useless to beat myself up about it without more information.

I was nursing a watered down whiskey that I couldn't afford in the back corner of a dark, quiet bar called The Golden Cove. It should have been called The Shithole, though you couldn't have given me a c-note to use its toilet. Past the rest room was an unlocked emergency exit that I could reach in a hurry if I needed to. I couldn't go back to my place, not with an angry troll looking for me, and I needed to take care of my broken rib, but for the moment I was still catching my breath.

Of course, what I was really doing was hiding out. Yerba City is a big city with lots of nondescript places like this neighborhood bar to lay low in. Finding a single person among the hundreds of thousands living at the tip of the Yerba Peninsula is like looking for a needle in a haystack. But the police have ways of tipping the scales in their favor. For example, all cell phones are equipped with a GPS location device, which allows anyone with the proper equipment to trace that phone's location to within three hundred feet if they know the phone number. That's why the first thing I did when I got my cell phone was to go into my privacy settings and disable my location services. Problem solved, right? Well, not entirely. With sophisticated equipment, the police can still track a phone by accessing data from its built-in barometer, altimeter, gyroscope, accelerometer, and magnetometer, as long as the phone is turned on and moving from one location to another. That's right, the smartness of smartphones makes them less private.

Knowing this, I have removed the apps from my phone that broadcast this data. It makes it harder for me to get weather notifications, but the tradeoff is worth it, as far as I'm concerned.

I considered my options. I was hoping that Miss Seafoam would pick me up and drive me somewhere safe, but I was giving up on that idea. I could walk to my own car if I was sure that Stonehammer wasn't lying in wait for me. The image of Stonehammer's snarling face caused the hairs on my neck to stand on end. They really do that when you're frightened enough. I'd seen horrors in the Borderland that I can't talk about, but which have haunted my dreams ever since. I'd seen monsters in alleyways here in the city that mothers warn their children about. I'd had guns pointed in my direction and knives pressing into my throat. I'd walked, or run, away from them all. I liked to think of myself as fearless. But the hairs on the back of my neck didn't lie. I was sitting in a dark, dirty bar, drinking bad whiskey, and I couldn't keep my eye off the front door, fearing that at any moment it would fly off its hinges and reveal an enraged troll with scorching red eyes aimed laser-like in my direction.

It occurred to me that I had a way of finding out whether or not the coast was clear. I prepared to summon my new pal Smokey. Something odd happened. I pictured the summoning sigil in my mind with unusual clarity, and as I wet my finger in my whiskey in order to trace the sigil on the tabletop, Smokey suddenly appeared with a whoosh and hovered in front of me.

"Whoa!" I drew back, surprised. "Where did you come from?"

"Alex called, Smokey come," the elemental whispered.

"I haven't summoned you yet. I was just about to trace the sigil."

Smokey whirled silently for a moment. Then it said, "Alex is different."

"Huh? How so?"

The elemental hesitated, then said, "The summoning is... inside Alex. And...." Again the elemental hesitated, as if searching for the right words. Finally, it continued. "Smokey doesn't know how Smokey came to Alex. Smokey doesn't understand."

I couldn't think of anything to say about that. I had never been able to summon an elemental without physically drawing a visible sigil on something. I'd have to explore this development later. Right now, I had work to do. I shook all distracting thoughts out of my head and focused on my current predicament.

"Okay, Smokey," I said. "Let's forget about all that for now. Here's what I need you to do. You remember that troll? Fly through the neighborhood and see if you can find him. If you spot him, come back and tell me. Otherwise, keep searching until I summon you again. Understand?"

"Smokey understands," said the elemental, and whisked itself out of the bar.

I waited five minutes and spent the time watching a news program that was playing on an old boxy television sitting on the corner of the bar. A reporter was interviewing Darnell Teague, our city's mayor. The reporter asked a softball question about the city's gang problem and stuck a microphone in the mayor's face. Teague put on a grim expression to let the viewers know that he was taking the question seriously. I'll bet a month's wages that he practiced that expression in front of a mirror. After a dramatic pause, in which he appeared to be formulating an off-the-cuff answer to the reporter's question, the mayor launched into a polished statement designed to assure his constituency that much was being done about the problem without actually revealing anything of substance. I had the impression that the mayor's response had been tested on a few focus groups before being unleashed on the general public.

After the mayor's rehearsed sound bite had been delivered, I left my unfinished drink and the last of my cash on hand on the table and stepped out of the bar. Smokey hadn't returned, which meant that it hadn't seen Stonehammer anywhere nearby. As an experiment, rather than drawing the sigil to summon the elemental, I just pictured the image in my mind. Smokey appeared almost immediately, whooshing through the air too fast to see and coming to a stop on my shoulder. I was going to have to investigate this change in my summoning abilities, but I was sure that it had something to do with whatever the elf had shoved into my forehead. I couldn't think of any other explanation, reasonable or otherwise.

"Any sign of the troll?" I asked Smokey.

"Smokey not see troll."

"Where did you search?" I regretted asking this question as soon as the words were out of my mouth. Conversations with elementals are limited to simple observations and easy to describe information. It was like when I had asked the elemental if it could tell me where Detective Stonehammer lived. Smokey, who travels through a network of air streams, had no way of communicating this information in terms of street names, intersections, and left and right turns.

Smokey bent this way and that, stretched and contracted, but could only say, "Smokey does not know how to tell Alex."

I pointed in the direction that I planned on walking. "Did you go as far as that pole with the three lights?"

"Yes."

"Did you fly beyond that pole?"

"Yes. Smokey fly over many poles with three lights."

Good enough. I would at least be safe for the next few blocks. Unless Stonehammer was waiting somewhere out of sight and planning to ambush me as I walked past. But what was I going to do, go back into The Shithole and hide out all day? Was this who I was now? A coward? Anyway, they'd throw me out on the street once they figured out that I was out of cash. Troll or no troll, I couldn't spend the rest of the day sniveling in a dark corner and licking my wounds. I told myself that it was time to get off the floor, cowboy up, and be a grown-ass man. But that didn't mean I couldn't take a few precautions. "Stay above me," I told Smokey. "I'm going to start walking. If you see the troll, come to me and tell me. Understand?"

"Smokey understands." Smokey then launched itself off my shoulder and disappeared from my view.

Either the troll was lying in wait for me, or he wasn't. It was just like in the Borderland. We'd all felt it. Today might be the day you buy it, or it wouldn't. Either way, you had to wake up and live it until you couldn't. I took a deep breath, shook off my apprehensions, and began walking to my car.

On the way I thought about where I could go to take care of my broken rib. It would need to be set and taped up so that it would stay in place. I ruled out going to a hospital. Stonehammer knew that I was injured, and if he was still looking for me then he would have the hospitals covered. I thought about some private clinics that I knew about. Some of them operated under the radar, but all of these would want cash up front, and I didn't have any. I thought about some people I knew who might do me a favor. I'm a loner by nature, but I have a few friends. The problem with calling on any of them, though, was that I would risk bringing trouble to their doorsteps. That didn't seem like the right way to treat friends. Too bad Miss Seafoam hadn't called me back. She probably had troubles of her own. Here I was, a tough son of a bitch, hard as steel, with a special ability to summon and command air elementals. Problem was, I couldn't figure out a way that even the most powerful elemental could help with a broken rib. I was on my own and fresh out of ideas.

Funny thing, though. As I made my way through the streets to my car it occurred to me that my rib wasn't giving me as much trouble as I thought it should. My side hurt all right, but not that much. I lifted my shirt and saw that my left side was covered by an angry red and yellow blotch. I gave the blotch an experimental rub with the palm of my hand. It was tender, but the pain was bearable. I poked at my rib with my finger. It felt bruised, but maybe it wasn't broken after all. That couldn't be right. I had felt it crack when Stonehammer kicked me. On the other hand, things had been moving so fast. Maybe it had only seemed to break. Or maybe this was another gift from the old elf. If I ever saw him again I'd have to thank him. And then I'd ask him what he wanted in return. Because if I've learned anything in my life it's that nothing in this world is free: there is always a catch. And the greater the gift, the greater the cost.

***

I reached my car without incident. Stonehammer was nowhere in sight, so I thanked Smokey and sent it off to take care of its own business, whatever that might be for a miniature burst of wind. Rustling leaves, I guess. Stonehammer was probably off somewhere getting his own medical attention. I'd done some damage to him. Served the bastard right. That'll teach him to mess with *this* mean motherfucker! Not that I'd want a rematch. I'd been lucky, and I knew it. He had only wanted to knock me around a little. Next time he'd mean business.

I pondered my next move. I no longer felt like I needed to be in a hospital. It was now about two o'clock. In ten hours, something might be happening at the old Placid Point Pier. The only thing I knew for sure was that I needed to be there. In the meantime, I needed to find someplace safe and prepare.

I still didn't like the idea of going to my place. I needed to lay low. A motel was out. My wallet was as empty as a pawnbroker's heart, and my bank account was close to it. I had a credit card that wasn't at its limit, but the police can trace credit card purchases. Reluctantly, I began to think about some friends who might be able to put me up for a few hours without anyone noticing.

I drove north. Fortunately, I had nearly a quarter tank of gas, which should be enough to last me a couple of days if I didn't waste it. I remembered that Stonehammer had somehow known about my trip to the pier that morning, so I kept checking in my mirror to see if anyone was following me. I didn't want to make that mistake twice. When I was convinced that I was safely outside of anyone's radar, I pulled over into a grocery store parking lot. Maybe I was feeling a little paranoid, but after I parked my car I did a thorough search to see if someone had planted a tracking device on the vehicle. I checked everywhere that I could think of, outside, under, and inside the car. I even used a screwdriver that I kept in my glove box to remove my dashboard cover and poke around inside. You can't be too careful.

I thought about Smokey then, and it occurred to me that someone might be using an air elemental of their own to watch me. A day ago, I wouldn't have had any way of knowing. I wondered if things might be different now. I closed my eyes and thought about what I wanted to do. Some sigils formed in my mind. I focused on them and arranged them into a spell that I made up on the spot. Sure enough, I could feel my senses begin to scan the skies. Cool!

The cold wind was gusting, so I figured that a few air elementals would be roaming the neighborhood, but I was shocked at the crowds of air spirits that I detected flying chaotically this way and that. Dozens of small elementals, Smokey's size or a little larger, whipped past me, drawn by the wind currents. More passed by, tacking against the current. I detected larger elementals whirling through the air higher up in the sky. And far above me, a half-dozen king-sized elementals floated majestically through the clouds, like gods. Summoning elementals was nothing new for me, but I realized that I had been summoning them blind. When I wanted an elemental, I would cast a summoning spell into the air like a fishing line, hoping for a bite. This was the first time I had ever seen the elementals flying about in their natural habitat. It was like putting on a scuba mask and seeing the scores of fish swimming beneath the ocean's surface for the first time. I didn't want to stop watching, but I had to take care of business. Reluctantly, I ended my spell.

The bad news is that I was surrounded by so many elementals that I couldn't tell if any of them were following me. My gut told me that I was okay, though. If an air spirit was paying any attention to me it wasn't being obvious about it. I'd have to settle for that.

More or less satisfied that no one was tracking me with technology, eyes, or nature spirits, I drove on to an old two-story office building at the north end of downtown. The building's small parking lot was full, and I spent thirty minutes searching for an available spot on the street before I found one six blocks away. It even had seventeen minutes left on the meter, so I wouldn't be getting a ticket right away. After that, well, I'd cross that bridge when I came to it. I would have to hope that the YCPD wasn't efficient enough to trace me through a parking ticket before I finished my business here and got myself out of the area.

Twenty minutes later, I walked into the office building and made my way up the staircase to the second floor. The office I wanted was at the end of the corridor. Written on the translucent glass window on the door of the office was the name Robinson D. Lubank, Attorney at Law. I opened the door and a cloud of pale blue smoke spilled out into the hallway. I fought through the smoke and stepped inside.

The office was thick with cigarette smoke. At the reception desk was a pleasantly curvy woman with dyed blond hair and a pretty girlish face. A lit cigarette dangled from her lips. Her buxom body was packed into a dress that was two sizes too small for her. On her desk was an ashtray with about a pack and a half of crushed-out butts. She looked at me, breathed in on her cigarette, and blew a puff of smoke upwards into the air. Without taking her eyes off me, she leaned her cigarette against the inside edge of the ashtray with practiced expertise. She smiled at me and said in a low husky voice, "Hi gorgeous. What's up?" Then lowering her eyes to my midsection, she added, "As if I didn't know."

"Hi, Gracie," I said. "You're looking luscious, as always. Is he in?"

"If I tell you that he's with a client, and that he'll be busy for another half hour, will you take me to the break room and let me show you my new tattoo?" Gracie's lips parted in a sultry smile.

"Sorry, baby. No time," I said with mock disappointment. "I've got an urgent thing going on."

"Yeah," Gracie sighed. "Me too."

"Graaaa-cie...." I chided.

"Okay, let me get him for you. He's pretending to work on a brief, but he's dying for an excuse to put it off." Gracie pushed a button on her intercom. "Robby? Alex is here with a thing. I offered to handle it for him, but he wants to see *you* for some reason." She smiled at me and batted her eyes.

"Leave him alone and send him in," said a gruff male voice through the intercom. "Tell him to put his pants back on first."

Gracie sat up straight and crossed her legs. "Mr. Lubank will see you now, sir," she said in an exaggerated professional voice. Then she smiled and winked at me. "Next time," she said, her voice filled with promise.

"You bet," I said, and went on in to see the city's shadiest lawyer.

The office was dominated by an oversized antique walnut desk with a deep-polished shine. Folders and loose papers were spread across the surface with no discernable order. A lit cigarette smoldered in an ashtray littered with old stubs. Peering out from behind a twenty-four-inch computer screen was an owl-eyed gnome with buck teeth and the world's most obvious toupee perched on his head like a dead hamster, wedged into place by a pair of enormous rounded ears.

"Th'fuck you want!" Lubank scowled at me.

"For starters, you can do something about the parking ticket I'm getting because you don't have any spaces in your shitty parking lot," I said.

"Fuck you," he said. "Take the bus next time."

Rob Lubank was one of my best employers. I'd done a lot of legwork for him over the years, digging up dirt on people that his clients were suing. No litigation was too sleazy for Lubank to pursue, and my work on his behalf often bordered on the bizarre. Several years ago he asked me to look into a case in which his client was suing a witch for malpractice. The young man had gone to the witch for a potion that would, let's say, enhance his manhood. It seems that he had a new girlfriend that he wanted to impress in a big way. The witch said that she would mix up something special for the young man and sold him a potion for a large chunk of change. The potion worked too well, and the next thing the young man knew he had a unit that was far too bloated to be practical for the desired purpose. That's when he contacted Lubank. According to Lubank, his new client couldn't have stuffed the tip of his tool into a stove-pipe hat. Worse, the effects were permanent. The client wanted to sue the witch, and the witch claimed that she had warned the young man that possible side-effects of the potion included severe hyperplasia of the penis. According to the witch, the eager young man had been comfortable with the risks. Lubank hired me to dig into the case. Quickly into my investigation, I discovered that the client's girlfriend had been none other than the witch's own teenaged daughter. The two of them had been keeping their relationship under wraps because the girl was already engaged to the son of one of her mother's friends. Unbeknownst to the pair, the mother was already aware of their secret trysts. They should have known better. I mean, she was a witch, right? Anyway, armed with this information, Lubank was able to convince the judge that the witch had plenty of motivation to bring harm to his client, and he was able to secure a large settlement for the grateful young man. In the end, it worked out pretty well for all concerned. The witch got what she wanted: her daughter's clandestine relationship came to an end, and the girl married the man that her mother had picked out for her. Last I heard, she had three healthy kids, her husband was loving and prosperous, and she was happy with her life. The client rented himself out as specialty entertainment for certain types of parties and did pretty well for himself. Also, I hear that he became popular with female trolls. Lubank got paid, of course, and so did I.

    Oh, by the way, Gracie was Lubank's wife. Marriages between humans and gnomes aren't common, but they happen.

Gracie was an outrageous flirt, and Lubank had the ethics of a slumlord, but they seemed like a nice couple. It was precisely because Lubank lived his life on the outskirts of respectability that I felt he could help me now.

"I need a favor," I said to Lubank.

"No," said Lubank.

"You don't know what I need."

"I don't care."

"You owe me," I said.

"For what?" Lubank asked, astonished.

"For the next time you need me," I said. "I'll work your job for half my fee."

"Bullshit!"

"Come on, Lubank. Just hear me out."

Lubank gave an exaggerated sigh. "All right, all right. What have you done this time."

"What makes you think I did something?"

"Out with it, Southerland. You're wasting my time." Lubank folded his skinny arms and rested them on his protruding gnomish gut. He looked like a reclining spider.

"We-e-ell," I said, drawing the word out, "I might have beaten up a cop."

Lubank rolled his eyes at me and said, "Lord Alkwat's pecker! You can forget about pleading self-defense."

I laughed a little and said, "If they get around to arresting me, the case will never get to court. I'll never make it out of the interrogation room. They'll throw me in the dumpster with the morning garbage. And then who will you get to dig up dirt so that you can blackmail your clients?"

"So if you don't want me to represent you in a lost-cause case against the YCPD, what do you want from me?" Lubank asked.

"I just need an out-of-the-way place to stay until tonight. And maybe some dinner. I had to run out of the apartment without my bankroll. Oh, and I need to use a computer and charge my phone."

"Th'fuck," Lubank said. "You want me to hide you? Lord's balls! Go hang out in the break room. There's a computer in there that you can use. Get a charger from Gracie. And tell her to give you a buck for the vending machine. No funny business from you two! I just got the couch in there reupholstered."

"Thanks, Lubank." I turned to go.

"You still have a key? Make sure you lock the front door when you leave." Lubank had given me a key to his office building the third time he hired me. He said that he was tired of having to come downstairs to let me in when he was working late and the building was locked down.

I turned to go. "And next time I hire you, I'm holding you to our deal," Lubank said to my back. "Half price. I'll have Gracie put it in writing."

"Yeah, yeah," I said as I walked out the door and into the lobby.

Gracie grabbed a charging cord from a drawer in her desk and led me to the break room. After closing the door, she slid the right side of her dress high up her leg and showed me her new tattoo—a tiny blood-red rose with a dark green stem—on her upper thigh. I told her that it was pretty. She giggled and slinked back to her reception desk, where she arranged for a nearby diner to deliver me a steak sandwich and a cola. While I ate, I spent some time on the break room computer. When I was done, I settled in on Lubank's newly upholstered couch and waited for the night to arrive.

Chapter Five

"Elf Hunt" was the name of the year's most popular game app. I had downloaded it to my phone a few weeks ago, and sometimes when I had time to kill I spent it hunting down villainous animated elves and pelting them with cartoon vegetables. It was a stupid game, but it could make two hours seem like twenty minutes. After I pelted my one thousand two hundred fifty-seventh elf with a rutabaga and watched him vanish in a puff of green mist, I wrenched myself away from the game and cleared it off my screen.

I still had time to kill, so I decided to experiment with my enhanced abilities with air elementals. I pictured sigils in my mind and practiced finding and summoning small, Smokey-sized elementals. I found that I no longer needed to physically draw the sigils in order to work any of my spells. Soon I had a dozen little whirlwinds parading around the break room in formations like tiny soldiers. I tried to send commands to the elementals telepathically, but that didn't work. Although I could summon elementals with my mind, I still had to actually speak to the elementals in order to command them.

After playing around for an hour or so, I realized that I was now thinking about elementals in a new way. Previously, elementals were nothing more to me than forces of nature that I could control in limited ways. They were useful, but I had never before thought of them as living things with emotions or feelings, or at least not since I was a kid. My schoolteachers had beaten those ideas out of me. They taught me that personifying elementals was childish. Elementals weren't human, my teachers told me. Nor were they pets. Elementals were tools that I could access and manipulate when I needed them and then discard when I was finished. I was taught to take my work with elementals more seriously. After meeting the elf, though, something in me had changed. The elf had given me an affinity with the elementals that I had never possessed before. I now saw each elemental as unique, and I found that it was easier to work with some than with others. It wasn't just that some were more efficient, while others seemed careless. It was that some seemed eager—even happy—to obey my commands. When I praised them, they responded by whirling a little faster, or by stretching themselves taller and thinner, or in some other physical way. Others were more reluctant and resistant to my commands. These were sometimes slow to obey or careless with their tasks. Before meeting the elf, I *used* elementals. Now, I worked *with* them. I felt exhilarated by my new level of understanding, but, again, I wondered what the price would be.

"Alex is different." That's what Smokey had told me at The Shithole. I was finding out what that meant. For one thing, I missed Smokey, as if the little guy were a trusted associate, or maybe even a friend. Screw my teachers—what did *they* know! I wondered whether I could summon Smokey from where I was. Lubank's office was about twenty miles from the Black Minotaur, and the smaller elementals tend to travel within small territories. I decided to try. I formed Smokey's summoning sigil in my mind and put my will into the spell. I waited. It took about half a minute, but then there it was, whirling on my shoulder.

"Hello, Smokey," I said.

"Smokey doesn't know where Smokey is," Smokey said, a tremor in its whisper.

"It's okay," I assured the elemental. "Why don't you fly off and orient yourself. Then come back."

Smokey streaked away. Five minutes went by, and it reappeared on my shoulder.

"Smokey understands," it said, and its whisper sounded steadier. Hmm. Elementals get nervous and insecure. I was learning more about them by the minute.

"Can you get back to the crowded place from here?" I asked it.

"Yes. Smokey knows which winds to follow."

"Excellent," I said, and I sent it on its way.

I dismissed the other elementals, too. The sun had disappeared over the horizon nearly an hour ago, and the clock on the wall showed 8:17. It was time to go.

My computer research had turned up some pertinent info. Detective Stonehammer's captain was Gerald "Gerry" Graham, human. He was the head of the general crimes investigative division for the department's field operations bureau, a position that gave him far-reaching authority. Captain Graham was a twenty-two year veteran of the YCPD. He had a graduate degree in criminology and had worked his way up the ladder from patrolman. He was highly decorated. Probably ambitious. In any case, he was willing to use his underlings to intimidate common working joes, such as simple private investigators. I looked at his official department headshot and saw a smiling friendly face with a clean-shaven manly jaw. His eyes were gentle, and his salt-and-pepper hair was neatly trimmed and combed. I didn't like him.

I also found some information on the Claymore Cartel and the Northsiders. It was the usual gang shit: drugs, drive-by shootings, turf wars, and so forth. The Cartel was the larger of the two gangs, citywide with branches in other cities up and down the coast, whereas the Northsiders were an up-and-coming local gang operating on—wait for it!—the north side.

Leaving the building, I walked the six blocks to my car, tore the traffic ticket from my windshield wiper, stuck it in my glove box, and headed for Placid Point. If the festivities were scheduled for midnight, I wanted to be at the pier by nine.

Driving through the city is a slow business, even on the fringes of downtown. The city is built on hills, and many of the slopes are severe. Cars tend to go too slow up the inclines and too fast down. Drivers regard the traffic lights as mere suggestions. Left turn lanes in the downtown area are rare. The smart way to make a left turn in the city is to drive up a block make three right turns, instead. Most drivers lack the patience for such a complicated and personally inconvenient maneuver. They would rather sit in the middle of intersections, stopping the traffic behind them, while they wait for the oncoming traffic to clear. This rarely happens until well after the light changes, which means that these drivers now find themselves blocking the traffic trying to cross. All the while, thousands and thousands of moving cars merge and diverge, approach and withdraw, accelerate, decelerate, and veer away and toward each other like a million ants on an anthill, avoiding destruction and disaster (for the most part) only because of painted white lines, signal lights, and a shared knowledge of the rules of the road, both written and unwritten.

For these and other reasons, most people find driving in the city to be a stressful experience, especially at night. I'm not one of these people. I love driving in the city after dark. Cars accelerate and brakes screech. Horns honk in various tones. Drivers shout and curse. It's all part of the music of the city. Accompanying this urban symphony is a cacophony of glaring colors. Twin streams of red lights float ahead of me, pair after pair of bright white lights move toward me. The greens, yellows, purples, and blues of the electric neon signs on both sides of the road cast a polychromatic glow into the streets and on the sidewalks, illuminating the crowds of men and women of various species on their way to stores, restaurants, and bars, their shouts of greetings and anger harmonizing and amalgamating into the nighttime spectacle that is downtown Yerba City. I eased back in my driver's seat, breathing in the bracing dirty air, tinged with gasoline and exhaust fumes, through my unrolled window, watching the ever-merging pools of color, and listening to the urgent sounds of downtown until I left it behind and the lights and echoes faded into the night sky.

At 8:55, I parked my car on Fremont Street a block east of the entrance to the old Placid Point Pier. Clouds blanketed the sky, blocking out the moon and stars. The few muddy street lights that still worked struggled in vain to illuminate this remote edge of the city. That was fine with me. The darkness would keep me safe from prying eyes. At least I hoped so. As I walked to the pier, however, I was struck by the clarity of my surroundings. My vision had adjusted remarkably well to the night, and I found that I could see the world around me as if the sun were low in the sky rather than well on its way across the other side of the globe. When I focused on an object, I could make out the details as if I were looking at it in daylight through a telescope. Another gift from the elf, I supposed. Another item on the bill.

    I took up a post between two abandoned souvenir shops close to the main road. I wanted to be able to duck out of there in a hurry if the situation demanded it. I scoped out the pier's parking lot with my new night-vision. It was as deserted as it had been that morning. I saw nothing around the abandoned museum, restaurants, and shops. I looked down the wharf. It was empty, too. Not even an elf.

    I waited. A cold wind whipped off the ocean and blew sand across the lot. I had rushed out of my office in just a thin suit coat, and now I was paying the price. Stonehammer hadn't given me any choice in the matter, but I wished that I had thought to ask Lubank if he had a spare overcoat. Or if Gracie had a spare shawl. Anything at all would have been a help. Some old writer had once said that he had never spent a colder winter than one summer night in Yerba City. I suppose that a soldier in Lord Shango's army might have taken issue with this idea when he was laying siege to Lord Ao Qin's northern capital in the Huaxian Empire during an early winter as the thick snowfall threatened to bury him in the plains far from his home, but at that moment I could see the old writer's point.

    As I waited, I listened. Waves lapped against the pilings of the old wharf and broke over the shore. The wharf creaked and groaned. A paper sandwich wrapper from somewhere tumbled across the parking lot and smacked into the wall of one of the abandoned buildings. The wind moaned as it made its way through the surrounding structures. In the distance, a car honked and tires squealed. The sound of a siren came to me from even further away. I concentrated and heard the faint sound of a shouting voice from several blocks away. I turned my head in another direction and caught the distant tones of a trumpet solo over a slow blues beat from a piano and bass guitar. I heard all of these sounds distinctly. It seems that, along with my vision, my hearing had been enhanced. I wonder what other surprises I had waiting for me. Could I fly? I jumped up, but returned straight to the ground. Guess not. Then I had an even better idea. I tried to "think" myself warm. No dice. I guess that the ability to stand up to Yerba City's cold nights wasn't one of the elf's gifts to me. Bastard!

    Nothing happened for a long time, except that the wind kept swirling and the temperature kept dropping. I thought about sheltering myself in one of the abandoned buildings, but I didn't want to lose my ability to move around freely. So I sucked it up, huddled into my suit coat, blew warm air into my hands, and used the souvenir shop that I was sitting against as a windbreak.

    At about 10:30 I heard a vehicle approaching cautiously from the direction I had come. Soon, a van appeared. Its headlights were turned off, and it carefully made a right turn off Fremont into the lot, dodging broken slabs of asphalt, but not always avoiding the potholes. I got to my feet and pulled back from the lot into the darkness, and then pressed myself up against the side of the empty souvenir shop. The van pulled up to the abandoned museum and stopped. Eight figures got out of the van. They wore dark, loose-fitting overcoats, and three of them carried what appeared to be gym bags, probably filled with weapons. Bandanas were tied around their foreheads and knotted at the sides of their heads. Before I met the elf, I wouldn't have been able to see the colors of the bandanas in the darkness, but with my new night-vision I could see that the bandanas marked these newcomers as members of the Northsiders. Interesting. Nothing in Miss Seafoam's story had indicated that the Northsiders were part of tonight's deal. Were they setting up an ambush? Probably. One of the gangbangers jimmied open the museum door with a crowbar, and they all entered the building, where I'm sure they kept themselves nice and toasty. The van drove away, probably to park nearby. As the van passed, I got a look at the driver. Like the other Northsiders, he had a bandana tied around his head, but it was nearly buried in an avalanche of curly black hair. I got a good look at his face and was shocked at how young he looked. I didn't think that he was more than fifteen, but maybe he was just babyfaced.

Another thirty minutes crept past like a retiree in commuter traffic. Suddenly, my new sensitive sense of hearing picked up the light scuffle of approaching footsteps in the near distance. The sound came from down Fremont rather than from the direction I had taken to get there. A moment later, two figures carrying a ladder turned into the lot. I owned a rod, but I'd left it in my desk drawer when I made my hasty retreat earlier that day, and under the circumstances I felt naked without it. A quick examination of my immediate surroundings revealed nothing that I could use as a weapon. Maybe I wouldn't need one. Maybe the elf had made me super stealthy and no one would ever know that I was there. Yeah.

The two figures were wearing heavy coats and bandanas over their heads that matched the color of the Claymore Cartel. The night was getting more interesting by the minute! They took the ladder behind an abandoned shop across the lot from me. Soon I could hear them climbing the ladder to the roof of the building and dragging the ladder up behind them. Creeping up near the front of the souvenir shop, I saw the two figures peering over the rooftop from prone positions. One of them had a pair of binoculars, which he used to scan beyond the shore. The other kept an eye on the entrance to the lot. These, I concluded, using all my vast reasoning powers, were lookouts.

I crept to the back of the souvenir shop and tried to find a spot behind the structures where I could see out into the ocean without being spotted by the lookouts on the rooftop, or by the ones that I knew must be watching out the windows in the museum. The Claymore with the binoculars was looking offshore for something. I wanted to know what it was. I found the spot I needed and gazed out to sea. It didn't take me long to find what the lookout was searching for: a sporty-looking vessel lying low in the water without lights. Even with my enhanced vision, the vessel was hard to detect at first, but grew more visible by the second as it headed straight for the pier at a high speed. At 11:50 on the dot, it reached the wharf, and a man leaped out of the vessel and tied it down. I had a clear look at the ship as it docked. I recognized it as a "go-fast boat," about twenty-five feet long, sleek, and powerful. It was a favorite vessel for smugglers.

From across the lot, I heard a quiet voice speak, saying, "The boat is here and the area is clear."

Well, clear except for the eight Northsiders hiding in the museum, but I guess you don't know about them. Or about me, either, though I had no plans to change that.

Moments later, I heard vehicles approaching on Fremont from the west side of the pier. I scurried back to my original vantage point between the souvenir shops and watched two vehicles enter the lot. The lead vehicle was a van. The second vehicle was a dark sedan. Headlights blazed from both. They weren't sneaking in. The two vehicles turned left at the entrance to the pier and pulled into the middle of the lot, winding their way through the broken asphalt. The doors to the van opened and a horde of figures wearing Claymore Cartel bandanas poured out. I counted twelve of them. It couldn't have been a comfortable ride. When the van was empty, two figures climbed out of the sedan, one average sized and the other towering over him. The average sized man was Captain Gerald "Gerry" Graham. The huge figure, a heavy bandage covering his left eye, was my new drinking buddy and sparring partner, Detective Octavian Stonehammer.

***

Graham directed the Claymore Cartel gangsters toward the wharf, and they did what he told them to do. The two lookouts climbed off the rooftop and reported to Graham, who told them to drop the ladder next to the van and join the rest of the group. Like the other gang members, these two followed Graham's orders. It was clear that Graham was running this show. Questions about why a respected police captain was in charge of a street gang presented themselves to me, but I filed them away for later. At the moment, I didn't have the time for speculation.

As I watched, Graham, Stonehammer, and six of the Claymore soldier boys stepped onto the wharf's walkway and approached the vessel tied to the end of it. All of them except Stonehammer had both hands stuffed deep into their coat pockets, probably holding handguns. Dangling from the detective's left hand was an attaché case, the perfect size and shape for carrying a shitload of bundled c-notes. The other eight Claymore soldiers waited in front of the wharf, standing guard I guess. I stayed where I was, waiting to see how it would all play out. As Graham and his entourage drew close to the vessel, two men emerged from it. One of the men held a flashlight. The other held a small boxy container of some sort. I couldn't tell what it was.

Graham's group stopped a few feet in front of the two men from the boat, partially obstructing my view. I assumed that they would now exchange their package for the attaché case that Stonehammer was carrying, and that seemed to be what was happening. I saw Stonehammer step forward and put the case down in front of him. He stood up and waited, and the man with the flashlight knelt over the case. He appeared to be checking out the case's contents, but it was hard for me to see him past the other bodies. Apparently satisfied, the man stood, and Graham stepped forward. I couldn't see what he was doing, but after a moment, he reached forward and shook hands with the two men in front of him. He turned, and I could see that he was now holding the container that the men in the vessel had brought in.

One of the men from the boat was now holding the attaché case. Graham nodded at his entourage, and they all began walking back to the lot.

Off in the distance, a foghorn sounded over the water, and, as if on cue, two things happened with sudden swiftness. The front end of the vessel at the end of the pier jerked into the air and the entire boat was pulled into the water. A huge wave rose from the spot where the boat had been and splashed over the wharf. Before they could react, the two men from the boat—along with the attaché case—were swept into the dark waters of the ocean. At the same time, the Northsiders burst from the museum firing pistol rounds into the crowd of Claymores guarding the wharf. I reflexively covered my ears at the popping of the firearms, my overly sensitive hearing overwhelmed by the sudden explosions. The first salvo put five of the Claymores to the pavement. Blood began to flow from beneath their fallen bodies. The other three scattered and drew firearms of their own from their pockets. The eight Northsiders continued to charge, trying to do as much damage as their element of surprise would allow.

At the end of the wharf, a troll-sized figure shot out of the water like a big game fish. The figure cleared the railing and landed on the pier. I could see right away that it wasn't a troll. The fern-like skin emerging from either side of his neck gave it away. So did the glittering scales that covered his naked body from the soles of his feet to his upper abdomen. First an elf, and now a male adaro. What a day. Short of a dragon crossing the sky, I'd pretty much seen it all.

Graham and his contingent of Claymores ran as fast as they could toward the parking lot. Stonehammer stood his ground, cracking his knuckles in the same way that he had when he had greeted me at the front door of my office. In another moment, the troll and the adaro were locked in each other's arms, each trying to wrestle the other to the deck.

The adaro opened his mouth and bit down hard on Stonehammer's shoulder. Stonehammer howled in pain and shoved the adaro away from him. The two began to circle each other, looking for an opening. Stonehammer threw a lightning-quick left hook, but the adaro ducked under the punch. When he popped up again he lashed out with his own left hand and clawed at the bandage covering Stonehammer's eye. Stonehammer jerked his head back, and the adaro fired off a right hook that connected with the damaged eye. Stonehammer spun around and went down to one knee. The adaro closed fast, but Stonehammer launched himself into the adaro's midsection and then crushed the adaro to his body in a powerful bear hug. The adaro's body arched backwards, and he brought his elbow down on top of Stonehammer's head, once, twice, and then a third time. The third blow broke the troll's hold, and the two once again began to circle each other warily.

Meanwhile, the gunfight in the lot had descended into chaos. Two more of the Claymores were down, but the lone Claymore standing at the edge of the parking lot was joined by his friends running off the wharf with handguns drawn. With my hands still clapped over my ears, I crouched low and watched the gunfight unfold from my vantage point between the souvenir shops. Now would have been a good time to beat feet out of there, since I didn't have any way to defend myself from firearms, but no one had seen me yet and I didn't feel threatened. Three more of the Claymore gang had been shot down, leaving six still standing, but the Northsiders had not fared well since losing the element of surprise. Only four Northsiders were still on their feet.

Three of the Claymores advanced on the Northsiders, one leading the way with the other two lagging just behind. Another of the Claymores veered well off to his right to flank the Northsiders, who were advancing on the Claymores in their own ragged line. The remaining two Claymores hung back. They appeared to be out of ammo. They glanced at each other and backed away from the fighting. After a few steps, they turned and ran out of the parking lot, disappearing behind the blackened ruins of the Fujita's Boarding House building. That evened the odds at four to four.

My attention fell on one of the Northsiders, positioned on the left end of their line. He was shorter and slimmer than the others, and, unlike the other Northsiders who had folded their bandanas into headbands, this one wore a scarf with Northsider colors that covered the entire top of his head, including his ears and hair. As I watched, two of the Cartel gangsters pointed their guns in the direction of the undersized Northsider. Before they could get their shots off, the little Northsider fired a round at the further away of the two, who grabbed his stomach and went down to the asphalt in a heap. A split second later, the round from the closer of the two Claymore shooters ripped past the Northsider, doing no harm. The little Northsider didn't appear to flinch. Then the air was filled with the sounds of shots, too fast and hot for me to follow.

One of the Cartel gangsters crept alongside Graham's car, parked just to the left of the Northsiders, attempting to come around the other end and catch the Northsiders by surprise. But a tall, lanky Northsider shooter with a gunslinger handlebar mustache saw what the Cartel gangster was up to. Handlebar mustache sprinted toward the car and shot the Claymore gangster in the center of his abdomen as soon as he showed himself. The Claymore shooter staggered away in my direction for several steps before falling not far from where I was crouched. He tried to rise, and I could see that his coat was soaked with blood. He let out a ragged wheeze that was hard to hear. He staggered to his feet and stumbled out of the parking lot to Fremont Street, where he collapsed on the sidewalk. He didn't move again.

Meanwhile, the Claymore gangster who had fired at and missed the smaller Northsider now found himself engaged with two of the other shooters. One of the Northsiders shot him in his gun hand, forcing him to start shooting left-handed. He lacked the skill to pull it off. Although he fired off round after round, he failed to damage anything except brick and asphalt. During the exchange, one of his Northsider targets stepped into a pothole and fell to the asphalt, but the other kept his feet. He and the left-handed shooter were standing no more than ten yards apart, and the two of them had probably fired off a dozen rounds between them, but, other than the Claymore shooter's right hand, neither appeared to be any the worse for wear.

As the combatants began to break ranks and scatter across the parking lot, the smaller Northsider held his position as if he were the eye of the hurricane. I couldn't help but admire his grace and calm on the battlefield. He appeared to me to be handling himself like a trained combat veteran, and I should know. I wondered if he had served in the Borderland. He looked too small to be a soldier, but he was proving to be lethal in a firefight.

The cool little Northsider turned to his left and fired at the gangster who had been attempting to flank his crew, wounding him in the gut. The injured gangster staggered away in my direction, but kept his feet. Handlebar mustache followed him, and the two exchanged fire as they ran past me toward the street. The Northsider who had tripped and fallen now picked himself up and ran in their direction. He soon fell again, struck in the back by the left-handed gunman, but was able to scramble to his feet. He trailed blood as he ran by me, but he continued to fire off rounds. Either he or handlebar mustache finally struck gold. When the gut-shot Claymore reached the street, he turned to shoot at his pursuers. As he did, a bullet smacked into the center of his forehead, and the back of his head exploded in a red mist. Two members of the Claymore gang now lay unmoving on the sidewalk just outside the parking area. Handlebar mustache and the wounded Northsider headed back to the center of the action, and I sank back a little further into the shadows as they jogged past me. Only about thirty seconds had passed since the first shot in the four-against-four standoff had been fired.

A thunderous roar came from the far end of the wharf, and, with great care, I eased myself forward until I had a good view. I saw Stonehammer standing over the adaro, who was sprawled on his back. Blood was streaming down from the bandage covering the detective's bad eye, as well as from a cut in the center of his forehead and from a gash in his shoulder where the adaro had sunk his teeth. The maddened troll launched a kick at the adaro, and when he connected, I rubbed my own left side in sympathy. The adaro, however, managed to grab on to Stonehammer's leg. Rolling over, he yanked the troll's leg under his own body. Stonehammer slammed to the wooden walkway so hard that I thought the pilings supporting the wharf would crack. The adaro pounced and wrapped his arms around the fallen troll's head and neck. The adaro let out a tremendous howl, and the muscles in his arms swelled as he attempted to twist Stonehammer's head from his shoulders. The troll refused to cooperate. He managed to get his legs under him and rose to his feet. Grabbing the adaro's right wrist, he yanked the adaro's hand to his mouth, bit down hard, and shook his head with bestial ferocity. Blood gushed from the adaro's hand. He released the troll's head and staggered backward in obvious pain. Stonehammer spit the adaro's bloody finger to the wharf and roared so loudly that the soldier boys stopped shooting at each other and turned to see what was happening. As we all watched, Stonehammer launched a sudden haymaker that connected solidly with the adaro's jaw. The sound of the bone snapping was nearly as loud as the shots from the pistols. The adaro fell backwards to the edge of the wharf, rolled over once, and dropped over the side into the ocean. Stonehammer sniffed once and rolled his head one way and then the other over his shoulders. Then he turned toward the parking lot, his one good eye glowing like a red-hot coal beneath his lowered brow.

 At that moment, I saw Graham disappear around the side of one of the buildings on my side of the lot. He was holding the container from the ship closely to his chest. The nimble little Northsider that I had noticed earlier also saw him and rushed off in his direction. I darted to the back of the souvenir shop just in time to see Graham emerge onto the remains of a paved alleyway behind the buildings. He hesitated for a moment, and the Northsider came crashing into him from behind. The force of the Northsider's blindside charge sent them both to the ground. Graham's head hit the pavement and he didn't move. The Northsider stood and poked at Graham with his foot. When Graham remained motionless, the Northsider stooped and picked up the boxy container that had fallen from Graham's arms. He kicked at Graham again, turned, and began walking in my direction.

Or, rather, she did. As the Northsider approached to within a few feet of me, I got a good look at her. Her scarf had fallen from her head when she tackled Graham, and dark blue hair now streamed down the sides of her face. It was the face of Cora Seafoam.

No, that's not right. It was a younger, wilder-eyed, more unkempt version of Cora Seafoam: the girl from the photo on my phone. I guess that at least some of Miss Seafoam's story had been on the level after all.

I was just about to step out and intercept Mila, when a booming voice shouted, "Don't move!" Mila froze. Twenty yards behind her stood Stonehammer, blood covering his face and streaking down the front of his coat. The troll was aiming a shotgun at Mila's back.

"Turn around," Stonehammer shouted. Mila turned. "Put the box down."

With a sigh, Mila did as she was told.

"Put your hands behind your head and get down on your knees," Stonehammer ordered.

Mila complied.

"Are you carrying a rod?" Stonehammer asked.

"No," said Mila. "I dropped it over there." She waved her right arm vaguely toward the lot.

"Keep your hands behind your head!" Stonehammer bellowed, and Mila returned her right hand to its place, dropping it casually below her left hand to the back of her neck.

The troll strutted toward Mila with a decided lack of caution. When he reached Mila, he put his shotgun into a holster hidden underneath his long coat and wiped his sleeve across his face, smearing the blood. After trashing a male adaro, Stonehammer didn't appear to consider a female one to be much of a threat.

A lascivious smile spread across Stonehammer's face. "Stand up," he said. "I'm going to have to search you."

Mila stood. Stonehammer stooped, and, leering at Mila, reached out and ripped open her coat. Buttons spilled to the ground. Blood dripped from Stonehammer's teeth. He reached out with his left hand and grabbed the adaro's breast.

In a flash, Mila's right hand ripped through the air and plunged a knife into Stonehammer's neck.

Stonehammer stood still for a moment, confused. Then he straightened up to his full height and towered over the adaro girl. The knife was ripped away from Mila's grasp as it remained buried in the troll's neck. A fresh stream of blood began to spill down Stonehammer's coat, and he staggered backwards. But he remained upright and glared hard at Mila with his single burning eye.

As I watched, transfixed, my attention was drawn by a movement back where Mila had tackled Graham. Blood dripped from a gash in the captain's forehead, but he was alive. He rubbed blood off his face and looked at it. He groaned and climbed to his hands and knees.

There's a time to observe and a time to act. It was time to act. Pulling my suit coat over my head to hide my face, I sprang into the alleyway and ran toward Mila. I scooped up the box from the ground with one arm. Then I wrapped my other arm around Mila, pinning her arms to her sides. I leaned to her ear and said in a near whisper, "Your sister says hello. Follow me." I released her and began to sprint up the alleyway toward the road, trusting that Mila would follow. The staccato sounds of gunfire still ringing out from the parking lot punctuated a series of long deafening roars from the wounded troll as I raced through the night.

I reached the road, made a left turn, and ran as fast as I could across the street toward my parked car. Mila was right behind me. A few steps down the road, I heard Mila shouting, "Shit! Shit! Shit! Where the fuck is he?"

I looked back at her.

Mila had slowed to a jog. "Quapo was supposed to park the getaway van here, but the little bitch must have cleared out when the shooting started. Fucking pussy! Shit!"

"I've got a car up ahead," I said. "Don't stop running! I'll get you out of here."

She glared up at me with contempt, and for a second I thought she was going to tell me to fuck off. Then her eyes were drawn to the container that I had picked up in the alley. She nodded once and followed me to my car.

As we drew near my car, I took my key fob out of my pocket and pressed the button twice to unlock the doors. I climbed in on the driver's side, and Mila hurried into the passenger's seat. I glanced back through my rear window and saw Stonehammer supporting Graham as the two staggered out of the alleyway to the road. I started the car, and, leaving the lights off, I drove away into the darkness.

Chapter Six

After I had put a couple of blocks behind me, I switched my headlights on and turned my head to see Mila glaring at me like a caged tiger.

"My name is Alex," I said.

"I don't fucking care!" Mila said, still glaring.

This was going well.

"You can give me that box and drop me off at the corner," Mila suggested, snarling.

"Not yet," I said. "I need to talk to your sister first."

The glare didn't diminish. "What's she got to do with this?"

"She sent me to find you," I said. "She's worried about you."

"Well isn't that sweet," Mila said, her voice dripping with sarcasm.

"She wants me to bring you to her."

Mila's eyes lit up in alarm. "No fuckin' way! Okay? Give me the box and drop me off. Now!"

I looked at her. "You don't want to see her?"

"Of course not, you fucking idiot! I didn't take that box away from Graham just to give it right back to him."

That left me a little confused. "What's this box got to do with anything?"

"Are you kidding?" Mila's eyes widened and she shook her head, incredulous. "Just give it to me and let me out."

"Not until I call her," I said.

"Fine!" Mila huffed. "Call her. I'd like to talk to that bitch myself."

I put the box on my left side so that Mila couldn't easily grab it and run. When I had picked it up in the alley, I hadn't really paid it much attention. I noticed it now for the first time. It was a black box made of thick metal, about a foot long, maybe four inches wide, and another four inches deep. The box was closed and locked. Two keyholes awaited a key. I didn't have a key, but that wasn't going to be a problem. I could bust it open if I had to. The box was heavy, weighing between five and ten pounds, and it was cold to the touch, colder than I would have expected. I wedged it securely between my left leg and the car door and took my phone out of my pocket. Making sure to watch the road, I found Miss Seafoam's number in my recent calls and tapped it. The call took me directly to voice mail and I disconnected without leaving a message.

"She hasn't been answering me," I said. "To be honest, I think she might be in some trouble."

"It would serve the old whore right if she was," Mila scowled. "She needs to mind her own fuckin' business."

"Hey," I said. "She's your sister, and she's genuinely worried about you."

"Fuck! Her!" Mila spit out the words. "She's not answering your call, so I think we're done here. I've got things to do. Give me the box and I'll dust."

"Uh-uh," I said. "What did you mean when you said that you didn't take the box away from Graham just to give it back to him?"

Mila rolled her eyes. She was sweating heavily, and her musky scent was filling my car. She was an adaro female, still burning adrenaline, and I was finding it a little hard to concentrate. "What do you *think* she's going to do with the box? Graham fuckin' *owns* her!"

I glanced quickly at Mila, and she must have seen some confusion in that glance.

Mila continued, exasperated. "You're completely clueless, aren't you. Look. Just give me the fuckin' box and go home."

I hesitated. I mean, she was right. I *was* clueless. Why had Seafoam come to me with her half-assed story? What was the rumble at the pier all about? What was the deal with this box?

Maybe the best thing for me to do was to give the box to Mila and walk out of this whole shitstorm while I could. But I couldn't let it go. I wished I could talk to Miss Seafoam, but I was having bad feelings about that. She would have called me hours ago if she was okay.

"I need to get some questions answered first. I'm taking you to your sister," I said.

Mila threw her hands in the air. "Great!" she said. "Just go back there and find Graham. We can all go together." When I didn't respond, she said, "You *do* know that she practically *lives* with Graham, right?" She stared at me, eyes wide. "He's got a wife and family down in the 'burbs, but he set my sister up in this luxury fuck pad in the city, and he spends all of his time there."

I concentrated on the road, trying to hide my surprise.

Mila continued to stare at me. "Wow," she said. "You didn't fucking know that, did you. Ho. Lee. Shit."

I kept driving. We were in downtown traffic now, still heavy even though it was after midnight, and every time I stopped the car I worried that Mila would open the door and jump out. But she didn't. She wasn't going anywhere without the box.

We rode in silence for a minute, both of us watching the road. I stopped at a light and took the opportunity to look her over. She shared enough features with Miss Seafoam to convince me that they were sisters, if that had ever been in doubt. Same eyes, same mouth, and, I suspect, the same hair if this wild creature could be convinced to take care of it. Mila was definitely the younger of the two, and by a good five years, if not more. Miss Seafoam appear to be in her mid-twenties; Mila couldn't have been more than eighteen. Of course, I was applying human standards, and I didn't know if they applied to female adaros. The difference in age between the sisters was more than physical. Miss Seafoam radiated sophistication. Mila was rough, edgy, prickly, and I would have said the same even if I hadn't seen her plugging thugs and stabbing trolls without hesitation or mercy. They shared at least one important thing in common. I glanced down and read the numbers 254877 tattooed on Mila's left wrist, and I knew that I would find a similar number on Cora's wrist if she ever allowed it to show.

Mila turned her head toward me and followed my eyes to her wrist. She looked back up, eyes flashing. "Say something about it!" she challenged in a menacing hiss that reminded me of a feral alley cat. I just shrugged and directed my gaze back to the road.

Mila continued to fire daggers at me with her eyes. Then she said, "So you were supposed to bring me to her, right?" Mila said, speaking to me as if I were an ignorant child. "What are you, some kind of fuckin' private dick? Yeah, that's something she would do. Well, *Dickhead*, where did she tell you to bring me? Did she check into a hotel or something?"

I didn't want to answer, but I said, "We didn't actually get that far. She came to my office this morning and wanted to hire me to find you. I turned her down."

Mila was having trouble sorting that out. I didn't blame her. I felt blood rising into my cheeks. I turned my face to hide my embarrassment.

"It was only after Stonehammer came to scare me off that I decided to help her," I explained. "I texted her to call me, but I haven't heard from her."

"Th'fuck!" Mila started pounding her head with her fists. "What did she tell you about me?"

"She told me you had fallen in with a bad crowd." Mila let out an exasperated breath, and I knew that I was touching on a familiar point of contention between her and her sister. "She said that you and your friends were going to be trading a cache of drugs to the Claymore Cartel tonight for weapons, and that she wanted me to drag you out of it and bring you to her."

"Fuck," Mila said in disgust. "She's a lying bitch." Looking up at me, she added, "I bet she didn't even mention the box, did she?"

"No, she didn't," I admitted.

"Figures," Mila snorted. "She's a moron. You're a moron. You're all fucking morons!"

"What's in this thing, anyway?" I asked, expecting more verbal abuse in return.

But Mila just looked away. "I don't know," she muttered. "All I know is that it's valuable. Graham was having it smuggled in. According to...my sources...it's supposed to be worth a fortune." She looked back at me. "It would be all mine right now if it weren't for you."

"Hey," I said. "I got you out of there, didn't I?"

"Are you kidding?" Mila asked in disbelief. "I had everything under control. If you hadn't come along, I'd have the box. And I'd be taking care of...." Her voice faltered, and she looked away. "Never mind," she muttered.

"Taking care of who?" I asked. "The rest of your gang? Wait. The adaro. Of course."

Mila's eyes fell, but she said nothing.

"Who is he?" I asked.

"What do you care," Mila said sullenly.

"What's his name?" I asked gently.

Mila frowned at me and let out three inhuman blooping noises that sounded like bubbles bursting from a pool of oil.

"That's his name," said Mila. "You can call him Kraken. It's a stupid name, but he likes it, and humans can pronounce it." She looked down again and muttered, "Stupid son of a bitch better still be alive."

"What is he, your brother?" I asked.

"No-o-o!" She used three syllables to say it in a sing-song voice that told me I was an idiot for asking. "He's not my *brother*. He's.... We're a thing! You know." She actually seemed a little flustered, and it struck me how young she was. "The fucking moron!" she finished.

I had a swell idea. "Maybe we should find him," I said.

She whipped her head around and stared at me openmouthed. "Seriously?" She asked with a hint of a tremble in her voice.

"Sure," I said. "I can't reach your sister, and, from what you've told me, we can't go to her. I'm not letting go of this box right now. Don't ask. I've got my own reasons." Truthfully, I wasn't quite sure myself what those reasons were. I felt like the box was the key to something, though, and I wanted to hang onto it until I got some answers.

Mila just snorted.

"Tell me about tonight," I said. "What was it all about?"

Mila sighed. "Kraken heard that something was coming in tonight at midnight. Something worth a lot of dough." She looked up at me. "When I talked about my sources earlier? Well, that's Kraken. He's my source. Anyway, Kraken and I decided to intercept it. I got some of the boys together for the job. I'm a Northsider!" she said, beaming with pride. "I'm the only girl they allow to fight with them!" She paused. "We figured that Graham would be there with some backup, but we weren't expecting the Claymore Cartel to be working with the cops. That's some serious shit!" She frowned for half a second and then continued. "Anyway, Kraken followed the boat to the pier. The plan was that after the merchandise was delivered to Graham, Kraken would come from the water, and we would come out of the museum. We thought we could get the drop on the cops and get them to hand the merchandise over without bloodshed." She looked up at me again. "Obviously, that didn't work."

"If Kraken knew about the box, why didn't he just sink the boat at sea and take it?" I asked.

"Kraken said that something was coming in, but he didn't know what it was exactly. We didn't know what he should be looking for. I told him that we should wait for something to be transferred to Graham and then we could take it away from him."

"Did you know that Kraken was going to have to fight a troll?" I asked.

"We figured he would be there. Stonehammer is like Graham's personal bodyguard. But Kraken said he could take him. I was hoping that we would surprise them and that they would just hand the merchandise over. We were going to be pointing a lot of guns at them. Like I said, we didn't know that the Cartel would be there." She sighed again. "And, well, things just kind of went kablooey." Then she glowered at me. "But I got the box! You had no right to take it away from me!"

"Take it easy, kid," I said. "The box isn't going anywhere, and Graham doesn't have it."

"So what do you want?" asked Mila. "A cut? Maybe we can work that out."

"We'll see," I said. The effect of Mila's scent was getting stronger, and I felt myself starting to lose my focus. I lowered the window a crack and tried to clear my head.

"I saw you during the gunfight. You handled yourself well," I told her.

Mila shrugged. "I drilled a couple of the motherfuckers."

"Have you had any military training?" I asked.

"What? No!" she said. "Who the hell is going to give *me* military training? Th'fuck!" She rolled her eyes, letting me know what an idiot I was.

"Did you really lose your piece out there?" I asked.

"Ran out of ammo," she said with disgust. "I got pissed and threw my rod at some fucker who was shooting at me. Missed him, but one of my boys shot at him and he ran like a fuckin' pussy." She grinned. She thought that firefights were fun.

I glanced at Mila as I drove. Only her face was visible to me over her high collared coat, but it struck me that she had pretty blue eyes.

I put the brakes on that train of thought before it could get started, reminding myself that she was a female adaro emitting dangerous vibes, and that I was at least ten years older than her. I also reminded myself that she had killed several people tonight without a hint of remorse in order to get her hands on the box I was holding, and that she would have no problem killing one more in order to take it and run. The memory of her sticking a knife in Stonehammer's neck shook the fog out of my brain and brought me back to full awareness. Underestimating this girl would get me dead in a hurry.

"Hey," I said, changing the subject. "Your sister didn't use her real name when I talked to her. What is it, anyway?"

"What name did she use?" Mila asked.

"Cora Seafoam."

Mila laughed without humor. "Figures," she said. "That's her professional name."

"Professional name?"

"Yeah," said Mila in a voice that sounded like she was sucking a lemon. "At the escort agency. She's a whore. Didn't you know *that*, either? An expensive whore. You said that she came to see you this morning? Did you fuck her?" She let out a little laugh. "Nah. Not you. You couldn't afford her."

So, high-end sex trade, just as I thought. "What's her real name?" I asked again. "Among humans, I mean."

"Leena. Leena Waterfowl. Pretty stupid, huh. And I'm Mila Waterfowl. That's the kind of name you get when government bureaucrats assign them to you. You get it? We come out of the water, so we get cute water names. Fuckin' shitheads!" She paused. "But anyway," she said with enthusiasm. "Let's go find Kraken. We need to go back the other way. I'll show you."

"Hang on," I said. "First I want to find out what's in this box and then put it somewhere safe."

Mila's eyes lit up, and I knew that she was as anxious as I was to open the box and find out what was inside.

***

By now, it was going on one in the morning. Yerba City's nightlife was always active, even during the middle of the week. It took me another half hour to make my way out of the downtown traffic and into a quieter light industrial zone. I pulled the car into a parking place on the street near a street light. I got out of the car, bringing the box with me. Mila got out on her side, and we both walked to the front of the car. I set the box on the hood, and we both examined it.

Mila looked at the keyholes and frowned. "How are you going to open it?" she asked.

"You don't have the key?" I asked her in mock surprise.

"No," she said as if I had asked her whether she could fly. "I don't have a fuckin' key!"

I laid the palms of both of my hands on the box. It was cold. Colder than it should have been.

"Don't you have a crowbar or something?" Mila asked. "We should be able to pop those locks."

I paused, thinking. "Feel this box," I said, and she reached out with one hand and touched it.

"It's freezing!" she exclaimed.

"Yeah," I agreed. I looked at her. "You don't know what's in here?" I asked. "No idea at all?"

"No," Mila admitted grudgingly. "I only know that it's valuable, and that a captain in the YCP fuckin' D arranged to have it smuggled in to an abandoned pier in the dead of night."

I didn't say anything.

"You think it's booby-trapped or something?" Mila asked.

I shook my head. "No. Probably not."

"Then what?" Patience was not one of Mila's virtues. She was about a second away from trying to snatch the box and run.

"Think about it," I said. "Why is this box so cold?"

Mila thought.

I didn't let her think too long. She might have come to the wrong conclusion. "Whatever's inside must need to be kept on ice," I explained. "If we open it, we might damage the contents." An idea popped into my head, and I leaned down and pressed my ear to the box. I heard a clear humming sound from deep inside.

I stood back up and said, "See if you hear anything."

Mila pressed her ear to the box and kept it there for several seconds. Then she straightened and said, "Yeah, it's humming. I can barely hear it, but it's definitely humming. It's not wired to explode, is it?"

"No, there's a freezer unit of some kind in it," I said. "That's why the box is so cold. Must be battery powered."

"What would need to be kept frozen?" Mila asked. She was suspicious, thinking that I was trying to pull some sort of grift.

"I don't know," I said. "Maybe a drug of some kind?"

That seemed to make some sense to Mila. She drew inward, thinking. Finally she said, "Let's go see Kraken. Maybe he'll have some ideas."

I pictured myself alone with two adaros, one of them a male capable of rolling over a twenty-five-foot smuggler's boat and wrestling with a troll.

I said, "I want to hide this box first."

Mila narrowed her eyes at me. "Hey," she said. "What are you trying to pull?"

"The police are looking for us," I reminded Mila. "The longer this box is in our hands, the better chance they have of taking it away from us. We need to put it somewhere safe before we go meet Kraken."

Mila looked ready to pounce.

"Stand down, Mila," I said. "Trust me. I'm not trying to screw you over. I'm not sure I want any part of this thing, but I don't want Graham to have it any more than you do. Let's stash it and go see Kraken."

Mila's eyes smoldered and I prepared for a charge. I was a good eight inches taller than the little adaro and outweighed her by a hundred pounds, but I'd seen her in action, and I wasn't putting anything past her.

The moment came and went, and Mila relaxed a bit. Maybe it might have been a different story if she hadn't lost her rod and her blade, but she knew she couldn't take me on emptyhanded.

"All right," she nodded. "Whatcha got in mind?"

"A lawyer I know has an office near here," I said.

"He must keep late hours," Mila said.

"He won't be there, but I can get in and hide the box for the night. We can come back for it when it's safe."

Mila hesitated, but then gave in. "Okay, let's go do it and find Kraken. But don't try nothin' funny!"

I drove us to Lubank's office building. When we got there, I unlocked the door to the building and we went upstairs. The building key also opened Lubank's office, and we went inside.

"Th'fuck!" Mila exclaimed, coughing. "Someone likes to smoke!"

"You can wait in the hall if you want," I offered.

"No way!" said Mila, waving her hands in front of her face. The thick blanket of smoke hung undisturbed.

I smiled and looked for a good place to stash the metal box. Not finding anything in the reception area, I opened Lubank's inner office door and walked in. He had a closet in his office where he hung extra shirts and suits. Various items had been stuffed on a shelf at the top of the closet. I pushed the box into the back corner of the shelf up against the wall where it would be unnoticed by anyone who wasn't looking for it. Not even Lubank would know it was there.

I turned to leave, but then stopped. Hanging in the closet was a fur-lined leather raincoat. I hesitated, and then took it down and put it on. It was too tight for me to button, and it barely hung past my waist, but it was warm. Turning, I saw Mila looking at me with an arched eyebrow and the hint of a smile. I knew I looked ridiculous, but I was desperate. Swearing that I would make it up to Lubank, I led Mila out of the office and back into the street, making sure to lock the doors behind me.

Once we were standing beside my car, I asked, "Okay, so how do we get to Kraken?"

"Back toward the pier," Mila said. "I'll show you."

I noticed that she took one last look back at Lubank's office building, but, with a deep breath and a shrug, she got into the car and we took off.

Chapter Seven

"What did you think Graham was arranging to pick up?" I asked Mila as we headed back in the direction of the pier.

"I don't know," Mila said. "Diamonds maybe. Or drugs. Maybe some priceless artifact. We figured that once we had it, we'd find a way to sell it."

"You and Kraken?"

"Yeah." Mila grew thoughtful. "We've been seeing each other for a while. Not that it's any of your business!" She leveled another fierce glare at me. I was getting used to that glare. It seemed to be her default facial expression. Then she looked away and muttered, "Leena fuckin' hates him."

So Seafoam, or Leena, knew about Kraken and Mila. Something else she had failed to mention to me. I wondered about Leena's part in all of this. Had she really been unaware of what was going to happen at the pier? What had she actually wanted me to do? She knew all along that I wasn't going to be able to talk Mila into leaving Kraken behind and going with me voluntarily. Had she wanted me to take Mila away by force? But she must have known that Kraken would be there to stop me. Did she know that Stonehammer would be there to stop Kraken? Then she would have known that Graham would be there, too, or at least that Stonehammer would have been there on Graham's behalf. Was she working with Graham? But if that were the case, why had Graham sent Stonehammer to keep me from interfering? Was she working *against* Graham? Why? And why come to me?

My head was spinning. None of this made any sense. And now I was on my way to meet a wounded and possibly enraged adaro who was capable of yanking ships to the bottom of the sea. Not to mention that I'd been driving his girlfriend around for the last hour, and for all I knew he could be the jealous type. What was I doing? What reason could I have for being involved in this mess? Curiosity? Pride? If I survived the night, I was going to have to seriously consider finding a therapist. Or go on a bender. Maybe I would go on a bender with a therapist.

I became aware that Mila was staring a hole into the side of my head.

"What?" I snapped.

"Kraken is not going to be happy that you stashed that box," she said. "He's going to wonder why we didn't bring it to him."

"I know a guy who can open that box without damaging its contents," I told her. "He's got a lab, so if it's some kind of drug he'll be able to tell us what it is."

Mila narrowed her eyes at me. "What do you mean he's got a lab?"

"He's a chemist," I said. Technically, that was true, but only barely. Tom Kintay did not have a degree in chemistry, or in anything else for that matter, having dropped out of school when he was sixteen. But he did, in fact, work with chemicals. To be precise, he synthesized chemicals into illegal designer drugs for the Hatfield Syndicate, one of the biggest underworld operators in western Tolanica. Back when I was an M.P. I had arrested Corporal Kintay for stealing pharmaceutical supplies from the army hospital. He never held it against me, though. After his dishonorable discharge and my honorable one, we both wound up in Yerba City. Although our career paths differed, we ran across each other from time to time, and even though we weren't exactly friends we at least got along pretty well.

Mila thought about this for a bit. Then she nodded and told me to make a right turn at the next light. We entered Placid Point and found a parking place a couple of blocks east of the old Placid Point Pier.

"There's an adaro settlement down that way," Mila pointed in the direction that led away from the pier. "That's where I live. We need to get to the shore down over there." She led the way.

Soon we climbed down to a small beach covered with driftwood, kelp, and trash and surrounded by a low cliff. "There's a cave over there," said Mila pointing off to our right. "You'll never find it in the dark, so keep up with me."

Actually, I *could* see it, thanks to my newly acquired night-vision, but I had no reason to reveal that nugget of information to Mila. She might be thinking of me as a business partner, but that could change in a flash once we found Kraken. I followed close behind her and we reached the entrance to a broad cave that the ocean waves had carved out of the side of the cliff.

"You're going to get wet," Mila told me. "The water will be up to your knees. Hope you can stand it, human."

Great. I transferred my wallet and phone from my pants pockets to my suit coat pocket, hoping that they would now be less likely to get soaked. I wished that I had left them in my car. The ground was too rocky to take off my shoes, and I resolved to endure soggy socks and ruined slacks without complaining. Oh well. I stepped into the water and followed Mila into the cave.

Kraken was sitting up in the water at the back of the cave. His face lit up when he saw Mila, who glided into his open arms. As he embraced his gal, though, he gave me a stare designed by nature to freeze prey in its tracks. Strange gurgling noises emerged from his mouth, sounding to me like *bloorp, broorup, gloorl*. In response, Mila turned and glanced at me.

"Oh, don't worry about him, baby," she said in a reassuring tone. "He's with us. For now, at least."

Gee thanks. That ought to soothe the beast.

Up close I could see that the adaro was a bit smaller than Stonehammer, except that he was broader in the chest and shoulders. He had a handsome face, though his dark blue eyes seemed to lack spark. Wet golden locks hung limp over his forehead. When I last saw him, he was a raging monster from the sea. Up close, I could see that he was as young as Mila, at that awkward stage between late adolescence and young adulthood. Massive muscles bulged from every part of his body, including the ridges above his eyes. He looked to be in remarkable shape for someone who had fought a troll an hour ago, other than the fact that he was missing most of the ring finger on his right hand. It had been reduced to a purple stump, but it wasn't bleeding.

Mila took the big fellow's hand and kissed the wounded stump. "Poor baby," she cooed. Then she balled her hand into a fist and pounded it hard into Kraken's chest. "You asshole! You said that you could take him!"

Kraken's face softened. He made apologetic burbling noises.

"Speak human!" Mila ordered. "We have a guest."

Kraken turned his killer stare back on me. "Who are you?" he demanded in an accent that sounded vaguely Polynesian.

"That's Dickhead," said Mila before I could answer.

"I'm Alex," I said.

"Leena hired him to find me," Mila continued. "She wanted him to get me away from the pier before the trouble started. He's a private cop."

Kraken gurgled a question at Mila.

"A private detective. Like a cop, but one you can hire. He works for himself, not the police department," Mila explained.

The confused look didn't leave Kraken's face, and I gathered that he didn't spend much time out of the ocean. He burbled at Mila some more.

"I told you to speak human!" Mila admonished. "Be polite!" She went on, "He snatched the box. I had to go with him because Quapo pussied out and dusted when the lead started flying. I'll deal with him later."

"Quapo left you?" Kraken growled. "That *borrgloop-borrbl*! I'll rip his head off!"

"Don't worry about Quapo," said Mila. "We don't need him. Me and Dickhead got the box away from Graham."

"It's Alex," I said.

Kraken snapped his head toward me. "Give me the box!" he roared.

"We don't have it with us," Mila explained. "There's something funny about it. It's keeping something real cold. If we open the box wrong, it might damage the contents."

Kraken grappled with these thoughts. It was going to take him a while to process what he was hearing. Mila plowed on. "Don't worry, baby. Dickhead stashed it somewhere safe for the night. Me and him'll get it back in the morning and take it somewhere where it can be opened safely, and then we'll find out what's inside. Hey, baby—it's okay! I've got this!"

Mila's words appeared to soothe Kraken, who was now staring at her with a tender look on his face. His breathing was starting to get slow and heavy.

Uh-oh.

Mila melted into her boyfriend's body and raised her face to his. Kraken lowered his face to hers and the two of them began to mash each other's lips with youthful passion. Their mouths were wide open. It looked like they were trying to eat each other.

I cleared my throat. It took three tries, each louder than the last.

After my third try, Mila tore her lips away from Kraken's and twisted her head in my direction. "What!" she said.

"Should I leave you two alone for a while?" I asked. "I could come back later."

Mila rolled her eyes at me. "Shut up!" she said. Kraken pulled open her coat, exposing her gills, which he began to kiss.

"Stop it!" Mila shouted at him. She reached behind Kraken's head and yanked it back by his hair. Then she slapped him across the face as hard as she could.

Kraken blinked twice and took a deep breath. Then he favored me again with his steely stare of death.

"Don't blame me!" I said. "We've got to figure out our next step. We can't stay here long."

Kraken turned to Mila for an explanation.

Mila kissed him on the cheek and said, "The police might be coming after us. I sort of stabbed Stonehammer in the neck."

"Really?" said Kraken. "With a knife?"

"Yes with a knife!" Mila snapped at him. "What do you think I stabbed him with? My butt?"

"Did you kill him?" Kraken asked.

"No, but he was real pissed," said Mila.

"Huh!" Kraken grunted. "Too bad you didn't kill him." He held up his hand. "The *brurrl-boorrrp* bit my finger off. See?"

"I know, baby, and I'm so sorry!" Mila kissed the purple stub again. "We need to hide out until we find out what's in that box."

"Stay here with me," said Kraken.

Mila thought for a second, and then looked at me. "What about him?" she asked, frowning.

I was waiting for this. I knew that I was in a tricky situation, and that it could go bad if I didn't do something about it fast. Mila was on the verge of deciding that she didn't need me. She knew where the box was and would have no compunction about storming into Lubank's office and taking it, possibly hurting Gracie and Lubank in the process if they stood in her way. All she had to do was say the word, and Kraken would take me out of the picture for keeps. I needed to make sure that they both knew I was necessary. It was time for some slick talking.

"Whatever is in that box is going to make you both rich," I began, "but only if you can get it out without spoiling it. The box is refrigerated, probably using liquid nitrogen or something like that. It's battery powered. Whatever's in there needs to be frozen. If you bust the box open, you'll lose the refrigeration and whatever's in it will thaw out. If that happens, it will be worthless. Depending on what it is, it might even be deadly. You'll get nothing for your troubles. You might even get killed."

I paused to make sure that they were both listening. They were.

"I'm going to retrieve the box after I've had some sleep and take it to a guy I know. He has a lab. He'll be able to open the box, take out whatever's inside, and keep it cold. If it's a chemical compound of some kind, which is what I think we're probably dealing with here, he'll be able to test it and tell you what it is. Then you can figure out what you're going to do with it."

Kraken's eyes narrowed as he tried to think. Thinking wasn't something he did a lot of, and it didn't come easy to him. "What if it's some kind of big *groorrl* that has to be kept frozen or it will explode? Like a *bruurbl-groorblup* or something like that."

"I don't think you can fit a nuclear bomb in a little box like that, baby," Mila explained in her talking-to-a-child voice. "And I don't think you can keep a nuclear bomb from going off by freezing it." Mila looked at me. "Do you think it could be something they use to *make* a nuclear bomb?"

"Like plutonium?" I said.

"Yeah, I guess so," said Mila.

I shook my head. "No, plutonium is transported in powder form in a sealed container. It doesn't need to be frozen."

"Hunh," said Mila. Kraken just looked on with those narrowed eyes, mouth contorted into an "oh." At least I had them thinking.

"But," I said, "it could be some kind of chemical weapon, or maybe a disease virus. If you expose it to the air...." I let them work out the rest for themselves.

"Th'fuck!" Mila exclaimed. "We could kill off the whole city! We might even wipe out all life on the planet!"

That was a stretch, but I wanted to put a little fear in them.

They got the picture. "Okay," said Mila. "We'll do it your way. But you aren't leaving my sight until we get the box, and I'm going with you when you give it to the lab guy."

"Fine," I said, "but I can't stay here."

Kraken frowned as he worked out the implications. He looked at Mila with alarm. "So you're going to leave me?"

Mila caressed his cheek. "I have to, baby. Just for a day or two. But it'll be okay. I just need to make sure that Dickhead doesn't take the box and run. I don't trust him."

Terrific.

Mila continued to comfort the overgrown child, "Don't worry. When this is over, we're going to be fuckin' rich! Then we can go wherever we want and do whatever we want. Not even my sister will be able to stop us."

Their eyes locked and it looked like they were about to heat up again, so I said, "Right. I'm going back to my place. Mila, you don't have to come with me, but it would probably be best if you do. You don't trust me, and I don't trust you."

Kraken didn't like this idea at all. "I don't want him with you. He's a *gruuub-grurr* human. You know what they're like."

"It's okay, baby," cooed Mila. She looked hard at me. "He won't touch me. He's seen what I do to men who touch me when I don't want them to."

I threw my hands up in surrender. "No problem from me," I assured them both. "I'd rather live. This is strictly business." Mila and Kraken both grimaced at me, exposing their pointed shark-like teeth.

I stepped out of the cave and returned to shore. After a couple of minutes, Mila joined me. She wouldn't meet my eyes, but she had a shy smile on her face. "Let's go, Dickhead," she said.

***

"Did you fire your housekeeper?" Mila asked me after I let her into my office.

"I think I mentioned that Stonehammer tried to talk me out of taking your sister's case," I said. "We argued about it."

"Th'fuck!" Mila exclaimed. "How are you still alive?"

I crossed the room and picked up the bloodstained glass shard with the still intact bottleneck at one end. Holding it up, I said, "You saw Stonehammer's bandaged eye?" I slashed the glass through the air at half speed, demonstrating my earlier strike.

"Holy shit—*you* did that to him?" Mila fixed me with an openmouthed stare. "I may have underestimated you."

I wasn't sure whether to be flattered or insulted, so I let it go. It had been a long day, and I was nearly dead on my feet.

"We can sleep upstairs," I said.

Mila narrowed her eyes at me.

"Don't worry," I assured her. "You can take the bedroom. I'll sleep on the living room couch. There's a door between the two rooms. You can lock it if you want."

"I'm not worried about you," Mila said with artificial bravado. "I can handle myself if you give me any trouble."

"I'm not attracted to children," I said.

She inhaled sharply. I'd insulted her by calling her a child. Then her lips spread slightly into a coy smile, "Sure," she said. "I'll pass the word to any children I happen to run into."

Mila followed me upstairs and I showed her the bedroom and bathroom.

"I'm going to take a shower," she announced.

"That's okay, but let me use the facilities first. Then I'll get out of your way."

"You don't want a shower?" she asked. "You're a fuckin' mess, you know. And you smell like shit."

"Thanks, I'm aware," I said. "But I'm too tired. Maybe in the morning."

"Suit yourself," she said, her coy smile back in place. I was starting to feel a bit lightheaded, and I had to remind myself that I was alone with a young female adaro, and an attractive one at that. I stepped into the bathroom and locked the door behind me.

After using the toilet, I made a few swipes at my face with a wet washcloth. I wasn't any cleaner when I finished, but I felt a little better. I opened the bathroom door and Mila stood just a few feet away, waiting for me. Her eyes were wide, wet, and innocent. Her lips were soft and inviting. She reminded me of

Cora—Leena, that is. Tendrils of fog tickled my brain. Forcing my way out of a growing lethargy that threatened to overwhelm my reason, I kept my face blank and did my best to ignore the kittenish adaro. I stepped past her, but couldn't help watching her out of the corner of my eye. She walked slowly toward the bathroom, pulling her shirt over her head with one hand as she moved. Without turning, she stretched her arm high over her head and let her shirt fall to the floor beside her. She glanced back at me with a suggestive smile and stepped into the bathroom, leaving the door open behind her. I grabbed a couple of spare blankets from my closet and hurried out the connecting door to the living room. She knew what kind of effect she had on human men, and I knew that she was playing with me. I had called her a child, but we both knew that wasn't true. Now she was getting some revenge by making me uncomfortable. Maybe, too, she was letting me know that she had power over me. I didn't know what she would do if I responded to her game, and I didn't want to find out. The image of her gunning down gang members was still fresh in my mind. I also wanted her to know that I was too cool and jaded to succumb to her charms.

But it wasn't easy. I left her in the bedroom, closing the door behind me. In a few moments, I heard her call out in a voice that was as smooth as velvet, "Sweet dreams, Dickhead." Then I heard the shower running. I arranged the blankets on my couch, stripped down to my boxers, and started to settle in.

A thought struck me, and I summoned Smokey. In seconds, the little elemental whooshed in through my narrowly opened window and floated to a stop in front of me.

"I'm going to sleep until a little after sunrise," I said. "Watch the building from outside. If anyone approaches the door, come back in and wake me up. Understand?"

"Smokey understands," said Smokey, and whooshed back out the window. Good. If Stonehammer or anyone else came looking for me, I'd have some warning.

Feeling more or less secure, I lay down at last and allowed my eyes to close. Sleep embraced me like a hungry grizzly bear.

Chapter Eight

I dreamed that I was a drop of water falling toward a vast ocean. For a moment I was plunging toward a rolling sheet of blue and silver water that stretched to the horizon in every direction, and then I sank below the surface. All at once, I *was* the ocean and the ocean was me. I was aware of every drop, and every drop was the whole. Everything was clear to me; nothing was hidden. In the deepest core of my being, I knew the wordless answer to every voiced question. I was entirely at peace, supremely enlightened, and utterly serene.

Something splashed on my forehead, and I reached up to brush it away. Something splashed me in the temple, and I pulled the blanket over my head. I could still remember feeling peaceful and serene, but the actual sensations of peace and serenity were gone, leaving nothing but emptiness in their wake.

A tiny breathy voice whispered in my ear, "Alex, wake up. Wake up, Alex!" The blanket flew off my head and a gust of wind blew into my face. "Wake up now!"

Against my will, I opened my eyes just in time to see Smokey zooming up from downstairs. The elemental blew a stream of water at my face. Smokey had been sucking up drops of water from the puddles on my office floor and then flying upstairs and splashing it on my head to wake me up. It was in an agitated state, stretching, contracting, and bending this way and that, all the while spinning with reckless speed. I became aware that someone was knocking at my office door downstairs.

"Men are here," said Smokey. "Men are here now!"

The final strands of my dream vanished. I gathered my thoughts and asked, "Is Mila okay?"

Smokey didn't respond.

"Mila," I repeated. "The adaro in my bedroom."

"Adaro not there anymore," Smokey told me.

"What?" I sat up. "When did she leave?"

"After Alex sleep, adaro leave building."

I didn't ask Smokey why it hadn't woke me up when Mila left. I hadn't told it to. My fault.

The knocking from downstairs grew louder, and a voice boomed, "Open up! Police! We know you're in there, Southerland. Open the door!"

I groaned and clambered to my feet. I entered the bedroom. The bed was unmade, but Mila was not there. Neither were her clothes. My immediate thought was that she had gone for the box. Had I misjudged her that badly? I was lucky she hadn't killed me in my sleep.

I was halfway dressed when the cops kicked my door in. I heard them curse when they saw the condition that my office was in. I was tying my shoelaces when they got upstairs and found me in my bedroom.

"Gentlemen," I said. "Is there something I can do for you?"

Two uniformed policemen stood side-by-side before me. Both were young. Neither smiled. One of them said, "Alexander Southerland? You're wanted for questioning. Come with us."

"What for?" I asked. "Go ahead and ask your questions now. I'll answer them."

"They want you downtown," said the cop. "Let's go."

"What's it about?" I asked.

"You'll find out," the cop said, and repeated, "Let's go!"

The two young cops were just pick-up and delivery. They didn't know why I was wanted. Giving them a hard time wasn't going to get me anywhere. I resigned myself to the inevitable, grabbed a jacket, and let the cops drive me downtown.

At the station, I was processed, fingerprinted, and my phone was confiscated. They ushered me into an interrogation room and left me alone at a table for about an hour with a cup of weak coffee and a strawberry jellyroll. I had few illusions about any of this turning out well for me, but I did have an ace up my sleeve, or, in this case, cupped in my hand.

Smokey was still with me. The elemental had followed me all the way into the interrogation room. Only two inches tall and practically invisible, it had passed through the police station unnoticed. The cops had cuffed my left hand to the underside of the table, but my right hand was free. I curled it into an open fist on the table in front of me, and Smokey flew inside. I leaned over and muttered some instructions to the elemental, who had troubles understanding some of them. After we puzzled everything out to my satisfaction, Smokey whisked itself away through a ventilation grill near the ceiling. I sat back and waited.

When the door to the interrogation room opened, Stonehammer walked in, carrying a folder. He had a fresh bandage over his left eye, another bandage on the left side of his neck, and I suspected that he had one under his shirt on his right shoulder, as well. He walked into the room with a slight, but noticeable limp. But his suit was clean and neat, and he was smiling. He was ready for some fun.

"Hello, Southerland," he said, and he sat down on the other side of the table.

"Hello, Detective," I said. "How's the eye?"

The troll let out a loud, boisterous, and phony laugh. When he was done, he nailed me with a quick backhanded slap to the face. I went flying from my chair. Only the bracelet cuffed to my left wrist kept me from flying all the way to the wall. On the down side, I was jerked hard to the floor. I ran a hand over my jaw. It wasn't broken, but it was going to turn some interesting colors after it swelled up. The metallic taste of blood filled my mouth, but my teeth remained in place. Not bad, all in all, but then we were just getting started.

I climbed to my feet and plopped back down on the chair.

Stonehammer fixed his burning eye on me. He wasn't smiling anymore. After a few seconds, he reached into his folder and took out a photo. He looked at it with interest and then put it down in front of me. The photo showed sixteen figures lying side-by-side on an asphalt surface. It had been taken from far enough up to include all of the figures, but I could see blood splashed on most of them. They were all wearing scarfs marking them as members of either the Northsiders or Claymore Cartel. I studied the photo for an appropriate length of time and looked up.

"Recognize these guys?" Stonehammer asked me.

"Should I?" I asked back.

"These guys shot each other up last night at the old Placid Point Pier," Stonehammer said. "You know, the pier you visited earlier that morning. The pier that the nymph sent you to."

"I turned that job down, remember?" I responded.

"Sure you did," Stonehammer said. "And you left it alone, right? There's no chance that you might have gone back later, say, around midnight?"

I clammed up, not wanting to get caught in a lie if I had been spotted on the scene.

"Nothing?" Stonehammer said. "Well, that's okay. I've got more pictures."

He picked up the first photo and took another out of his folder. He placed it on the table in front of me. It showed Kraken entwined in a net and dragged onto the rocky sand in front of his cave. The picture had been taken in the dark, and the adaro was illuminated by a searchlight. The fierce look on his face indicated that he was alive and angry.

"From the gills, I'd say that's an adaro," I said.

"Anyone you know?" Stonehammer asked.

"I'm not sure," I said. "Adaros all look alike to me."

"Is that right," Stonehammer said.

"That one looks mean, though," I said. "I wouldn't mess with him if I were you."

Stonehammer glowered at me from deep under his brow. Then he picked up the photo and put it in the folder. "I've got one more for you," he said. And he smiled. He reached into the folder and pulled out the third photo. He held it up and studied it for a good ten seconds. Then he put it down in front of me. He looked straight into my face, watching for a reaction.

It was hard not to give him one, but I tried. It was a photo of Mila from the shoulders up. She was lying on a sidewalk. Her eyes were open, but dull. Dark blue bruises surrounded both of her eyes. Her nose was crooked. A stream of dried blood stretched out of the right corner of her mouth and down her chin. A hole from a small-caliber bullet defiled the perfect skin in the middle of her forehead. A pool of blood covered the cement behind her head. A serial number was stamped on the photo: 254877. The numbers I had seen tattooed on the back of Mila's left wrist.

Poor Mila. Yes, she was uncouth, foulmouthed, and dangerous. Maybe even homicidal. She had been doomed by circumstances to a hard life and probably a bad end. But she had been young, passionate, and full of life. She hadn't received a formal education, but she had been street-smart and gifted with a natural intelligence. Who knows what she could have accomplished or what she could have been under different circumstances. Now she was a corpse. Questions filled my head, but I didn't like my chances of getting any of them answered.

I looked up to see Stonehammer still studying me. I shrugged.

"Are you going to tell me that you don't know who that is?" he asked.

I let out a breath that I didn't know I'd been holding. "No," I said. "That's Miss Seafoam's sister, Mila. "That's who she wanted me to find."

Stonehammer reached into his folder and pulled my phone out. He tossed it to me and I caught it with my free hand. On the screen was the picture of Mila that Cora—Leena—had transferred to me. I looked up at Stonehammer. "Yeah," I said.

"Did you find her?" Stonehammer asked.

"I didn't look," I said.

Stonehammer stared at me for half a minute. I stared back into his glowing red eye and didn't squirm. Stonehammer blinked first. I felt a little pride in myself for that.

My pride vanished when Stonehammer backhanded me again in the same spot he had hit me before. Again I crashed to the floor. This time, I spit one of my back teeth out of my mouth with a clot of blood. I remained on the floor for what felt like a long time, my left hand stretched over my head and attached to the table. I was in no hurry to get up, but eventually I climbed back into the chair. With my tongue, I felt for the space where the tooth had been. The piercing pain in my jaw told me that it was cracked. I might have groaned. I sure felt like groaning.

Stonehammer pounded the table, and I flinched. Couldn't help myself.

"You think I wouldn't recognize you just because you covered your face?" the troll snarled, anger in his voice. "You were still wearing your motherfucking suit! Same suit you were wearing when you went running out of your office like a pussy." Stonehammer shook his head. "Still think you're smarter than this stupid troll?"

I didn't think his question needed an answer, so I slouched in my chair and shut my eyes. I didn't think I'd had enough sleep the night before, and I felt like catching up.

Stonehammer didn't cooperate. He pounded the table again, and my eyes flew open. Better the table than my jaw, but I didn't think Stonehammer was done having his fun.

"Tell me where the box is," he demanded. "And unless you want another crack in the jaw don't try to deny that you took it. I saw you pick it up and run away with the nymph. Where did you stash it? My men have been all over your place, so I know it's not there. Where is it?"

Before I had a chance to answer, he said, "Wait! Don't tell me right away. I want to have to work for this." He smiled at me, and it was an evil smile.

I thought fast, and maybe not clearly. "I don't have it," I said. Stonehammer raised his hand. "No!" I said. "I really don't.

And I don't know where it is. Mila took it from me last night when I was sleeping. I don't know what she did with it."

Stonehammer stood and walked slowly around the table. He reached out with one hand and gripped my shoulder. He pulled me up from my chair to my feet. He paused to smile at me. Then he punched me square in the stomach with his other hand. I doubled over, not breathing. Stonehammer released my shoulder from his grip and I fell to the floor in a heap. The last thing I remembered was my stomach spilling coffee and chewed-up jellyroll all over the floor.

***

I dreamed that I had been bitch-slapped and punched in the gut by a troll. I woke and realized that I had simply been reliving my most recent memory. Great. Not even sleep had brought me relief from reality. I groaned and kept my eyes shut. I didn't want to know where I was.

Eventually, curiosity got the best of me and I allowed my eyes to open. I was in a bed, lying on a mattress that was too thin. I didn't know how long it had been since my interrogation, but, given how I felt, it couldn't have been more than an hour. My stomach ached and my jaw felt like it had been pierced by a railroad spike. My mouth tasted like vomit with a metallic tinge. I cleared my throat and shot a disgusting bloody glob of spittle to the floor. Not very polite of me, but I wasn't a guest here by choice.

I was in a holding cell, about ten feet by five. The air smelled like decades of old sweat and stale cigarettes. The accommodations consisted of a metal bed, a cement floor, bare walls, and a door with a barred window. Next to the door was a twelve-ounce plastic bottle of water. I rolled out of bed and stood. My head didn't spin and my stomach didn't lurch. Could have been worse, I supposed, but the day was still young.

I walked to the water bottle and picked it up. I removed the cap, took a sip, and swished the water around without swallowing, cleaning out my mouth. I spit on the floor again. The contents looked cleaner this time. I drained the rest of the bottle in three gulps. Then I walked to the corner of the cell furthest from the bed, lowered my trousers, and took a long piss on the wall. I noted a trace of blood, but not as much as I had feared. Still, I had to admit that round one with the troll hadn't gone well for me. The second round probably wouldn't, either, but I was anxious to get it started. The less time I had to spend in this cell, the better. It was getting filthier by the minute!

I didn't have to wait long. Two uniformed cops came for me just a few minutes later. They opened the door and one of them cuffed my hands behind my back. The other wrinkled his nose and did a double-take at the stain on the wall. He looked at me with disgust. I glanced back at him and shrugged. He shoved me out the door hard enough to make me stumble, but the other cop had a firm grip on my arm, so I didn't fall. Small favors.

They led me back to an interrogation room. It was probably the same one I'd been in before, but it was hard to tell. They all look alike. After I was seated, the cop who had prevented me from falling uncuffed my right hand and attached the bracelet to the underside of the table. As he did so, he leaned close to me and muttered under his breath, "Sorry about this." I glanced at him and saw a square-jawed thirtyish man with short black hair and dark brown eyes. He held my gaze for a second, looking sad, then stood and left the room with the other cop. I was ready for round two.

But I was in for a treat. This time, it wasn't Stonehammer who entered the room. Captain Gerald "Gerry" Graham himself stepped in. He held the door open, and Leena Waterfowl, known professionally as Cora Seafoam, walked through. Graham closed the door and took the chair across the table from me. Leena remained standing.

The door opened again, and a uniformed officer walked in with a clean ashtray, which he set on the table in front of Graham. Having accomplished his duty, the officer left the room. Without speaking, Graham pulled an open pack of cigarettes out of his shirt pocket. He tipped the pack to the side and tapped the bottom of the pack until a cigarette poked its way out of the top. Graham pulled the cigarette out of the pack and put it between his lips in one smooth motion. He replaced the pack in his shirt pocket with one hand and pulled a silver lighter out of his pants pocket with the other. A stylized 'GG' monogram was displayed on the front of the lighter. It was a serious lighter. It must have cost someone some serious coin. Not Graham, though. I'm guessing that it was a gift from his wife. Graham flicked the lighter, and it lit after the first try. He fired up his cigarette and took a long drag. He blew the smoke into the room and pocketed the lighter. He took another shorter drag, and placed the cigarette in the ashtray. Having finished letting me know how insignificant I was in his world, Graham looked up and met my eyes for the first time.

"Mr. Southerland," said Graham. "I'm Captain Graham. But I guess you already know that."

I looked up at Leena. She was looking at the floor.

Graham didn't turn around, but pointed back at Leena with his thumb. "You know Leena Waterfowl," he said, "though maybe not by that name? I understand that she used a different one when she came to see you."

I kept my eyes on Leena. She didn't meet mine. I wondered what she was doing there.

In the photo I'd seen, Graham had appeared friendly. He didn't look friendly now. He looked harried, like a man who has just realized that despite weeks of work he's not going to get his taxes filed on time. He ran a hand through his salt-and-pepper hair, looked at it, and then wiped it off on his thigh.

He folded his arms on the table and leaned forward. He got down to business. "Yesterday morning, Miss Waterfowl hired you to kidnap her sister, Mila. She knew that her sister was involved in gangs, and that her gang, the Northsiders, was going to be battling it out with another gang, the Claymore Cartel, at the old Placid Point Pier at midnight. She wanted you to take her sister out of the fight by force. That's conspiracy to kidnap. Miss

Waterfowl loved her sister very much. For that reason, we can forgive Leena for her misguided attempt on her sister's behalf."

Graham picked up his cigarette and took a puff. I waited.

"After Miss Waterfowl left your office," Graham continued, returning the cigarette to the ashtray, "you went to the pier to scout it out." He hesitated. "You were seen there by one of our officers."

Graham didn't mention that he had known that Miss Waterfowl would be coming to meet with me, and he left out the part where he had sent Stonehammer to warn me off the case. He was also vague on how it was that an officer had seen me at the pier.

Graham cleared his throat. "Detective Stonehammer was waiting for you at your office when you returned. He attempted to bring you back to the station for questioning. You assaulted the detective, doing serious damage to his eye, and ran out the back door of your office."

A wry chuckle escaped from my throat. I couldn't help it. I wondered how Stonehammer felt about this part of the story. How long was he going to hear about how a mere human had "assaulted" him and escaped his custody? He was never going to live that down.

Graham cleared his throat again. It was apparently something he did after he lied. I wished that I could play poker with him some time.

"Later, you went back to the pier, where you witnessed the gang fight," Graham continued. "You managed to capture Mila and drag her out of the fight. You might think that you were saving her skin, but if she was unwilling to go with you, then that's kidnapping." He paused and frowned. "Mila had something on her, a locked black metal box. She gave it to you, or, more likely, you took it from her. Then you drove her to your apartment."

Graham paused again, and his frown deepened. He tapped his finger on the table while he collected his thoughts. "Out of consideration for Miss Waterfowl," said Graham, "we're not going to get into what the two of you did once you got to your apartment. We're not interested in your sordid little life, Mr. Southerland."

I looked up at Leena, who was still looking at the floor. I didn't say anything. What was the point? Graham was just trying to rattle me, and I wasn't going to let a little weasel like him get under my skin.

"Now here's where things get a little fuzzy," Graham said. "One of two things happened. Either you stashed the box somewhere, or Mila got away from you while you were sleeping, took the box, and then *she* stashed it somewhere."

Another pause. More tapping.

"In any case," Graham finally said, "you went after Mila. Either you thought that she was going for the box, or that she had taken it and run. Regardless, you went after her, and you caught her. And then you beat her up and shot her in the head."

That's when Leena looked up and met my eyes. Her own eyes were filled with fury. She tried to set me on fire with those eyes. I had killed her sister, and she wanted me to pay with my life, but only after watching me suffer some serious pain. Now I knew why she was here.

"You got it wrong, Graham," I said. But I knew that there was nothing I could say that would change anything. The story had been carved in stone. It was a done deal. Mila had been murdered, and I was set up to be the fall guy.

I was fucked.

Chapter Nine

"You can go now, Leena," Graham said without turning. Leena never took her eyes off me as she opened the door and left the room. I'd only met her twice, and this was the second time she had left a room lighting my face on fire with her glare. I could still feel my forehead burning after she left.

When the door closed behind her, I turned to Graham. "This is bullshit, Graham, and you know it. Who do you think will believe that I shot Mila, left her body for you to find, and then went back to my apartment and waited to be arrested?"

"All of the people who need to will," he said. "I'll make sure of that."

I knew he was right.

I plowed forward anyway, "You did it, didn't you. You or Stonehammer. You couldn't beat the location of the box out of her, so you killed her."

Graham ignored me. "Where's the box? We know you have it. Tell me where it is, and we can forget this whole thing. We've got you on conspiracy, assaulting a police officer, kidnapping, and murder. Trust me when I say that we can make all of these charges stick. But if you deliver the box into my hands, right now, then all charges will be dismissed. You have my word on that. I'll even see that you get a ride home."

I sat back and said nothing. No matter what he was telling me, I knew that the only reason I was still alive is that he needed the location of the box from me. I wasn't going to give that up no matter what. Once he had the box, I was a goner. Despite Graham's promises, I'd vanish faster than a snowflake on a hot radiator grill.

"Fine," Graham said in a resigned voice. "You had your chance." He stood. "Time to get Stonehammer back in here."

My whole body tensed at the thought of another bout with the troll, but just then the door opened and Rob Lubank came bursting through. "Don't say a word!" he told me. "We're getting out of here. Now."

"What the hell are you doing here!" Graham shouted, startled.

"Getting my client," said Lubank. "You have no right to hold him here without counsel."

"What are you talking about, Lubank!" said Graham. "I can do whatever I want to this murdering scumbag."

"Is that so?" said Lubank. "Do you really want to play it that way?"

The stalwart captain with the iron jaw and the potbellied gnome with the ridiculous hairpiece stared daggers at each other. Neither moved for a full ten seconds. Finally, Graham looked away. "Take him," he growled. "Get him out of here. But don't think this is over, you fucking parasite!"

"Language, Captain, language," Lubank admonished. "What would your children think?"

"Get out!" Graham roared.

They had to bring in the cop with the key to my cuffs to unclasp me, but, to my surprise and relief, I soon found myself following the gloating gnome past dozens of glowering cops and out of police headquarters.

When we were in Lubank's car, I asked him, "How did you do that?"

Lubank glanced at me, "A little 'thank you' would be nice."

"Thank you," I said. "How did you do that?"

"You're welcome," said Lubank.

"Lubank!"

The gnome gave me a sly grin. "Oh, I've got the goods on good ol' Graham. Don't worry about him. He'll dance to my tune."

"You're blackmailing a captain in the YCPD?"

"Blackmail is an ugly word," said Lubank. "Let's just say that Graham's been a naughty boy. He's also ambitious. Being a captain isn't good enough for him, but if some of the things I know were to hit social media, he'd be lucky to get a job selling shoes."

"I know that he keeps an adaro sex-worker in a downtown apartment," I said.

Lubank just snorted. "Even his wife knows about her. No, I've got dirtier dirt on him than that. The stuff he's done with little girls, well, if I told you it would make your hair curl."

"Hmm," I said. "And he looks like such a clean-cut family man in his photos."

"But forget about that," said Lubank. His expression changed from triumphant to angry faster than a hummingbird's blink. "Did you steal my raincoat? You fucking bastard! I love that coat! If you damaged it I'll sue you so hard you'll be begging the cops to send you to prison just so you can have three square meals and a fuckin' place to shit!"

"Sorry," I said. "It was cold last night, and I couldn't go back to my place."

Lubank scowled at me. "You can give it back to me after I drop you off at your place."

"I'll, uh," I stumbled. "I'll have to get it cleaned first."

Lubank slammed his hand on the steering wheel. "You bastard! You fuck! Alkwat's pecker! How bad did you hurt it? Is it torn? Did you damage the lining?"

"Yeah, thanks for asking about me. As you can see, I'm a little banged up. My jaw's probably broken, and I lost a tooth, but I'll be okay," I said. "Thanks for your concern."

"Fuck you!" Lubank shouted. "I don't care if you're breathing your last fucking breath! You know how much that coat cost? A fortune, that's what! It was a birthday gift from Gracie, but, of course, I had to pay for it. Gracie loves that coat, too! She's going to hate you for ruining it."

"It's not ruined," I said. "It just got a little wet. And muddy. I'll get it cleaned and it'll be good as new."

Lubank grumbled something I didn't catch, but let it go. He probably had a dozen coats just like the one I borrowed. He just liked busting my ass.

After a while, I said, "I take it that my elemental managed to deliver my message to you?'

That got Lubank going again. "You and your fuckin' air demons! You crazy fuck! I'm in my office and all of a sudden Gracie is screaming at me from the other room. 'Robby, get in here right now! Robby, help!'" Lubank's imitation of his wife's gravel-throated screech was hilarious. "So I go in there," Lubank continued, "and there's this fuckin' tornado in Gracie's ashtray kicking ashes and cigarette butts all over the room. It fuckin' messed up Gracie's dress but good! You can bet that she'll make me buy her a new one. That's another thing you're gonna have to pay for, you fuck!"

"Put it on my tab," I said.

"Fuckin' right I will!" said Lubank. "Anyway, the tornado is hissing at us—'Alex! Police station! Trouble! Help!'—over and over again. It was fuckin' eerie, let me tell you! And I'm like, 'Southerland's in trouble? Who cares?' But Gracie's got a thing for you, you know. Can't see why she'd look twice at a crazy bum like you when she's got the Rob Monster in her life. You know what they say: 'Once you go gnome, there's no going home.' But go figure out women, right? So anyway, she insists that I gotta go riding to your fuckin' rescue like a fuckin' knight in shining armor. And here we are!" He chuckled at me. "Oh how I love sticking it to the police. Gotta admit that you made my day." He paused. "And by Lord Ketz-Alkwat's pecker, pal, do you ever owe me! Gracie's gonna have to draw up a contract for an installment plan! Wait till you see what I'm going to charge you for my legal services! You know that attorneys bill by the minute, right? You're going to make me rich enough to retire!"

"My thanks aren't enough?" I said. He just laughed softly, like a slimy weasel who had me by the balls.

"What happened to the elemental?" I asked.

"How the hell do I know?" Lubank shouted. "It followed me to my car and that's the last I saw it. Keep that fuckin' demon away from me! Demons drive away clients!"

I thought about Smokey. The little guy had really come through. In the interrogation room, I had asked it if it could find its way back to the faraway place where we had met before. It had said that it could. I told it to go there and then turn left out the door and go to the door at the end of the hall. That had confused Smokey. It was frustrating. I could get the tiny elemental twenty miles away to Lubank's building and up to the break room on the second floor, but I couldn't figure out how to get it to understand how to go an additional hundred feet down the hall to Lubank's office. Finally, I told him to go out the break room door and look for smoke. That was something the little elemental understood. I told Smokey to find the source of the smoke and to shout a message to whoever was in the room. I knew that the message would have to be simple, so I settled on "Alex! Police station! Trouble! Help!" I told Smokey to shout as loud as it could. Hell if it hadn't worked!

"What are you smiling at, asshole?" Lubank asked me.

"Nothing," I said. "Not a thing. Hey, um..." I hesitated.

"What!" Lubank said.

"I, uh, left something in your office last night. I need to get it."

Lubank stopped behind a line of cars waiting for the light. He turned and stared at me. "What is it?"

"A locked box," I said. "I put it up in the top of your closet. You didn't happen to see it, did you?"

Lubank continued to stare at me. "The police wouldn't happen to be after it, would they?"

"I don't know about the police," I said, "But Graham is. And his goon, Stonehammer."

"Fuck! You!" Lubank said. "And you left it in *my* office? Gracie's in there by herself, you fuck!" He stepped on the accelerator, made a tight U-turn across the road divider, barely missing the car in front of him, and swerved into the stream of traffic going the other way. I braced myself against the dashboard, but through some miracle Lubank, honking his horn like a maniac and screaming obscenities out his window, managed to avoid hitting any cars.

"All right," he said to me as he drove back to his office. "Spill! Why do I have hot merchandise in my closet that I didn't know about?"

I gave him a sparse, fact-based narrative of events, beginning with my encounter with Stonehammer in the Minotaur. He listened without speaking, nodding at key points and weaving his way through the heavy traffic like a crazed stock car driver. I had to admire his driving skill, even as I feared for my life.

When I got to the part about Graham showing up at the old Placid Point Pier, he interrupted me, asking, "Graham was in control of the Claymore Cartel?"

"He was in charge of that particular bunch, at least."

"Hunh," he grunted. "That's interesting. For that, I'm going to deduct a percentage of what you owe me. Go on."

When I finished bringing him up to date, he shook his head. "Poor little adaro girl. She was in over her head." After a pause, he asked me, "Why do you think she left your place? Was she coming after the box?"

"I guess so," I said. "I thought that I had convinced her to let me handle it, but she must have thought up some scheme of her own."

"Who do you think shot her? Graham?"

"That would make sense," I said. "Either Graham or Stonehammer. Or maybe someone else working for Graham. They caught her and tried to beat the location of the box out of her. She wouldn't talk, though. Otherwise, they'd already have the box and I'd be dead."

"Tough little cookie," said Lubank. "But why would they shoot her if they didn't get the location from her?"

This bothered me, too. "I don't know," I admitted. "Frustration?"

"Hmm," said Lubank, unconvinced. After a while, he said, "Maybe her death had nothing to do with the box. Lovely little lady walking down the street all by herself. Maybe she was mugged."

"She wasn't walking," I said. "It's a good twenty miles from my place to your office. She wasn't gonna go after the box on foot."

"Someone came and picked her up?" Lubank asked. "Who? Did anyone even know she was at your place?"

"Kraken did," I said.

"And you say that the police caught Kraken?"

"Looks like it. He might have told them where she went."

"Not easy to squeeze the truth out of a male adaro," said Lubank.

"No," I agreed. "It's not."

"She had a phone, right?" said Lubank. "Someone could have called her. Maybe her sister?"

"Maybe," I said. "But Mila wouldn't have told Leena anything. She didn't want her to get anywhere near that box. Graham owns Leena."

"Lord's fuckin' balls!" said Lubank. "I'm out of ideas."

We rode in silence the rest of the way to Lubank's office. I was tired, hungry, and I needed a drink. My jacket was stained with blood. Oh, and my stomach ached, my jaw was broken, and I was missing a tooth. It had been a good hardworking tooth, my favorite one. Plus, I was getting a cramp in my right bicep from bracing myself against the dashboard. And the police wanted to torture me into revealing the location of the mysterious box. Once they found it, they'd rub me out and hide the body. I didn't even know what was in that box, but a young girl had died for it, thanks to me. If I hadn't pushed my way into her life, she would probably have sold the contents of the box by now and be living happily ever after with her dimwitted stud of a boyfriend. Other than that, this was shaping up to be a fine day.

***

"Oh, honey!" exclaimed Gracie when she saw me. "What happened to you?"

"He's fine," Lubank said. "Have the police been here?"

"No, baby," said Gracie.

"Did they call?" Lubank asked.

"No. You have a couple of messages from clients, and one from Judge Gillespie. I put them on your desk."

"Anything urgent?"

"One of them is from Mr. Djengo," said Gracie. "He seemed upset."

"He's an idiot," said Lubank. "It'll keep. I'm going to be in my office with Lover Boy. We won't be long."

"Don't you boys do anything I wouldn't do," Gracie said.

We went into Lubank's office and he shut the door. I went to the closet, retrieved the box, and put it on his desk.

Lubank studied it closely. "So this is it, huh? Strange." He put his hand on it. "It's cold all right." He bent down and listened to it. "Yup. Probably a battery of some kind, just like you said." He knocked on the surface. "Hard. So what now? Are you going to take it to this Kintay fellow?"

"That's the plan," I said.

"Good. The sooner you get this fuckin' thing out of my office the better," Lubank said. "If the police show up I'll tell them to take a fuckin' hike."

"Sorry to get you involved in this," I said.

"Fuck you," he said. "Now get lost. Tell Gracie to call you a cab. And don't forget to get my raincoat cleaned."

Gracie was waiting for me outside Lubank's door as I walked into the reception area. "Where are you going, baby?" she asked.

"Home," I said. "Mind calling me a cab?"

"Honey, you aren't going anywhere until I clean you up," said Gracie. "What happened? You look like you went a couple of rounds with a freight train!"

"Pretty close to the truth," I said.

"Let me take a look." She leaned in close to examine my jaw. "Whew! Baby! I hate to say it, but your breath would kill a moose!"

"You got a mint or something?" I asked.

"Better than that," she said. She walked to her desk, opened a drawer, and pulled out a pint bottle of whiskey and a shot glass. "For emergencies," she said, and filled the glass. She handed it to me with a smile.

"Thanks," I said. After using up a second to ponder the wisdom of taking a shot on an empty stomach, I lifted the glass to my lips. I poured the entire shot into my mouth, swished it around a couple of times, and swallowed. The drink burned all the way to my stomach, but it was a nice burn. The burn soon turned into a pleasant glow that warmed my chest and face.

"This is good stuff," I said.

"Nothing but the best for the Lubanks," said Gracie. "Genuine avalonian whiskey. Robby gets it by the case from a client. Don't ask me about the details. I'll get you a cab, but you're going to have to let me clean some of that blood off your jacket before I let you out into the public."

Gracie got on the phone. I noticed that her dress was smudged here and there from the ashtray incident. Her ashtray was nearly empty, but the room was as neat and clean as ever. When she hung up her phone, I apologized for the mess that Smokey had made.

"Oh, don't worry about that," she said. "It didn't take me long to clean it all up. I'll put this dress in the wash tonight and it will be good as new. If the stains don't come out, I'll have Robby buy me a new one."

"He'll charge me for it," I said.

"No he won't. Remember, I do all the billing. But, sweetie, that little imp scared me half to death! I'm going to have to figure out a way for you to calm my nerves." Her lips parted in a suggestive grin.

I let her take me into the rest room, where she scrubbed away at my jacket with some wet paper towels. When she was done, she leaned in close to my ear and said in a low seductive voice, "You take care of yourself, baby. Don't let anyone mess up that pretty face of yours again." And then she kissed me lightly on my bruised jaw.

"Thanks, Gracie," I said.

She slapped me on the butt and said, "Get outta here, tiger, before I lose control of myself. Your cab should be here by now."

She walked me out of the office and I waved back at her as I left. She blew me a kiss and closed the door behind her. I went downstairs, and, sure enough, the cab was waiting.

Once I was in the cab, I thought about where I wanted to go. I didn't have any cash on me, but I had a credit card, and I was no longer worried about it being traced. I wasn't on the run anymore, but the police still suspected that I had the box. I didn't want to bring it home with me. In fact, I needed to get it out of my hands as soon as possible.

So I told the cabbie to take me to the central downtown bus station. Once I was there, I rented a locker and stored the box in it. Then I walked a half mile to the post office, where I used my credit card to buy an overnight envelope and postage. I addressed it to my office and mailed myself the key to the bus station locker. Then I walked back to the bus station, bought myself a ticket, and boarded a bus for home.

Once on the bus, I took out my phone and called Tom Kintay. After four rings, a weary voice said, "Kintay."

"At ease, corporal," I said.

"I didn't do it," said Kintay.

"Didn't do what?"

"Whatever you think you've got on me, copper," Kintay said, altering his voice to impersonate a famous old-time movie gangster.

"Aw shucks, man. I've got nothing on you," I said. "You're clean as a whistle."

"Far as *you* know, flatfoot," Kintay said. "Still digging up dirt on us innocent working-class citizens?"

"Whenever anyone is willing to pay me for it. What about you? Anything exciting going on in the criminal underworld?" I asked.

"Nothing much," said Kintay. "Same old shit. I'm so bored that I'm thinking of going legit."

"Don't do that," I laughed. "I don't want to think about you in a buttoned-down brown suit and spit-shined loafers."

"Me neither," Kintay agreed. "I hope you've got something for me."

"Funny you should mention it," I said. "I've got something that might make your life interesting for a change. Can I stop by sometime tomorrow afternoon or the next day?"

"Hey, my time is your time," said Kintay. "Stop by whenever you want. You know where I am."

"Thanks, buddy," I said. "Try to stay out of jail until I get there."

"Can't make any promises," said Kintay. "See you around."

I disconnected the call and slid my phone into my inside jacket pocket. Sliding down in my chair in a relaxed slouch, I turned and watched the city slide by the bus window. The bus was climbing up a hill in the financial district past skyscrapers of varying architectural shapes and styles. The afternoon sun fought its way through the clouds and reflected off the windows and glass doors. The sidewalks were crowded with businessmen in dark suits and fedoras, homburgs, and newsboy hats, smart-looking women in scarfs, sophisticated dresses, and high-heeled shoes, tourists in sweatshirts and ball caps, the odd troll in heavy woolen suits, glowing red eyes peering out beneath heavy brows, a sneering hirsute dwarf here, a strutting self-satisfied gnome there, and homeless indigents of all species sitting or lying against the walls of the buildings begging the passers-by to help fill the overturned hats on the sidewalks in front of them with some of their spare cash. The Yerba City wind blew hot-dog wrappers, polystyrene foam coffee cups, and palm-sized empty cardboard shrimp trays up the street fast enough to keep pace with the bus as it negotiated the stop-and-go traffic.

It was well past lunchtime, and my stomach was letting me know about it. But the pain in my jaw was mostly gone. I rubbed my palm across it, and, while it was still tender to the touch, it was well on its way to healing. I wondered if my tooth would grow back. Probably not, but I had no reason to complain, and I was grateful for what I'd been given. I hoped that I was done getting my bones broken for a while, though. I felt no need to push my new healing powers any further than I already had.

The bus pulled up to a stop a couple of blocks from my place. I got off and started walking down a sidewalk lined with coastal cypress trees. A block away from my building, I stopped. Stonehammer was standing in my office doorway, peering down the street away from me. So there it was. Stonehammer was going to force the location of the box from me, and then I would disappear so completely that I wouldn't even be a memory.

"No fuckin' way," I said to myself. Running wasn't an option. It was time for these jokers to find out once and for all just who they were dealing with.

Chapter Ten

I put a cypress between me and Stonehammer and cleared my head. I called up sigils in my mind and mentally put them together. The world of the air opened up to me, and I saw elementals coasting with the wind currents and floating through the clouds. I wasn't looking for the Smokey-sized ones this time; I needed a weapon. A slowly swirling column of wind was drifting with a current about a hundred feet above me. I formed a sigil and sent out a summons. The elemental changed its direction and descended toward me, dragging pieces of low-hanging clouds in its wake. Seconds later, it touched down on the street in front of me, a wide swirling wind eight or so feet tall with a diameter nearly as wide. Cold displaced air rustled the leaves in the trees lining the street. I pulled the collar of my jacket up over my neck and waited for the breeze to blow itself out.

A low-pitched howling moan issued from the elemental: "Greetings, summoner."

In the past when I summoned an elemental this large, it would resist my control. The larger and more powerful the elemental, the more willpower it took to subdue it. An elemental the size of the one in front of me was about the largest that I could hope to command, and not without a severe struggle. I prepared myself for the battle.

As I gathered my will, however, I found that the elemental had no intention of fighting back. It merely awaited my wishes.

"Are you ready to do what I ask?" I said, trying to hide my surprise.

"This one is ready," came the reply. Interesting.

I pointed toward my office. "Do you see the troll standing near that building?" I asked.

"This one does."

"Drive it away," I said. "Feel free to damage it."

"This one will."

As I watched, the elemental intensified its whirling. It stretched upwards until it was twelve feet tall. It whirled faster and faster and grew darker and darker. Faster than my eyes could follow, it enveloped a cypress tree a few yards in front of me. The tree crackled and snapped, and jagged branches and pieces of tree trunk now whirled within the spinning elemental. Lubank liked to call the elementals he'd seen me summon "air demons." This one truly fit that description. It was terrifying, and I was glad it was on my side. At least I hoped it was.

The elemental shot toward my building, and I followed it at a run. I saw Stonehammer turn in our direction and watched his eyes widen in alarm. Suddenly, debris from the tree flew from the elemental straight toward the troll. Stonehammer had just enough time to raise his arms and duck his head before he was pummeled by broken branches and wooden shafts. The flying debris slammed Stonehammer against my office door, and he crumbled to his hands and knees.

The onslaught was over in seconds. As Stonehammer shook his head and stumbled back to his feet, the elemental retreated and bounded upon another cypress tree. As the sounds of wood crackling and breaking filled the air, I waved to catch Stonehammer's attention.

"Hello, Detective," I said to him. "Having a bad day?" Then, with great and unnecessary dramatic flair, I extended my arm toward the whirling elemental, paused, and then, striding toward the troll, whipped my arm forward in a throwing motion, finishing up by pointing my index finger directly at Stonehammer. "Attack!" I exclaimed.

The elemental leaped toward the troll and fired off a new volley of debris. Give Stonehammer credit: he knew when he'd been beat. He rushed away from me down the street, chunks of wood pelting him as he ran. I shouted after him, "Tell Graham to stay the hell out of my face!" Stonehammer dashed into an expensive looking silver sedan. His tires screeched as he sped away.

That went well. And then I saw the collateral damage of the elemental's assault. My office door was a mess. The signs on the door were nowhere to be seen. A tree branch had plunged through the paneling where the signs had been attached. Deep scars and brown scrapes covered the door and the walls surrounding it. Troll blood stained the walkway in front of the building. Lord's balls, I thought. There goes my cleaning deposit.

But it was worth it. I was basking in the glow of triumph. For the first time since Stonehammer had tried to muscle me at the Minotaur, I felt like I was in charge of my life again. I still had work to do, starting with cleaning up and repairing my home, and I was still in serious need of some dough, but I felt like I could look at myself in the mirror again without recoiling in shame, and that was something more precious than gold.

I turned away from my door to see the elemental floating in front of me. Its wind speed had slowed to a gentle circling breeze that merely rustled the twigs and wood chips littering the sidewalk and walkway to my office door. I gave it a salute.

"Nice job," I said.

"This one is pleased that you are pleased," it answered in its low howling moan.

I thought for a second, searching for the words I wanted. "You offered no resistance to my will," I said at last.

"No," it said.

"Why?" I asked.

"This one knows you," it said. "This one has been riding the wind in this place since long before you were here. Once, this one would have refused to submit to your commands. But you have been touched by the elf. You are different. This one will serve you now."

Wow. I had assumed that it was the elf that had enhanced my abilities with elementals, as well as my vision, hearing, and powers of healing, and now this elemental had provided me with confirmation. I was also learning just how much the elf had given me. I didn't want to think about how much debt I was accruing. Instead, I thought about how to best take advantage of my new strengths.

"Will you let me name you?" I asked the elemental.

"This one will."

I tried to think of a truly bad-assed name. Treehammer? Nah. Treenado? Uh-uh. Storm of Broken Wood? Hmmm. I was really bad at this. And then it came to me. "I'm going to name you Badass," I said. Hey, creativity may not be my strong suit, but this name fit like a glove.

"Badass," moaned the elemental. It stretched itself tall and whirled in what I interpreted as pride. "Badass will come to the one touched by the elf and serve when called."

"Sweet," I said. "For now your service is ended. Happy flying!"

Badass bowed slightly and dissipated into the air.

***

I hadn't eaten since heaving up my breakfast, and it hadn't been much of a breakfast. I went inside, and, after picking my way through the broken glass in my office and trying to ignore the sour wet carpet smell, I went upstairs to find food. I found a frozen pizza and popped it into the microwave. When it had heated long enough to be edible, I pulled it out and devoured it in two minutes flat. As I wolfed down the pizza, I noted that my jaw, while still sore, no longer felt broken. I knocked back a bottle of beer. Five seconds later, I shook the walls with a series of booming belches. I grabbed a bottle of whiskey and a shot glass out of a cupboard. Soon, any lingering pain from my earlier beating faded into a pleasant numbness. Life was good.

I spent some time deciding whether to take a nap or to go downstairs and start straightening out my office. Realizing that I wouldn't be able to see any clients, and thereby earn some much needed income, until I'd cleaned the office, I got up and started to head downstairs. But at that moment, my phone rang.

I pulled the phone out of my jacket pocket and read the number on the top of the screen. It looked familiar, and then all at once I remembered who it belonged to. I opened the connection.

"Southerland," I said.

The voice belonging to the woman that I still wanted to think of as Cora Seafoam said, "Hello, Mr. Southerland. This is Leena Waterfowl." Her voice was low and uncertain. It was not the voice of the woman who had given me a death-stare as she walked out of the interrogation room at the police station. It was the voice of the woman who had sought me out to beg me to find her sister.

I didn't say anything, and after a pause, she said, "I owe you an apology."

I remained silent. She continued, "I know now that you didn't kill my sister. I've been a fool, and I'm sorry."

"So who killed Mila?" I asked.

"I don't know," she said, her voice so quiet I could barely make it out. "But I suspect that it was Gerry. Captain Graham, I mean. He wants to frame you for the murder."

"Why me?" I asked.

She didn't answer right away. "It's complicated," she said, finally. "I need to talk to you about it. There's so much to explain. Can I come to your office?"

"I'm afraid not, Miss Waterfowl," I said. "My office is undergoing repairs."

"Oh," she said, and I could hear her unspoken questions.

I had some questions of my own. "Is there somewhere we can meet?" I asked.

"Yes," she said, sounding as if she had made an important decision. "Yes, let me give you an address. Are you ready?"

I grabbed a pad and pen and said, "Shoot."

"Okay it's the Spillman Building at 321 Ford Street. Go to the sixth floor and look for office number sixty-three. It will be to the right of the elevator."

"I got it," I said. "When."

"Give me an hour," she said, and we disconnected.

So Leena wanted to talk to me. That was good, because we had a lot to talk about. Question was, could I trust her? According to Mila, she was Graham's girl, bought and paid for, and Graham wanted the box. How much did Leena know about the box? She hadn't mentioned it to me when we'd met the day before, but that didn't mean she didn't know all about it. Maybe Graham confided in her. Maybe he didn't, but Leena might be in a position to know things about his business, both official and unofficial. How close was she to Graham? Had it been Leena's own idea to call me, or did Graham tell her to? In going to meet Leena, was I falling into a trap set by Graham? Maybe, but there was only one way to find out.

I left my apartment and hoofed it to the parking lot to get my car. When I got there, my parking place was empty. Lord Alkwat's balls!

I found Mac in his booth, head bent over some sort of logbook, cigarette dangling from his lips. "Mac," I said, keeping my voice calm. "I need my car."

Mac didn't even look up. "Smith's Towing Company," he said.

"What?"

"That's who I called to tow your car away." He checked off some boxes on a page in his logbook.

"You had my car towed?"

"You had till noon. It's after noon." Mac still hadn't looked up from his logs. Cigarette ash dropped from his cigarette to the open page, and he brushed it off in my direction.

"You couldn't give me another hour?" I said.

He didn't bother to answer me.

"Shit!" I said. "When I get my car back, you can forget about me coming here again with my business."

"Good!" Mac exclaimed, and he finally looked up from his logs. "I've got a *paying* customer coming in to take the spot. I don't have room for deadbeats. And you still owe me money, including a late fee. You'll be getting a bill in the mail. Pay it or I'll sue. Now get the hell out of here."

I glared at him, but he wasn't having it. He was being a hard-ass about it, but I had to admit that he was well within his rights. That didn't stop me from wanting to kick the skinflinted son of a bitch in the teeth, though. Fuck him! Having no further recourse, I walked away.

I called a cab, and it arrived in fifteen minutes. I told the cabbie to take me to 321 Ford Street, and I seethed all the way there. Not only would I have to pay my lot rental fee—plus the late charge—but now I would have to pay the towing company for the tow and a storage lot to reclaim my car! I needed dough, and fast. The sense of triumph I had felt after running off Stonehammer just an hour ago had already faded into a distant memory.

Ford Street was in a run-down commercial-slash-residential neighborhood in the western part of the city, an area known as the Humback District for reasons I don't know. Probably named after some rich politician from days gone by. Some people celebrated the district for its artist enclaves, its spirit of personal freedom, and its nonconformist avant-garde social scene. Others denigrated its inhabitants for their massive drug use, alternative sexuality, and unwarranted artistic pretensions. Two ways of seeing the same thing, I suppose. I liked some of the restaurants there, though I thought that many of the residents might benefit from paying more attention to their personal hygiene.

The cab dropped me off at a six-story building of indeterminate color (possibly white when it was new) that had been dumped on the street about a hundred years ago and left to rot ever since. Graffiti covered every available space up to the third floor, and generations of seagulls had decorated the rest. All of the building's windows, along with the main entryway, were square at the bottom and arched at the top. After the architect had implemented this halfhearted attempt at creative design, he or she had given up on the exterior and left it a big, ugly, concrete block. Carved over the main entryway, but left colorless, were letters spelling out the words "Spillman Building." I was at the right place.

The interior had been restored and decorated about thirty years ago. Stained rust-colored carpeting covered the floor of the downstairs lobby. The matching cloth chairs that lined the wall of the lobby all featured broad orange, yellow, and red stripes, although the colors had faded at different rates of speed. A woman with dyed red hair sat at a desk at the end of the room furthest from the front door. She was engrossed in a magazine and didn't look up from it when I walked in the door. She looked old enough to have been the building's original receptionist. A directory on the wall near the stairway made her job unnecessary. I examined the directory and found that most of the offices in the building were vacant. Somehow, that didn't surprise me. The occupied offices included a variety of businesses, including several graphic artists, a few photographers, a publisher, a couple of lawyers, and a private investigator named Nigel Larramy. I wondered if he did divorce work. Office number sixty-three was occupied by something called Classic Escorts. I had a pretty good idea what they were about.

A creaking elevator brought me safely to the sixth floor, but it was a near thing. I resolved to take the stairs when it was time to leave rather than risk that elevator twice in one day. Office number sixty-three was to the right of the elevator, just as Leena had told me it would be. I stepped out of the dingy hallway into an office with a crisp, clean pale blue carpet and polished wood-paneled walls. Standing lamps filled the office with light that was soft and cheery. The blades of an ornate ceiling fan glided through the air in languid revolutions that created only the barest of breezes. A beautiful restored antique walnut-colored desk dominated the room. On the walls were pictures of stunningly gorgeous women of various species, including human, adaro, sprite, gnome, dwarf, and even troll. All were dressed in sensual lingerie or underclothing. The photos were stimulating, but not lurid. I thought they were tasteful, which is to say that I'd seen worse. Much worse.

Sitting behind the desk was a middle-aged man who spent a great deal of time on his own appearance. His wavy jet black hair was as thick and rich as chocolate syrup. His black mustache was waxed to fine points that stuck out from the ends of his upper lip in perfect symmetry. His enameled teeth were so white that they gleamed, except for one upper front tooth that was capped in polished gold. A gold hoop earring hung from one earlobe, and a diamond stud pierced the other. He wore a black button-down shirt with red pinstripes. It was tight across his muscular chest, tapered to show off his trim abs, and short-sleeved to accentuate his bulging biceps. A tattoo of a nude woman with large breasts and round full hips decorated his right forearm, and the watch he wore on his left wrist would have paid the rent on my building for the rest of the year. He favored me with a toothy smile and rose when I entered the office.

Leena sat in a chair across from the desk. She was dressed much as she had been when I'd seen her in my office, fashionably, but without ostentation, in a pink silk dress that reflected the soft light in a way that made the dress seem almost liquid. She didn't rise, but she gave me a rueful smile and held up her gloved hand for me to take.

"Hello, Miss Waterfowl," I said, taking her hand lightly with thumb and fingertips and then releasing it.

"Mr. Southerland," she said. "Thanks for coming. And, please, call me Leena."

"Leena," I said. I didn't ask her to call me Alex. I wasn't ready to be her friend.

I looked up at the man standing behind the desk. His smile crinkled the light brown skin under his dark brown eyes and seemed to simulate warmth without quite being genuine. It was a practiced, professional smile, one that said, "I'll do business with you, but don't bother inviting me to your backyard barbecue." He stuck out his hand and said, "Hi Mr. Southerland. My name is Tony. Tony Atwater. I'm Leena's former employer."

He gave my hand a manly squeeze. "Please," he said indicating the chair next to the one Leena was sitting in. "Have a seat. Leena asked me to join your discussion and help fill in some details. I might even be able to help you both out a little. You know, with some advice, if nothing else."

"That's fine with me," I said. Looking at Leena, I asked her, "Where do we start?"

Leena looked deep into my eyes. "Let me start by telling you the truth," she said.

Chapter Eleven

"I was processed into the adaro settlement in Yerba City when I was a child," Leena began. "I carried my sister Mila in my arms into the settlement. She was barely more than a baby. We had been separated from our parents and were raised by the adults in the settlement." She glanced into her lap for a beat and then lifted her eyes so that they met mine. "Mr. Southerland, please understand that I'm not telling you this to elicit sympathy. But I think that knowing a little bit about my background will help you to understand some of the decisions that I made as I grew older."

I nodded, and she picked up her story. "As you know, the adaro settlement is quite impoverished. The living conditions are downright squalid. We don't fit in well with humans, and humans are uncomfortable in our presence. Adaro men terrorized human sailors for centuries, becoming monsters in folk tales that have been handed down for generations, and they can't live for long on land. As for adaro women, well...." She trailed off and left her thought unfinished. It was okay. I knew what she was saying.

"As I grew up," Leena continued, "I learned about the effect that adaro women have on men of other species, and I all too quickly discovered the degree to which men are attracted to me in particular. You'll have to excuse me for being blunt, Mr. Southerland, but I want to be completely candid with you. It's the least I can do for being less than honest with you in our first meeting."

"I appreciate that," I said.

"I'm not going to beat around the bush. The plain fact is that I was determined to escape the poverty of the adaro settlement, and that meant taking advantage of the assets that I possess," said Leena.

"That's when I came into the picture," said Atwater. "My agency isn't just some cheap house of prostitution. I provide beautiful, classy ladies for sophisticated gentlemen. My ladies accompany these gentlemen to dinners, private parties, or other evening entertainments, and I expect the gentlemen to treat my ladies well. Then, in the later hours, my ladies treat the gentlemen well. We're licensed and legal, and my ladies are proper professionals. They are also very well compensated for their services."

I could have done without this guy's sales pitch, but I just nodded.

"Anyway," Atwater said, "Leena came to my agency about four years ago. I had one of my ladies teach her the ropes, and, after a few months of smoothing away her rough edges, I fixed her up with a client. Leena is gorgeous, as you can see, and she proved to be a natural in our business. Word spread, and she became highly sought after. She and I developed a nice, respectful professional relationship. She's been good for me, and I think I've been good for her." Atwater aimed his toothy smile at Leena, and she gave him an affectionate grin in return. She reached across the desk and briefly clasped his hand.

Isn't life grand.

Leena turned back to me. "I enjoyed my time with the agency," she said. "I really did. I learned what it meant to have nice things and how to live well. I acquired polish. You can't imagine what these things meant to a scrubby little orphaned refugee who was brought up in a slum." She closed her eyes for a moment and took a long, slow breath. I watched her breasts swell beneath her dress. I would have been a fool not to.

When she opened her eyes, Leena said, "And then I met Gerry. Gerry Graham, that is. Captain for the Yerba City Police Department. I wasn't the first lady that he had contracted from the agency. He had been a client for years. He took me to dinner, and then to the penthouse suite at the five-star Summerplace

Hotel. He was a perfect gentleman to me, even as I performed my service. He saw me three more times over the next three weeks, and then he called Tony and offered to buy up my contract."

"I hated to lose Leena," Atwater said, "but Graham's offer was very generous. And I was happy for Leena."

"I knew about Gerry's family, of course," said Leena. "But he bought a suite in the Langston Arms." Even a low-rent Joe like me knew that the Langston Arms was one of the most exclusive high-rise condominium complexes in the city.

"I moved in," said Leena, "and he provided me with everything I asked for: clothes, a credit card, a car, domestic servants—everything! And he spends more time with me downtown than he does at his home in the peninsula."

It didn't take a genius to figure out that a police captain's salary wouldn't begin to cover the costs of keeping Leena in luxury. In fact, he must have already been supplementing his income when he first began calling on Classic Escorts. One thing you could say about Atwater's ladies—they weren't cheap!

Leena paused for several seconds. The tip of her tongue slid slowly over her lower lip. I sensed that we had reached the turning point in her story. "My life with Gerry was very satisfactory for several months," she said, finally.

"Very satisfactory?" I said.

She blinked at me. "Get real, Mr. Southerland. I wasn't in love with him, or anything like that," she said, and she smirked a little as she said it. "This isn't a fairy tale. But for a little girl who had only known the settlement for most of her life, this was a dream come true."

"I get it," I said.

Her expression softened, and she went on. "I was living well. But, recently things...changed. I really don't know why. Maybe he got tired of me, I don't know. He started becoming less attentive. We began having arguments. And then, a few days ago, out of the blue, he said something about ending our arrangement."

That was interesting. It sounded as if Graham had begun to develop an immunity to the adaro's pheromone-induced charms. I could picture Leena trying to manipulate Graham into buying her something, or doing something for her, only to be resisted and refused. How confusing that must have been for her! I remembered her reaction to me when I turned down her case. She wasn't used to hearing men tell her "no."

An adaro's eyes always seem to be moist, but Leena's now glistened more than usual. "I was scared, Mr. Southerland. Having come this far, I wasn't ready to be discarded. But if Gerry was going to toss me back to the streets, I was going to go down swinging!"

Leena paused, and her jaw clenched. "I'm not naïve, Mr. Southerland. I think you know that. I knew that Gerry had ways of making money outside of his normal job. Ways that were illegal. This past Monday, I overheard Gerry on the phone. He was talking to someone about some kind of package that would be smuggled in at midnight on Tuesday at the old Placid Point Pier."

I had been listening, but now she really had my attention.

"Gerry referred to the package as 'the box.' I gathered from the conversation that the package contained something illegal and valuable, but that's all I could find out about it."

"What did you do?" I asked.

Leena looked at her hands, which were folded in her lap. "You have to understand, Mr. Southerland. I was upset. I...I didn't want Gerry to complete this deal. He was going to get richer, and I wasn't going to be part of it. I knew that what he was going to do was illegal, and I wanted him to get caught. I wanted him to be punished. I know that my thinking wasn't rational, but I didn't care. He was going to throw me out!" She looked back up at me. "I wanted revenge, I guess," she said in an unsteady voice. "I wanted to hurt him."

She reached up and smoothed a stray lock of hair from her forehead. When she spoke again, she put some steel in her voice. "I called Mila and told her about the smuggling operation.

I knew that Mila had gang connections. I asked her if she could talk her gangster friends into going in and stealing the package. My plan was to make an anonymous call to the police and alert them to upcoming criminal gang activity at the wharf. I wanted them to send a gang unit to the pier on Tuesday night. That way, policemen from outside of Gerry's department would be on the scene to catch him red-handed trying to smuggle in some illegal contraband. It seemed like a clever idea to me. I didn't tell any of this to Mila, of course."

After a pause, I prompted her to continue by saying, "But...?"

Leena's lips parted in a wistful smile. "Mila," she said. "Mila was very disrespectful to me. She thanked me for the information, but she said that she already knew that something valuable was being smuggled in at the abandoned pier. She told me that she was already planning to get the package for herself. She said that she was getting help from a young adaro man who has the hots for her, and that he would sink the smuggler's boat while it was at sea and grab the package. That wouldn't work for me at all. I managed to talk her into letting the boat dock first, and to wait for someone to take the package out onto the pier. Otherwise, I told her, she might lose the package at sea, or the contents would be damaged by the water. She agreed to do that much, but she insisted that no one was going to walk away with the merchandise except her."

"What would have been wrong with that?" I asked.

Leena shook her head. "I was worried about Mila. Remember, I carried her in my arms into the settlement. I was only a child myself, but I raised Mila. We didn't have parents at the settlement. I was the closest thing to a mother that Mila had. And she was more like a daughter to me than a sister." Leena reached up and wiped at her eye with her gloved hand. When she spoke again, it was with a hardened voice. "But she never really saw me that way. She was always willful and disobedient. And then later, she never understood why I became what I became. She never approved. She never shared my burning desire to escape the slum that we had been forced into. We had become somewhat estranged. I regret that deeply."

"And so you wanted to protect her," I said.

"Exactly, Mr. Southerland. When I heard her insisting that she was personally going to try to seize the package at the pier, my heart sank. I knew that Gerry would be there, and I knew that Stonehammer would be with him. Stonehammer is Gerry's attack dog, and he's very loyal. I knew that he wouldn't hesitate to hurt, or even kill Mila in order to keep her from taking the box. And I also knew that I couldn't go through with my plan to get a gang unit on the scene. Not with Mila there. I didn't want the police to get their hands on her."

"And so you came to me," I said.

"Actually," she said, "I called Tony first."

"That's right," said Atwater. "Leena called me Monday afternoon and told me the whole story. "She asked for my advice. I suggested that she should hire someone to get Mila out of the way in case things got ugly." His ever-present smile widened. "I'm the one who gave Leena your name."

"How did *you* get my name?" I asked.

"You did some work for a friend of mine," he said. "Joe Bentley? He needed an item retrieved, and you got it for him. He has a lot of good things to say about you."

I remembered Joe Bentley. He was an exec for an investment banking firm who had misplaced a file containing some sensitive information. I found out that the file had actually been stolen and arranged for Bentley to buy it back. The case had been far from routine, but in the end I retrieved the file and saved Bentley's job. I hoped that he had dropped my name to some people who were more respectable than Atwater.

"So you came to me with a story about a missing person and a drug deal and asked me to snatch up your sister," I said to Leena. "Why not just tell me the truth?"

"If I had told you that a captain of the YCPD was involved, or that he was going to be there to receive smuggled goods, would you have taken the case?" Leena asked.

I shrugged. "I might have. You should have given me the benefit of the doubt."

"For all I knew," said Leena, "you would have picked up your phone and called Gerry. That's what most sensible men would have done. Gerry might have even rewarded you for the information." She glanced back at Atwater, who looked away. There was something about that brief exchange that made me think I had missed something. But Leena was eager to continue her story, so I let it go for the moment. "Also," said Leena, "I wanted a neutral party to be at the pier to witness Gerry smuggling in something illegal. Someone other than a gangster. I had given up on my plan to send in a police unit, so I decided on a private investigator." She shrugged and showed me a half-smile. "To be honest, I hoped that I could use you as leverage against Gerry if he successfully brought in the package. I was going to tell him that someone had witnessed his operation, and that I was prepared to go to a higher authority and have him prosecuted. Of course," she added with a slight shake of her head, "I couldn't tell *you* that."

I thought about her story. It *seemed* plausible, but I still had questions. "I tried to text you after you left my office," I said. "Why didn't you respond?"

"I didn't see your texts at first," she said. "When I got back to the condo, Gerry was waiting for me. I don't know how, but he knew that I'd been to see you. He was furious!"

I nodded. "He knew by Monday night that you were planning to come see me," I said.

Leena's expression showed surprise. "What?" she said.

"He sent Stonehammer to try to scare me off. Stonehammer told me that you would be coming to my office with a missing person case, and he told me to turn it down."

"So...."

"But that's not why I rejected your case," I interjected. "I turned you down because you weren't being honest with me."

"But...."

"And then I regretted it." I paused. "Maybe Stonehammer intimidated me a bit," I admitted. "But I should have given you a better chance to make your appeal. I'm sorry."

Leena pressed her lips together but said nothing.

"That's why I texted you," I said. "I wanted to give you another chance."

She sighed. "How did Gerry know?"

"Your phone call to your former boss here," I nodded at Atwater. "Graham must have heard your end of it somehow. Did you mention my name? Did you mention that you would be using the name Cora Seafoam? And that you'd be asking me to find someone?"

They both thought about it. It was Atwater who spoke. "You did, Leena. You repeated Mr. Southerland's name when I referred him to you, and you said that you were going to use the Cora Seafoam name to protect yourself if things didn't go well."

"How did he hear me?" said Leena. "He wasn't anywhere near me when I called you."

"Lots of ways," I said. "He could have planted a listening device on your clothing. He could have had an agent of his nearby. Who knows," I said, an idea popping into my head. "He might have had some non-human help, like an elemental."

"Hey," said Atwater. "Do you suppose I should be worried about myself? Do you think Graham knows that I was the one you called?"

I thought about it. "Maybe not," I said. "If you haven't run into Graham or Stonehammer yet, then you probably won't. They've already gone after Mila to get the box, and they've come after me. If they haven't come after you, then maybe Graham only heard Leena's half of your conversation, and he didn't know who she was speaking to."

Atwater nodded slowly, not quite convinced. I wasn't that convinced myself, but I didn't have any better answers. "Well, if they *do* come after me," said Atwater, "I'll be prepared. I've got some well-paid trolls on my staff, you know, to keep the ladies safe. They keep me safe, too. If Graham's goon comes after me, he'll find himself outsmarted and outnumbered."

I wanted to get this conversation back on track. "Leena," I said. "You still haven't answered my question." She looked up at me with a quizzical expression. "Why didn't you return my text messages?"

"Oh," she said. "Like I said, when I got back to the condo, Gerry was waiting for me. He was very angry! He grabbed me and dragged me out of the building without my purse and into his car, and then he drove me to the police station. He actually put me into a holding cell! I couldn't believe it! He said that he didn't want me to interfere with his 'big deal.' He kept me there until morning! You better believe that I was incensed!"

I'll bet. "And your phone was in your purse?" I asked.

"Yes. I didn't see your messages until I got it back."

"Okay, that adds up," I said. "What happened in the morning?"

Leena's eyes welled up. "Gerry came to get me out of the cell. That's when he told me about Mila. He told me that you had beat her and shot her in the head. I think I went a little crazy then. He told me that he had you in custody, and I demanded to see you."

"So why don't you think I did it?" I asked.

"He let you go!" Leena exclaimed. "Why would Gerry have let you go if you had done it? I thought about it and realized that you couldn't have been guilty of killing Mila. It didn't make sense. That's when I figured out that it must have been Gerry. Either he did it or he had someone else do it for him. When it comes down to it, he's soft. He doesn't like to dirty his own hands when he can order someone else to do the work for him." Leena slammed her fist into the arm of her chair. "All for his precious box! What's in it? What does he want so badly that he will kill for it?"

We were all quiet for a while after that. I thought about Leena's story, looking for holes. It seemed solid enough, but I had a gut feeling that something was wrong with it. I couldn't put my finger on it, though. Too much had happened in too little time. And even though my broken bones had healed, maybe I was still feeling the effects of too many blows to the head and too little sleep. The details of this affair swirled in my mind like one of my elementals. I couldn't quite get a grip on it.

Finally, I said, "So what next? I'd like to find out what I'm in the middle of, but to be perfectly frank, I'm not getting anything out of any of this." I looked at Leena, "I know that I turned down your case, but now I'm in it up to my neck. And I'm not getting paid. If I'm going to help you find out about this box and prove that Graham killed Mila, someone is going to have to hire me to do it."

"Of course," Leena said, and I detected a bit of frost in her voice. Too bad, baby! I needed the dough. And, after all, I had the box. Neither Leena nor Atwater knew that, though maybe they suspected. Either way, I wasn't going to take another step without being compensated.

We negotiated my fee plus expenses, and Leena wrote me a check that was big enough to keep me housed, fed, and drunk for the next month. Finally! I needed to get it into my bank account as soon as possible, and that wasn't going to happen while I was sitting in this glorified pimp's office.

"Okay," I said. "We need to do two things. First, we need to find out what's in that box. Second, we need get enough dirt on Graham take him out of the picture. It won't be easy to get the district attorney's office to prosecute a captain in the YCPD. We'll need solid evidence that he committed major crimes. I was at the pier Tuesday night, and I can testify that Graham picked up smuggled goods. I can also testify that he used a street gang to help him out."

"Do you think that the D.A. will be interested in going after a police captain for smuggling?" asked Atwater.

"That's going to depend on what's in the box," I said. "But if we really want to get the D.A.'s attention, we have to prove that Graham murdered Mila." I turned to Leena. "Do you happen to know where she was murdered?"

"I think I do," she said. "I heard bits of a conversation between Gerry and Stonehammer after you were released. I'm pretty sure that they found the body on Fremont Street where it runs through the adaro settlement."

"Well," I said, thinking about it, "I don't know that I'll find anything, but the scene of the crime seems to be as good a place to start as anywhere. I'll head over there now. Uhhhh...." I stopped.

"What?" said Leena.

"As it happens," I said, "I'm without a car at the moment. It would help if I had one."

Atwater smiled. "Borrow one of mine," he said. "I can spare one, if you promise to be careful with it."

"That's very generous," I said. "Thank you."

Atwater's smile broadened. "I think you'll like this one. Come! Let's go get it for you."

We got up, and Atwater led us out of the building and around back to a rear parking lot.

Chapter Twelve

I found a pair of sunglasses in the glove compartment of Atwater's car and put them on. I didn't need them—I was driving away from the setting sun—but I wanted to hide my face on the off chance that I might pass someone I knew. I didn't want to be seen behind the wheel of this ridiculous automobile. The car's windows were tinted, but I needed to be sure. The vehicle seemed to be as large as my living room. Four full-sized trolls could have fit side-by-side on the back seat without complaining about lack of leg or head room. The dashboard panel had more meters and dials than a passenger plane. The entire interior of the car was done up in thick red leather. The exterior was black as a moonless night with purple racing stripes stretching down the length of both sides. A four-piece jazz quartet could have held a jam session on top of the hood, which was decorated with an elaborate decal of a purple winged woman, bare breasts exposed, rising from purple flames. A dozen bodies could have been stuffed into the trunk. I cruised through the streets and tried hard not to take up more than one lane at a time. I needn't have worried. Cars veered as far away from me as they could when I drew near.

It took me nearly an hour of careful driving to get to the city's adaro settlement, which was sprawled out on either side of Fremont Street on the other side of a low hill that rose up east of the old Placid Point Pier. No sign marked the entrance to the settlement, technically I was still in the Placid Point district, but as I drove through the intersection of Fremont and Bay Street it was easy to see that I had crossed an invisible border into a unique section of the city. It was almost like entering a foreign country. On either side of me I could see hastily constructed shelters made of wood and scrap metal, with rag-covered openings serving as windows. The shelters were clustered along narrow roadways that wound through the settlement. Trash blew through the streets and up against the walls of the shelters. As I continued to drive down Fremont, I passed an ugly two-story concrete brick office complex surrounded by a chain link fence. A wide gate in the fence provided the only entrance into the complex. A sign on the gate said "Adaro Settlement Center" in large letters. Smaller letters underneath said, "All visitors must register at front desk." A car in front of me pulled into the gate and stopped at a guard station, where the driver was greeted by a bored-looking troll who examined his identification card and passed him through.

On impulse, I pulled into the gate and stopped at the guard station. I lowered my window as the guard approached.

"Can I help you?" the troll rumbled, giving Atwater's monster automobile a quick going over.

"Maybe," I said. "An adaro girl was killed somewhere around here early this morning. The police were there investigating. Do you know where that was?"

The troll glared down at me with his red glowing eyes. "Lots of crime in this neighborhood," he growled.

"I was acquainted with the girl," I said. "I just want to see where it happened."

"Well, you sure ain't no cop," said the troll. "Not with this car."

"I'm a private investigator," I said.

The troll considered this, and then shrugged. "Yeah, a girl got capped a little further down Fremont. I saw the crime tape this morning, but I don't know if it's still there. Down close to the entrance to Pelican Pier."

I thanked the guard and made a U-turn back onto Fremont. Pelican Pier was at the far end of the settlement, about six blocks down. About two blocks past the settlement center, I saw a place called Sirens on my left. Although the settlement was a slum, Sirens was a popular, if notorious night spot in the city. My work had taken me there a couple of times. In the main room, a beautiful half-dressed golden-voiced adaro singer performed in a cage that was suspended six feet above the floor. Fully nude adaro women danced on elevated stages on either side of the singer. Other adaro women mingled with the audience, luring the men off into private rooms for lap dances. The singers were always excellent, the dancers were always sensuous, and the lap dances were...popular. Sirens was owned by the Hatfield crime family, and the troll bodyguards who patrolled the place showed no mercy to drunken patrons who tried to make any trouble on the premises. But the unlit streets and alleyways surrounding the night spot were the place to go for cheap street drugs and even cheaper sex.

The sun was low in the sky as I drove past Sirens. A car in front of me stopped at a light, and I pulled to a stop behind him. A thin adaro waif of a girl in a loose white blouse and tight shiny blue shorts slipped between our cars and came up to my driver's side window, which was still lowered. She had large false eyelashes, and her lips were caked with bright red lipstick. Thick makeup failed to hide a blotchy pock mark on one cheek. She folded her arms across my window sill, and I spotted the needle marks on both forearms. She couldn't have been older than thirteen. She blinked her large, moist sea-green eyes at me, leaned close to me through the window, and said in a thin child's voice, "Hi, baby. Are you looking for some action?"

The numbers tattooed to her left wrist reminded me of Mila, and I was overwhelmed by a wave of irrational anger. "Beat it, kid," I said.

"Oh, don't be that way," the girl cooed. She looked into my back seat. "You've got plenty of room in this car of yours. You must be rich!" She lifted a hand and pulled at the side of her blouse, exposing a small bare breast. She licked her bottom lip with the tip of her tongue. "Want some?"

"Not interested," I said, and started to raise the window.

The girl jumped back. "Fuck you, cocksucker!" she screamed at me, her voice much more shrill than it had been.

The girl kicked at my car with her platform shoe and moved on to the car stopped in front of me. The car's driver saw her coming in his rear-view mirror and lowered his window. The girl leaned in to make her offer. While they were engrossed in their conversation, the light changed. The car didn't move. After a couple of seconds, I politely honked my horn, which was as loud as the car was big. The girl looked back at me and showed me her middle finger. Still angry, and getting angrier, I yanked on my steering wheel and squeezed the beastmobile to the right of the idling car. With two wheels on the sidewalk, I made an aggressive right turn into the crossing traffic. I heard the squeal of braking tires. A horn honked, and someone shouted, "Fuck you, asshole!" But no one wanted to mess with a vehicle the size of the one I was driving, and I managed to force my way into the line of cars without banging into anyone.

My plan was to make two left turns and get back on Fremont, but the road I was on wasn't straight. It wound its way through a residential area consisting of small temporary huts that were exact matches of the huts on the army base in the Borderland. For a brief moment, I thought that I had returned to the war zone. These huts, trucked in and planted on plots of bare sand, appeared to be almost new. One look at the structures told me that they had to be government-issue housing for the incoming adaro women. As I wound my way through the housing, I saw an adaro woman standing just inside the front door of one of the huts. She had a baby at her breast and was speaking with another adaro woman just outside her hut. The other woman had a firm grip on the hand of a skinny little girl who looked to be about five years old. The women stopped talking when they saw me driving by in Atwater's monster and stared at me with angry eyes. The little girl reached down, picked up an old decaying apple core that was half-buried in the sand, and threw it in my general direction. Her aim was bad, and the apple core landed somewhere behind the car as I drove on by.

I was a little disoriented, but I made a left turn as soon as one became available. When I did, I found myself behind a line of cars moving at a crawl down the narrow avenue. Wondering what the hang-up was, I lowered my window and leaned out as far as I could. Up ahead, I saw three rough-looking young men in jackets with gang colors. They were stopping each car as it approached. I was pinned into the line of traffic, and there was nowhere to go but forward.

When I reached the three gangsters, one of them leaned into my window and held out a small plastic bag with three tiny crystals inside. Without looking at me, he said, "Rock?"

"Rock" was the street name for a type of cheap crystallized cocaine that was sweeping the poorer neighborhoods of big cities. Users smoked it in pipes, and, if they were lucky enough to have a clean product, experienced the same invigorating life-affirming buzz that was provided by commercial coke. Its sale and use were illegal because it cut into the profits of the legitimate pharmaceutical corporations. Politicians railed against it, and stories of rock-related deaths flooded the media. But the cops turned a blind eye to the rock trade, first because it was impossible to control, and second because it wasn't yet hurting anyone who mattered.

"No thanks," I said to the gangster. "I just made a wrong turn."

"Then drive on," said the gangster, backing away from my window.

"Wait," I said. "How do I get back to Fremont?"

The gangster was annoyed. "Left and then left. Now move on, motherfucker. You're wasting my time."

I drove on, took a left and then another left through the shabby slum housing, and found myself back on Fremont. I passed by a series of depressing strip malls with unlit parking areas, bars on every window, litter scattered everywhere. Young adaro women and human men, dressed in torn clothing and smoking cigarettes, crowded together on the street corners, glum expressions on their faces, milling about with nothing better to do. I tried to picture a young Leena Waterfowl growing up in this neighborhood, but I couldn't get my mind around it.

As for Mila, she had seemed too vibrant a personality to exist in these surroundings. I shook my head, understanding why they had wanted out of this dismal place.

***

As I drew close to Pelican Pier, the neighborhood became less crowded. I could see the bay off to my left, just past some dunes. I was a half-block from the entrance to the pier when I passed some police tape surrounding a section of sidewalk to my left on the ocean-side of Fremont. I found a place to park Atwater's beast of an automobile and stepped out of the car. The sun was just disappearing over the ocean, and I paused to take in the view. The sunset seemed clean compared to the settlement, and its beauty was refreshing. Who says I don't have a soft side! I thought about Gracie's avalonian whiskey and wished that I had a bottle of the stuff with me to keep me warm.

I waited for the last of the sun to drop out of sight, crossed the street, and headed back up the incline toward the area marked off by the police tape. Maybe this was where Mila had met her end, and maybe it wasn't, but it was worth checking out. The sidewalk I was on was bordered only by broken concrete, weeds, and sand, which sloped down a hillside to the shore. A trickle of traffic flowed by in both directions, but I saw no one else about. I drew closer to the police tape and stepped into a puddle of water that covered the sidewalk.

The instant that my foot fell on the puddle, water rose up my sides and over my head, immersing me in freezing cold salty water as if I had stumbled into the deep end of the pool. I lashed out with my arms and legs, but to no avail. I was trapped inside a man-sized bubble of water. The water bubble followed every movement of my body and kept me enclosed.

I realized that I had been ambushed by a water elemental, and I couldn't find any way out of it. I punched, and the wall of the bubble moved away from my fist. I kicked and the bubble expanded to avoid my foot. Not only was I going to die, I was going to die frustrated. I couldn't remember being so powerless. Water trickled into my nose and mouth. I shut my air passages up tight, stomped down hard on my cough reflex, and continued to jab and kick, knowing that it was useless but refusing to give in.

My lungs felt close to bursting, and I fell to one knee. In desperation, I tried rolling down the hill, hoping that the elemental would break on the rocks and broken concrete, but the water bubble rolled right over every obstacle. I came to a stop on level sandy ground near the shore. My temples were pounding, my eyes burned, my ears were filled, and I was on the verge of passing out. My lungs weren't going to hold out much longer. In a matter of moments, I was going to inhale, fill my lungs with water, and drown.

Just as I was figuring that I had bought it, I saw a dark blur through the water. Something slashed through the elemental. Unable to hold my breath any longer, I gasped—and air filled my lungs! My head was free. Something ripped through the elemental, and water splashed away from me and into the sand. I crawled to my hands and knees, coughing up foul-tasting water, but gulping precious air into my lungs. It seemed that I was going to live after all.

When I had regained enough strength to move, I sat back on the sand, using one arm to help support myself and using my other hand to wipe saltwater out of my eyes. I coughed again and spat to one side. I looked up and saw Kraken standing in front of me, water dripping from his naked body. Even after my near-death experience, I couldn't keep my attention from being drawn to the package between his legs, which had been hidden under the water when I had seen him in the cave. Let's just say that his junk was proportional to the rest of his massive frame. That made me wonder about female adaros, but I wasn't prepared at the moment to let my thoughts wander any further along those lines. I mentally slapped myself across the mouth and shook my head. Kraken reached down and helped me to my feet.

"You okay, Dickhead?" he asked.

"Alex," I corrected him. "Yeah, I think so. Thanks to you."

Kraken grunted, "Stupid *gruurbluurbl*!" he said. Or something like that. "It won't bother you again."

"I hope not," I said. "That was too close for comfort. I'm sure glad you were nearby when it attacked. I thought it was checkout time for me. You really saved my skin!"

"Unh!" he grunted. I got the feeling that the elemental's attack no longer concerned him. It was in the past, and he was already bored by it. Kids today. Short attention spans.

"Where's Mila?" he asked. "I've been waiting for the two of you all day. Now you're here and she's not. Where is she?"

The poor guy didn't know. And I was going to have to tell him. Wonderful.

"I'm sorry, Kraken," I said. "Mila is dead. Someone got her before we could get to the box."

He stood still, scrunching his face and trying to process what I'd told him. "Mila's dead?" he said when the message registered. "She can't be dead. What're you talking about?" He grabbed me by my shoulders and squeezed.

"I'm sorry!" I said, trying to peel his hands away. "She walked out on me last night. Someone caught up to her and killed her."

"Who!" he barked.

"I don't know, kid! I'm trying to find out."

"Who was it!" he bellowed.

"I told you, I don't know! Let go of me, you big oaf!" I was afraid that he was going to snap my collarbone. It would be ironic if I survived certain death from the water elemental's attack, only to be crushed to death by the adaro who had saved me.

With a yelping cry, Kraken let me go and turned away from me. He walked down the sand a few steps and stopped. "Mila's dead!" he cried. Then he fell to his knees and began sobbing.

I walked over to him and put my hand on his shoulder. "I know, kid. It's a tough break. Mila was a great little gal."

The big adaro was taking it hard. His shoulder trembled beneath my hand as big wracking sobs escaped through his lips. And then suddenly he whipped his head around and fixed me with a shark's dead-eyed stare. "Did you kill her? Did you kill Mila?"

"Hey, take it easy, kid," I said, drawing my hand back from his shoulder. "You're not thinking straight. I didn't kill Mila. I *liked* the girl. I'm trying to find out who did it."

He kept his shark's stare on me for another few seconds, but couldn't maintain it. "Find out who killed Mila," he said, lowering his head. "Find him and bring him to me."

"I'll find him," I said. "But I need your help. I need you to answer some questions. Can you do that?"

Kraken reached up and wiped tears from his face. He nodded.

"Mila and I were going to go get the box this morning," I said. "But during the night while I was sleeping, she took off. I think that she was going to get the box on her own, but she never got there. She met someone, or someone caught up to her. They beat her up pretty good. I guess they were trying to make her tell them where the box was, but she didn't tell them. Tough girl! Anyway, someone shot her in the head, probably because she wouldn't talk. The police found the body this morning."

I paused and let Kraken take it all in. His expression was glum and defeated, and his eyes were blank. After a good ten seconds, he nodded, and I continued.

"There's some police tape on the sidewalk up the hill." I pointed to indicate the spot. "I think that might be where Mila was killed." Kraken looked up to see where I was pointing. He got to his feet and started walking.

"Wait, hold up!" I said, following him. He climbed the hill, and I scrambled after him. When he got to the tape, he stopped and stared at the section of sidewalk enclosed by the tape, as if he were seeing Mila's body. I hoped that no one was there to see him. I couldn't imagine how someone would react to the giant naked adaro standing in the moonlight. People called the emergency hotline for all kinds of things these days, and I didn't want a bunch of cops and firefighters descending on us from all sides.

I approached the tape cautiously, remembering the water elemental. I searched for puddles, but saw none, not even in the spot where I had been ambushed. Satisfied, I looked over the tape to the enclosed sidewalk that Kraken was still staring at. There was nothing to see. No body, of course, but no obvious traces of blood, either. No indication that anything had ever happened there. Just sidewalk. I ducked under the tape and knelt to examine the sidewalk more carefully. It was well past sunset, but up close with my enhanced vision I could see the sidewalk as if it were lit up by a spotlight. I studied every part of it, but saw nothing out of the ordinary. I rapped on the sidewalk with my knuckles in various spots. I bent down and put my ear on the cement. Nothing. I sniffed and smelled bleach. The police had cleaned the pavement. I stepped back outside the crime tape and examined the area around it. In the movies, the intrepid hero would have found some tiny but important clue that the police had overlooked. But this wasn't the movies. A wave of disappointment swept over me. There was nothing to learn here.

Except that I'd been ambushed here by the elemental. That had to mean something. But before I could consider the possibilities, Kraken turned and began to pace back down the hill toward the shoreline.

"Wait!" I called after him. "Where are you going?"

Kraken turned his head without breaking his long-legged stride. "Mila was there," he said.

I ran back down the slope after him. "Hang on, you big dope!" I yelled. I felt sorry for the kid, but I was starting to feel like an idiot chasing him up and down this blasted sand dune. My shoes were filled with wet sand, my clothes were soaked from the elemental's attack, and I was in danger of succumbing to hypothermia. I really needed a drink, or at least a couple of cups of hot coffee.

I caught Kraken at the base of the dune and grabbed him by the arm. "Stop! Take it easy for a second. I still need to ask you some questions."

Kraken stopped and looked at me with a surprised expression, as if he had forgotten that I was there. Then he sagged and sat down cross-legged on the sand. I knelt in front of him. "Mila was there," he said.

"How do you know that?"

"I smelled her blood on the hard land inside the big ribbon," he said. "She was there."

"You smelled blood?" I said. "Through the bleach?"

He nodded. "Female adaro blood. It was Mila's."

"You can do that?" I asked.

"I am adaro," he said, as if that explained everything. Maybe it did.

"How do you know it was Mila's blood?" I asked.

He stared at me. "It was Mila's," he insisted.

It was a stretch, but I had to agree with him. Leena had told me that this was the area where Mila's body had been found, and the crime scene tape told the rest of the story. But even if this was where Mila had been killed, I was no closer to finding out who had killed her. The police had done a thorough job cleaning up.

I tried to think. Something was trying to rise up from the scattered pile of information in my brain. What was I missing? Something about Mila? Something about Kraken? Then I remembered. "The police showed me a photo this morning," I began. "It showed you tied up in a net just outside your cave. What happened?"

Kraken snorted. "The *gruuub-grurr* cops showed up after Mila and you left, while it was still dark. I was drifting in the water, getting strong after fighting the troll. He broke my jaw, you know, and the water hadn't finished healing it. Anyway, the cops got me in a *gruuub-grurr* net and dragged me to the land. They couldn't hold me, though. *Gruuub-grurr* weak land-slugs!" He smiled at the memory. "I ripped their net apart. The *gruuub-*

grurr cops ran away like *blurruplupples*. One of them shot me here." He showed me a reddish spot on the left side of his torso. "It's better now."

The adaro words bubbled up from somewhere deep in Kraken's chest and reminded me that I was having a casual conversation with a legendary creature that most humans never see. It was like being in the middle of a children's bedtime story. The world began to seem strange and unfamiliar, and I was struck by how little I knew about it. I felt like I was floating.

"You heal fast," I said, trying to bring my feet back to solid ground. I wondered if his finger would grow back.

He shrugged. "The ocean." As far as he was concerned, no other explanation was necessary.

"I'm glad you got out of that net," I said. "They didn't come back for you?"

"No. I wish they would!"

"What have you been doing since?" I asked.

"Swimming. Waiting for Mila." He trailed off, his face sagging. He looked like he wanted to cry again.

"Look," I said. "That water elemental wasn't there by accident. Elementals don't just sit around waiting to attack anyone who might be passing by. Someone sent it there for a reason. How long have you been here? Did you see anyone besides me in the vicinity?"

Kraken wrinkled his brow in thought. After a time, he said, "I didn't see anyone. This is a quiet place. Nothing much ever happens here. I was swimming through the water back there, back and forth from my cave. I was waiting for Mila, but I don't like sitting still. I came up on the land a few times. I didn't see nothing until you came rolling down the hill with the *gruurbluurbl*, the elemental, as you say. I didn't like that! *Gruurbluurbls* do what I tell them to! I didn't tell it to kill anyone."

"Well, someone did," I said.

But why? Was it guarding something? If so, what? Nothing that I could see, and I'd taken a good close look. Had the elemental been targeting someone? Like, maybe, me? But who knew that I was going to be here? Just Leena and Atwater. Was one of them trying to kill me? Maybe I was being paranoid, but I had to at least consider the possibility. Leena had said that she was coming clean with me, but was she? I had the feeling that she was still telling me only what she wanted me to hear. What was her angle in all of this? As for Atwater, I couldn't think of any reason why he would want me dead, but how much did I really know about him? Until this afternoon, I hadn't even known that he existed. I tried to remember the part of our conversation that had led me to come up to the adaro settlement. Leena had said that she overheard parts of a conversation between Graham and Stonehammer, and that what she had heard had led her to believe that Mila's body might be found somewhere in the settlement. Had she and Atwater pressured me to investigate, or had that been my own idea? I couldn't remember for sure, but I thought that I had been the one to suggest it. Had I been manipulated? It was possible. But Leena had written me a check. I was working for her, trying to find out about the box and who killed Mila for it. That didn't mean that she was above suspicion, but it counted for something. No, most likely the water elemental had been there for some reason that had nothing to do with me. Maybe I'd been wrong. Maybe it *had* been minding its own business and I'd just had the bad luck to step in it.

I wrenched my mind back to the present. "You sure you didn't see anyone hanging around up there?" I asked Kraken.

"No."

"You didn't see the police earlier, putting up that tape?"

"No. I must have been somewhere else when they did that. Maybe in my cave."

I was getting nowhere. Time for a different line of inquiry. I sat down close to the big adaro on his downwind side, trying to use him as a windbreak. At some point soon, though, I was going to have to get into some dry clothes.

"All right," I said. "Let's leave that. Let's talk about the box. Mila said that you were the one who told her about it. How did you find out about the box?"

"The elf told me," he said.

That staggered me. All I could say was, "What?"

"The elf," Kraken repeated. "I saw him at the old pier a few days ago. He told me that a ship was carrying something, and that I should take it. He said that it was valuable."

"The elf?" I couldn't get my brain to work. "What elf?"

Kraken looked at me as if I were stupid. Maybe I was. "The elf!" he said. As far as Kraken was concerned, no further explanation was necessary.

"Does this elf sometimes fish off the old pier?" I asked.

Kraken snorted. "I don't know. Maybe. He goes wherever he wants. Sometimes I see him on this shore, sometimes on the islands." He waved his hand westward.

"Where was he when he told you about the box?" I asked.

"On an island," said Kraken. "I don't know the human name for it. It's small. I went there and he was waiting for me. He told me about the merchandise and said I should take it." Kraken shrugged. "So I told Mila about it. She said that she would get some friends to help. She told me to wait until the boat reached the pier, and then we would take the merchandise and get rich. She said we could buy an island and we would live there." Tears began to well up in his eyes.

"Tell me about the elf," I said, partly because I wanted to know more about him, and partly to draw Kraken's attention away from Mila.

"He's just the elf," said Kraken. "There aren't many elves around anymore, you know. He's the only one I've ever seen, but the old adaro men say that others live far away. This one talks to the old men sometimes, but this was the first time he ever talked to me." Kraken looked at me and smirked. "He probably doesn't talk to humans."

"Why not?" I said.

"Duhhh!" said Kraken, treating me like an idiot. "Because of the way humans turned against the elves during the fight against the Dragon Lords!"

"Turned against—what are you talking about?

Kraken sighed, showing his impatience with me. "Everyone knows that elves and humans fought against the Dragon Lords. They might have won, too, but then the humans made a deal with the Dragons Lords behind the elves' back and turned against them. That's how the Dragon Lords beat the elves and took over the lands." He frowned. "Now they're trying to take over the oceans, too. They've forced the women out of the water. But the men are still fighting!" His eyes lit up. "We'll take the oceans back and rule them like we used to!"

I was fascinated by this version of ancient history, so different from everything I'd been taught. But if it was getting us any closer to finding out who killed Mila, I couldn't see how. I'd have to look into this.

"Huh!" I said. "Maybe we can discuss this more later, but let's get back to Mila. You mentioned her friends. These were the Northsiders?"

"Yeah, that's what she called them. She said that they were a gang, and that she was a member. She said that they would help her get the merchandise, but then she would take it and we would go away together. Then we were going to sell it and keep the money for ourselves." He sighed. "But I don't want it anymore, now that she's dead." He looked at me. "You can have it. If I see the elf again, I'll tell him that I can't do what he wants without Mila." He made as if he were going to stand.

"Wait," I said. "Just another couple of minutes."

"Okay," Kraken said, settling back into the sand. "But I have to get back into the water soon. It's not good to be out of the water for too long, you know."

I hesitated. "So it's true that adaros can't spend too much time out of the water?" I asked.

"True for adaro men, yes," Kraken said. "In the saltwater, we're strong! No one can defeat an adaro man in the ocean. But dry land makes us weak. If we leave the ocean for too long, we die."

I filed that away for later and turned back to my subject. "Did Mila have any troubles with any of the Northsiders?" I asked. If she had always meant to take the box for herself, maybe one of her gangsta friends had got wind of her plan. Maybe he had caught up to her, tortured her for the location of the box, and killed her when she wouldn't talk. It was a possibility.

Kraken made a humphing sound. "Quapo," he said.

"The driver who left the scene when the shooting started?" I asked.

"Yeah," said Kraken with contempt. "He's a *bluurrblen* pussy! Mila said that he was supposed to drive her away after she got the box. But he left her there on her own!" He launched into a series of burbling noises that I interpreted as impolite words in the language of the adaro. Then he continued in "human language" for my benefit. "Quapo hung around Mila like a *bluubrondaaanb* around a shark. I don't know your word. The little fish that attaches itself to a shark and eats the crumbs that the shark leaves behind."

"Remora," I said.

"Whatever. Anyway, he liked Mila, and Mila strung him along." He paused, seeming embarrassed. "Mila kind of did that to boys. They followed her around, and she liked to tease them. She never liked any of them the way she liked me, though!" He said, fixing me with his deadly gaze.

"I'm sure of that," I said.

Kraken dropped his eyes. "Anyway, Quapo would do anything Mila told him to. So she told him to drive everyone to the pier and to wait for them down the street. Mila told the rest of the gang that he was going to be their 'getaway driver.' But she was going to take the merchandise and run to the car by herself and make Quapo drive her away. Then she was going to leave Quapo and bring the merchandise to me." He paused and narrowed his eyes. "Hey!" he said, as an idea seeped its way into his head. "Do you think Quapo killed her?"

I thought about it. My money was still on Graham, but I had to admit that Quapo made a good suspect. He had succumbed to Mila's inhuman allure, as most young men would, and Mila had encouraged him while keeping him at bay. At some point, Quapo would have become frustrated, especially if he knew about Kraken, which he probably did. I doubt that Mila had kept her relationship with the young adaro hunk a secret. Maybe he knew that she was going to use the gang and then dump them. I doubt that Mila had been all that careful around Quapo. She probably thought that she had him wrapped around her finger. She could have been a little loose with her lips around him. Maybe Quapo had some second thoughts about her and ditched her. Had he called Mila last night? It was possible. Mila might have thought that Quapo would be a more cooperative business partner than I would. She might have told Quapo to come and get her and then drive her to Lubank's office to get the box. But she didn't tell Quapo where they were going, just when to turn and when to keep going straight. So Quapo developed plans of his own. Snapping out of Mila's spell, he tried to force the location from Mila, and when that didn't work, he killed her. As any cop will tell you, in far too many men there's a fine line between sexual attraction and hate, especially when the attraction is unfulfilled. I worked it around in my head, and it made sense.

It didn't bother me that the crime scene up on the sidewalk was not between my building and Lubank's office. Quapo could have moved the body and dumped it there. There were still too many details about her murder that I didn't know. But I knew that Quapo was a lead I had to follow.

"Do you know where the Northsiders hang out?" I asked Kraken.

"They go to a bar near here to drink and play that dumb game with sticks and balls on a table," said Kraken.

"Want to go there with me? Now?"

Kraken said, "To find Quapo?"

"Maybe. I'd like to talk to some of the Northsiders. It would help if you were there with me," I said.

"Give me a few minutes," Kraken said. "I need to swim."

With that, Kraken stood and jogged to the shoreline and into the water. He dove in and disappeared. After a few seconds, I saw him leap into the air like a dolphin about a hundred yards from shore. A few seconds later, I saw him leap again several yards from where he had been. Kraken swam and leaped for about ten minutes, and then he climbed out of the water and back onto the land.

When he reached me, I said, "Better?"

He grunted. "Let's find Quapo." He started to walk toward the dune.

I hesitated. "Ummm.... Do you have any clothes?" I asked.

He didn't even pause. I shrugged and followed him up the dune.

Chapter Thirteen

After catching up to Kraken, I led him to Atwater's car. Kraken's eyes lit up when he saw it. "Sweet ride!" he said.

When we were inside, he looked this way and that, examining everything. He was a kid in a candy store. He touched the meters on the dash and felt the cold red leather on the seats. "Do you think we could fill this with water?" he asked. "That would be *broorblin* awesome!"

"Just tell me how to get to this bar," I said.

"It's back there past the settlement," he said. "On the other side over the hill. It's called Medusa's. Look for the lady with snakes in her hair."

I made a U-turn on Fremont and we drove back through the settlement. I was relieved when we crossed Bay Street and left the settlement behind. I had felt something close to the same kind of relief at the end of my tour in the Borderland. The two places were different kinds of undesirable, but equal in their need to be seen receding in the rear-view mirror.

Kraken couldn't keep his hands off the red leather interior of Atwater's beastmobile. He made me lower the window on his side of the car so that he could stick his head outside and watch the buildings and other cars go by. He reminded me of a large puppy. The ride temporarily took his mind off his loss, and, for that, I was happy to indulge him. As we pulled into the dirt parking lot at Medusa's, though, Kraken's face became grim and his eyes threatening. I wondered if bringing him here was a good idea. On the other hand, wandering into a gang bar without some serious backup wouldn't have been one of my smarter decisions.

Medusa's Tavern was not a place that was going to attract any tourists. The brown wooden exterior looked to be losing a decades-long war against the damp salty winds blasting sand in off the coast. If it hadn't been for a few motorcycles and a couple of cars in the parking lot, and a weak beam of light peeking through two shuttered windows on either side of the front door, I would have thought that the place was abandoned. A carved wooden figure barely recognizable as the mythical Medusa was nailed above the door. Faded red paint in one of the windows spelled out 'Medusa's Tavern" in letter's about two inches tall. I doubted that I would have been able to read them without my enhanced night vision. If you didn't know this place was here, you would never have found it, which meant that it wasn't a place for strangers.

"You've been here?" I asked Kraken.

Kraken nodded. "Mila brought me here a few times. This is where her gang meets." His features hardened, and I knew that he was thinking about Mila. If Quapo was here tonight, Kraken might kill him on the spot.

"Remember," I said. "We don't know that anyone in here killed Mila. I'll ask some questions, and I want you there to back me up in case they don't want to answer. But don't do anything unless I tell you to, or you have to. We need answers, and they won't be able to give them to us if they're dead. Understand?"

Kraken nodded.

"Do you know who's in charge of the Northsiders?" I asked him.

"Yeah," he said. "A guy named Ten-Inch. That's his motorcycle over there." Kraken pointed to a tricked-out bike parked closest to the front door of the bar.

"Ten-Inch. Right. Betcha a fin he's exaggerating," I said.

"What?"

"Never mind."

I looked Kraken up and down. "Uhhh," I said. "Are you sure you don't need some clothes?"

"I don't wear clothes," he said.

Of course not. "Okay," I said. "Let's go."

We got out of the car, not without some reluctance on Kraken's part, and walked into Medusa's Tavern. The interior of the bar was a good match for the outside. Through the dim, smoky light, I could make out ten or so tattered barstools pushed up against a no-frills bar on the left side of the room. A handful of tables and chairs of unfinished wood were scattered about the floor, which was covered with empty bottles, bits of shattered glass, and cigarette butts. A few cushioned booths lined the wall on the right side of the room. Stuffing poked out of rips in every cushion, except for the ones in which all of the stuffing had been yanked out long ago. Knives had been used to carve slits, scars, initials, short messages, and crude drawings, mostly of male genitalia, big-breasted women, and various sex acts on every wooden surface in the place. In the back of the room was a single pool table, surrounded by about a dozen tough looking thugs wearing jeans, denim jackets, and rolled-up headbands displaying Northsider colors. The pool area was nearly as large as the dining area. Most of the Northsiders were holding beer bottles and smoking cigarettes. Empty bottles and butts littered the floor, and the mingled smell of beer, tobacco, and pot filled the air. The gangbangers were the only people in the bar, and all of them were watching Kraken and me as we walked toward them.

"Is Quapo there?" I asked Kraken under my breath.

"No," Kraken growled back at me.

"Which one is Ten-Inch?" I asked in a whisper.

"Over there." Kraken whispered back, and he gave a nod at a figure sitting against the wall on our right.

Ten-Inch was dressed like the rest of the gang, his headband failed to disguise a receding hairline, and, in contrast to the other Northsiders, his hair was cut short. Permanent frown lines cut across his forehead, and deep lines marked the dark puffy skin under his eyes. The black stubble from his three-day growth failed to mask a faded scar that stretched down the right side of his face from his cheek to his chin. A cigarette dangled from his lips, and he regarded me with bemused curiosity as I approached.

A thug with a pool cue in his hand stepped forward to intercept us as we drew near. "Hey, Kraken," he said. "Who's the old guy?"

"That's Dickhead," said Kraken nodding toward me.

"Actually, my name is Alex," I said.

The thug gave me the briefest of glances before turning back to look up at Kraken. "What's he want?" he asked.

"I want to talk to Ten-Inch," I said before Kraken could answer. "It's about Mila."

That got their attention.

"Where is she?" asked the homeboy with the pool cue.

"She's dead," I said.

Murmurs punctuated by profanity filled the room. "Th'fuck!" pool cue guy muttered under his breath. Some of his gang brothers began to step in our direction. One of them yelled, "What are you, a cop?"

"I'm not a cop," I said.

"He's a private cop," said Kraken. I looked at him and frowned. "Keep quiet," I muttered.

"A cop's a fuckin' cop," yelled another of the homeboys. "We don't like cops," he added. A general murmur of approval followed this pronouncement. Several of them began to crowd toward Kraken and me. Pool cue guy took a quick glance behind him to make sure that he had support from his buddies, and then he swung the business end of the cue at my head. I have to admit, the kid was good. He was quicker than a striking rattlesnake. But Kraken was quicker. Before the cue handle could dent my skull, Kraken's arm darted out, and the stick slammed to a stop in the palm of his hand, inches in front of my face. With a jerk of his arm, the giant adaro yanked the pool cue away from the astonished Northsider. Kraken broke the cue over his own knee, put the two pieces of the stick into one hand, and tossed them back over his head toward the dining area, where they bounced off the tables and chairs with a raucous clatter.

"Leave Dickhead alone," Kraken said without a trace of tension. The homeboys who had been advancing on us all stopped in their tracks. One or two of them may have gulped.

Ten-Inch leaped to his feet. "You two," he said, waving his hand at Kraken and me. "Come with me, please." He turned and opened a door in the back wall of the bar. He stepped through and held it open. Well, he *did* say "please." So Kraken and I strolled past the other Northsiders with casual indifference, while they all stared at me with cold eyes. They ignored Kraken, however. Apparently, "No shoes, no shirt, no service" didn't apply here, at least not to a seven-foot tall naked adaro. Between him and me, I was the odd man out in this place.

We walked through the open door into a small office, complete with an old desk that looked like it had come from a secondhand store and several wooden chairs matching the ones in the dining room area. A single bare forty-watt bulb hung from the ceiling above the desk, but Ten-Inch didn't bother to switch it on. A dark smudge at the bottom of the bulb suggested that it was burned out. A bright moon cast light through a partially shuttered window in the back of the room, and horizontal shadows from the shades filled the office. The top of the desk was covered with folders, loose papers, paper clips, a tape dispenser, and various other desk items, along with an obsolete computer, a landline phone, and a dirty metal ashtray. Papers and logbooks of various sites were stacked on the floor around the desk. A pile of empty beer bottles were stacked against the wall near an overflowing wastepaper basket standing against the back wall of the room. Ten-Inch closed the door behind us and navigated himself around the debris to take a seat behind the desk. He didn't offer us a chair.

"Who are you and what happened to Mila?" he asked.

"My name is Alex Southerland," I said. "I'm a private detective. Mila's sister hired me to make sure that she got safely out of the ruckus on the pier last night. I was there, out of sight, when it all happened. Mila got away from the firefight, but I guess your driver cleared out when the going got tough."

"Quapo." Kraken squeezed the name out of his throat with a dangerous growl.

"I offered Mila a ride out of there, and she took it," I said.

Ten-Inch breathed in smoke from his cigarette and didn't say anything.

"After we got away," I continued, "She took off on her own. This morning the police found her. She'd been beaten and shot through the head." Kraken gave off a low growl at this, but didn't move. "The cops knew that her sister had hired me to find her, so they brought me in for questioning. They made a halfhearted attempt to pin the murder on me, but I didn't do it, and they knew it, so they let me go. Now Mila's sister wants me to find out who murdered her. I thought that I would see if anyone here might know anything useful."

I stopped and watched Ten-Inch blow a stream of smoke out to one side. I noted that Ten-Inch was not as young as the other Northsiders. He appeared to be a little older than me, for that matter, but maybe the incipient baldness made him appear older than he was. I also noted that his thoughtful eyes contained a spark of intelligence. This was no dummy. I'd have to be careful what I said to him.

"Why would Mila go with you?" he asked.

"I told her that her sister had sent me," I said.

He gave me a hard look. "Mila hates her sister," he said. "You'll have to do better than that."

He was right. I let out a breath. "Okay," I said. "You know why she went to the pier, right?"

Ten-Inch didn't say anything. He knew. He waited for me to continue.

"I got my hands on the merchandise," I said. "She went with me because she wanted it."

"Where is it?" Ten-Inch asked me.

"I've got it hidden away," I said. "Mila knew where. She was with me when I stashed it. I think that she was going for it when she left me. I think that someone caught up with her before she could get it and tried to beat the location out of her. When she wouldn't talk, he shot her."

Ten-Inch thought about it. "And who do you think killed her?"

I shrugged. "Might have been the cops," I said. "I assume that you know about Captain Graham?" Ten-Inch motioned me to continue. "He was smuggling in the merchandise. He knew that the two of us had run off with it." Ten-Inch nodded, but Kraken shifted his feet and nudged me hard enough to force me to catch my balance. I looked up at him, and then back at Ten-Inch. "Kraken here," I said, "thinks that Quapo might be the killer." Kraken growled.

Ten-Inch took another puff of his cigarette and blew out more smoke. He hadn't offered one to Kraken or me. I didn't smoke, and I doubted that Kraken did, either, but offering us a smoke would have been the polite thing to do.

"Why Quapo?" he asked me, not looking at Kraken.

I answered before Kraken could. "I gather that Quapo had a thing for Mila," I began.

Ten-Inch coughed. "Something like that," he said. "A lot of the guys in that room did." He shrugged. "I might have had a little thing for her myself." His eyes flicked up at Kraken. "Not that I would have done anything about it, of course." He looked back at me. "She was the kind of girl that men had things for."

"Kraken says that Mila encouraged Quapo a bit, maybe more than she did the others, but never gave him what he wanted," I said. Ten-Inch's lips parted in a brief smile, but he didn't say anything. "He bailed on your gang. It may be that he called Mila a little later and convinced her to meet him. He knew about the merchandise, and maybe he convinced her that the two of them should go get it. But he might have had his own plans. Maybe he thought he could get the location of the merchandise from Mila, ditch her like he did the rest of the gang, and keep it all for himself. Maybe Mila wouldn't cooperate with him. Maybe he was sick of the way Mila was leading him on. Maybe he beat her up and got a little too excited." I shrugged.

"Lots of maybes," said Ten-Inch. He took one last puff from the cigarette and crushed it out in the ashtray. "Why didn't he wait for Mila to take him to the merchandise before turning on her?"

"I can't tell you," I admitted. "I don't know what went on while he was driving her to the spot. Like you said, lots of maybes. But when you combine Mila, a frustrated admirer, and the prospect of a lot of dough, I can see how the whole thing might explode."

"Hmmm." Ten-Inch took his cigarette pack out of his shirt pocket and lit up another smoke. Now would have been the time to offer us one, but he put it back in his pocket. I guess he wasn't that polite.

"Quapo never made it back here," said Ten-Inch. "I don't know where he is." He took a puff. "I'm not happy about that," he said.

Ten-Inch leaned back in his chair and looked up at the ceiling. Kraken shifted at my side. He was getting impatient. He hadn't come here to flap lips. He wanted to hit something, or someone.

Ten-Inch must have sensed the same thing I did. He leaned forward and smiled up at Kraken. "How you holdin' up, big fellow?" he said.

"I want Quapo!" Kraken growled. "I want to ask him if he killed Mila!"

"I'd like to ask him that, too," said Ten-Inch, "among other things. Like why he bailed on his tribal brothers. Don't worry, well find him." Ten-Inch stood from his chair and walked around his desk to stand in front of Kraken. He reached up and gripped Kraken's arm. "We all loved Mila, big fellow. She was a Northsider! We'll all miss her. But I know that it's worse for you. She was your lady, and now she's gone. That's hard, man! That's fuckin' hard."

Kraken blinked away tears from his glistening eyes before they could form. He sniffed and nodded.

"If you need anything, just let me know. You might not be a member of the tribe, but I'll always be here for you, big fellow, for Mila's sake." I wanted to believe that this overaged gangbanger was insincere, but I have to admit that he sounded like he was speaking from the heart.

Ten-Inch squeezed Kraken's arm. Then he walked back behind his desk. Before he sat, he said, "Kraken, can you open that door for me please?"

Kraken nodded, stepped back and opened the door.

Ten-Inch sat down and shouted, "Doc, get in here!"

After some scuffling noises from outside the door, the tall, lanky gangster with the handlebar mustache that I'd seen at the pier walked in. His right arm was pressed to his side and held there by a homemade sling made from a dirty towel.

"This is Doctor Death," said Ten-Inch, waving his homeboy over to his side. As Doc made his way around the desk, Ten-Inch told me, "Doc here was the only one of the tribal brothers who returned from the pier last night. Doc, did you see Mila leave the firefight?"

Doctor Death lowered his eyes, "Sorry, Ten-Inch," he said. "I was kind of occupied. After the last of the Claymore scum ran off, I checked around and saw that I was the only one there that was still breathin'. What a fuckin' bloodbath!"

Ten-Inch looked at me, inviting me to ask questions. "Did you see Graham or the troll leave the pier?" I asked.

Doctor Death turned to Ten-Inch, who nodded at him. Then the gunslinger looked at me and said, "I didn't see Graham leave. I saw the troll. He went running out of the parking lot, but I didn't see where he went after that. I heard him yelling, though." Doctor Death glanced at the purple stump on Kraken's hand and then quickly looked away. "After that," he continued, "I got shot in the arm. I got the motherfucker, though!" he finished.

"You didn't see Mila after that?" Ten-Inch asked.

"No. I saw her plenty during the action, though! Let me tell you, that bitch was fuckin' deadly!" He looked up at Kraken with shining eyes. "You would have been proud of her, big man!" He choked back a sob.

"Did you ever see Quapo after he dropped you off at the pier?" Ten-Inch asked.

"No, man," Doctor Death said with disgust. "I looked for him when it was all over. I went to where he said he would be, but the punk-ass bitch was gone, and he took the van with him! I saw some good brothers die out there last night. Fuckin' Quapo has a lot to answer for!"

Ten-Inch clutched the back of Doctor Death's hand. After a moment, he said, "Okay, Doc, wait for me outside. Close the door when you leave."

After Doctor Death left, Ten-Inch leaned back and studied me without speaking. When he finally spoke, he said, "What did you say your name was?"

"Alex," I said. "Alex Southerland."

"Veteran?" Ten-Inch asked.

"I did my time," I said.

"In the Borderland?"

"Yes sir," I confirmed.

"What unit?"

"Twenty-seventh," I said.

Ten-Inch nodded. "Isthmus?"

I took a long look at him and nodded. "How about you?" I asked.

"Thirty-third," he said, and it was my turn to nod.

"I know them," I said. "The Hawk was in command while I was there."

"Loo-tenant Hawkins," Ten-Inch said. "He was in command while I was there, too."

"Good man," I said.

"The best," Ten-Inch agreed. Then he asked, "You know Sergeant Hillerman?"

"I knew him," I said. "Before he was evaced out."

"I knew Hilly while he was in," said Ten-Inch. "He told me a story once about a crazy sergeant in the twenty-seventh named Southerland. Said he was a stone-cold killer, but someone you could count on when the shit was flying."

"He liked to talk through his ass," I said.

Ten-Inch nodded. He took another puff on his cigarette, which had been languishing in his ashtray. A long chunk of ash fell off, and he crushed out the rest. He stood and held out his hand. "We'll find Quapo," he said. "Or you will. Either way, we'll get to the bottom of this. If there is anything you need from us, let me know."

"Likewise," I said, shaking his hand.

Ten-Inch looked up at Kraken, who was looking sullen and bored. "Kraken, you stick with this man, okay? He'll help you find Mila's killer."

Kraken blinked at me like he'd forgotten who I was.

Ten-Inch and I exchanged contact numbers on our phones, and then he walked us out the door. His brothers looked at him, questions in their eyes.

"This here is Alex Southerland," said Ten-Inch. "He's looking for Mila's killer. So are we. Also, we're both looking for Quapo. We need some answers from him. If you find him, I want to know about it. Now somebody get us all a beer."

A couple of the homeboys went behind the bar and brought out a case of cold beer. Each of us, including Kraken, popped open a bottle and held it up.

"To Mila," said Ten-Inch.

"To Mila," we all echoed.

"She was a fuckin' cock-tease and a motherfuckin' bitch," Ten-Inch said, "but she was a true tribal sister and a loyal Northsider. She was also the best streetfighter in this room, and I'll kick any fucker's ass who says otherwise.' Everyone smiled. Ten-Inch lifted his bottle to his lips, and we all did the same.

I decided not to mention that, with the possible exception of Kraken, Mila had planned to betray the whole bunch of them.

***

Kraken emptied his bottle in one long swallow. When he was finished, he looked down at me and muttered, "Find Quapo. Bring him to me. Someone has to die for Mila."

"Let's make sure that he's guilty, first. Okay?"

Kraken held his beer bottle up with one hand and squeezed, crushing the bottle into shards. He ignored the blood that ran down his hand.

Chapter Fourteen

Kraken and I left the bar soon afterwards. When we reached Atwater's car, I asked him if he needed me to drive him anywhere. He looked at the car with some longing in his eyes, but said that the ocean was just down the dunes, and that he'd walk. He had hoped to get his claws on Quapo, and, as far as he was concerned, the visit to the bar had been a bust. Now he was anxious to get back into the water, where I knew he'd grieve for Mila in his own way: immersing himself in dark dreams of retribution.

Before he left, I said, "I'd like to keep in touch with you if that's okay."

Kraken thought about that without responding, so I said, "If I find out who killed Mila, I want to let you know about it."

Kraken nodded then, and said, "If you want to reach me, go to the end of that old pier. Call for me. I'll come as soon as I can, but it might not be right away."

"You'll hear me?" I asked.

Kraken rolled his eyes at me. "No, but the fish will. They'll send word to me."

"You talk to the fish?" I asked. He just looked at me. "Of course you do," I said.

"Find Quapo, Dickhead" he told me.

I didn't bother correcting him. It was a lost cause. "I will," I said. "Go swim. Try to stay out of trouble. Let me handle this. I'll come for you when the time is right."

With that, Kraken turned and headed down the side of the bar and on to the water, walking tall under the moonlit sky. I watched him until he disappeared down the slope. Before last night, I had thought of male adaros as legendary creatures. They were the fearsome rulers of the deep, the kings of the ocean.

Through the ages, adaros had doomed scores of trespassing sailors to watery graves. And now, I had downed a beer with one of these legends, albeit a budding prince rather than a king. And while I could detect a hint of the storybook qualities of his fabled ancestors in the youth, he seemed in many ways to me to be as human as any land-bound teenaged boy I'd ever encountered, edging his way out of the simple black-and-white world of adolescence toward the confusing complexities of adulthood. But his world was different from mine, and I didn't know whether I'd see him again. I wished him the best, especially in his time of grief and loss, and hoped that he wouldn't do anything rash. I nodded after him and whispered, "Good luck, buddy. Stay cool." Then I turned back to the car.

Stonehammer stood looming before me, teeth bared in a broad smile. Before I could move a muscle, I felt his fist crunch into the side of my chin. The ground tilted, rose up, and struck me in the face. Blackness rolled over me, and I tumbled in.

***

Contrary to what you see in movies and television shows, it's almost impossible to knock a person out with one punch. Your brain sits in a pool of fluid that cushions it from the inside of your skull. Inside your brain are little electrical way stations called neurons, which are fed by electrolytes (potassium, calcium, and sodium). To be knocked out, you have to be hit so hard that your skull slams into your brain with enough force to knock the potassium out of your neurons. Usually, in most people, this takes more than one blow, and it helps if your brain bounces back and forth from one side of your skull to the other a few times in rapid succession. When the potassium leaves, calcium rushes in to take its place, and when your neurons get overloaded with calcium your brain shuts itself off until it can restore the proper balance of electrolytes. The shutdown generally lasts anywhere from a few seconds to several minutes, but, if the damage to your brain is severe enough, you might never recover consciousness at all. Most of the time, though, you will wake up with a concussion. You will probably feel fine in a few days, maybe a few weeks if the damage is bad enough. But the effects of a concussion linger, and if you happen to be the kind of guy who gets his head whacked around a lot, the cumulative effects of multiple concussions can lead to personality disorders, dementia, or even death. One way to prevent all of this misery is to protect your head by not allowing it to be used repeatedly as a punching bag by an aggressive troll. I felt that this would be a good lesson for me to learn some day. I had the feeling, though, that today wasn't going to be the day.

Oddly enough, a blow that's hard enough to knock you out doesn't hurt. Pain occurs in the brain, and an unconscious brain doesn't register pain. I felt Stonehammer's fist when it hit my chin. It hurt like a son of a bitch. But the blow to my chin knocked me down, not out. What knocked me out was the ground slamming into my face. I didn't feel any pain when the ground hit my face. I should have felt it when I woke up, because of the resulting concussion. But I didn't, and I wondered why.

When I regained consciousness, I found myself sitting in a metal chair with my hands cuffed behind my back and my feet tied to the legs of the chair. My chin was slumped down to my chest and my jaw was swollen like a balloon. But I didn't hurt. Not in my head, not anywhere. My whole body was numb. My first thought was that I was paralyzed, but a quick check revealed that I could move my fingers and toes with only a normal amount of effort. I could have moved my arms and legs if they hadn't been restrained. The numbness extended into my head, and I was having difficulty focusing my thoughts. I just wanted to sleep. After a while, it occurred to me that I'd been drugged.

I must have moaned or groaned or something. In any case, Stonehammer came stomping in from somewhere and sat in a chair directly across from me just a few feet away. He was nattily dressed in yet another pinstripe suit, this one pale blue with yellow stripes. In my dazed state, he made me think of blue skies and sunshine. I started to dream about running around on the beach when I was a kid.

"Wakey, wakey," Stonehammer said in an irritating sing-song.

"Hey, Detective," I said, noting the slur in my voice. "Howzzit hangin'?"

"I'm fine. Thanks for asking," said Stonehammer. "What's going to happen now, is that we're going to have a little chat. Before we do, though, I should tell you that you've been shot up with a little chemical compound that will keep you from calling up your wind spirit pals." He leaned in toward me. "But," he said, "if I see anything strange come into this room.... If I so much as feel a breeze on my check...." His arm darted out and he wrapped his huge mitt around my throat, giving it a squeeze. "I'll snap your neck. You got me? Nod if you understand."

I couldn't have moved my head if I had wanted to, but Stonehammer took his hand away and smiled, satisfied. I glanced around the room, but my brain was having trouble processing any details. I didn't see any windows, but, other than that, I couldn't have provided a useful description of the room I was in. Light was shining from somewhere, but I couldn't tell where. I wondered how much time had passed since Stonehammer cold-cocked me outside Medusa's. What day had that been? Tuesday? No, Wednesday. Was it still Wednesday night or Thursday morning? I had no idea.

"The box," said Stonehammer, interrupting my scattered thoughts.

"The box," I repeated.

"That's right," said Stonehammer. "We're going to talk about the box. You picked it up and ran off with it, remember? Our guys didn't find it in your building, so I need to know where you tucked it away."

The box? Oh, right. Mila's box. Poor Mila. Who had killed her—Stonehammer? The van driver, what was his name.... Quapo! Yeah, that's right. Kraken thought it was Quapo. Poor Kraken.

"Hey! Southerland!" Stonehammer snapped his fingers in my face. What was Stonehammer doing here? Where was I, anyway? "Southerland!" Stonehammer shouted. He slapped me in the face. A light slap. Just enough to get my attention.

"Sorry," I said. "Did you ask me something?"

Stonehammer leaned in until his broad, ugly face was inches from mine. His one good eye shone with a menacing red glow. His pointed teeth were yellow and his breath smelled like he'd been eating roadkill. I recoiled and said, concentrating on each word, "Lord's balls, man—you ever heard of mouthwash?"

Stonehammer slapped me again, a little harder this time. I hardly felt it. The drugs, I realized. I started to say something about that, but decided that it would be a good idea not to. I didn't want to encourage him to try harder.

"Where did you put the box?" he asked, enunciating every word.

"Box," I said, allowing my chin to slump. "Box. Sorry. Can't remember."

I thought that Stonehammer would slap me again, but he didn't. Instead, he sat back and thought for a bit, as if debating something in his mind. Finally, he got up and crossed over to another part of the room. When he came back, he was holding something long and sharp. An icepick, I realized.

Stonehammer resumed sitting. He held up the icepick. "Here's the way I figure it," he explained to me. "You cut my fuckin' eye. That's gonna cost you. They say that it'll never recover, and that I'll have to either wear a fuckin' patch over it or get myself a glass eye to replace it. I think that the patch would look kind of cool. What do you think?"

I tore my gaze from the ice pick. "Hmm," I said, giving it some thought. "I don't know. It kind of suits you. I think that the chicks would dig it."

"They might," he agreed. "You need a little swagger to pull it off, and I've got plenty of motherfuckin' swagger." He nodded, thinking about it. "But I think I'm going to go for the glass eye. It's more dignified, and I'm a fuckin' dignified motherfucker. Right?"

"Absolutely," I agreed, still slurring over the 's's. "You could pop it out and clean it when you're torturing helpless suspects. It'll freak 'em out." I smiled.

Stonehammer nodded. "True, true," he said. "It's settled, then. The glass eye it is." He leaned forward and held the tip of the ice pick up to my left eye. "So which will *you* choose? The patch or the glass?"

I held myself as steady as I could. I tried to conjure up the sigil for Badass, but my brain was too scrambled by the concussion or the drugs. Probably both. The image of the sigil was on the fringe of my memory, but I couldn't quite bring it into focus.

Instead, I focused on the ice pick. It was hard not to. It was inches from my eye.

Stonehammer held the pick steady. "Personally," he said, "I think you should choose the patch. A homemade brown one, cut out of your cheap fake leather shoe. You should tie it around your head with your shoelace. It would go with your downscale lifestyle." I wanted to tell him that he was wrong about my shoes, that they were made of genuine leather, and that they weren't cheap. I opened my mouth, but my throat was too tight, and the words wouldn't come out. He leaned closer to me, until his mouth was right up to my ear. "Now," he said in a near whisper. "I'm going to ask you again. Where. Is. The. Box."

I forced myself to look away from the ice pick. I put a dreamy smile on my face and slumped down into my seat. "Ohhh," I said, drawing it out. "The *box*! You mean the one I took from the pier? The one that Graham smuggled in? *That* box. Yeah." I paused and raised my eyes upwards and to the left, as if remembering. "Oh yeah. I put it in the trunk of my car. But my car got towed away. I couldn't pay the lot rental fee. So that bastard dwarf called a tow truck. Fuckin'...fuck...." I let my voice trail off, closed my eyes, and let my chin fall, making sure to avoid the ice pick.

Stonehammer sat still, thinking about what I'd told him. When I was in the army, some shadowy characters in an even more shadowy agency had taught me some shit to do if I ever found myself being tortured. It wasn't a pleasant experience, but I learned a few useful things. One of the things they taught me was to try to give up plausible, but false information rather than the truth if I was in a position where name, rank, and serial number wasn't going to cut it. After Lubank had snatched me out of the police station, I knew that Graham would keep after me. My greatest fear was getting trapped in a lonely spot where I could be questioned without anyone else's knowledge. And here I was. But I'd had time to develop some misdirections, and one of them had been this story about the box and my car. If Stonehammer bought it, I might gain some time while Graham tracked my car and checked the trunk. Once they found that I'd been lying, of course, I'd be in even bigger trouble, but I'd hoped that something would be gained by buying time.

Without a word, Stonehammer stood up and stomped out of the room. I guessed that he would now call Graham. I kept my eyes closed and tried to think about my options. It was hard, though. My brain still felt like it was stuffed with cotton. I couldn't concentrate. Sleep called to me. An ocean surrounded me. I was a drop of water, merging with the ocean. My senses expanded. I could see everything. I knew everything. Illusions of myself as an independent lifeform fled from me. I was one with the universe, at peace with the cosmos. There was no place, no time....

A sharp slap to my face forced me back to the moment. I was still sitting in the metal chair, feet and hands bound. I did not feel enlightened. I felt numb.

"We're going to check on your car," Stonehammer said. "If we don't find anything, I'll take out both of your eyes." He held the icepick up to my face again. "Maybe I should take out one of them now, just for the fun of it."

I thought of the endless ocean and put my dreamy smile back on. "Go ahead, Detective," I said, exaggerating the slur in my voice. "You've pumped me full of so much dope that I won't feel a thing. If you're going to do it, now's a good time."

Stonehammer considered this. Then he pulled the icepick back and said, "Later then." With no warning, he plunged the pick into the side of my neck and yanked it out again. Blood spurted down my shirt. Initially, I didn't feel a thing. I expected the pain to come in a second or two, but I was too hopped up for that. The drug took my mind to funny places. I was distracted by the realization that I wasn't wearing my jacket, and I wondered what had happened to it. That made me remember Lubank's raincoat. I still needed to get it clean. Good thing I wasn't bleeding on it. I smiled when I thought how mad Lubank would get if I got blood on his precious raincoat. Then the pain came, but it was a distant pain. It was happening to someone else, not me. It was funny. They could inflict physical pain or they could dope me up to keep me from focusing my summoning skills. They couldn't do both. Advantage Southerland. My last thought before I lost consciousness was that I hoped I wouldn't bleed out.

**

I didn't bleed out. Stonehammer was too skilled for that. He knew exactly what he was doing. The pick missed my jugular vein and every other vital spot on its way through my neck. I regained consciousness to find Stonehammer applying a clean bandage to my wound. When he saw that I was awake, he said, "*There* you are. Sorry about sticking you like that. What am I going to do about that temper of mine, eh?" He chuckled.

Stonehammer, still dressed in his sunny blue and yellow pinstripe suit, was in a jolly mood for some reason. I soon found out why. After he finished with my bandage, he reached down to the floor beside him and picked up a half-gallon sized wooden mug. A potent alcoholic aroma drifted up from the mug to my nose, causing it to burn. My eyes began to water and my throat closed, cutting off my air for a full three seconds. Stonehammer put the mug to his lips and took a slow sip. He swallowed and let out a long, satisfied breath, which made me gag all over again.

All in all, I preferred being stabbed in the neck to this new form of torture.

I soon found that I had another reason to be uncomfortable. "Detective," I began, "I hate to cause you any trouble, but if there's a restroom in this place I could really use it."

"Eh? Yeah, I guess it's been a while for you, hasn't it," Stonehammer said. I wondered how long a while it had been. Based on the pressure I was feeling in my bowels, I guessed that I had been out all night.

Stonehammer thought it over for a moment. "Hmmm, well, all right," he said. "I'll uncuff you and take you to the toilet, but no funny business! Give me any trouble and I'll, I'll…"

"Snap my neck?" I offered.

"Yeah!" Stonehammer swayed a bit as he stood. He pulled a key ring out of the right front pocket of his slacks. He pushed aside several large gold keys until he came to a smaller silver one. He used this key to unlock the cuffs on my ankles, and then the same key to unlock the cuffs on my wrists. He returned the key ring to his pocket. I kept my eyes on that key as long as it was in sight. Then Stonehammer grabbed the back of my shirt and tried to yank me to my feet. My body refused to cooperate, and I sagged in the troll's grip. He didn't mind. He dragged me across the room to an adjoining bathroom and dropped me to the floor in front of a jumbo-sized toilet bowl. "Think you can manage from here?" Stonehammer asked with a smirk.

"Any chance for some privacy?" I asked.

"Nope." Stonehammer leaned back against the bathroom wall across from the toilet and took a long drink from his mug. His glowing eye seemed to glaze over, and he slid down the wall until he was seated on the floor. He wasn't going anywhere.

I unfastened my pants and managed to get to my feet. I pulled my pants down to my knees and plopped down on the toilet seat. I struggled to balance myself on the oversized seat to keep from falling in. Stonehammer sneered at me with amusement. As humiliating experiences go, this one was pretty bad.

As I was completing my business, I noticed a faint dull ache in my swollen jaw and a dim pain in my neck. Whatever jungle-juice Stonehammer had injected me with was starting to wear off. My mind was still too dazed to conjure up a sigil, but I knew that I just needed a little more time. I couldn't let Stonehammer know that, of course. He didn't know about my body's newly acquired healing abilities, and I suspected that I was coming around quicker than he thought I would. I wondered how long ago I'd been drugged. Daylight was coming into the room from somewhere. I looked up above a seven-foot long bathtub and saw a partially open window that was letting in sun. Green plants were growing on the other side of the window, and I realized that it opened at ground level. That meant that I was in a basement. Judging from the fact that this bathroom was obviously troll-sized, I guessed that Stonehammer had taken me to his own home. Looking up made me dizzy after a few moments, and I had to tear my eyes away, but I was becoming a little more aware of my surroundings.

"Hey!" I said, trying to make my voice sound even more dull and listless than it was. "What day is it?"

"Unhh, let me see." The sluggishness in Stonehammer's voice sounded genuine. "Yesterday was Wednesday, so today must be Thursday. Yeah, Thursday." He looked up at the window. "Looks like it's morning." He turned and looked at me with disapproval. "Thanks to you, I've been up all night! Asshole!" He took another drink from his mug, and muttered, "Sure be glad when the captain gets back to me about your motherfuckin' car." He glared across at me and said, "Hey! You done yet? I ain't finished having fun with you! I wanna fuck you up some more!" He pushed himself back into the wall and slid back to his feet.

I stood, pulled up my pants, and fastened them. If I was going to be knocked around again, I at least wanted to be properly dressed. "Aren't you going to let me wash my hands?" I asked.

Stonehammer crossed over and grabbed me once again by the back of my shirt. "Come on!" he said, and dragged me back into the main room. He plopped me back onto my chair and reattached the cuffs to my wrists and ankles, returning his key ring back to his pants pocket when he was done.

"Now where were we," said Stonehammer. "Oh yeah!" With that, he backhanded me across the cheek that wasn't yet swollen. My head snapped around, but I barely felt the blow. I slowly turned to face the troll and met his eye.

"Shit!" said Stonehammer. "It ain't no fun if it don't hurt!" He drained the last of his drink and wiped his mouth with the back of his hand. "Hang on," he said. "I need a refill."

Stonehammer walked behind me, and I could hear him opening a refrigerator. When he reappeared, he was holding a full mug. Big mug, too. I wondered how much more he could drink without passing out. Probably a lot.

Stonehammer took a big sip and frowned. He was thinking of how he could hurt me in my doped up state. An idea popped into his head, and he smiled. "You might not be feeling any pain now, but you'll fuckin' hurt plenty when the dope wears off! He got to his feet and punched me in the stomach hard enough to send the chair sliding back a few feet. I was too trussed up to double over, but I leaned my head down and vomited bile all over my lap. Blackness crept into my head.

Stonehammer wasn't done. He clawed at the side of my face, and blood trickled down my shirt. Then he slapped me hard across the face, and even in my drugged state I knew that he had broken my nose. Another blow shut one of my eyes, and I decided to close the other one, too. I wasn't quite unconscious, but I was headed that way fast. For what seemed like an eternity, Stonehammer punished my body with blow after damaging blow. But I was alive, and I knew that I was likely to stay that way until Stonehammer heard from Graham. The troll was controlling his punches. Even drunk, the detective was too much of a professional to let me die without his boss's say-so.

I began to go under, but Stonehammer wouldn't allow it. After a brief respite, I felt my head being yanked up by the hair. Water splashed into my face. I sputtered and opened my undamaged eye. I watched as Stonehammer pulled back his right fist and measured me for an uppercut. I braced myself. But then Stonehammer relaxed. "Nah," he said, smiling. He reached down and mussed my hair. "I'm tired of beating you up when you're too hopped up to fight back. It's not fuckin' fair! And it's no fun!" He scratched his chin, and then bent down and picked his mug up off the floor where he had left it. "You know, you're not a bad guy. You're all right. You're my pal. I like the way you fuckin' take a punch. In fact, I could fuckin' punch you all day long. Hey," he said, his face brightening. "I know! I'm going to give you a drink!" He looked one way, and then the other. He turned in a full circle, staggering a bit. "Now where did I put that drink.... Ah, here it is—it's in my fuckin' hand!"

The mug was, indeed, in Stonehammer's left hand. "Can you fuckin' believe that?" he said. "I must be all fucked up!" This thought seemed to please him. He looked from his mug to me and scowled. "You look fuckin' awful! You need a drink. Don't you think you need a drink? I think you do." He held the mug under my nose and laughed. "This stuff'll fuckin' kill you," he informed me.

I didn't doubt it. The fumes rising from the mug were enough to make me go blind.

Stonehammer pushed the mug to my lips. "Come on, pal. Have a drink!"

I pulled my head back and tried to turn away. Stonehammer grabbed the back of my head and forced it back around. He jammed the mug past my lips into my teeth. "I said have a drink!" he shouted. "What, you don't want to drink with me, you fuckin' asshole!" He tipped the mug until the contents splashed on my face. I tried to turn away, but the troll held my head firmly in place. A stream of the burning liquor trickled into my mouth and down my throat. It was like drinking molten steel. I let out a cough, but then I couldn't inhale. I was going to suffocate.

Stonehammer pulled the mug away and laughed. "Smooth, isn't it! Pure home-brewed troll moonshine, straight from the ranch!" He brought the mug to his own lips and gulped down three big swallows. Then he let out his breath in a long sigh of pleasure. It was only then that I was able to inhale again. I coughed uncontrollably for what must have been a full minute.

"Come on, pal, have another," said Stonehammer.

"Please, no," I whispered to myself. Stonehammer grabbed my head and forced another mouthful of liquefied fire down my throat. I gasped for breath, but, truth be told, this second mouthful went down more easily than the first. It sure wasn't Gracie's avalonian whiskey, but I no longer thought that it would kill me, at least not right away. And I noticed something else: my head had cleared a little. Maybe it was the fiery drink, or maybe it was adrenaline. Either way, I was more awake now than I had been since I first opened my eyes that morning. But that didn't mean that I ever wanted to touch another drop of that dragon venom!

"Getting used to it, aren't you?" Stonehammer smiled at me. "Can't beat home brew." Stonehammer stepped back to his seat and plopped his ass down. He took a slow sip. "My family brews this shit, you know. It's from a secret recipe passed down in my family for fuckin' generations. My sister sends me a batch every summer. My little sister." The troll's face softened. He felt like talking. I wanted to let him. I needed a break. "I didn't always live in the city, you know," he said. "You humans may think of trolls as city folk, but that's not true of all of us. My family has a cattle ranch up north, and that's where I was raised. Spent the first hundred twenty-seven years of my life up there. Then a little over twenty years ago I got the itch to come to the city. I kicked around the streets a little and became a cop eighteen years ago. It's a fuckin' good life, and I'll never go back to the ranch. But, motherfuck, I miss the home brew!" He held up his mug, smiled, and took a long pull.

He went silent. I needed him to talk. "You have a sister?" I said.

Stonehammer frowned at me, "What's it to you?" he asked through clenched teeth.

"I'm just trying to get around the idea of a big goon like you having a sister," I said.

"Watch your mouth, asshole! My sister is none of your fuckin' business." The troll lifted his mug to his lips and took a small sip. "She's proud of me, you know." His mouth widened into a dreamy smile. "She thinks that I'm a good honest cop. Can you believe it?" He looked off into the distance and held up his mug, toasting his sister. Then he shook his head and took a long drink. When he spoke again, his words were slurred almost to the point of incoherence. "I'm her hero. I write her letters every month. I tell her how I examine crime scenes and look for clues. I tell her how I put the clues together and solve cases that no one else can solve. She thinks I'm a genius!" His smile vanished, and his one good eye grew moist. "She doesn't know what kind of cop I really am. 'Graham's Goon!' That's what they all call me at the department. Not to my face, of course. But I still hear them. Assholes! But my sister don't know that. And she ain't never gonna know, either!" He raised his mug and slammed down a quick gulp.

Stonehammer's alcohol-soaked mood was swinging all over the place, and it had just swung toward angry. I didn't want that. "Tell me about Mila," I said, forcing my words through my swollen lips.

"Hmm, what? Who?"

"Mila. The adaro girl who was murdered. The murder that Graham wants to pin on me."

"Oh, yeah," Stonehammer nodded and his expression softened. "Cute little frail." He smiled a sleepy smile. "The little nymph stabbed me in the neck!" He shook his head. "Spirited little bitch, I'll give her that."

"Who shot her?" I asked.

"Huh? Heh! I can't tell you that." He gave me a sly smile. "Nice try, though."

"Did you do it?"

"What? Me? Of course not!" he scoffed. "No, no, no. Not me."

"I didn't think so," I said.

"No? Why not?"

"Mila was shot with a low-caliber bullet," I said. "You don't use a gat that fires a little slug like that, do you?"

Stonehammer made a jeering noise. He reached up and wiped away the spittle that had dribbled out the side of his mouth. "Shit no," he said. "I couldn't even fit my finger on the trigger! Only thing I carry is a motherfuckin' shotgun! That's a weapon for a Hell-born troll!"

"But you know who did it, don't you," I stated.

Stonehammer got sly again. He made an effort to refocus. "Who, me? How would I know? I'm just an ol' country troll. I don't know nothin' 'bout nothin'!"

The ol' country troll lifted his mug, but it was empty. His eye blinked in confusion. I was certain that he was on the verge of telling me everything he knew about Mila's murder. He just needed a nudge.

"You know plenty, Detective. We both know that you aren't dumb. You're a smart guy. You're smarter than Graham, that's for sure! He's a sap. That adaro twist of his has him wrapped around her little finger."

Stonehammer scowled. "Graham! He thinks I'm a fuck-up. Thanks to you, asshole!" His eye again grew moist, and a tear leaked down his cheek. "Why didn't you do what I told you to?" he said, anger again bubbling to the surface. "Why didn't you back off when Leena told you to find her sister? Then you cut up my fuckin' eye!" He wiped away his tear. "And then you sent that fuckin' tornado after me! Th'fuck! Fuckin' thing kicked my ass! Graham was fuckin' hot! He told me one more fuck up and he'd demote me to parking attendant. Fuckin' asshole!"

Stonehammer frowned and grew thoughtful. "Fuckin' Graham," he muttered. "He used to be an all right guy. Real smart. He had his fingers in all kinds of pies. He helped me make some money, let me tell you! Yeah, he put a lot of jack in my pocket. Him and me, man. No one could stop us. But it all changed when he hooked up with that fuckin' nymph!" Stonehammer spat on the floor. "She's got him so pussy-whipped that he can't think straight. She ripped out his balls and turned him into fuckin' weakling! It's disgusting! I *hate* what he's become. Fuckin' spineless wimp. Makes me sick!"

"Fuckin' right!" I agreed. "Why should you always do what he tells you to do?" I said. "Come on, Detective! It's just you and me. Two pals. Let me in on it. I think you know who plugged Mila. Why don't you tell me? Show me that you're smart!"

Stonehammer swayed in his seat. "Ha! If I told you, then I'd have to kill you." He laughed. "Come to think of it, that's not a bad idea. I'll tell you, and then I'll kill you!" He started to push himself out of his chair.

Just then, I heard a buzz, like an alarm.

"Uh-oh," said Stonehammer. His eye widened and his mouth tightened into a circle, as if he'd been caught with his hand in a candy jar. "Someone's at the door. Might be the captain." He staggered to his feet, catching himself on the back of his chair. He took a breath and tried to regroup. He took another breath, and, taking great care, made his way across the room. "You stay here," he said. Like I was going to be going anywhere.

I watched him reach a staircase that I hadn't known was there. I realized that a fog was lifting from my brain. The drug was wearing off. Or maybe the troll brew had shocked me out of the worst of my daze. In any case, I felt like I was close to being able to focus on a summoning spell. If I could relax for just a few more minutes....

But I wasn't going to get the chance. From upstairs, I heard a door open and then Graham's voice.

"You're drunk!" Graham said.

"Nah," Stonehammer replied. "Just a little buzzed."

"It's nine o'clock in the morning!" Graham said.

"I've been up all night," whined Stonehammer.

"Never mind," said Graham. "Where is he?"

They came down the stairs and stood in front of me.

"You're a mess," Graham said.

"Find my car?" I asked.

Graham nodded. "Oh, we found your car all right. But you know what we didn't find in it? The box!"

"What?" I said.

"What?" Stonehammer echoed.

"Seems that our boy lied to you," Graham said to Stonehammer.

Stonehammer growled. "I'll kill him!" He lurched towards me.

Graham grabbed his arm and stopped him. "Hang on," he said. "It's okay." Then he turned to me and smiled. "We got the box."

Chapter Fifteen

My heart sank, and I could feel the drug starting to pull me back into the fog once again. How had Graham managed to get his hands on the box?

As if reading my thoughts, Graham said, "I thought that you might be lying about the box being in the trunk of your car, so I sent a couple of men to your building to see if anyone might be bringing the box to you. Your lawyer, perhaps. By the way, I've got men watching him, too." He smirked at me, letting me know how smart he was. "First thing this morning, an overnight courier service delivered an envelope to your office. One of my men received it from the courier. He opened it up and found a key with a number on it. My man recognized it as a key to a locker at the central bus station. He called me, and I sent him to the bus station, where he opened the locker. And wouldn't you know it, he found my box in the locker. He's on his way to the station with it now, but I made a little side trip here to let you know the good news in person."

"That's very kind of you," I said. "But are you sure it's the right box?"

"Very sure," Graham said. "I had my man describe it to me over the phone. Black metal, cold, heavy, two keyholes, faint humming sound. Not many boxes like that around."

I tried not to let my disappointment show on my face.

"Oh, by the way," Graham said. "Thanks for not trying to open it. I've got the only key. And if you try to open it without the key, if, say, you try to pry it open or pick the locks, then a glass vial in the box will break open and spill acid all over everything in it, rendering the contents worthless. If that had happened, I would have been very upset."

"I'll bet," I said. "Hey, what's in that box, anyway?"

Graham smiled. "You'll never know." He turned to Stonehammer. "I'm going to the station," he told the detective. "When I'm gone, finish him and hide the body. We'll pin the adaro girl's murder on him and close the file on that case. When you're done, come to the station and report to me. Oh, and you might try sobering up first. Got it?"

"Yeah, Captain," said Stonehammer. "I got it."

"Good!" said Graham. "Don't fuck it up. Shoot him up with a triple dose of that zombie juice you injected him with. That should do it. And then bury him somewhere where no one goes."

"Don't worry, Captain," Stonehammer muttered. "I'll handle it."

Graham gave me one last hard look and headed up the stairs. After he heard the front door close, Stonehammer turned to me and said, "Any last requests?"

"Yeah," I said, keeping my voice casual. "How about having a drink with me? Let me raise one last taste of your family's home brew."

Stonehammer was taken aback. "Really?" he said.

"Sure," I said. "If this is it, I want to go out with a bang."

"Fuckin' A!" said Stonehammer, looking pleased. "One more shot of the family recipe before you go." Stonehammer went to the kitchen area behind me. I heard the refrigerator door open and close, and when he returned, he was holding two mugs, one in each hand.

"Here we go," he said. He looked from one hand to the other. "Umm. How should we do this?"

"Why don't you unlock my hands?" I said. He frowned at me, and I smiled. "Oh, come on. What am I gonna do? My legs are locked down." Stonehammer still looked dubious. "It's my last drink, buddy. Let me take it with some dignity."

Stonehammer hesitated for another beat, but then relaxed. "What the hell," he said. "It's the least I can do." He set the mugs down on the floor and dug out his key ring. Crouching behind me, he released my wrists and returned the keys to his pocket. He came back around and picked up the mugs. He handed one of them to me and I took it with my right hand.

As soon as the mug was in my hand, I flung the contents straight into Stonehammer's face. The liquor burned his good eye. With a roar loud enough to shatter a plate glass window, the troll dropped his mug, reared up, and covered his eye with both hands. I thrust my left hand into his right pants pocket and pulled out his keys. I ducked down and searched for the silver key. Finding it, I reached down to uncuff my ankles.

I wasn't quite quick enough. Stonehammer lashed out blindly and batted me to one side. I tumbled to the floor and slid across the room with the chair still cuffed to my ankles. But I managed to hang on to the keys, and before the blinded troll could find me, I had freed both of my feet.

I tried to stand, but my legs were as limp as noodles. Stonehammer, still unable to see, bellowed and kicked out with his feet hoping to land a lucky blow. He connected hard with the chair, but I rolled away and, with my second try, managed to get to my feet. I wasted no time. I made for the stairs and stumbled up to the main floor. I fell twice on the way but was out the door before Stonehammer knew I was missing. I could hear him roaring all the way down the street.

***

I spent the next half hour putting as much distance between myself and Stonehammer's house as I could. Then I collapsed on the sidewalk. I had been lucky, but I wasn't out of the woods yet, and Graham had the box. I considered letting him keep it and calling it a draw. But I knew that I couldn't do that. He had pissed me off, and I couldn't let it go. Besides, the slimy son of a bitch was still trying to pin Mila's murder on me! There was no way that I could let that stand. Not to mention, that he'd still want to kill me if he knew that I was alive. I still didn't know what was in the box, but if Graham wanted it, then he wasn't going to have it. Not after everything he'd put me through. It was as simple as that.

I needed a plan to take the box from Graham, but for now all I could do was catch my breath. The run had pushed the last of the drug out of my system, and the fog in my head had cleared away. The bad news was that my body was now wracked with pain. One eye was swollen nearly shut, I had a hole in my neck, my nose was broken, both of my jaws were swollen, several bones in my body were severely bruised, if not fractured, and everything hurt. I felt like I'd been run over by a bus. Twice. Graham was right: I was a mess. Even with my healing powers, I probably belonged in an intensive care ward. I didn't have the time for that, though. I didn't know what Graham was planning on doing with whatever was in that box, but I needed to stop him before it happened.

The first thing I wanted to do was to get cleaned up before I was arrested for scaring small children. That meant getting home, showering, tending to some wounds, and putting on clothes that weren't stained with dried blood and vomit. I searched my pockets and was relieved to discover that I still had my wallet, keys, and phone. With my phone and a credit card, I could do anything. I checked the street signs and discovered that I was in a residential area on the east side of the peninsula, not far from the bay. Pretty fancy district. Stonehammer wasn't lying when he said that he was doing well. I called for a cab and waited.

A half hour later, I climbed out of the cab in front of my building. I scanned the street, but saw no signs of the cops. Graham had assumed that I would be taken care of, and I wondered whether Stonehammer had informed him otherwise. I doubted that the detective was anxious to admit to yet another fuck-up. As far as Graham knew, there was no reason to station men at my building anymore. At least, that's what I was hoping. I needed to get in and out before Stonehammer dug up the nerve to tell him I was still alive and kicking.

The cops hadn't cleaned up my office for me. Shit. And I thought they were supposed to be public servants. If anything, it was worse. Empty beer cans and cigarette butts had been added to the debris on the floor. Slobs! I noticed that the door of my safe was hanging open. All of the best safecrackers worked for the YCPD. Fortunately, I didn't keep anything valuable in my safe. It was more for show. Clients like it when their private investigator has a safe.

I went upstairs and, of course, the police had tossed everything up there, too. My couch was turned on its side, my oven door was open, and my clothes were spread all over my bedroom floor. I ignored the mess and cleaned myself up as quickly as I could. Getting out of my clothes was an exercise in pain management, but the hot shower was pure ecstasy. Looking at myself in the mirror proved to be too depressing, so I hung a towel over it and tried to distract myself by thinking about food. I was famished! I didn't want to spend any more time in my apartment than I needed to, but after I was dressed I decided to take a few extra minutes to heat up a frozen beef pie in the microwave. When it was good and hot, I devoured it in three bites. I followed it up with a beer and a shot. The shot seemed pretty tame after my experience with Stonehammer's hooch, but at least I could breathe after downing it. I'd been home for less than a half hour, but I felt much better. It wasn't a week on a tropical island, but it would do.

I was ready to go somewhere, but I wasn't sure where to go. I called a cab anyway and made sure that I had everything I would need. A cold wind was already blowing, so I put on my trench coat. I also reached into the top of my closet and dug out a brown fedora that my landlady, Mrs. Colby, had given to me. It had belonged to her grandson, Clint, and she said that she wanted me to have it. I accepted it and was grateful, but I almost never wore it. I was supposed to be dead, though, and I wanted to be as inconspicuous as possible. So I put it on and pulled the brim down over my forehead in the hope that it would hide some of the bruising on my face. The last thing I did before I walked out the door was to get my shoulder holster out of my closet and my thirty-eight out of my desk. I was glad that the police hadn't taken it, but I guess they really didn't have a reason to. After taking a few moments to make sure that the gun was loaded and ready to fire, I strapped on the holster and armed myself. Under the circumstances, I felt much more comfortable with a piece under my coat.

By the time the cab arrived, I'd decided what I was going to do. My first step was to have the cabbie drive me to my bank. I had him wait for me while I deposited Leena's check and withdrew some ready cash. It's amazing how much better you feel when you've got some dough in your pocket. Then I had the cabbie drive me to Medusa's Tavern so that I could pick up Atwater's car. I found the car in the parking lot where I left it. The rest of the lot was empty. I checked to make sure that the car was intact, and I found a piece of paper tucked under the windshield wiper. A handwritten note on the paper said, "Seriously? Ten-Inch." Funny guy. I got into the monstrosity of an automobile, started it up, and drove to a nearby cheap motel.

I had a few reasons for wanting to hole up in Placid Point. My gut told me that the area was in the center of something, and that I should be there. I felt a need to be close to the old abandoned pier, where I'd met the elf and witnessed the gang fight, and where I could give the fishes a message for Kraken. I also wanted to be close to Medusa's so that I could stay in contact with Ten-Inch and the Northsiders. I was more or less working with them now, trying to find Quapo. And there was another reason for being in Placid Point, too. The man I wanted to visit had a used jewelry shop just a few blocks from the motel.

I checked into the motel and found my room, which was about what I'd expected it to be. The carpet only had one hole of any significance, and the room looked like it had been recently vacuumed, so I counted that as a plus. The heavy cloth curtains over the front window were stained by decades of cigarette smoke, but they were designed to keep occupants safe from prying eyes. The radiator was functional and less noisy than a passing freight train. I didn't know if the television worked, but I wasn't planning on turning it on anyway. I soon discovered that the toilet worked, and the water running out of the spout over the bathroom sink was suitable for cleaning hands, if not necessarily for drinking. The walls under the faded floral wallpaper were probably thin, but, as far as I could tell, neither of the adjoining rooms were occupied. At least not yet. The whole room smelled of mold and mildew, but that's one of the reasons it didn't cost an arm and a leg, so I had no reason to complain.

I sat on an ancient thinly padded chair that would have cost less than a fin in a strip mall thrift shop. It was pushed up to a small reading table. I switched on a small shaded lamp that sat on the table, leaned back in the chair, and called up Smokey's sigil. I opened the door a crack, and he streaked through less than half a minute later.

"Hello, Smokey," I said to the tiny hovering whirlwind.

"Alex brings Smokey to strange places," whispered the elemental.

"Do you want to check out your surroundings?" I asked.

"Smokey would like that."

I let the elemental drift outside for a few minutes. When it returned, I closed the door and sat down in the chair.

"Do you remember the building called the police station?" I asked.

"Smokey does."

"Can you find it from here?"

"Smokey thinks so."

"Good," I said. Earlier, I had set up my notebook computer, which I had picked up at my apartment. I had it cued to the headshot of Graham on the YCPD website. "Do you think that you could recognize this man if you saw him?"

The elemental studied the photo for several seconds. "Smokey does not know. Smokey can try."

I guess that was the most I could ask for. "Okay," I said. "I want you to go into the police station. Keep out of sight, but look for this man." I pointed at the image of Graham. If you find him, return here and tell me. If, after searching the building, you *don't* find him, come back here and tell me. Understand?"

"Smokey understands."

"Great!" I said. I got up and cracked the door open. "Up, up, and away!"

Smokey stretched itself up until it was a full four inches tall and hovered in the air, spinning fast enough to blow dust off the lampshade on the table lamp in front of me. Then it bent itself away from the door before flinging itself toward and through the opening and into the skies. Hunh! Was Smokey developing some flair? The little swirl of air seemed to be enjoying its work!

I didn't know what to expect. My experience with elementals told me they had trouble distinguishing between humans of similar appearance. I was asking Smokey to identify one from a headshot on a computer screen, and that might prove to be too much for the little air spirit. But I wanted to know if Graham was at the station. If he was, then he probably still had the box with him. I hoped that was the case. It was only about noon, and I didn't think that he'd had enough time to do anything with it, but I couldn't be sure of that. I was gambling, but it seemed a safe bet.

A little more than seventy-five minutes passed. Without warning, Smokey streaked into the room from somewhere and whirled in front of my face. I had been fighting off the urge to sleep, but Smokey's sudden appearance had startled me into full wakefulness. Looking at Smokey, I sensed somehow that the little elemental was excited.

"Smokey found the man!" it whispered loud enough to be the equivalent of a shout from the tiny air spirit.

"How did you get in here?" I asked. "Never mind." This room wasn't exactly hermetically sealed, after all, and an elemental as small as Smokey could zoom through any opening big enough to let in air. "Are you sure he was the man I showed you?"

"Smokey is sure!" it said, sounding as confident as a whisper could sound.

"That's great news!" I said. "You did a terrific job!"

Smokey whirled in a way that seemed to radiate pride.

"Now, here's what I want you to do. Go back to the police station. Find the man again. His name is Graham."

"Graham," Smokey repeated.

"Stay out of sight, but watch Graham. If he leaves the building, follow him. Stay with him until I call you back to me. Understand?"

"Smokey understands."

I hesitated. "Does Smokey like to serve?"

Smokey hopped back and forth in the air in front of me. "Smokey is happy to serve Alex," it said.

"Nice to know," I said. "Okay, go!"

Smokey hopped around a bit more and then vanished, leaving whirls of dust in its wake.

***

After Smokey left, I got into Atwater's car and drove northwest toward the coast to the Nautilus Jewelry and Novelty Shop. I pulled into a two-story parking garage that was going to charge me way too much to park my car, but there was no point in bitching about it. The supply of parking spots in the city was low, and the demand was high. At least the lot took credit cards. After parking the car, I walked the block and a half to the shop. A dozen or so small open cases displayed diamond rings and jeweled necklaces behind the shop's large double-paned barred windows. A painting of a fierce-looking male adaro wearing a jeweled crown and holding a large spiral shell in his cupped hands covered the shop's glass double-door entrance. I walked through the doors into a well-lit showroom featuring two rows of jewelry displays under locked glass covers. Behind the counter at the far end of the showroom was a short, wiry forty-something man with thinning gray-streaked hair and thick glasses. He was seated on a tall stool and hunched over an e-tablet. No other customers were in the shop, and the man behind the counter glanced up at me when I entered.

"If you need any help, just ask," he said, and he returned his attention to the tablet.

I took off my hat and walked to the counter. When I reached it, I said, "Do you have any actual diamonds in here, Crawford, or is it all just shiny glass?"

The man's head shot up and he gave me a sharp look. Then his face relaxed, and he said "Alex? Lord's iron balls, man, you look like shit!"

"I get that a lot," I said.

"Seriously, man, what happened? Did you get run over by a streetcar?"

"Nah," I said. "Just a troll."

"That sounds worse than a streetcar," said Crawford. "Do you know that your nose is crooked?"

"Is that bad?" I asked.

"Lord's iron balls! And your eye is a mess! Have you been to the hospital?"

"No time," I said. "I need a favor."

Crawford hesitated, and his eyes narrowed. "What have you got yourself into?"

"Oh, you know. A smuggling operation, a murder, a corrupt police captain. The usual."

"Sounds intense," said Crawford. "Soooo.... What do you want with me?"

"Not much," I said. "I just need you to infiltrate police headquarters and help me steal something."

"Uh-huh. Right." Crawford stared at me. I stared back. After a few moments, he said, "You serious?"

"Yup," I said.

Just then, a young couple, identically dressed in dirty sweatshirts and torn jeans, walked through the front door and into the showroom. Crawford said, "Hold that thought," and strolled out from behind the counter to greet them. Once off his stool, Crawford revealed himself to be less than five-feet tall and somewhat stooped. I couldn't keep myself from wondering if he had a hairless tail tucked under his pants, but it would have been rude to ask. Someday, though, I'd have to know.

Turned out that the couple was just browsing. I wondered if they were casing the joint, but I'm naturally suspicious. In any case, the couple left after a few minutes. When they were gone, Crawford flipped a switch near the door, and an electric "open" sign switched to "closed." Crawford began to pull his displays out from the front windows.

I waited for him to finish and return to the counter. When he was seated on his stool, he turned to me and said, "Tell me more."

I nodded. "A police captain named Graham had something smuggled in a couple of nights ago. It's packed in a heavy black metal box about this big." I held my hands apart to indicate the size of the box. "The box is unusual. Whatever's inside needs to be kept cold, and the box has some kind of battery-powered freezer unit in it. It's also locked. It has two keyholes in the front. I'm told that anyone trying to open it without the key will break open a glass container of acid that will destroy the contents of the box."

"How heavy is the box?" Crawford asked.

"Pretty heavy," I said. "Between five and ten pounds, I'd say."

Crawford nodded, and I continued. "I believe that the box is currently somewhere in Graham's office at the police station downtown. I'm not sure what he intends to do with the box, but he might be moving it soon. I want to get that box before he does."

Crawford let out a whistle. "You don't want much, do you!"

"Interested?" I asked.

"Maybe," he said. "What's in it for me?"

"My thanks?" I said.

"Hmmph!"

"Maybe dinner and a beer?"

"Hmmph!"

"Can we leave that open for now?" I said. "I'll owe you."

"Yeah you will," said Crawford. "What if this box is in a locked safe or something? I won't be able to get to it."

I shrugged. "We'll improvise. If nothing else, I'd like to know exactly where Graham is keeping the box. Once I know that, then we can go from there."

Crawford frowned at me. Then his features relaxed into a smile. "Ah shit, Alex," he said. "You knew when you walked in that I wouldn't be able to resist. Breaking into police headquarters? Stealing a mysterious box out from under the nose of a corrupt cop? Walking out with it through an entire department of our city's finest? When do we start?"

"Whenever you want," I said. "I'll drive you downtown whenever you're ready, and we'll get you started."

"Let me finish locking up," said Crawford. "It's been a slow day. Next Tuesday is the first of the month, and business should pick up then. This shouldn't take me long."

Fifteen minutes later, Crawford grabbed a long gray coat and a gray homburg and announced that he was ready. "Let me just grab a snack for the road," he said. "You like cheese balls?"

"You're such a cliché," I told him. He gave me a shrewd grin.

Chapter Sixteen

Crawford laughed out loud when he saw the car. Once he caught his breath, he declared, "I love it!"

"It's not mine," I said.

"Of course not," he said. "What'd you do, steal it?"

"No, I didn't steal it," I said. "It was loaned to me."

"By who?" said Crawford. "A pimp?"

"Something like that," I admitted.

Crawford just shook his head. He reached into his shirt pocket and pulled out a pair of sunglasses. "Let's go, boss!" he said. "And be sure to take the long way! I want to be *seen* in this boat!"

When we were out in traffic, Crawford wanted to roll down the window and lean his elbow on the sill. He complained that no one could see him through the darkened glass. I wouldn't let him. "I'm trying to be inconspicuous," I said.

"That ship has sailed, my friend," he told me.

"As long as no one can see us, I'm okay." Crawford smiled and shook his head, but said nothing.

On the way downtown, we discussed some of the logistics of our operation. "Do you think you'll have any problems getting into the station?" I asked.

Crawford made his humphing noise. "There isn't a building that rats can't enter," he said. "Trust me, the building is already filled with them. Did you know that if you are anywhere in a city, there's a rat no more than fifty yards from you? And if you're downtown, there's one no more than thirty feet from you, on average? In an old building like the police station? They're crawling through every pipe, vent, and crumbling wall. Getting in won't be a problem. Getting out with a heavy metal box, though? That might be a problem."

I thought about that. "Even locating the box will be hard," I said. "I'm sure that it will be locked up somewhere in Graham's office."

"Do you know where the office is?" Crawford asked.

"No, but I might get some help with that," I said.

"Well, once I'm in the office, I can take a look around. Maybe the box is out in the open."

"Maybe," I said. "Let's hope."

We rode in silence for a while, and then I said, "So, tell me how it works. Are all of the rats…you?"

Crawford nodded. "They're all me when they separate. Then they all go off and have their own experiences. When two or more of them merge, so do their memories. When we all come together, then I have all the memories."

"But you can't communicate with each rat when they're scattered?"

"No," said Crawford. "We have to come back together."

I thought about this. "How many of them have to come together before you're you again?"

"Most of them," Crawford said. "I can divide into a hundred seventeen rats." He hesitated, then said, "I used to be able to divide into a hundred forty, but I've lost some over the years."

"Ouch!" I said.

"Yeah. I'd just as soon not talk about that. It's a hard world we live in, my friend." He sighed theatrically. "Anyway, when a hundred of them merge, I'll be able to talk to you. I'll just be a little smaller than I am now." He smiled.

"A hundred," I said. "Nice round number."

"Apparently not a coincidence," Crawford said. "I've talked with other were-rats, and communicated with a lot of them online. We've got quite a network, you know. The condition isn't hereditary, so it isn't easy to find someone to teach a young were-rat about what he is. The internet has made a *huge* difference in our lives. Anyway, it's the same with all of us. One hundred is the magic number."

"What happens if you're down to ninety-nine?" I asked.

"Then you wind up with either one large rat or up to ninety-nine small ones, all with short life spans."

I whistled. "Well," I said, "try to keep yourself together for a few more years, okay?"

"Ah, listen to you, you old softy," he said. "Don't worry—I'm pretty cagey!"

"Aren't you all?" I said.

He snorted, "Stereotyping? Hey, not all were-rats are as well-adjusted as me. A lot of them are crazy! It's something we all have to fight with, especially when we're young. But some of us never learn to deal with it." He turned to look at me. "I'm serious. If you ever see a were-rat, and it isn't me, don't antagonize him. Or her. Just back away slowly. You know what they call a group of rats? A mischief of rats! I shit you not!"

I looked at him to see if he was serious. "A mischief? That's it? I think I can handle a little mischief."

"Let's see what you say when a hundred criminally insane rats are digging their teeth into your flesh," said Crawford, an evil smile on his face.

I shuddered in spite of myself. "Point taken," I said.

"Speaking of which," Crawford said. "Did this Graham character have something to do with that face of yours? If you want him to suffer a little...." He left the rest unsaid.

"Tempting," I said, "but no. I don't want you to get into that kind of trouble. Trespassing and maybe some burglary will be enough. Besides, he's got a troll protecting him."

"Ugh," Crawford's face screwed up. "I hate troll. Okay, no feasting on human flesh tonight."

I turned toward him. "Uh," I began. "Do you often feast on human flesh?"

"Often? No." He smiled, and then laughed when he saw the expression on my face. "Not for a long, long time," he said.

"I don't want to know," I said, and I felt my skin grow cold. Actually, I was dying to know, but this was not the time.

***

I parked in a city lot a block away from the police station. "How do you want to do this?" I asked Crawford.

"I'll walk to the back side of the station and then send in a rat," he said. "You said something earlier about getting help finding the right office?"

"Yeah, hang on a sec," I said. I unrolled my window a crack, focused, and soon Smokey was whirling on top of the dashboard.

Crawford drew back with a start. "Whoa!" he exclaimed. "An elemental? I thought that you had to write down some kind of symbol or something to summon one."

"Long story," I said. I did the introductions: "Crawford, this is Smokey. Smokey? Crawford. Say hello."

"Hello Crawford," Smokey hissed.

"Hello Smokey," said Crawford. "Pleased to meet you."

I turned to Smokey. "Is Graham still in there?"

"Graham is there," Smokey whispered.

"Has he been there this whole time?" I asked.

"Graham never leave building," Smokey replied. "Graham move around inside building sometimes."

I paused. "Did Graham ever carry anything with him when he left his office?"

Smokey thought about this question. Finally, the elemental said, "Yes."

I thought about how to phrase my next question. "Did he ever carry a box about this size?" I mimed the proper dimensions.

Smokey didn't hesitate. "No."

Hmm. Most likely, then, the box was locked somewhere in his office. Graham wouldn't have left his office with the box sitting out in the open. Oh well, one thing at a time.

"Okay," I said. "Let's all go back behind the station. Stay with me, Smokey."

We left the car and made our way to the back of the police station. I kept my hat brim low, because I didn't want anyone to recognize me. The afternoon was getting late, and, as usual, the wind was getting more and more brisk. It seemed that about half of the men I saw around me were wearing trench coats or something similar, and pulling the brims of their hats low to keep them from flying off their heads. I was just another pedestrian with somewhere that he needed to be.

Pedestrian traffic was light on the backside of the police building. Crawford scanned the base of the building as we walked. Juniper bushes had been planted near the walls of the building in a vain attempt to introduce a bit of nature to the concrete jungle.

Crawford came to a sudden stop. "There," he said, pointing with his chin.

I couldn't see anything unusual about this part of the building, but I nodded. "Okay, here's what we'll do. Send off two rats. One can relay messages back and forth if necessary." Crawford nodded. "Smokey? I need you to help the rats find Graham. Can you do that?"

Smokey whirled in front of me, almost invisible in the wind. "Rats?" Smokey asked.

I turned to Crawford. "Smokey needs to see the rats."

Crawford bent and reached his hand to the ground, palm up. Two small rats, one gray and one white, leaped out of his hand. It looked like a trick by a street magician. The rats turned to me and stood on their hind legs. They each waved at me with their right foreleg.

"Cute," I said. "Smokey, can you guide these two rats to Graham?"

"Rats," Smokey said. "Smokey can take them to Graham."

"Good!" I said. "Okay, then—off you go!"

The rats leaped into the juniper bushes, and Smokey followed.

***

Crawford and I spent the next forty-five minutes fighting off the wind and talking about the second-hand jewelry business. Or rather, Crawford talked, and I tried to listen. As a rule, I try to learn as much as I can whenever someone talks about his or her business, because I never know when some trivial piece of information will be helpful to me in a future case. Once, during the course of a conversation with an insurance adjustor, I learned that a certain type of double door featuring lots of glass separated by wooden lattice-work and capped by a large arch-shaped window had first been introduced in upscale residential homes built about thirty years ago, and that the design had not existed in houses before that time. This obscure fact helped me to discover that a person I was investigating had lied about where he had lived as a child, a key factor in helping me to break the case. After listening to Crawford go on and on about how slight differences in mountings and settings can make big differences in the resale value of rings and brooches, however, I was finding it hard to keep from falling asleep on my feet. After the events of the last couple of days, I could have used about sixteen uninterrupted hours of shuteye. I found myself nodding along and making appropriate noises during pauses without taking in much information.

After one long pause, I looked up to find Crawford staring at me with an odd expression on his face. "Sorry, what was that?" I said, trying to look interested.

"Your nose," said Crawford.

"What about it?"

"I think it's straightening."

I reached up to touch my nose. Sure enough, it was no longer crooked. The pain had receded by several degrees, too.

"We'll have to talk about that some time," I said. "When we can sit and relax over a few drinks."

Crawford nodded. "Let's," he said. He changed the subject. "I wonder what's going on in there. Is this what you do all day? Stand around waiting for something to happen? I used to think that private investigators had exciting lives, but if it means collecting bruises and standing around in the cold, then you can have it!" He rubbed his hands together in front of his face and blew on them to try to warm them up. "Hey," he said. "Have you ever thought about getting yourself a money clip?"

For the next ten minutes, Crawford treated me to a lecture on the pros and cons of clips vs. wallets as the means of storing paper money. I gave up trying to learn anything useful after thirty seconds.

Finally, in the middle of a sentence I hadn't been following, Crawford bent down toward a juniper bush. A rat leaped into his hand and seemed to sink right into it. Crawford stood up and stared into nothing for a few seconds. Then his eyes refocused, and he glanced up at me. "Your elemental guided the rats through the heating vents to Graham's office. They had a good view of him from there. They didn't see anything that looked like your box, though."

"Has Graham been in his office the whole time?" I asked.

"Yes, and the rats have been watching him. Nothing interesting happened until just a few minutes ago when he got a call. It was on his cell phone, not his office phone. As soon as he found out who the call was from, he got up and closed his door. The rats could only hear his side of the call, but it was obvious that he was talking about the box. Someone is coming to his office at five thirty—a half hour from now—to talk to him about it in person. Graham said that he has the box in his office safe."

I thought about this. "Did Graham say whether he was going to show the box to his visitor?" I asked.

"He didn't say anything about that," Crawford said. "It'd be great if he did, though, wouldn't it?"

I nodded. "Yeah. It would help a lot if he took it out of his safe so that his visitor could examine it. It would be even better if he gave the box to his visitor." I thought some more. "You know, one of those possibilities is likely. Why else would the other party be coming here in person?"

"Yeah," Crawford agreed. "I think you're onto something."

I looked at Crawford, sizing him up. "If that box makes an appearance, what would be your chances of doing a grab and run?"

Crawford screwed up his face in thought. "The grab would be easy. The run? Not so easy, especially if the door was closed. Sorry." He shrugged.

"Could you get the box into the heating vent?" I asked.

"Hmm." Crawford considered this. "If I had enough time, I might. If it's no bigger than what you said it is, it should fit, but just barely. A hundred rats might be capable of pushing a ten-pound box up a wall and into a vent, once I pushed the grill off. But with a couple of men trying to stop them? Hard to see that working," he said.

"I might have a way of making it happen," I said.

After I explained my plan to Crawford, he laughed. "That's pretty incredible! You think that lame-brained stunt would actually work?" He shook his head. "Sounds like a real stretch to me."

"Well, what's the worst that could happen?" I asked.

"It wouldn't work, and I'd lose more rats than I could survive," said Crawford. "Couldn't you, I don't know, storm into Graham's office and knock them out or something? Then you could just grab the box and walk out of there. That's how they do it in the movies."

"Sure," I said. "I'll bluff my way into the station, stroll on over to Graham's office, grab the box, and shoot my way past a department full of cops with a gat that never runs out of ammo."

"Sounds as good as *your* plan," said Crawford.

"Maybe. But I forgot to tell you. It's possible that Graham thinks I'm dead. If that's the case, I'd like to keep it that way for a while."

"Oh, great!" Crawford said. "And your plan won't give that away?"

I hesitated. "It might. But he won't know for sure."

We gnawed away at the plan for a few minutes more, but finally agreed that it was the best idea we were likely to get.

"If nothing else," said Crawford, "we'll be making some *mischief* that Graham will never forget!"

I tried, but I couldn't keep myself from groaning.

***

Crawford sent two rats back to Graham's office to find out if there was any new information that we needed to know. Five minutes later, one of the rats returned, and Crawford told me that Graham hadn't moved from his desk or received any other calls on his cell phone. Crawford sent the rat back in.

I summoned Smokey and thanked the elemental for doing a good job. I started to release it, but then thought of something else that it could do. I gave it new instructions, and Smokey told me that it would be happy to serve. I sent it back into the building.

Several minutes later, a rat returned, and Crawford told me that Graham's visitor had arrived. I cleared my mind and called up the sigil I had designed for summoning Badass. I focused, and seconds later the elemental appeared on the sidewalk in front of me, bobbing slowly up and down like a giant bubble.

"Holy shit!" Crawford exclaimed. "This might work after all!"

"Hello Badass," I said.

"Greetings, Alex." The elemental's moaning howl seemed to emanate from the evening winds.

I told Badass what I wanted it to do, and Badass indicated that it understood. I sensed that it was both eager and amused.

"Okay," I said to Crawford. "You know what to do."

Crawford shrugged and laughed. "Here goes nothing!" he said. All at once, Crawford's clothes deflated and dropped to the sidewalk. His homburg and eyeglasses plopped down on top of the pile of laundry. One hundred fourteen rats swarmed out of the clothing and disappeared under the junipers. Badass leaned toward the path that the rats had taken and a slim tendril of whirling air extended from the bubble and followed after them. As the tendril stretched, the bubble grew smaller, until, several minutes later, the entire bubble had squeezed its way through the junipers and disappeared into the building. All I could do now was wait to see whether my harebrained scheme had worked. Knowing that the chances were slim, I shook my head and prepared for bad news.

Chapter Seventeen

"You should have seen it!" Crawford's face was red, and he couldn't keep himself from laughing out loud. "Where's that waitress?" he shouted. "The next round's on me. This," he paused, building up the drama, "was the most fun I've had in years!"

It had been an hour since we cruised back into Placid Point, and we were celebrating in a booth at a popular sports bar called the Boatyard Bar and Grill. We were devouring spicy chicken wings and washing them down with a good locally brewed lager. By now, I was familiar with most of the details of our caper, but Crawford couldn't stop repeating his story.

"So we're all lined up in the heating vent, one hundred seventeen rats strong," he told me for at least the fourth time. "The little elemental is spinning around near the front. The big elemental was spread out in the heating vents all over the building. The guy's in there with Graham, and he wants to see the box. So Graham goes to his safe, opens it, and pulls it out. Matches your description perfectly!"

"You've told me all this," I interrupted.

"I know, I know!" Crawford said. "But in bits and pieces, and all out of order. I want to start from the beginning and get everything right. So anyway," he continued, "We went into action. We jammed ourselves into the grill—and it wouldn't move! By now we're making so much noise that Graham and the other guy come over to the wall and look up to see what's going on. We pushed harder and harder! And then, the grill snaps off and falls right on Graham's face! A bunch of us went right down with it, and the rest of us came swarming out. We fell all over Graham and the other guy! Lord's iron balls, you should have seen the looks on their faces! They were flailing away at us with both arms and running all around the room! It was hilarious!"

"And you didn't get hurt?" I asked.

"Oh I got a little beat up," Crawford said. "A couple of the rats broke some bones, but none of them died. Now that I'm all together, I've got some bruising here and there, but nothing serious. I don't look as bad as you do, that's for sure!" He poked at my jaw.

"Hey!" I said, pulling my head away.

"Hunh!" he said. "Doesn't look as bad as it did earlier. Must be the light. Anyway, the box was on Graham's desk. A bunch of us swarmed to it and pushed it to the floor. That got Graham's attention real fast, let me tell you!" He paused again for maximum dramatic effect. "And that's when the big elemental came blowing out of the vent! You call it Badass? Good name! Those poor bastards didn't know what they were in for! Anyway, a bunch of us pushed the box up on our backs. Only a few of us could fit underneath it, and, Lord's iron balls—it was heavy! But we're stronger than we look, and we managed. The hard part was getting it into the vent. Most of us had to pile ourselves into a ramp, and the rest of us had to push the box. Fortunately, when we are all pressed together like that, we basically have one brain. It's pretty much me at that point, even if I'm a pile of rats. So it was a coordinated effort. That helped a lot. But, still, it took some time."

"And that's where Badass came in?" I asked, already having heard this part of the story.

Crawford's smile lit up his face. "You should have seen it!" he shouted again.

I held my finger to my lips to shush him. The Boatyard was not a quiet place by any stretch of the imagination. The bar was filled with rowdy sports fans watching a variety of sporting events on the television screens that lined the walls and hung over the bar. Still, I didn't want word of tonight's events to become public knowledge.

Crawford lowered his voice a decibel or two. "You should have seen it! The big elemental blew itself up until it filled half the room. It picked papers and files off Graham's desk and whirled them around. What a mess it made! Then it blew Graham's cigar box off the desk and started shooting cigars at the two guys! And that was just for starters! Those guys got pelted with staplers, pens, scissors—pretty much everything that was on Graham's desk! I think that Graham wet his pants! The other guy actually pulled out a gun!" Crawford snorted. "What did he think he was going to do, shoot the elemental?" Crawford stuffed a chicken wing into his mouth.

While he was chewing, I said, "And your rats weren't hurt by all this?"

"Let me tell you," Crawford said around his partially chewed chicken wing. Sauce dripped down the sides of his mouth. "That big bag of wind has control! Graham and his buddy were getting whipped by gale-force winds and desk supplies, and the air in our half of the room was as calm as a summer day. We finally got the box into the vent. Probably took less than a minute, actually, but it felt like an hour. Good thing it fit! It was pretty tight, but we were able to push it along okay. The other elemental, the little one, showed us where to go. I don't know if you're a genius or if we were just lucky, but your harebrained scheme worked like clockwork!"

Just before Crawford had turned himself into a swarm of rats and entered the police station, I had sent Smokey back into the vents with instructions to find a way from the central heating vent in Graham's office to an exhaust outlet that I had spotted high up on the back wall of the building. After the rest of my crew had entered the building, I found a trash can nearby and pushed it through the juniper bushes until it was up against the wall under the grill that covered the outlet. Then I climbed up on top of the trash can and used my mailbox key to undo the two bottom screws holding the grill in place. It wasn't easy, and I'll probably have to replace the key, but it worked.

Several long minutes passed before I heard a metallic scraping noise coming from the partially opened grill. Smokey popped out first and lit on my shoulder, spinning like a maniac and bouncing up and down with excitement. Then the box banged against the grill. I climbed on top of the trash can again and bent the grill out as far as I could. The box pushed out a little further, and I was able to pull it out the rest of the way. I leaped to the ground and watched a seemingly endless swarm of gray and white balls of fur spill out of the grill and tumble into the juniper bushes below. The rats streaked to Crawford's pile of clothing, which I had dragged to the sidewalk below the exhaust outlet, and, as I watched, the clothes inflated like a man-shaped balloon. Soon, Crawford was grinning at me and giving me an enthusiastic thumbs up. Then Badass blew through the outlet like a shot from a cannon. The grill tore loose from the wall and tumbled into the middle of the street. It bounced off a passing car, which screeched to a stop.

"Run!" I shouted, feeling like a child who had just thrown a ball through my neighbor's window. As Crawford and I ran for my car, I thanked the two elementals for their service and released them for the evening.

***

It was after ten when I drove Crawford to the back of his shop. A staircase behind the shop led up to his apartment on the second floor.

"Are you sure that the box is secure?" I asked him. We had stopped by and stashed the box in a vault at the back of Crawford's shop before going to the Boatyard.

"Don't worry about it," he said. "I keep my most precious stones in that vault. Nothing short of a nuclear bomb can open it without the combination, and I'm the only one who knows the combination."

"All right," I said, satisfied. "I'll be back in the morning to pick it up."

"Sure you don't want to come up for a nightcap?" Crawford asked. "You can even spend the night on the couch if you want."

"Thanks, it's tempting," I said. "But I'll just go back to the motel." I really needed a good night's sleep, and a bed sounded better to me at that moment than a couch.

"Suit yourself," said Crawford. "Goodnight. See you in the morning. And, hey, thanks for making my day! I've never burgled a police station before. The expression on their faces!" He laughed as he got out of the car. I watched him climb the stairs and unlock his apartment door. He gave me a wave and went inside.

As I drove away, I realized that, long as this day had been, I was too keyed up to go back to the motel. Loose pieces of information swirled in my head, bouncing off each other and looking for a place to stick. Tired as I was, I knew that I wouldn't be able to sleep until a few of these thoughts came together and formed something solid. The night sky was clear, and a nearly full moon hung in front of my windshield like a beacon. On a whim, I drove toward it. I felt like driving, and the moon was as good a destination as any. It led me to the northwest, and after a few minutes I found myself driving southwestward on Fremont past a rocky beach between the old and new Placid Point Piers. Traffic was light. I drove slowly and let my mind wander.

I came to a stop sign. Spray painted on the sign was the "CC" insignia of the Claymore Cartel. Something jogged in my head, but I couldn't quite grasp it. I continued driving in the direction of the new pier and reached another stop sign. It was also tagged with the "CC" gang sign. Unlike the graffiti I'd seen at the old pier, neither of the Cartel tags on the stop signs had been overridden by "NS" insignia. I was on undisputed Claymore Cartel turf.

An idea struck me like a slap in the face. It wasn't so much an idea as a collection of loose jigsaw pieces coming together and forming a recognizable section of the puzzle. I pulled the car off the road and got out. I walked away from the road past some trees until the ocean came into view. I stood against a tree and watched the waves roll in under the stars. As my head cleared, I examined my new puzzle section from different angles, looking for holes. It seemed solid. Solid enough to run with.

A cold wind blew in from the ocean, and within a minute I could feel my face going numb. I rubbed my jaw on both sides of my face. I still ached, but the swelling was nearly gone. Both of my eyes were open, too, although the area around the injured one was still tender to the touch. My nose had straightened, and I could breathe through it without any trouble. My other injuries were well on their way to healing. I felt bruised, but not battered.

I listened to the crashing and roar of the waves. I was where I needed to be. My next step was to find some Claymore Cartel homeboys. I took a deep breath and filled my lungs with the salty mist. As I did, I detected a foreign scent, something that didn't belong. It didn't take me long to figure out what it was. Beneath the pleasant smell of salt water, the sharp tang of washed up seaweed, and the putrid fishy odor of rotting sea creatures was the faint but pungent stink of gasoline. I sniffed the air like a bloodhound, trying to place the scent. It seemed strongest down the coast toward the new pier. Maybe someone was having a cookout on the beach? Straining to listen, I heard the sound of voices. One of the voices was louder than the others. It was a shrill voice, and not a happy one. I jogged down toward the beach.

After a few minutes of jogging through the sand I reached the top of a sand dune, and, thanks to my night vision, I saw figures on the otherwise deserted beach about five hundred yards away. The smell of gasoline was stronger now, blowing my way in the stiff ocean breeze. With nothing but the moon to illuminate the night, I was certain that none of the figures would be able to see me until I was right on top of them. I ran down the dune in their direction, slowing only when I drew close.

Four figures were on the beach. Claymore Cartel bandanas covered the heads of three of them. Two of them were holding nine-millimeter gats. One was holding an open gas can.

The fourth figure was the unhappy one. I couldn't blame him. He was standing in the middle of a neck-high pile of tires, arms pinned to his sides and unable to move. As I approached, the gangster with the gas can poured gasoline all over the tires and over the head of the man trapped inside them. An enormous shock of tightly curled hair spilled out of the victim's head and covered most of his boyish brown face. The last time I'd seen the young man with that face, he had been driving a van out of the parking lot of the old Placid Point Pier.

"Say goodbye, Quapo," shouted the gangster holding the gas can. He pulled a lighter out of his pocket.

"No, don't do it!" screamed Quapo. "Please!"

I pulled my thirty-eight from my shoulder holster and fired it into the air. The explosion from the pistol echoed through the air like a thunderclap, and all four of the figures yanked their heads in my direction. I crouched and moved to my left, circling them, counting on the darkness to keep the gangsters from getting a clear view of me.

"Drop your guns!" I shouted, still moving. "And get rid of that lighter!"

No one dropped anything, so I shot at the sand near one of the gunman's feet. He yelped, jumped back, and let go of his gun, probably by accident. I fired near the feet of the other gunman. "Next one goes into your head!" I yelled.

They all strained to see me for a second, and then the second gunman tossed his gun to the sand. "Now the lighter," I said, getting closer to the group. The gangster with the gas can sighed, and tossed the lighter away.

"Get him out of those tires," I said in a calm voice. None of them moved. "It's all right," I said. "Captain Graham's been looking for this guy. He wants him alive."

The three Claymore gangsters looked at each other. The one with the gas can said, "You work for Graham?"

"That's right," I said. "Sorry about the shots. I had to get your attention before you polluted the beach with this lowlife."

"He's been creeping around where he doesn't belong," said gas can guy. "He says that the Northsiders want to kill him. We were going to save them the trouble."

"Maybe Graham will give him back to you when he's finished with him," I said. "But for now, I need to take him to Graham alive. So let's get him out of there."

The three gangsters all looked at each other, consulting without words. Finally, gas can guy said, "Whatever," and the three of them pulled the tires off Quapo. The two gunmen held him to keep him from running, and gas can guy punched him in the stomach, knocking the wind out of him.

"Okay," gas can guy said. "He's all yours."

I grabbed a handful of Quapo's gasoline-soaked locks and yanked him to his feet. I put the business end of my thirty-eight on the base of his spine. "Come on," I said, making my voice gruff. "Give me any trouble and I'll make you a quadriplegic." I released Quapo's hair and grabbed him by the arm. Smiling at the Claymores, I said, "Thanks, guys. Have fun!" I walked off with Quapo before the gangsters had a chance to think about what was happening. They watched us disappear into the night.

When I was over the dune, I released Quapo and put my piece in its holster. "You all right?" I said.

Quapo looked at me, openmouthed.

"Relax," I said. "I just saved your life."

"Who are you?" Quapo said. "Did Graham send you?"

"Never mind who I am," I said. "I've got a car just ahead. We'll talk there." We walked the rest of the way to my car in silence.

When Quapo saw my car, he whipped his head around to take another look at me. "This your ride?" he asked.

"It's not mine!" He continued to stare at me. "Someone loaned it to me."

"A pimp?" Quapo asked.

"Just get in," I said.

We got in and I drove us away.

I headed in the general direction of downtown. We rode in silence. Despite the cold night air, I had to open the car window to let out the gasoline fumes coming off Quapo. I concentrated on the road while Quapo sat sullen, looking at nothing. When we had traveled a few blocks, I turned to him and said, "So how long do you think it took Ten-Inch to figure out that you were Stonehammer's snitch?"

Quapo muttered something that I didn't catch.

"What was that?" I asked.

Quapo looked at me and shouted, "Informant! I'm not a snitch, I'm an informant!"

"Anything you say, sport," I said.

Quapo went sullen again. "Wasn't nothing I could do," he said. "Stonehammer had me dead to rights, possession with intent to sell. He said that I had two choices. Thirty years in the pen, or I could earn some extra scratch informing on my homies." He turned to me. "Can you imagine what life in Q would be like for a good-looking kid like me?" He looked away again. "Wasn't much of a fuckin' choice."

"You're breaking my heart," I said.

"Yeah, like you give a flying fuck," he muttered. Speaking up, he said, "About two seconds. That's how long it would have taken a smart motherfucker like Ten-Inch to know that someone had been informing once he heard that Graham had brought a squad from the fuckin' Cartel to the pier. That's why I fuckin' hauled my ass out of there as soon as I saw them pull in."

That's the way I had figured it, too. It had been sitting there in the back of my mind, surfacing only when I saw the Claymore Cartel tags on the stop signs. Why had Graham arrived at the pier with a small army of gangbangers just to pick up a package? It could only have been because he was expecting to be ambushed by a larger force than his troll bodyguard could handle by himself. How could he have known? Who could have told him? Leena, maybe. She had known that the Northsiders would be there. In fact, according to her it had been her idea to bring them along. So why would she turn around and tell

Graham? No, either Leena was playing some complex game that I couldn't figure out, or one of the Northsiders was a snitch. And Quapo had bailed on his gang family, making him a likely candidate. So I cast out my line, and Quapo snatched the bait.

"Why did you assume that Ten-Inch would identify you as the sn... informer?" I asked.

"I didn't," said Quapo. "But I wasn't going to hang around until he found out. You don't know Ten-Inch. That coldblooded motherfucker is a psycho! Once he knew that one of his boys had informed on him, he'd start cutting off balls until someone confessed."

"Okay," I said. "So where have you been since Tuesday night?"

"Hidin' out. I've been trying to call Stonehammer, but the son of a whore won't return my calls! I figured that he'd hung me out to dry."

Quapo was probably right. Once he had abandoned his gang at the pier, it would be obvious that he was the one who had ratted them out. At that point, he was no longer useful to the police, so Stonehammer had ghosted him.

"What were you doing in Cartel territory?" I asked him.

Quapo sighed. "I thought I could go over Stonehammer's head to Graham. I knew that the Northsiders would be looking for me. I needed Graham to bring me in. Hell, he owed me! He and Stonehammer. It was their fault that I was in this shit! Anyway, if Graham was in charge of a unit from the Cartel, then he must have made some kind of deal with Jaguar. I thought that if I could talk to Jaguar, I could convince him to connect me with Graham."

Jaguar? Must be the local head of the Claymore Cartel. I filed that away.

We were stopped at a light. I gave Quapo a long look. "You thought that the Cartel would let you in? Because that's what gangs do with traitors, right?"

Quapo squirmed in his seat. "Okay, it was a fuckin' longshot. But I didn't know what else to do! And it seemed solid.

I mean, if I'm working for Stonehammer, and the Cartel has a deal with Graham, that meant we were all on the same side, right? That's how I was gonna explain it to Jaguar. But I never got the fuckin' chance. That Cartel crew didn't want to fuckin' listen to nothin'!" He looked up at me. "Good thing you came along. I guess that Stonehammer got the word to Graham after all."

I didn't say anything.

"I mean, you said that you work for Graham, right?"

I glanced over at him and smiled.

"Oh shit," he moaned. "Shit! Shit! Shit! Don't tell me that Ten-Inch sent you!" He pounded on the dash with both fists. "Fuck me!"

"Hey! Easy on the car!" I said. "Ten-Inch didn't send me. Not exactly, anyway. I'm a private detective. I'm investigating a murder." I turned to look at Quapo. "I'm trying to find out who killed Mila."

Quapo went rigid. "Mila's dead?" he asked. "Mother-*FUCK*!" His fists flew to his face and covered his eyes.

"Ten-Inch thinks that you killed her," I said.

"What? No way, man. No fuckin' way!" Tears ran down his cheeks, and he choked back a sob.

"Kraken thinks that you did it, too." I was pouring it on, but I wanted to know for sure.

"Shit!" Quapo choked. "I didn't kill Mila. I couldn't! I— I *loved* her! Shit! Kraken's going to kill me! I'm fuckin' dead!" He rubbed at his eyes with his sleeve. "Someone killed Mila? Ah fuck. Poor little bitch. Fuck."

He was either the world's best actor, or he was just now finding out that Mila was dead.

"Take it easy, kid," I said. "I'll keep Kraken off your back. Ten-Inch, too. But you're not entirely innocent, are you. It was you who lured Mila out into the open."

Quapo looked up at me and nodded. "Stonehammer told me to do it," he admitted through his tears. He called me early Wednesday morning. He said that Mila had something that

Graham wanted. He told me to call Mila and get her to let me pick her up. He said that nothing would happen to Mila if she cooperated. I had to do it!" He started sobbing again. "I had to do it!"

When his sobbing subsided, I said, "Tell me what happened."

He nodded. "Okay, okay. Stonehammer told me to call Mila, like I said. I called her. I told her that I knew she had the package from the pier. I said that Stonehammer and Graham were looking for her. She said that she didn't have the package, but she knew where it was. I said that I could pick her up and that we could go get it together. I told her that we didn't have to get the brothers involved, that it would just be her and me, and Kraken if she wanted him in on it. So she said something about the fuckin' package being hard to open, and I'm all like, 'Don't worry! We can handle that!' I told her that I knew some people. Man, I was just talking out of my ass, you know, but she fuckin' bought it." He stopped talking and bit back more tears. "So she told me where to pick her up, and I drove there to get her. Fuckin' Stonehammer and Graham were hiding in the back of the van. When Mila got in, Stonehammer grabbed her and dragged her into the back. Graham told me to drive to the adaro settlement. They all got out there on Fremont Street, and Graham told me to get lost. So I did." He put his head in his hands. "And that's the last I seen of any of them, I swear!"

"And you didn't think they'd kill Mila?" I asked him.

He didn't look up. In a quiet voice, he told me, "I didn't want to know about it. I just didn't want to fuckin' know about it."

In spite of myself, I felt sorry for the kid. And he *was* a kid. Couldn't have been more than fifteen. Between Mila, Stonehammer, and Graham, he'd never had a chance. He hadn't just been in over his head; he'd been born at the bottom of the deep end, and he'd never come close to the surface. But that didn't make him innocent. It just made him pathetic.

I drove him to the central bus station. I took some bills out of my wallet and held them out to him. "Take this," I said. "I don't care what you do with it, but if you're smart you'll buy a bus ticket and get out of the city. A lot of nasty people are looking for you, and if they find you, they'll kill you. And it won't be a quick death."

Quapo nodded and took the cash. He left the car and I drove away without waiting to see what he'd do next. He'd given up Mila to be tortured and killed. Yeah, he'd had to do it in order to save his own skin, and that's the only reason I hadn't bundled him up and left him on Ten-Inch's doorstep. But that was all he was going to get from me. As far as I was concerned, I'd given him a chance, but what he did with that chance was his own decision. Callous? Maybe. I've been called worse. All I knew was that I was done with Quapo. He was out of my hands.

Chapter Eighteen

I was awakened by a rhythmic knocking on the wall at the head of my bed. The knocking was accompanied by grunts and moans, punctuated by shouts of "Oh daddy! Oh daddy!" I didn't know where I was at first, but after a few moments I remembered that I was in a cheap motel room, and I realized that the noises that had disturbed my sleep were coming from the next room. I fumbled on the table next to my bed and found my phone, which told me that it was 3:23 a.m. That meant that I'd been asleep for about an hour and a half.

I was too exhausted to move, so I decided to wait it out. I doubted that I'd have to wait long. After a few seconds, the speed of the knocking increased and the "Oh daddy!" shouts became louder. There was a loud masculine moan, and the sounds stopped. I closed my eyes and stepped into oblivion.

"Oh daddy! Oh daddy!" My eyes popped back open. I checked my phone. It read 3:48. Shit. Were they going to be at it all night long? I really needed sleep. I got up and grabbed a pint bottle of whiskey that I had brought into the motel room to help me wind down after dropping Quapo off at the bus station. Only a few sips remained, and I finished them off. Then I tore the covers off the bed, grabbed my keys, and went outside. I unlocked Atwater's car and climbed into the back seat with the bed covers. The seat was only slightly smaller than the motel bed and probably more comfortable. In seconds, I was swimming through a black velvet void.

I woke up with the sun pouring into my eyes and a stream of drool sliding down my cheek. I sat up and wiped my face with the bedcovers. I was naked except for my boxers, so I kept the covers wrapped around my body as I left the car and re-entered the motel room. I checked my phone and discovered that it was

7:13 on Friday morning. I'd had about a third of the sleep I needed, but it would have to do.

I stood in front of a mirror and took stock of myself. My eyes were blackened, the right more than the left, and my jaws were purple. The wound on my neck had scabbed over. I had angry welts all over my ribs, chest, and shoulders. But I felt better than I looked. Any bones that had been broken had knitted and seemed well on their way to being whole. Other than feeling stiff all over, my biggest problem at the moment was an overwhelming desire for black coffee and strong booze.

I knew one thing for sure: I wasn't going to spend another night in this fleabag. After I was dressed and packed, I went to the motel office and paid off my bill. The clerk gave me a survey card so that I could rate my stay, but I tossed it in the trash can outside the office when I left. The couple in the room next to mine would undoubtedly give them a better review than I would.

I found a convenience store with gas pumps just up the block from the motel. After I filled the tank of Atwater's car, I went inside the store and bought a large cup of coffee and a pint of whiskey. Deciding that I needed something solid to go with my liquid breakfast, I also bought a couple of doughnuts. Perfect! I was ready for the day.

I had a lot to do. First, I needed to drive back to Crawford's place and pick up the box. Before starting the car, I called him to make sure that he was up. He was not only up, but he was excited.

"You know that man in Graham's office?" he said. "That was Lawrence Fulton!"

"Who's that?" I said.

"Lawrence Fulton!" Crawford repeated. "You know. Mayor Teague's lawyer and chief advisor!"

"No kidding?" I said. Now that Crawford had jogged my memory, I remembered Fulton as the shadowy figure who, according to the media, did the mayor's dirty work and shielded him from the fallout. It was rumored that Fulton had ties to underworld crime families, and that he was instrumental in covering up Mayor Teague's many alleged indiscretions before they could blow up into major scandals. Teague himself was charismatic and well-loved by his constituency, and a staff of lawyers and fixers worked twenty-four/seven to keep him one step removed from the dirt he tended to kick up. Fulton directed that staff.

"I read an article in a local online news outlet called The Voice of the Bay," said Crawford "Are you familiar with it?"

"Yeah," I said. "They're not what I would call a trustworthy news source."

"True," Crawford said. "They've got some clever writers, though. Anyway, the article says that Captain Graham was attacked in his office by some thug who had escaped from the holding cells. It says that the attack came late in the day while Graham was in a meeting with a representative of the mayor. Most of the details are bullshit, but here's the kicker—they posted a picture of the two of them and identified Graham's visitor as Fulton! You should see the bruises on their faces! That elemental of yours really worked them over. But the man they identified as Fulton is definitely the man that I saw with Graham in his office."

"That's interesting," I said, meaning it.

"Do you think that Graham was smuggling in something for the mayor?" Crawford asked.

"Kind of looks that way," I said.

"What have you gotten yourself into?"

"Whatever it is," I said, "I need to get that box out of your hands as soon as possible. Preferably before anyone finds out that I got you involved."

"No time like the present!" said Crawford.

"I'm on my way."

***

The box was in the vault where we'd left it. It was still cold to the touch, and I could still hear the hum of the battery. I didn't know how much juice the battery still had in it, but hopefully I wouldn't need it to continue working much longer.

Crawford walked me to my car. As I was about to get in, I thanked Crawford for his help and added, "Hopefully no one will know that you were ever involved in this. But Graham will have figured out by now that a were-rat stole his box. Don't be surprised if you get a visit from him or one of his cops."

Crawford smiled. "Not many people know about me, but I'm not worried about it. I haven't always been the respectable shopkeeper you see before you now. One of these days we'll get together and I'll tell you some stories from the carefree days of my misspent youth."

"Well, take care," I said. "Especially over the next few days. Call me if the cops give you any trouble."

"Will do!" He held up an upturned hand, and a rat appeared. The rat waved at me as I drove away. Cute, but creepy.

***

My next step was getting the box to Tom Kintay. His lab was located in an industrial section down the peninsula in South Yerba City. I called Kintay to let him know I'd be there in an hour. He said that he'd be waiting.

On the way to Kintay's lab, my phone rang. Keeping one hand on the wheel and both eyes on the road, I took my phone from my pocket and answered the call.

"Hello?"

"Alex Southerland?" asked a nondescript male voice.

"Who's this?" I asked.

"The last thing I said to you was 'Sorry about this,'" said the voice.

"I get that a lot," I said.

"I was cuffing you to a table at the time."

I remembered the cop with the sad dark eyes who had led me from the holding cell to the interrogation room.

"Okay," I said. "What's up?"

"I need to talk to you," said the voice. "Somewhere private. I've got information that you'll want to hear."

"Is Graham putting you up to this?" I asked.

"You're suspicious, and you have a right to be. But Graham doesn't know about this. Pick a time and place and I'll be there, alone. No funny stuff, I promise."

"What's your name?" I asked.

"I don't want to say anything on the phone," he said. "They say that cell phones are secure enough, but I don't want to take any chances. Especially where Graham is concerned."

I thought about it. "Okay," I said. "How about noon? We can talk over lunch. You know a place called Monty's Grill on Dillon Street?"

"Down on Grayshore Point?"

"That's the one."

"Yeah, that's perfect. I'll be there at noon." He disconnected the call.

Had I just agreed to walk into the jaws of a trap? Maybe. But no risk, no reward. A cop on the inside was offering me information, and I needed information. It was a chance that I had to take.

I'd be careful, though. Careful as a songbird at a cat convention.

***

I pulled into a spacious industrial park filled with factories and old two-story office buildings. I wound my way through the parking lot to a small detached one-story building in the back of the concrete park. The building had no windows and only one small door. Above the door was a sign displaying the digits "1240." There was nothing to indicate what the building might house, but I knew that this was Tom Kintay's lab, and that he would likely be the building's only occupant. I parked in front of the building and carried the box to the door. At the door, I pressed a buzzer and smiled at the hidden camera that I knew was located in the door frame. When I heard an answering buzz and the click of the lock mechanism being released, I opened the door and walked through. The door closed and locked behind me.

Kintay was sitting at a lab table cluttered with equipment. As I expected, no one else was in the room. The air in the room had a light chemical smell, like the waiting room in a dentist's office. I heard the gentle whirring of wall fans, but they didn't seem to have much effect. Kintay looked up when I entered and frowned. "What the hell happened to you?" he asked.

"It's nothing," I said. "Just got into a heated discussion with a troll."

"What'd you do, insult his mother?"

"Nothing like that," I said. I held up the box. "He wanted this, and I didn't want him to have it."

"And you're still alive?" said Kintay.

"You should see the troll," I said.

Ex-Corporal Tom Kintay was one of the palest men I'd ever seen. He had skin so colorless that it was almost white, light blond hair, and eyes the color of a robin's shell. He looked like he had never experienced direct sunlight in his life, and he probably hadn't seen much of it since he left the army. He didn't live in his lab, but the cot and sleeping bag in a far corner of the room surrounded by empty food boxes and plastic cola bottles indicated that he spent a fair amount of his life there.

Kintay stared at the box in my arms.

I jiggled it. "Wanna take a look?" I said.

Kintay's pale eyes were open wide, and he reached for the box like an addict reaching for a needle. "Gimme!" he said.

I gave him the box. He held it up close to his face. Then he turned his head and put his ear on the surface. He put the box down and rubbed his hands together. "So what's the story here?" he asked.

"It was smuggled in by a go-fast boat and picked up at the old Placid Point Pier by a corrupt cop last Tuesday at midnight," I said.

Kintay put the box on the table and looked up at me with disbelief. "You're fuckin' shitting me!" he scoffed.

"It *does* sound a little hard to believe," I admitted.

Kintay stared at me for a few seconds. Then he smiled, shook his head and whistled. He asked, "Let me guess—no key?"

"Yup," I said. "And I'm told that the lock is booby-trapped. One wrong move will cause the contents of the box to be doused with acid."

"This gets better all the time!" said Kintay. "Okay, let's get it open." He walked over to a drawer and began to dig through it. When he came away from the drawer, he was holding a thin metal case. He returned to his seat and opened the case, revealing a series of blank keys. He took one out, looked at it, and put it back. He took out another and closed the case. Clearing a spot on his table, Kintay laid the key on it and picked up a small scope. He examined the key through the scope and then used it to get a closer look at the two keyholes on the box. "This will take a few minutes," he said. "Do me a favor and get me a cola out of that refrigerator over there."

When I returned with his cola, I saw that Kintay had put on goggles with dark lenses. He had poured a trickle of liquid into each of the keyholes and was now shining a thin beam of red light from what appeared to be the world's smallest flashlight into one of the locks. He turned to a computer screen and entered some keystrokes. "Hmm," he muttered. "Clever." He entered some more keystrokes.

Looking up at me, Kintay said, "This is pretty cool. These locks are unusual. Any idea what's inside?"

I shrugged. "Your guess is as good as mine."

"Something dangerous, I hope?"

"If you're lucky."

"We'll know in a few minutes!" Kintay resumed working. I sat down a few feet out of his way and watched him work.

After studying his computer screen for a minute or two, Kintay opened a drawer and took out a metal cylinder with a slot on one end and a cable on the other. He plugged the cable into a

USB port in his computer and inserted the blank key into the slot. He pushed a button on the top of the cylinder, and I heard the sound of grinding metal. When the grinding stopped, Kintay slid the key out of the cylinder and mounted it on a brace. The key was no longer blank; it now looked ready to open a lock. Kintay took a small nail file out of a drawer and began smoothing out the ridges and slots. Occasionally, he turned his laser light on the key and consulted his computer screen. After about five minutes, he put down the file and the light, took off his goggles, and removed the key from its brace.

"The key is ready to go," said Kintay, "but I want to open the box in the clean room."

I hesitated. "Am I going to have to take a shower or something?"

"Fuck no," Kintay said. "This isn't the federal space agency. But we'll have to put on robes and slippers."

Kintay brought me to one side of the room and opened a closet. We took out paper robes, paper slippers, and puffy little paper hats. Kintay took out a couple of paper masks, too, and we put them on. Then we walked through a door into a sort of airlock and stood while a spotlight bathed us in purple light.

"Will I still be able to have children?" I asked.

"Only if you can find some woman desperate enough to have them for you. I wouldn't get my hopes up."

When we were fully prepped, we entered the clean room. It looked like any other room, but cleaner. Kintay put the box down on a table. He held the key up, smiled, and said, "Here goes nothing."

"Should I cross my fingers or something?" I asked.

"Nah," he said. "If I fucked this up, a couple of crossed fingers won't help."

"But you're pretty confident?" I asked.

He just smiled and plunged the key into the keyhole on the right side of the box. He gave the key a quarter turn and pulled it out. Then he slid the key into the other keyhole and gave it a half turn. He pulled the key out and put it back into the first keyhole. He gave it another quarter turn, pulled the key out, and flipped open the box. "Ta-da!" he said.

I came over to get a closer look. A cloud of cold mist emerged from the open box. Kintay waved away the mist and we both peered inside. In the middle of the box, surrounded by glass tubing and small metal blocks, were six soft plastic tubes, each filled with translucent off-white liquid and sealed with a plastic stopper.

"See this glass container over here in the lid?" Kintay pointed at it with the key. "That's the acid. You weren't mistaken when you said that the locks were connected to a booby trap. One wrong move, and everything in the box would be a sludge of goo. I'll take it out of there. I want to take a look at it later. Might be useful." He found something that looked like a jeweler's tool and, with great care, detached and removed the container.

"What do you think is inside those tubes?" I asked.

"No idea," said Kintay. "Could be a drug. I'll have to open one of the tubes and test the contents."

"How long will that take?" I asked.

"Hard to say," said Kintay. "I might know something later today, but I can't make any promises. I've got some other work that I have to do, but it's not as exciting as this. I'll do as much with this today as I can."

I nodded. "Well, be careful," I said. "Try not to start a pandemic, or blow up the city, or anything like that."

Kintay wiggled his eyebrows up and down. "Wouldn't that be fun!" he said.

"Right! Well, do me a favor and call me as soon as you know what this is," I said. "I'll owe you bigtime."

"No problem," Kintay said. "You know me. I'll probably be needing a favor from you one of these days."

"No doubt," I said.

I turned to leave, and then stopped. "Oh, one other thing," I said. "I'd appreciate it if you didn't tell your bosses about this. It's just you and me, okay?"

Kintay nodded. "Goes without saying," he said.

I gave him a long look.

"Trust me," he said.

Right. Kintay was a career criminal who developed designer drugs for a crime family. He wanted me to trust him. But it was a chance I was going to have to take. We said our goodbyes and I left him to his work.

Chapter Nineteen

I turned into the parking lot of Monty's Grill at about a quarter to noon. I scanned the lot, but didn't see any cops hiding behind cars and whispering into radios or waiting to ambush me as I walked into the restaurant. Nor did I see any police helicopters circling overhead. Now if I could just avoid stepping into any suspicious-looking puddles of water....

I decided to wait for my mysterious cop friend in the restaurant. I didn't want him to see me stepping out of Atwater's loaner vehicle. If I had to explain what I was doing with it to one more person, I'd have to shoot him. I went inside and got a table near the window. A perky brunette waitress in a mini-dress came to my table with a menu and asked me if I wanted water. I told her that I was waiting for a friend, and that I would love a cup of coffee, black please, while I waited. After a minute, the waitress returned with the coffee and another menu. I watched her hips sway as she walked away.

At twelve o'clock sharp, I saw a police car pull into the parking lot. The dark-eyed uniformed cop got out and scanned the lot, looking for me. He saw me through the window and came inside to join me. We regarded each other in silence for a moment. Before either of us could speak, the perky waitress appeared and asked the cop if he'd like water or coffee. The cop ordered coffee, and the waitress gave him a smile that would charm a tax auditor and twirled away.

"I think she likes you," I said.

The corners of his mouth raised about a quarter of an inch. "I'm afraid my husband would object," he said.

"Ah," I said.

"Mr. Southerland, my name is Marc Littlecrow," said the cop.

"Call me Alex," I said, and we shook hands over the table.

"I don't have much time, so I'm going to get right to the point. I work undercover for Internal Affairs. We're investigating Captain Graham, and I'm embedded in his unit."

"I see."

"Graham is as dirty as they come," said Littlecrow. "We've got enough now to get him kicked him off the force, but some of the shit he's involved in is big. We're close to getting enough on him to force him to flip on some bigger fish."

"Let me guess," I said. "Mayor Teague."

"Got it in one," said Littlecrow. "Sounds like you've been doing some digging yourself."

"A little," I said. "But that one was easy. I saw a story today that he'd been attacked in his office during a meeting with the mayor's fixer."

"Larry Fulton, yeah," said Littlecrow. "A real piece of scum." His eyes met mine and narrowed. "But I suspect that you know more about that attack then what you read in an article."

He hadn't asked me anything, so I didn't respond.

Just then, the perky waitress appeared beside our table and asked if we were ready to order. I ordered a roast beef sandwich and Littlecrow ordered a salad. "I'm a vegetarian," he told me. Whatever.

"So why did you want to meet me?" I asked when the waitress left.

"Graham went to the abandoned Placid Point Pier Tuesday night to pick up a package that he had arranged to be smuggled in," said Littlecrow. "We think that he was acting on behalf of Mayor Teague, and that he was going to hand the package over to Fulton when he was attacked yesterday afternoon. The package was stolen during the attack." His eyes bored into mine. "We think that you had something to do with the attack. Do you have the package?"

"What makes you think that I have anything to do with any of this?" I asked.

Littlecrow nodded. He'd anticipated my response. "Let me lay my cards on the table, and then we can stop dancing around," he said. "I know that Graham had you arrested early Wednesday morning, the morning after he picked up the package at the pier. An adaro girl named Mila Waterfowl was murdered earlier that morning. Graham wanted to pin the murder on you." He paused. "What I *think*," he said, "is that you and the adaro girl somehow intercepted the package and hid it somewhere." He looked at me for confirmation. I stayed silent.

After a few moments, Littlecrow continued. "I believe that Graham and Detective Stonehammer, whom you've had the pleasure of meeting, caught up to Mila and tried to force the location of the contraband from her. At some point, Mila was killed. Murdered. By Graham or Stonehammer, I assume, though I don't actually have any solid proof. It's possible, I suppose, that they could have released her, and then she could have been killed by someone else." Again, Littlecrow searched my face, trying to determine if I could shed any light on his suspicions. I let him wonder.

"In any case," Littlecrow continued, "Graham acquired the contraband yesterday morning." He paused. "An officer in his unit was stationed at your office, Mr. Southerland. A courier delivered an envelope to your office, and the officer took it. The envelope contained a key to a locker at the central bus depot. Graham sent the officer to the bus depot to open the locker. The officer did so and found a locked metal box, which he delivered to Graham." Littlecrow paused again. "Mr. Southerland, I was that officer."

"Why didn't you keep the key when the courier delivered it to you and give it to internal affairs?" I asked.

"When I got the key, I first called my superior at IA," Littlecrow said. "He told me to let the process play out. He wanted Graham to reacquire the contraband and complete his deal with the mayor's office. Our department is working directly with the Office of the District Attorney, and the DA is after the mayor. Anything we get on Graham is going to be kicked upstairs. Mayor Teague is the ultimate target, not Graham."

I nodded. It made sense. Graham was small fry. They wanted to land the whale. But that wasn't *my* agenda. And it wasn't my client's. Leena and I wanted Graham to pay for his part in Mila's murder. And I wanted Stonehammer swept up in the net. For me, it was personal.

"Okay," I said. "So what do you want from me?"

Littlecrow leaned in and lowered his voice. "We want you to return the contraband to Graham so that he can deliver it up the line to the mayor."

Like hell! Still, I thought it best to play along. Littlecrow had told me on the phone that he had information I wanted. I hadn't heard much yet that I didn't already know.

So I nodded and sighed. "Okay, I get it," I said. "And I can help you. But would you mind answering a few questions for me? Just to satisfy my curiosity?"

"Sure, go ahead and ask," said Littlecrow. "I'll answer if I can. I owe you that much."

"What's in the box?" I asked. "Drugs?"

Littlecrow sighed, "I was hoping that you could tell me. We honestly don't know. All we know is that the mayor wants it badly. It fits in with some kind of scheme of his. And there's really only one thing that he wants, and that's power."

"Money is power," I said.

"True," said Littlecrow, "and maybe that's all there is to it. Maybe whatever is in the box is something that he can sell for a lot of dough. But maybe it's something else. Something that brings power in and of itself."

"Like what?"

Littlecrow shrugged. "I couldn't begin to imagine," he said.

"Maybe some kind of disease strain? Like ebola?" I said. "He could hold the city hostage with something like that."

Littlecrow smiled. "Well, this isn't a spy movie, and Mayor Teague may be a lot of things, but I don't see him as some kind of comic book villain. If it's something like that, he's more likely to sell it to a government research lab than threaten the city with it."

"Well then, I'm stumped," I said. "All I know is that whatever's inside has to be kept frozen, or at least refrigerated. You touched the box, so you know what I mean."

"Yeah," said Littlecrow. "I'm guessing some kind of designer drug. Teague could make a fortune selling it off to one of the crime syndicates."

"Umm," I said. "Makes sense."

Our food arrived then. The waitress smiled at Littlecrow and said, "Enjoy your meal."

When she left, I said, "You should tell our waitress that she's not your type."

"Why spoil it?" Littlecrow said. "She seems nice, and I like the service. She's earning a generous tip."

"Sure she's not tempting you to the other team?" I asked.

"Hey," he said. "I'm a happily married man. Luke and I have an anniversary coming up. Our fifth."

"Congratulations," I said.

We spent the next few minutes filling our stomachs, me with good red meat, him with green leafy rabbit food. To each his own.

When I sensed that he was ready to answer more questions, I asked him, "So what do you have on Graham?"

Littlecrow swallowed. "Extortion, accepting bribes, influence peddling.... Basically the same shit we'd find if we investigated most of the administrative officers in the force."

"That can't be all of it," I said. "You wouldn't be targeting him if that's all you had."

"Yeah, there's more," he said. "We think we can get him for some serious abuse of power. Stonehammer's a monster, and he does what Graham tells him to do. We can implicate both of them in witness intimidation, assault, and even murder."

"You'd let him skate on murder in order to get Teague?" I asked.

"Not entirely," said Littlecrow. "But the DA would offer a reduced sentence. Hard time instead of the death penalty."

"Did you know that he was running a crew from the Claymore Cartel at the pier on Tuesday night?" I said.

Littlecrow nodded. "Yeah, that's something else we've got on him. How do you think that would play in the media? 'YCPD Captain Runs Street Gang!' We've got him for worse, but that's the one that would make the headlines."

"I know a guy who says that Graham is a pedophile," I said.

Littlecrow raised an eyebrow. "I don't know if he's a pedophile," he said, "but we both know that he keeps an adaro escort in a luxury condominium downtown."

I nodded.

Littlecrow scowled, "Leena Waterfowl. What a piece of work *she* is! She's got Graham on a leash so tight that it's choking him. To be honest with you, I wouldn't be surprised if she's behind every crooked deal that he's into, including this smuggling scheme."

"What do you mean?" I asked. This was where I wanted our conversation to go, and I wanted to catch everything that the embedded IA cop had to offer on the subject.

"There's only one thing that interests Leena Waterfowl. Money. And she's been squeezing Graham dry. The poor idiot would steal gold from Lord Alkwat's own hoard for her. And the bitch never has enough." Littlecrow shook his head. Then he leaned in and pointed a cautionary finger at me. "Look," he began. "I know that she came to you for help. Don't believe a word that lying bitch says! She lies as easily as most people greet each other in the morning."

"She says that Graham is losing interest in her," I said.

Littlecrow shook his head, "Don't believe it! Graham is practically her slave."

"Didn't he put her in a holding cell the other day?"

Littlecrow snorted. "For about fifteen minutes! He was furious with her for going to see you. Especially after that other P.I. blew the whistle on her."

What?

"He was smart enough to call Graham as soon as she left his office," Littlecrow continued. "You can imagine Graham's reaction when he found out that his girl toy was trying to interfere with his smuggling scheme. That's when he put her under surveillance, which is how he found out that she was going to try again with you."

I tried to keep my expression blank. "Yeah, he sent Stonehammer to scare me off."

Littlecrow grinned. "Graham was royally pissed when you stood up to his pet troll and went out to the pier. And he was even more pissed when Stonehammer came crawling back to the station later on with a limp and a slashed up eye." He took a sip of coffee. "You know, you're becoming a bit of an underground hero among some of YCPD's finest. Not a lot of them like Stonehammer very much. They call him 'Graham's Goon.'"

"What did Graham do?" I asked.

"He sent Stonehammer off to get patched up and sent me and some other guys out to try to find you. But it's a big city." He smiled. "I don't suppose you care to tell me where you went."

"Not a chance."

"Didn't think so. Anyway, I gather that you showed up at the pier that night and ran off with the contraband. Don't bother denying it," he said. "Anyway, we got it back—for a while!"

I wanted to find out more about Leena's part in all this, so I said, "And Leena only spent fifteen minutes in the holding cell?"

"Maybe a little longer," Littlecrow said. "No more than an hour, though. Graham couldn't stand the idea that he might have offended his little goddess." He smiled again, remembering. "You should have seen her with Graham after she was released. She was spitting fire! Graham begged her to calm down. Literally begged her! It was disgusting." He shook his head. "Let me tell you something for free, Southerland. Graham has a small circle of flunkies, but he's never had much respect from most of the cops in the department. He's a little man with no morals and big ambitions, and a troll enforcer who is weirdly loyal to him. Since Leena came into his life, he's lost most of the respect that he ever had."

So Leena had lied to me about how long she had been in the holding cell, which meant that she was lying to me about her whereabouts when Mila was killed. "Where was Leena when Graham went to the pier?" I asked.

"I don't know," said Littlecrow. "She told Graham that she was done with him, and that she was going back to the condo to pack."

"But she didn't leave him," I said. "She was in the room when Graham was interrogating me on Wednesday morning."

"Yeah, yeah," Littlecrow scowled. "She was just bluffing. Graham's her meal-ticket. She wasn't going to let him off the hook that easily. Graham brought her to the station that morning. Let me see...." He paused, thinking. "After you were released, she was in Graham's office for about an hour with the blinds drawn." He smiled. "Maybe they were 'making up.' Anyway, she left looking like a black widow who had just bitten the balls off her mate. Which means that she had Graham where she wanted him again. No more holding cells for her!"

We concentrated on our lunch for a few minutes. He seemed to be enjoying his salad, and the pretty waitress kept coming by to refill our coffee cups and exchange pleasantries with Littlecrow. She only glanced my way when she had to. I guess she wasn't attracted to facial bruising. I thought about telling her that Littlecrow had beat me up to make me confess to a crime that I didn't commit, but I decided to let it go. She probably would have taken his side.

When the waitress was gone, I said, "You know, Graham almost succeeded in having me killed."

"I was going to ask you about that," said Littlecrow. "I think that Graham believed that you *had* been killed. He thought Stonehammer had done you in."

"He came close," I said. "I got away."

"Well, Stonehammer somehow managed to avoid revealing that little tidbit of information until after Graham was attacked." Littlecrow looked across at me, studying my face. "I guess he showed you a little sample of his hospitality. I'm surprised that you aren't in a hospital."

"I heal fast," I said.

Littlecrow looked doubtful, but nodded. "You want to tell me how you escaped?"

"No."

"Suit yourself," Littlecrow said, "but maybe we can use this. If you're willing to testify, we can get Graham and Stonehammer both for attempted murder."

"Do you really need it?" I asked.

"Not if we can get them for the adaro's murder," Littlecrow said. "Anyway, Stonehammer is really in Graham's doghouse now. After he realized that his contraband had been taken, he got Stonehammer on the phone and literally screamed at him. Graham knows that you were the one who took his stuff. We could hear him all over the station. 'You told me he was taken care of! You told me he was taken care of!' And the things he called Stonehammer! I mean, there are words you just don't use with trolls. I don't know if that relationship is going to survive."

Hmm. Graham without Stonehammer? That would be interesting. But a rogue Stonehammer, running around unsupervised? That didn't bode well for anyone, especially yours truly.

"One last question," I said. "Did you happen to get a look at Mila's autopsy?"

"That's not something that they would share with a lowly officer like me," Littlecrow said. "I'll check around, though. I might be able to persuade someone to give me a peek. I'll call you if I find out anything."

We finished our lunch and I didn't object when Littlecrow picked up the check. He wanted to know what I was going to do with the box, and I assured him that I would make sure that Graham got it. I was lying, of course, but Littlecrow bought it. He left the restaurant first, waving to our disappointed waitress as he walked out the door. I had another coffee refill, giving the cop a chance to clear out, and then got into Atwater's car and drove off into the afternoon.

***

In the stop-and-go freeway traffic, I thought about my conversation with Littlecrow. The big revelation was that Leena had been lying to me. I assumed that she had been less than honest here and there. That was pretty much a habit with her. But that didn't keep me from being blindsided by two pieces of information. First, that she had consulted another P.I. before coming to see me. Second, that she hadn't been in a holding cell when Graham was picking up the box or when Mila had been killed. That was interesting, to say the least. I had questions, and she owed me some straight answers. I decided that now might be a good time to return Atwater's ridiculous automobile. I headed for the exit to the Humback District.

Chapter Twenty

It was midafternoon by the time I pulled into the lot at the back of the Stillman Building, and the wind was whipping itself into a frenzy. I got out of the car, pushed the brim of my hat down to keep it from blowing off my head, and pulled my coat collar up around my neck. I hesitated before walking away from the huge boat of an automobile. For reasons I couldn't imagine, I was reluctant to lose this car now that it was time to give it back. The black and purple horror was certainly an eyesore, and it was as big as a tank, but the baritone rumble from its powerful four hundred forty-two horsepower eight-cylinder engine was both solid as a block of granite and somehow soothing and comfortable. The four-speed stick glided into each gear with just a flick of my wrist. And, yes, the red leather interior and the naked woman on the hood were way too lurid for a low-key average joe like me, but my last good night's sleep had been in the car's spacious back seat. Had I bonded with this preposterous metal monster?

Telling myself that I was nuts, I forced myself to walk out of the wind and into the Spillman Building. The receptionist was once again engrossed in a magazine, and I had the strange feeling that she hadn't moved since I last saw her. Avoiding the treacherous elevator, I walked up six flights of stairs to the office of Classic Escorts. About halfway up, I started wishing that I had called ahead. If Atwater wasn't in his office, I was wearing myself out for nothing.

I took a minute to catch my breath outside office number sixty-three, and then I walked in. A pretty young gnome, about four feet tall, with long yellow hair and a low-cut blouse that revealed a generous amount of cleavage, sat at the antique desk, seat adjusted to accommodate a woman of her height. She flashed me a friendly grin, which faded when she saw my bruised face. But she recovered quickly and said, "May I help you?"

"Is Mr. Atwater in?" I asked.

"Can I get your name?"

"Tell him it's Alex Southerland, and that I've got his car."

The receptionist picked up the receiver from the phone on her desk and, with an adorable flip of her head, threw her hair back from the side of her face. She lifted the receiver up to her gnome-sized ear and said, "Mr. Atwater? There's an Alex Southerland out here to see you. He says that he has your car?" After a short pause, she said, "Okay, thank you." She hung up the phone and her mouth widened into a dazzling smile. "Mr. Atwater will see you," she told me, as if I'd just won a major prize. "Right through that door." She indicated the only door in the room that didn't lead me back out into the hallway.

Atwater was standing in the office as I entered, smiling and ready to shake my hand. "How's my car?" he asked. "She do the job for you?"

"She was perfect," I said. "No problems."

"Good! She's fun to drive, isn't she?" He could have been talking about one of his ladies.

"That she is," I was forced to admit. "Though I'm not sure she's really my style."

"Well, giving you a taste of something strange and exotic is what we're all about here," he said. His obvious double entendre made me feel too much like one of his clients, and I was anxious to talk about something else.

"Would you like to sit?" Atwater indicated a chair.

"Thanks," I said.

"How 'bout a drink?" said Atwater.

"Sure," I said. "Whatever you've got."

Atwater poured two glasses of whiskey and gave me one. I took a sip, and it went down smooth, warming my whole body. "Good stuff," I said.

Atwater raised his glass and then downed half of it. He sat behind his desk and said, "So how goes the case? Have you nailed Graham's ass to the wall yet?"

"I'm still working on it," I said. "I've got a couple of questions that you might be able to help me with."

"Oh?" he said. "I don't how I could help, but fire away."

I swirled the drink in my glass and took another sip, enjoying the burning sensation in my throat as it made its way to my stomach. "Leena called another P.I. before she called me. Did you know about that?"

"Ahh, hmmm," Atwater looked down at the top of his desk. "Well, actually, yes. Yes I did." He looked across his desk at me. "You have to understand that my first concern is for Leena," he told me. "She is not always honest, and I agreed to back up anything she told you."

"Uh-huh," I said.

"And, well, I mean she has her own way of looking at things." Atwater downed the rest of his drink. "She's not human, and she doesn't always think like a human. I don't always know what's going on in that pretty little head of hers. But I know that she means well."

"Fine," I said. "She means well. So what's the deal with this other investigator?"

Atwater sighed. "I probably shouldn't say anything without talking to her first. But I don't see the harm in it." He hesitated, then went on. "It was sometime last week that Leena found out about this...stuff...that Graham was smuggling in. She came to me and told me about it. She asked me if I would be willing to go to the pier and observe Graham receiving smuggled goods. She wanted to be able to tell Graham that she had a witness who would be willing to testify that he was involved in smuggling. Well," Atwater continued, "that's not really my kind of work, right? But I told her that we had a private investigator right here in this building who might be willing to do what she wanted. I even offered to pay for his services."

"Nigel Larramy?" I asked.

"Yeah, that's him. Do you know him?"

"No, but I noticed his name in the directory downstairs."

"Of course," said Atwater, nodding. "Anyway, we went together to visit Larramy. Leena explained what she wanted him to do, and he agreed. I wrote out a check, and we figured that was that."

"What happened?" I asked, already knowing the answer.

"The motherfucker called Graham as soon as we left the office!" Atwater scowled. "Larramy told him everything! And Graham gave him a fat reward for the information. He was nothing but a cheap extortionist!"

"That explains why Leena was more circumspect when she came to me," I said.

"Yes," Atwater said. "When she called me on Monday, I gave her your name and recommended that she try again. I assured her that you were more honest than Larramy, but she wanted to take a different tack with you. She'd been burned once, so I can understand how she felt. Given her experience with Larramy and her background with men," he paused a beat before continuing, "well, she thought that you would be more motivated by a 'damsel in distress' than by the desire for justice. She thought that if she could just get you to the pier when Graham was in the middle of his smuggling operation, she would have the threat she needed to use against him."

It made sense, even if she had been wrong about me. If she had been straight with me in the first place, I would have been more willing to help her get dirt on a corrupt cop. I might have been able to get Lubank in on it, too. He might have been able to find a way to make the charges against Graham stick. Or maybe he would have just filed the info away in his blackmail files. At any rate, we might have been able to avoid the mess that came after. Who knows, Mila might even still be alive. In any case, Leena had made a mess of things.

"You know," I said, "I'd like to have a talk with this Larramy fellow."

"That might be hard," said Atwater. "I'm afraid that I got a little angry with him after what he did to Leena. I had him kicked out of the building."

"You can do that?" I asked.

Atwater smiled. "The Spillman Building is owned by one of the city's more notorious families. By way of several cut-outs and shell companies, of course. You'll forgive me if I don't provide any specifics. The head of that particular family and I are...associates. And friends, too. I told him that I was displeased with Larramy, and within twenty-four hours, I discovered that the fellow had cleared out his office. Haven't seen him since. I do hope that he's okay."

"Remind me not to make you mad," I said. He gave me a brief smile.

I wondered if I had the whole story. "Is there anything else you can tell me?" I asked Atwater. "Did Leena lie to me about anything else?"

Atwater looked thoughtful. "Not that I know of," he said. "But with Leena, you never know."

We sat in silence for a few moments, and then Atwater asked me, "Are you still going to help her?"

I thought about that. The smart thing to do would be to walk away, but two things prevented me from doing so. First, I was in this up to my neck. Graham and probably Stonehammer were still looking for me, and both had their own reasons for wanting me dead. It was personal now between me and Stonehammer. He had plenty of reasons to blame me for his falling out with Graham, not to mention the fact that I had injured him and made him look stupid. As for Graham, I had his box, and I knew too much. He needed me out of the way in a hurry. Second, I had deposited Leena's check, which meant that I still worked for her. And the job wasn't finished. Larramy may have sold her out, but most P.I.'s aren't like that. We're proud professionals. When we get a job, we do it. Sure, I'd have to have a talk with Leena about being upfront with people, but I still owed her an honest effort.

Unless, of course, she was guilty of more than just lying. If, for example, she had murdered her sister and was trying to set me up for it, I'd be more than justified in cutting her down at the knees. She had lied about where she was when Mila was murdered, which made her a suspect in my eyes, and the fact that she had written me a check didn't make her any less so.

That reminded me of something. "Atwater," I said, "when I left here on Wednesday, I found the place where Mila was murdered. It was right where Leena told me to go."

"Okay," said Atwater.

"When I got to the crime scene, I was attacked by a big water elemental," I said. "I almost drowned. You know anything about that?"

"Me? No, of course not!" said Atwater. His surprise seemed genuine. "Lord's balls! I can't imagine!"

"And then later," I said, "I was taken by the police. By Stonehammer, to be more precise."

Atwater's eyes were wide. "That's awful. I guess that explains your bruises. You're lucky to be alive!"

"Yes, I am," I said. "And I'm not happy about the coincidence of the whole thing."

"What do you mean?"

"Leena told me to go somewhere, and I fell right into a trap," I said. "Little odd, don't you think?"

"I wouldn't know," Atwater said. "Your business and mine are very different."

I stared at him. He shrugged, but held my gaze without flinching.

"I'm going to ask you a question, and I want an honest answer," I said.

"Please," Atwater said. "I've been as honest with you as I can be without hurting Leena."

"Yeah, but that might be the problem," I said. "My question concerns Leena."

Atwater shrugged again. "Go ahead and ask," he said.

So I did. "Can Leena summon water elementals?"

Atwater reached up and scratched under his chin. "She's an adaro. All adaros can summon water elementals. It's part of their nature. But if you're suggesting that she set you up to be killed by one, it doesn't make sense. Why would she hire you just to kill you? And why would she want you dead in the first place?"

Those were good questions, and I didn't have any good answers. If she had killed me that night, she had no reason to believe that she would ever get her hands on the box.

So I tried another angle. "Do you know if Graham has anyone under him who can summon elementals?"

Atwater frowned. "Wouldn't be surprised," he said. "But I don't know Graham all that well, and I don't know anything about his job. He was a paying client. He had more money than a police captain should, but I wasn't interested in where it came from." He slid back in his chair, letting me know that he was about to stand. "Sorry. Don't think I can help you."

He and I both stood. "Okay," I said. "Thanks for being straight with me about Leena. That helps. Thanks for the drink. And thanks for the use of your car."

"No problem," said Atwater. "Let me walk you out."

At Atwater's insistence, we took the elevator to the ground floor. I held my breath, but despite a few jolts and some suspicious grinding noises, the elevator compartment managed to chug its way to the bottom without killing us.

Atwater walked me out the back door of the building to the lot and accompanied me all the way to the car. I took the key off my key ring and gave it to him. He looked the car over.

"What are you going to do now, call a cab?" he asked me.

"Yeah, that's right," I said.

He opened the driver's side door and pulled back in alarm. "Lord's balls!" he exclaimed. It smells like gasoline in here!"

"Oh, sorry," I said. "The car's fine, but I had to give someone a ride last night. He'd been doused in gasoline. I opened the windows, but I guess I didn't get all the fumes out."

"Doused in gasoline?" Atwater leveled a stare at me. "Do I want to know about this?"

"Best you don't," I said. "I'm sorry, do you want me to have the car cleaned?"

Atwater's face broke into a quiet laugh. "Please!" he said. "Keep her for a while longer. Enjoy yourself! You like the way she rides, don't you? When you're ready, bring her back." He tossed me the key. "In good condition, mind you."

"Thanks," I said. "I appreciate your patience."

"And watch who you pick up!" Atwater said, smiling. "A man has to be careful about who he associates himself with."

I nodded. Good advice.

***

I had muted my phone before meeting with Atwater because I hate it when phones go off in the middle of meetings. After I left Atwater, I checked my phone for calls the first time I had to stop at a light. I had three voicemails. The first was from Leena.

"Mr. Southerland, this is Leena," said her recorded voice. "I haven't heard from you in two days, and I wanted to check with you to see if you were okay and if you had found out anything new. Call me, please."

I could understand why Leena might be a little concerned, but I didn't want to talk to her at the moment. I had no doubt that Atwater had called her as soon as he got back to his office and was filling her in on our visit. I could hold off talking to her until later.

The second call was from Littlecrow. I hadn't expected to hear from him so soon, and I was anxious to hear his message.

"Mr. Southerland, this is Officer Littlecrow. Call me. It might be important."

Might be? I wondered at this, but before calling him back I wanted to check out the third call, which was from a number outside my list of contacts. Usually when I get a call from a number I don't recognize, and the caller doesn't leave a message, I ignore it. But this caller had left a voicemail, so I touched the play button and listened.

"Hello, Mr. Southerland. My name is Lawrence Fulton. I think that you know who I am. You've got something that I want, and I'm willing to make you a deal for it. Please call me at your earliest convenience. I hope to hear from you this afternoon."

So the mayor's fixer wanted to hear from me at "my earliest convenience," and by that he meant right away. He had been dealing with Graham, and now he wanted to deal with me. That made sense. Graham no longer had the box. I did. The question was, how did Fulton *know* that I had the box? There was only one way to find out.

But before calling Fulton, I pulled off the street into a grocery store parking lot and called Littlecrow. He picked up after one ring and said, "Officer Littlecrow."

"It's me," I said, knowing that his phone had already told him who was calling.

"One moment," said Littlecrow. I heard him say to someone with him, "Sorry, I need to take this call. I'll be right back."

After several seconds, Littlecrow said, "I'm at the station, but I'm in a place where I shouldn't be overheard."

"What do you got for me?" I asked.

"It's about the autopsy," he said. "Turns out, there was no autopsy."

"That right?"

"Yeah. I talked to someone I trust, and she told me that officially the results of the autopsy were filed, but for some reason they aren't where they're supposed to be. Neither the computer file nor the hard copy. But she doesn't believe that an autopsy was ever performed, and neither do I," Littlecrow said.

I didn't believe it either. "Let me guess," I said, "the body was cremated?"

"I don't know," said Littlecrow. "The person I talked to doesn't have access to the bodies. But I wouldn't be surprised. I mean, the odds that an autopsy was done, and then the official paperwork just vanished, well, that doesn't happen. Not unless someone wants it to."

"Someone like Graham," I said.

"That would be my guess."

"Thanks," I said. "You've been helpful. I'd better let you get back to work before anyone starts looking for you."

"Okay, take care of yourself."

"You too," I said, and disconnected.

Someone didn't want the details of Mila's death to get out. I wondered why? She'd been beat up and then shot. They certainly didn't try to hide that from me when Stonehammer showed me the photo of Mila's dead body. It was graphic enough. Why try to hide anything now? What was I missing?

I'd have to hold that thought for now. While I was in the parking lot I called Fulton. I was expecting a secretary, but Fulton surprised me by taking the call himself.

"Mr. Southerland?" he asked.

"Mr. Fulton?" I asked back.

"I'm glad you called," he said. "As I said in my message, we need to meet. How soon can you be in my office?"

"Do I want to come to your office?" I asked him.

"That depends. Would you like to be rich?"

I thought about it for a few seconds, and then said, "I guess that would be okay. My rent's due in a few days."

Fulton laughed. "You won't have to worry about rent anymore once we make a deal. You'll be able to buy a home anywhere you want to live."

"I don't know," I said. "I'm happy where I am."

"Well at least you'll be able to stop worrying about where the rent is coming from each month," said Fulton. "Please. Let's talk. I gather that you've had a rough time lately. Let's put an end to all that and settle this matter like gentlemen."

"All right," I said. "Where's your office?"

He gave me the address and I agreed to come right over. Why not? I didn't have any place else that I needed to be at the moment. I considered that this might be a trap of some kind, but it made sense to me that Fulton would want to buy the box and its contents from me without a lot of messy complications. After all, he was willing to buy it from Graham, wasn't he? Wasn't that why he'd come to Graham's office? It seemed likely. So I started the car and headed back downtown.

Chapter Twenty-One

Fulton's office was located in City Hall. It was late enough in the day for me to catch the beginning snarl of the evening commute, and I didn't reach the hall's visitor parking area until after five-thirty. I left my hat in the car rather than risk losing it to a forty mile-per-hour gust of wind on the way to the building. That's one of the reasons I don't like wearing hats, especially in *this* city. I pulled the collar of my trench coat up to my ears, stuffed my hands into my pockets, and made my way to the main entrance. When I stepped through the door, I was met by a pair of security guards standing in front of a metal detector. One of them instructed me to put any metal objects that I was carrying in a basket on a conveyor belt. I took out my phone and my keys and placed them in the basket. Then I remembered that I was carrying a gun. I didn't pack heat often and had almost forgotten that I had it with me. I took it out and placed it in the basket. I stepped through the metal detector, which didn't beep. The second security guard gave me back my phone and keys, but told me that I would not be permitted to carry my thirty-eight into the building, and that I could retrieve it when I was ready to leave. He tied a numbered tag on my piece and gave me a card with the matching number. I put the card in my pocket and climbed up a short flight of stairs to the main hall.

I found Fulton's office a few doors down the hall from the mayor's office. He was near enough to the mayor to be close at hand when his presence was desired, but far enough away to do the furtive behind-the-scenes work that the mayor needed him to do without bothering him with the particulars. When I walked in, I was greeted by an attractive middle-aged receptionist who told me that Fulton was expecting me and would be available in a few minutes. I sat down in a plush office chair and waited.

After a few minutes, the receptionist answered an interoffice call, rose from her chair, and let me know that Fulton was ready to see me. She directed me through a door and down a short hallway to another door, which she opened for me. I walked in and found Fulton sitting behind a desk with his phone at his ear. He looked up at me and held up his index finger. I got the impression that he was a busy and important man.

The point made, Fulton hung up the phone and rose to greet me.

"Mr. Southerland," he said, grinning broadly. He held out his hand for me to shake.

"Mr. Fulton," I said, shaking his hand and taking note of the impressive ruby stones mounted on the wide gold bands that he wore on his middle and ring fingers. Those stones would make quite a dent if he decided to take a poke at somebody.

Lawrence Fulton wasn't physically imposing, but he carried himself like a man who had never lost a fight. He had a round face, a pug nose, and eyes that could only be described as intense. Above his left eye was a small bandage, the only visible souvenir from his encounter with Badass. I was impressed! His short wavy dark hair was streaked with gray, and it looked like it had been cut fifteen minutes ago at a clip joint where the barbers and customers told each other dirty jokes and shared the same conservative politics. He had probably shaved that morning, but he was ready for another round.

Fulton waved me to a chair, and I sat down. He came around his desk and took a chair near mine, turning it so that he was facing me. "It's late, and I want to go home," he said. "So let's get to it. As I told you on the phone, I want to make a deal."

"Okay," I said.

"You've got the box. You aren't going to dance with me, are you?"

"No," I said, "I've got it. Not on me, of course, but it's where I can get to it."

"Right," said Fulton. "Tell me that you haven't tried to open it."

"I haven't," I said. "I don't have the key, and, from what I've heard, if I try to bust it open I'll fry the goodies inside."

"That's right," Fulton said. "And even if you *have* the key, you'll 'fry the goodies' if you don't open the box properly. You were smart to leave it alone."

I nodded, and he continued. "I want that box. Or rather Mayor Teague does, and that's the same thing. I hired Graham to smuggle it in for me, and he botched the job. One job that man had!" Fulton shook his head. "One job! But Graham's a fuckin' turd. He's incompetent and he's a fool. When he found out you had the box, what did he do? He sent his goon after you. With the money I was going to pay him, he could have made a deal with you. But no. He has to do it the hard way. And now you are probably righteously pissed off, am I right?"

"I've had better weeks," I said.

"Fuckin' right you have!" Fulton nodded, showing me that he was on my side. "I can tell from the bruises on your face. You're probably hanging on to that box out of sheer spite, and I don't blame you." He paused for a beat, and then asked, "Do you even know what's in the box?"

"Nope," I admitted.

"Thought so," said Fulton. "How could you? And you wanna know something? Neither do I. But it's important to Teague, so it's my job to get it for him by any means necessary." He clenched his jaw and leveled his eyes at me from under his furrowed brow to make sure that I had caught the implied threat in his last four words. Then he relaxed his jaw, dialed down the intensity in his eyes a notch, and said, "But I don't wanna cause a lot of trouble for you. Let's do this the way it should've been done in the first place. You give me the box, and I'll make it worth your while. I mean, let's be reasonable. What's the box to you anyway? You don't know what's in it. All you know is that it's worth a lot of jack. Well, I'm willing to give you some serious jack for it. I get the box for the mayor, you get rich. I call that a win-win."

Truthfully, I thought that Fulton had a point. What *was* the box to me? It had been nothing but a headache up till now. I had kept it because Stonehammer had tried to muscle me into giving it up, and because Graham had tried to have me iced after he took it from me. And because of Mila. She had been killed because of that box, and I wanted her killer to pay. Never mind that I had only known her for a couple of hours. That part's not important. And now Fulton was offering to make me rich if I would just give him the goods. Would that make me happy? I didn't know.

"I can see that you are a reasonable man," I said, "but there are some points I'd like to get cleared up. I'd like to ask you a couple of questions, if that's okay."

Fulton leaned back in his chair. "Fire away," he said. "What would you like to know?"

"What about Graham?" I asked. "If I sell you this box, then I assume that he's going to get nothing from you for his troubles. He'll want to take that out on me. How am I going to keep him off my back?"

"Don't worry about Graham," said Fulton, waving his hand as if he were brushing Graham aside like an irritating fly. "He's through. Make a deal with me, and Graham will be out of a job and out of the city before he knows what hit him. Stonehammer, too. I despise incompetence, and those two motherfuckers are total fuck-ups."

"Graham killed a girl a couple of days ago," I said. "Or he had her killed. Stonehammer roughed her up good before she died. I'd like the public to know about that. Consider that part of my price."

Fulton nodded. "Sounds fair to me. I can handle that. We can even make this good and legal if you have any evidence."

"I don't have much," I admitted. "I had a witness, but I sent him out of town for his own safety. An autopsy would have helped, but according to a source I have in the department, no autopsy was ever performed. I'm guessing that the body was shoved into an oven as soon as Graham got it back to the station."

Fulton smiled at me, like a magician about to pull the card I'd been thinking of out of his ass. "Not necessarily," he said. "We're talking about Mila Waterfowl, right? Well, as it happens, a person or two in the YCPD actually work for me. Long story short: the girl's body is locked away in a safe place. And I can use that corpse to get rid of Graham."

I tried not to look stunned, but I'm pretty sure that I failed. If he was telling the truth, then Fulton was even more dangerous than I thought! I wouldn't want him as an enemy, and I hoped that we weren't headed in that direction.

Fulton knew that he had surprised me, but he had the decency not to gloat. He reached into the inside pocket of his suit and pulled out a rectangular piece of paper. "This is a cashier's check," he told me. He turned it around so that I could see the business side of it. It was made out to me. I looked at the line containing the amount. It was for more money than I had made in my seven years as a professional investigator. I forced myself to continue breathing.

"Give me the box, a box you have no use for, and this check is yours," Fulton said. "And, as a bonus, I'll see to it that Graham and Stonehammer go away for Miss Waterfowl's murder. Ball's in your court, Mr. Southerland. What's it going to be?"

He sat back and waited for me to speak. There's a saying among salesmen. When you've made your closing argument, shut up. He was shut up tight, waiting for me to accept his deal. I couldn't think of a single logical reason not to. I opened my mouth to say, sure, let's do it.

But what I said was, "That's a very generous offer, Mr. Fulton, and I appreciate the way you do business. I was thinking, though.... It's the only offer I've seen. If you, or Mayor Teague, want what's in the box, then maybe someone else does, too. What if I were to go online and put the box up for sale? I might find someone willing to outbid you."

Fulton smiled. "And would they give you the justice you seek, as well? No, Mr. Southerland, let me assure you. You could try to do what you are saying, but it would take a lot of time and trouble to set up such an auction. A lot of things could happen during that time. Graham is still after you. How much longer do you think you can keep yourself safe? As you've already seen, there are a lot of people out there who would be more willing to take the box from you than pay for it. And even if you managed to but the item up for bid, I'm positive that you would find my offer to be the best that you are going to get."

I nodded. "Fair enough. You're right. It's a lot of dough, and I agree that trying to start up a bidding war would be impractical."

"Believe me, it would." Fulton clammed up again. In his mind, the deal was closed.

But I wasn't quite done. "What would happen," I said, "if I said no?"

Fulton's expression didn't change. "Well, then, I'd be very, very disappointed." He got up and walked back behind his desk, slow and cool, like a man holding all the aces. He plopped down in his chair with a thud and leaned forward, putting his arms on his desktop and crossing them. "Would you like a cigarette?" he asked me, keeping his voice friendly.

"No thanks," I said. "That's the one vice I've avoided."

"A drink then?"

"Another time," I said.

"Suit yourself," said Fulton. "Mind if I smoke?"

"Okay with me," I said. He opened a wooden box on his desk and removed a cigarette. He took a gold lighter out of his pocket and lit up. He put the cigarette to his lips, breathed in, blew a stream of smoke off to one side, and put the cigarette in a clean ashtray.

Fulton sat back in his chair and looked at the ceiling. "When you came into the building," he said, "the guard at the door took away your firearm. We can't have people running through City Hall with weapons, right? But here's the thing. If you choose to be unreasonable and turn down my offer, I'll have someone use your gun to shoot Mila Waterfowl's corpse through the bullet hole that's already in her forehead. I might even do it myself, just to make sure that there are no mistakes. I'm an excellent shot, you know. I've got marksman awards to prove it." He paused to lift his cigarette out of the ashtray and take a brief puff. He returned the cigarette to the ashtray and said, "I will then arrange for an autopsy and a ballistics test which will show conclusively that your gun was the cause of Miss Waterfowl's death. You'll be arrested, tried, and executed." He paused and fixed me with a no-more-of-your-nonsense stare. "Any more questions?"

I knew that he could do what he said. I had two choices. I could take the deal, get rich, and see that justice was done for Mila. Or I could be hanged for Mila's murder. I hate it when I only have two choices. Thing is, that's rarely ever the case. There's almost always another option out there. It's just harder to find.

I nodded and sighed. "You've got me," I said. "As far as I can tell, my only move is to take your deal and be happy with it, which, I admit, would be an easy thing to do. Like you said, your deal is a winner all around. But," I said, "I'm not the smartest guy in the world. Hell, I'm not the smartest guy in this room. If it's okay with you, I'd like to run your offer by my lawyer, just to make sure that I'm not missing any loopholes. Can you give me that much? Tomorrow is Saturday, but he'll see me. I can have an answer for you by tomorrow afternoon."

Fulton took a puff from his cigarette and pondered this for a moment. "I should tear up this check right now," he said. "I could lift a finger and have your P.I. license revoked. I could make you for the girl's murder. But I don't believe that any of these things are going to be necessary. I'm confident that your lawyer is going to tell you to do the right thing. I plan to spend the weekend with my family, so I'll give you till Monday morning. Shall we say ten o'clock?"

"Thank you, Mr. Fulton," I said. "You've been very patient with me. And professional. Not like Graham, that's for sure."

Fulton rolled his eyes. "Graham! Now that's one pussy-whipped son of a bitch. That mistress of his has him on his knees barking like a dog and making him love it. Before she came along, he was a reliable associate. Not very imaginative, not smart, but reliable. We've done a few deals together, and he's always done his part. But when she entered the picture, he changed. He doesn't do anything now unless she tells him it's okay." He shook his head. "I thought that he was coming around. I had a talk with his pet ape, Stonehammer. He was working on Graham, trying to get him out from under the bitch's thumb. He told me that Graham was making progress. But she's like a drug, and he's addicted. And if there's one thing you can't trust, it's a junkie."

"What do you mean he was making progress?" I asked.

Fulton's face turned to stone. "Never mind," he said. "Nothing you need to know. Anyway, it doesn't matter now. Once we finalize our deal, he's through."

I smiled at him and said, "You're right." I stood. "Monday morning, then."

We shook hands and he put his left hand on my shoulder. "Do the right thing," he said. "Make yourself rich and get justice for the girl. Don't be a loser!"

"Goodbye, Mr. Fulton," I said. "Thanks for this opportunity. I feel good about it. Sorry to put you off, but I don't think there will be any problems in the end."

The intensity in Fulton's eyes shifted to maximum, and his grip on my shoulder tightened. "Let's hope not," he said, "for all our sakes."

***

I left City Hall with an empty holster. My piece would be used as evidence against me in a murder trial if I didn't sell the box to Fulton. If I sold him the box, I'd have enough dough to retire and live a life of leisure for the rest of my days. It was a no-brainer, right? And yet, even before I had left the building I knew that there was no chance of me accepting Fulton's deal. Fulton was a smart cookie, but he'd made a big mistake. He'd offered me too much money. If the box was worth that much to him, then I needed to know more about why he wanted it, or, rather, why the mayor wanted it, before I'd be willing to hand it over. Maybe I'm just stubborn. Maybe I'm crazy. I don't know. But the carrot was too big and the stick too extreme for me to simply hand over the box and walk away, even if I was walking away with more wealth than a working-class slob like me could wrap his head around.

I needed to know what was in the box. I thought about calling Kintay, but I didn't want to push him. He'd told me that he would call me when he knew something, and if I bugged him about it now it would just piss him off. I would just have to hope that he'd have some answers for me soon.

Anyway, I had something else that I needed to do. I'd told Kraken that I would let him know when I found Quapo, and nearly a day had gone by since I'd found him. It was time to head back to the old Placid Point Pier.

On my way to the pier, I decided to stop off and check on Crawford. I'd dragged the shopkeeper into my affairs, and even though he had gone willingly I wanted to make sure that he was okay. I parked my car and walked a block and a half to the Nautilus Jewelry and Novelty Shop. When I got there, the store was closed. The store hours posted on the window next to the front door indicated that the shop was open until nine o'clock on Fridays. It wasn't even seven yet. This wasn't good.

I leaned in and peered through the barred glass windows. Nothing looked amiss. Maybe Crawford had simply closed early. I walked around the shop to the back and climbed the stairs to the landing outside Crawford's apartment. I pressed the doorbell and heard the ringtones from inside. I strained my hearing for the sound of footsteps. Nothing. I knocked on the door. Nothing.

I tried the door handle and found that the door was unlocked. I didn't like that.

I opened the door and walked in, leaving the door hanging open. A pair of pajamas was sprawled on the carpet just in front of the door. Otherwise, everything seemed to be in order. No furniture had been overturned. The couch cushions hadn't been slashed. No bodies were lying on the floor bleeding into the carpet. I decided to take a look around.

Except for the empty pajamas, I didn't spot anything suspicious in the living room or kitchen. It was clear that Crawford led a quiet life, and he kept a clean house. Nothing was out of place. I went into his bedroom. The bed was unmade. That got my attention. In an otherwise tidy bedroom, an unmade bed stands out like a lit cigar on a debutante's window ledge. But I found no signs of violence and no indications of a search. I looked under the bed, but the only thing I could see was that Crawford did a thorough job when he vacuumed. I'm sure that if anyone looked under *my* bed, they'd by assaulted by dust balls. I stood and spotted Crawford's cell phone in a charging stand on top of a chest of drawers. Crawford's wallet and keys lay next to the charging stand. I found money and credit cards inside the wallet. I checked the drawers. They were filled with clothes. So was his closet. I went into the bathroom. There was a place for everything, and everything was in its place.

I went back into the bedroom and regarded the unmade bed. For an unmade bed, it was pretty much intact. It was a single bed. The single pillow was dented, the sheets wrinkled, and the blankets thrown open, but I detected none of the telltale signs of a person being dragged out of the bed by force. By all indications, Crawford had rolled out of his bed without disturbing it much and walked away. But where? And why hadn't he taken his phone, wallet, and keys? I thought that I knew most of the answer. The empty pajamas were a giveaway.

I reentered the living room and stopped short. In the center of the room was a white rat. As I watched, it stood on its hind legs and waved at me. Then it started to scurry toward the front door.

I followed the rat outside and down the stairs. The rat led me to a detached garage across the alley from the apartment and slipped through a partially opened side door. I pushed the door open and found Crawford, naked, leaning against the side of a two-door compact car, smiling at me.

"Hello, Flatfoot," he said. "How's it hangin'?"

Chapter Twenty-Two

"Aren't you cold?" I said.

"A little," said Crawford.

"You want to tell me what's going on?"

"Let's go upstairs to my apartment first. Is the coast clear?"

"There might be some people about," I said. "Are you saying that your neighbors have never seen you with your pants down?"

"That would be undignified for a respected small business owner like me," said Crawford. "We could make a dash for it, I suppose, but then you might have to explain to someone why you're entering an apartment with a naked man."

"I could tell them that I'm just here for a one-night stand," I said.

"No one would believe that you're my type," said Crawford.

"I'd offer you my coat, but it's about twenty sizes too big for you," I said. "A little guy like you would get lost in it."

"I'm willing to chance it," said Crawford, "unless you want to go up and get me some clothes."

"Too much trouble," I said. I took off my coat and gave it to Crawford, who wrapped it around himself like a towel. We went upstairs without incident.

In case you're wondering, Crawford didn't have a tail. At least not in his human form.

When we got inside, Crawford went into his bedroom and came out a few minutes later fully clothed. "Let me grab something out of the refrigerator. I'm starving! Do you want anything? I've got beer."

"Got any whiskey?" I asked. "It's too cold for beer."

"Sorry," said Crawford.

"Okay," I said. "I'll take the beer."

When we were settled in Crawford's living room, I said, "Okay, spill it. What happened?"

Crawford laughed. "A couple of cops came calling on me this morning. They told me that they wanted me to go downtown and answer some questions. One of them started to grab me. You should have seen his face when I melted into a swarm of rats!"

"Hmm," I said. "It didn't take them long to finger you as their burglar. Or maybe they were just rousting known were-rats. Either way, it means that they knew about you."

"Yeah, that sucks," said Crawford. "So much for my secret private life."

"So where have you been?" I asked.

"I ran off. I've got bolt holes all over this place for emergencies like this. Anyway, I split up and scattered. I stayed that way for quite a while, just to be sure. I gathered myself together in the garage and sent a rat outside to scout around every once in a while to see if it was safe to go back upstairs. But there's been a cop car stationed outside all day long. It left just before you got here."

"Hey, man," I said. "I'm really sorry about getting you into this."

Crawford screwed up his face and waved my apology away. "Don't worry about it. Like I told you, I can handle myself."

"What are you going to do now?" I asked him.

"Depends," he said. "You think the cops will be coming back?"

"Probably," I said. "You might not be safe here for a while."

"Or ever again," said Crawford.

"I wouldn't go that far," I said. "I think that this whole thing with Graham and that box is going to come to a head soon. I have a feeling that whatever happens, it's not going to end well for Graham."

"Good to know," said Crawford. "I have a place I can go for a few days. Just call me when the coast is clear."

"I'll do that," I assured him.

"Oh, by the way," said Crawford. "Didn't you tell me that you'd had a run-in with a troll?"

"Yeah," I said.

"Well earlier today a troll in a silver sedan double-parked next to the cop car that I told you about and had a chat with the cops in the car. I got the impression that the troll was in charge."

Stonehammer! I was going to have to do something about him.

***

My phone was ringing as I pulled Atwater's musclebound automobile into the old Placid Point Pier parking lot. I hoped that it would be Kintay and feared that it would be Leena. For once, I caught a break.

"Corporal?" I said.

"I'm still innocent," said Kintay.

"Sure you are," I said. "Got something for me?"

"Yes and no," said Kintay. "I know what it is in a general sense, but I'm still working on the specifics."

"Okay, tell me what you've got so far."

"It's not what we were expecting," said Kintay.

"Corporal?" I prompted.

"Sure you don't want to guess?"

I waited, knowing that he was as anxious to tell me as I was to hear it.

"It's not drugs," he said.

I continued to wait.

"It's not a germ."

I remained silent. He was ready to fold.

"Okay, okay," he said. "Are you ready for this? Stem cells! Those tubes contain stem cells!"

"Stem cells?" I said. "No shit?" Kintay was right, that *was* unexpected.

"Yeah! Isn't that cool? Motherfucking stem cells!" Kintay was excited. "I couldn't fuckin' believe it when I found them. Stem fuckin' cells! Ripe and ready for use. But here's the mystery: I don't know what kind of stem cells they are."

"What do you mean you don't know what kind?" I said.

"I mean I don't know from what kind of organism," said Kintay. "I've never seen anything like this! All I know is that they're humanlike, but not human. I'm going to test for gnome, troll, and dwarf, but I don't think I'll get a positive for any of them, either. They look more human than any of those other guys, but they're not quite human. It's almost as if they come from a human hybrid, but that's impossible. Humans have been doing it with people from the other sentient species for thousands of years, but they've never made a baby with one. The cells must be modified in some way, if that's even possible, or maybe they come from some kind different kind of human, if you know what I'm sayin'."

I knew what he was sayin'. In fact, I was beginning to think I had an answer, and I was starting to get chill bumps thinking about the implications. But I didn't want to say anything yet.

"Are you going to keep working on this tonight?" I asked.

"Are you fuckin' kidding me? Of course I am! I'll work all night if I have to. This is the most interesting job I've had since I synthesized that sick crystal meth compound that flooded the streets a couple of years ago. That was genius! But this, this is different. I can't wait to see where it takes me!"

"Okay," I said. "I'm tied up tonight, but I want to come see you first thing in the morning. That all right?"

"How's about ten?" he asked. "I'll have the answer by then, plus a couple of hours of shuteye."

"Ten it is," I said. "See you then. Oh, and have fun!"

We disconnected. If I was right, Kintay was in for a frustrating night. I hoped that he would be able to get the sleep he needed before I got there in the morning.

The sun had set nearly two hours ago, and the stars shined down through a clear sky. Only the slimmest edge of the moon reflected light, but the dark of the moon was plainly visible, even without enhanced night vision. The parking lot was deserted, and so was the wooden wharf that stretched out over the ocean. I walked out of the car, across the lot, and to the end of the wharf. I leaned over the railing where the fisherman had stood…when was it…just four days ago? It was hard to believe. I looked down into the water, unsure about what I was supposed to do next. Should I just call out for Kraken? I wished that he had a doorbell or something. Oh well.

"Kraken?" I shouted. I cleared my throat and looked around, feeling like an idiot, and thankful that the pier was abandoned. Then I shouted a little louder, "Kraken? Are you there? Anyone home? Hello?"

This was embarrassing, but it would be even worse if I had to leave a message with a fish. How would that work? Was there a receptionist fish down there somewhere?

Just then, however, I noticed a disturbance in the rolling surface of the ocean. Suddenly, a shape leaped out of the water and over the railing. A wave splashed over me, almost knocking me off my feet and soaking me from head to toe. I wiped the cold, burning saltwater from my eyes, and there was Kraken, standing beside me.

"Hello, Dickhead," he said.

"You know," I said, "my name isn't Dickhead. It's Alex. ALEX!"

Kraken smiled, but his eyes were sad. "I know," he said. "But Mila called you Dickhead, and when I call you Dickhead it reminds me of her."

I didn't know what to say to that. We shared a brief silence, and then Kraken asked, "Did you find Quapo?"

"I did. That's why I'm here. Look, Kraken, Quapo didn't kill Mila. I'm absolutely sure of that. So I let him go."

I expected Kraken to be mad. Furious, even. But he surprised me. He just nodded, and said, "You're sure? Okay, good. Do you know who did it?"

"I'm not one hundred percent," I said, "but I'm close. I don't think it will be much longer. I wanted to let you know about Quapo, though."

Kraken frowned. "Ten-Inch won't be happy that you let him go. Quapo bailed on the gang during the fight."

"Yeah," I said. "But what's done is done, and Ten-Inch will just have to deal with it and move on. I'm going to Medusa's to see him. Wanna come along?"

"No, not really," Kraken said, looking back at the ocean with obvious longing.

"That's fine," I said. "Look, when I find Mila's killer I'll let you know. Like I said, I'm close. Stick around the pier, okay? I really don't want to have to send a message by fish courier."

"No?" Kraken looked amused. "Some of those fish are pretty smart, you know."

"If you say so," I said, not sure how I felt about the idea of smart seafood.

"Oh, before I forget," Kraken said. "The elf says hello, and he told me to tell you that there is going to be a storm out at sea tomorrow. That means that the surface of the water on the coast is going to be pretty wild by tomorrow night. But he says that you shouldn't worry about it. Oh, and he said to make sure to tell you to keep hoping."

What? "Huh?" I'm sure I sounded less intelligent than Kraken's underwater messengers. "Why...?" I couldn't get the words out.

Kraken shrugged. "That's what he said. I don't know what any of it means, except that he's right about a storm forming out there. I had a long talk with him earlier today. He told me stories about the old adaro heroes. Pretty awesome shit, as you humans say. His stories made me feel a little better." Kraken grabbed my shoulder and gave it a squeeze. "Well, I'm off," he said. "Later, Dickhead!"

"Wait! What?" But the adaro had already leaped over the railing and into the rolling water. Perfect swan dive, too.

***

By the time I returned to the car I was close to freezing. I started up the car and let it idle with the heater turned on full blast. The heater did the trick, and about ten minutes later I was more or less dry, or at least dry enough. I pulled out of the lot and headed up the road to Medusa's Tavern.

The dirt lot at Medusa's was nearly full, and Ten-Inch's cycle was in its spot up front. Looked like it was all hands on deck tonight. I parked in the back of the lot and got out of the car. That's when I noticed that one of the Northsiders was standing just outside the entrance doing sentry duty. When he saw me, the sentry opened the door a crack and leaned in to alert someone inside. I took my time walking to the door. When I was about halfway there, Ten-Inch stepped outside. He stood next to the sentry and waited for me.

"How you doin', Sarge," Ten-Inch said when I arrived. He held up a hand for me to take, and we hooked thumbs and bumped shoulders.

"I'm all right," I said. "Tribal meeting tonight?"

"Somethin' like that," said Ten-Inch. "Glad you came by. There's something you need to see." He held the door open for me, and I walked past the sentry and into the bar.

About forty or fifty Northsiders were packed into the bar, all wearing their colors. They stood in a rough circle, holding wooden bloodstained clubs and long bloody knives, and facing the center of the room, where the battered and slashed body of Quapo hung limp and naked from a rope that hung from the rafters and was looped under his arms and around his chest. Blood dripped from the body and pooled on the floor beneath his feet. His face had been nearly obliterated by a blast from a high-caliber firearm, and Quapo was recognizable only by the distinctive explosion of tightly curled hair that spilled out of his head to his shoulders and nearly covered the remains of his face. His black curls were streaked with scarlet.

Before I could react, I heard Ten-Inch say, "Search him."

I was grabbed from both sides. Rough hands removed my coat and empty holster and then patted me down. "He's clean," said a voice from behind me.

"Show him a seat," said Ten-Inch, and I was forced into a chair near Quapo's hanging body. Two of the Northsiders stood on either side of me, each with a hand on my shoulders, holding me in place.

Ten-Inch pulled over a chair and sat in it facing me. He held me with a cold stare and folded his hands into a pyramid in front of his chest. "You found Quapo," he said in an accusing tone. "But instead of bringing him to me, you tried to put him on a bus out of town."

"Quapo didn't kill Mila," I said.

"That what he told you?" said Ten-Inch.

"Yeah," I said. "And I believed him."

Ten-Inch put his hands down on his thighs and shifted a little in his seat. "Well, maybe he did and maybe he didn't," he said. "But he was a snitch, and he deserted his tribal brothers in the middle of a firefight."

"He was just a kid," I said. "And Stonehammer didn't give him a choice."

"There's always a choice, Sarge," said Ten-Inch. "Like the choice you made when you tried to send him out of town."

I didn't say anything to that. The entire gang was crowded close to the two of us, staring at me with dead eyes, like a school of barracudas.

Ten-Inch went on. "Quapo had a choice. He coulda gone to prison. He'da been a hero in the joint, a 'gangsta' who chose doing time over ratting out his brothers. Or," Ten-Inch paused a beat, "he coulda taken your advice and lammed it outta town for good. But he was stupid. He came back here and begged me to forgive him. To let him back in the tribe. But that's not what you do with rats. Once they start snitching, you can't ever trust them again. I had to make an example out of him so that everyone knows what happens when you make the wrong choice."

The Northsiders all nodded their heads, and I heard murmurs of "Hell yeah," and "Fuckin' right," and so forth. Their dead eyes never left my face.

"So that brings us to you, Sarge," said Ten-Inch. "What am I supposed to do with you now?" He rubbed the side of his chin, as if considering the matter. I let him consider. "See, here's the thing. You're a veteran. I respect you. You got a rep." He put his hand down and leveled his gaze at me. "But you lost your edge. I don't think you woulda shown no mercy to a fuckin' deserter on the Border. You'da put him up against the wall and blown him away." He paused. "Have you gone soft?" he asked me. "Is that it?"

"I haven't gone soft," I said. "But we're not in the Borderland. The war's over for us."

Ten-Inch's jaw tightened and his eyes blazed. "The war's never over for me! I was no older than Quapo, and they said they were going to make me a man. They sent me to the Borderland and I fought like a warrior. I fought and I killed, and I watched my brothers get killed in a hundred different ways. I seen their arms and their legs and their dicks get blown off. I seen their heads explode off their necks. I seen things there that I'll never, ever unsee. You know how it was."

I nodded. I knew.

Ten-Inch continued. "And then they brought me back. Back out of the land of the dead and back to the land of the living. They thanked me for my service and turned me loose on so-ci-e-ty. Told me to be a good boy. Get a job. Fit in. But it was too late. I wasn't a boy no more. They turned me into a man, just like they said they would. And I stayed a man." He nodded at me, a slight smile on his face. "So what about you? Are you still a man?"

"What do *you* think?" I said.

"I think that we should find out," said Ten-Inch. "Let's fight it out, you and me. We fight until one of us surrenders or dies."

"What would be the point of that?" I asked him.

"Ain't no point," said Ten-Inch. "I just want to satisfy my curiosity. Are you still the crazy sergeant I heard about in the Borderland, or did so-ci-e-ty make you soft? 'Cause I've been avoiding the mainstream, living the life of an outlaw out here on the edge. But I'm getting' a little long in the tooth, you know. Got some gray in my hair. I may need to go do something else with my life one of these days. But I gotta be honest with you, Sarge. I don't know if polite society has a place for me. I don't want to lose my *self* in it. Did you? When you stopped being a warrior, did you stop being a man? It's something I need to know."

"Then let's find out," I said, and it was on.

Chapter Twenty-Three

The Northsiders pushed themselves to the edges of the dining area. Ten-Inch stripped to the waist, revealing a body full of thick muscle mass, and handed his clothing to someone in the crowd. He pulled up one of the legs of his pants and unfastened a knife sheath that was wrapped around his ankle. He handed it over to one of his followers. We left Quapo hanging from the rafters in the center of the room.

"You want to search me for weapons?" Ten-Inch asked me.

"No need," I said. "I trust you."

I took off my shirt, exposing the bruises on my ribs and shoulders. Ten-Inch stretched his legs with a couple of side lunges, first one way and then the other. I reached into the air with one arm, stretching my shoulder, and then repeated the stretch with my other arm. We locked eyes and, without any fanfare, began to circle each other.

Ten-Inch's expression was deadly, and his eyes focused on mine with a killer's intensity. Quapo had called him a psycho, and I knew that he was right. Ten-Inch had never left the Borderlands. He was still at war. It was all he knew. For me, surrender was not going to be an option. If I lost this fight, Ten-Inch had no intention of letting me walk out of Medusa's alive.

I decided that I needed to be aggressive, to strike hard before my opponent could get into the fight. I charged, feinted with my left, and aimed a straight right at Ten-Inch's chin. Ten-Inch pulled his head back and slapped my fist away with practiced efficiency. I never saw his right hand move, but it crunched into my jaw and sent me stumbling back the way I had come. I'd been in fights before—lots of them! Hell, it was like I fought someone almost every day when I was a kid. When I was big enough to do it, I put a long overdue beatdown on my father, and he was the one of the toughest motherfuckers in my neighborhood. But I had never mixed it up with someone whose punches were as lightning quick as the one that had just hit me. Ten-Inch followed me back and connected with a sudden left jab/right cross combo that sent me reeling back into the arms of a Northsider, who flung me back toward Ten-Inch. Ten-Inch wrapped his arms around me in a bear hug that forced the air out of my lungs. With a grunt, he lifted me off my feet and slammed me to the floor. He aimed a kick at the side of my head, which I partially blocked with my shoulder. I rolled away from a second kick and managed to get to my knees. The onlookers were shouting and cheering. I wasn't off to a good start.

"Get up!" Ten-Inch shouted, waving me in with his hands.

I climbed to my feet and adopted a boxer's stance, left hand forward. I tried to formulate a plan of attack. But Ten-Inch wasn't going to give me the time to think of one. He charged in, and I deflected a sharp left jab, then another. Then Ten-Inch launched his right foot at my groin. I turned my hips and caught the kick in my thigh, but the force of the kick was enough to buckle me. I never saw the right hook that sent me tumbling to the floor. I rolled over and regained my feet. Tasting blood in my mouth, I reached up to wipe at my nose. When I pulled my hand away, it was streaked with red.

Desperate, I tried to think of a tactic to turn the tide of this fight, but Ten-Inch was relentless. He charged at me and snapped my head back with a jab that seemed to come from nowhere. In full retreat, I stumbled into one of the Northsiders, who laughed and pushed me back into the center of the room, where I bumped up against Quapo's body. Ten-Inch aimed a right hook at me, and I used the hanging corpse to block his punch. I retreated behind it, trying to get my bearings and plan a counter-attack. But Ten-Inch caught me at the ankles with a surprise leg sweep and I fell hard to the floor, landing in the bloody pool under Quapo's body. As I tried to scramble to my feet, I slipped a little in the blood and fell to my hands and knees.

Ten-Inch charged around Quapo's body and kicked me hard in the ribs. I rolled away from a follow-up kick and continued to roll until I could get my knees under me again. Just in time, I saw Ten-Inch's spinning leg kick and blocked it with my forearm just enough to keep the kick from tearing my head off. Ten-Inch tried another kick, but now he slipped in Quapo's blood and fell to one knee. That gave me time to regain my feet. I didn't stay there long. Ten-Inch stood quickly and slugged me behind the ear with a punch I didn't see. I felt like I'd been hit with a crowbar, and once again I was on my back, staring at the rafters. I was getting trounced, and I hadn't landed a single blow. Ten-Inch was skilled, experienced on the battlefield and in the streets, and merciless. At the rate we were going, this fight would be over before I was even in it. I needed time to think. Was there some way that I could I turn this around and gain an advantage? Or was I simply overmatched?

    The Northsiders hooted and hollered. Ten-Inch loomed over me. He wasn't even breathing hard. If one of his goals was to reinforce his authority over his followers, he was doing a hell of a job of it. He'd impressed *me*, that's for sure. Ten-Inch casually lifted my arm up by my wrist with his foot and let it flop to the ground. His lips twisted into a predatory smile. The onlookers cheered. I turned my head and spat a gob of blood to the floor. Looking up at Ten-Inch, I said, "Give up yet?"

    The smile left Ten-Inch's face. He took a step back and said, "Get up!" I took a reluctant breath, started to oblige him, and made it to my hands and knees. I took another breath, and struggled to my feet. I resumed my fighter's stance and nodded, letting Ten-Inch know that I was ready for more.

    I had started this fight trying to take the action to my opponent, but that hadn't worked. I decided to focus on what Ten-Inch was doing and to try to respond with counter-moves. But Ten-Inch came at me hard and launched one blow after another at my head, too quickly for me to process and respond. I wondered if some of those punches were damaging his knuckles as much as they were damaging my skull, but I wasn't hopeful. I caught some of the punches with my arms, but a few of them connected, and one of them slammed into my temple hard enough to send me flying into the arms of one of the onlookers. I slid down to a seated position, but the Northsider gangster pulled me back to my feet and shoved me back into the combat zone. I looked for Ten-Inch and saw two of him closing in on me. I ducked away and tried to shake the double-vision out of my head. I retreated behind Quapo's body and used it to hold off Ten-Inch's charge while I gasped for air and attempted to clear my head.

A voice in my head was trying to get my attention. I realized that it was my own voice, speaking from somewhere in my brain. "What's the matter with you, Southerland," it said. "I thought that you were supposed to be a tough guy. Hard as nails. Turns out that Ten-Inch was right. You've lost your edge. You've gone soft."

Ten-Inch tried to leg sweep me again, but I pulled back in time to avoid it.

"I've got something left," I told myself. "This ain't over."

"Who you fooling!" said the voice. "You're done. Say goodbye."

No! When Ten-Inch charged around Quapo, I grabbed him in a clench, pinning his arms to his side. We staggered around the floor like a pair of dancing bears, me trying to catch my breath, Ten-Inch trying to free his arms. He managed to push me away and followed up quick as a cat with a left hook that sent blood spraying out of my mouth into the ring of onlookers. Coming at me like a juggernaut, Ten-Inch launched a kick and buried his foot squarely into my solar plexus. I saw stars, and then the world went black. Only semi-conscious, I covered my head with my arms just in time to block a money shot that would have ended the fight for good.

On the edge of dreamland and unable to see, I raised my arm to where my instincts told me the next punch would be coming from and, to my amazement, blocked it. I backed away and continued to retreat, hoping that my vision would clear. A roar filled my head, and I could no longer hear the taunts and cheers from the Northsiders. Then the roar subsided, and, though I could see that the Northsiders were still shouting, all I could hear was silence. My legs felt like lead, and my arms hung beside me like wet noodles. I was on a streetcar to oblivion.

Ten-Inch was nothing more than a shadow in the mist. Sensing victory, he launched a quick jab/jab/cross combination, but, armed only with my instincts, I blocked all three punches. Ten-Inch stepped back and tried a wild right hook. Without thinking about it, I turned my head and avoided the flying fist. Ten-Inch's head snapped back before I realized that I had somehow connected with a lightning counter-punch combination of my own. Then, without planning it, I sent him to the floor with a low-spinning kick that slammed into his knees.

Ten-Inch lay on his back, his mouth and eyes open in surprise. I took advantage of the lull to step back and regroup. What had just happened? Just as I thought I was done, the tables had somehow turned. Some dormant instincts had awakened, and suddenly it was as if I knew what Ten-Inch was going to do before he did it. I realized that my only chance of getting out of this fight alive was to stop trying to figure out a way to win and let those instincts take over.

I allowed Ten-Inch to regain his feet. Aggressive as ever, he charged in. Without thinking about it, I stepped to one side and used his own momentum to shove him face first into the onlookers. They prevented him from banging into the wall and helped him regain his balance. Ten-Inch closed with me again, feinted a left jab, and launched a kick at my groin. I sensed the move before his foot left the floor. I struck his foot aside with my forearm and slammed the heel of my hand into the bridge of his nose. Blood exploded from his nostrils.

Ten-Inch's eyes hardened, but, rather than attacking, he began to circle me, more cautious now, looking for an opening. I pulled my weary arms up into a fighter's stance, but then let them drop to my side and stood still. I stopped trying to meet my adversary's eyes and gazed instead at an imaginary distant horizon. The Northsiders had gone quiet, but I wouldn't have heard them if they had been screaming. The only sound in my head was the thump of my own heartbeat, still strong and slowing by the second. I listened to it and let my body relax. I slide-stepped to my left to cut Ten-Inch off as he continued to circle. Ten-Inch changed directions, and I slide-stepped to my right and a little forward, forcing him to retreat a foot or so. We maneuvered in this way for the next few seconds until Ten-Inch found himself backed into Quapo's corpse.

Ten-Inch's face broke into a snarl. He charged at me and threw a vicious left hook. Without lifting my hands from my sides, I twisted my head to the side and felt his fist fly past my chin. I shuffled to my right to prevent Ten-Inch from following up and turning his hook into a combination. Ten-Inch grimaced and aimed a spinning kick at my knees. By the time his foot snapped out at me, I was no longer standing where he thought I would be. He retreated in frustration, arms up to ward off a counter attack.

I stayed where I was, arms at my sides, calm as a summer breeze. Ten-Inch charged, bobbed, weaved, and fired off a haymaker that would have dented a steel girder. It never connected. Before his swing could get started, I was inside it. Time seemed to slow to a crawl as my right hand rose, the upper sections of my fingers curled back and the lower joints extended. My flattened hand slipped palm down beneath Ten-Inch's jaw, and I felt my knuckles slam deep into his throat.

Ten-Inch lurched backwards, eyes wide in alarm. Off balance, he tried to counter with a left hook from somewhere in the next county. I saw it coming like he was moving underwater. I let his fist fly close past my jaw, then reached up and grabbed his wrist with my left hand. Using the momentum of his swing against him, I pulled his arm on by and snaked my right arm around his elbow into an arm bar. While Ten-Inch was still following through, I twisted my body violently to the left and slammed my right shoulder against his left one. His momentum and my weight caused Ten-Inch to crash down to the floor, and

I landed hard on his shoulder with my own. Still holding onto his wrist and elbow, I pinned his shoulder to the floor with all my weight and yanked back as hard as I could. His elbow snapped.

Ten-Inch roared. To me it sounded like it was coming from far away. "Give up," I said. He shook his head.

I snapped back on his arm again and felt his shoulder pop. "Quit!" I shouted.

"No!" he screamed.

I yanked back on his separated shoulder again. Ten-Inch screamed, and then his body went limp. I released my arm bar and knelt beside him. I felt for a pulse. He was alive, but unconscious.

With a sudden roar, like a wave breaking as it approaches the shore, my hearing returned to normal. I became aware of the fact that, although my nose was bleeding, my breathing was steady and calm. I sensed my heartbeat, and it was as steady as if I were sitting at the Minotaur, sipping on a cold brew. I looked up at the Northsiders, and they were gawking back at me, transfixed and confused. No one was making a sound.

I stood up. "Someone help me with him," I said. "I need to patch him up."

***

An hour later, I was sitting with Ten-Inch in his Spartan one-bedroom apartment, about two miles from Medusa's. He was propped up on a bare mattress with his back against the wall. I sat in a threadbare cushioned chair across the small living room. That was all the furniture he had. He had transformed the apartment's bedroom into a gym, and it was filled with a collection of free weights, a homemade heavy bag that hung from his ceiling, and a treadmill. The apartment smelled like years of old sweat.

We had taken turns cleaning up in Ten-Inch's shower, and Ten-Inch had loaned me a pair of khakis to replace the blood-soaked pants that I had worn during the fight. They were a little tight around the waist, but the length was right. I had retrieved my shirt, along with my coat and holster, from the Northsiders before leaving Medusa's, and I had them on, too. Ten-Inch was stripped to his boxer shorts. His left arm was pressed against the side of his body with plastic cling wrap. He sat back, relaxed, his left knee pulled up and his right arm hanging loose beside him on the mattress, a half-empty bottle of convenience-store beer in his right hand. He wasn't smiling, but there was no tension in his face or his eyes. He could have been kicking back after a routine day at work.

"I'm going to have a hard time regaining the respect of my tribe," he told me. "I'm going to have to face some challenges to my authority."

"Bullshit," I said. "They saw you give me the beatdown of a lifetime, and you never quit. There isn't a single one of them who doesn't know that you could kick their ass, even with one arm pinned to your side."

Ten-Inch smiled at that. "True," he said. "But I'd be disappointed if a couple of them didn't feel honor-bound to try." He pulled the bottle up to his mouth, leaned his head back, and drained the rest of his beer. When he was finished, he sent the bottle rolling down his hardwood floor. Then he let out a belch long and strong enough to wilt an artificial rose. Looking up at me, he said, "How'd you do that? You were beat. I could see it in your eyes. And then I couldn't hit you anymore. You blocked everything I threw at you. And then, after not hitting me with nothing all night, you land a couple of killer shots and nail me with a submission move that came right out of your ass. Th'fuck, man! How'd you do that?"

I took a pull on my own beer, while I thought about what I was going to do with his question. Finally, I said, "I stopped thinking and trusted instincts that had been buried since I was at the Border."

Ten-Inch shook his head. "Those are some instincts. I guess I woke them up in you. You're welcome." He gave me a self-deprecating smile.

Ten-Inch was right to a point. He had awakened something in me that had been stored away in the seven years since I left the military life. But I knew that my ability to clear my senses and access those instincts had been part of a gift given to me by a creature that most people believed was long extinct. I also suspected that the giver of that gift was going to require more from me than thanks.

"Another beer?" I asked Ten-Inch.

"Yeah, do you mind?"

I got up and grabbed two bottles from his refrigerator. After Ten-Inch knocked back a swallow, he said, "Fuckin' Quapo, man. Fuckin' Quapo. You may not believe me, but I liked the kid. He had potential."

Ten-Inch glanced up at me, but I didn't say anything.

Ten-Inch took another drink. "He couldn't just stay gone, could he," he said. "He shoulda taken off when you gave him the chance. Those tribal ties are strong, though, and he wanted back in. I couldn't allow that. Man in my position can't show weakness."

"You were tough on him," I said.

"Had to be," said Ten-Inch. "He deserted his brothers during a firefight, and they all wanted his blood. So I gave them all a shot at him. I hung him up and let them come at him one at a time with clubs or knives. When it was all over, I put an exclamation point in his face with a forty-four." He looked up at me. "I was in the middle of a big speech about tribal unity when you showed up. Had them in the palm of my hand." He saluted me with his beer bottle and took a swallow.

"So your shot finished him off?" I asked.

Ten-Inch shook his head and waved his bottle at me in dismissal, "Nah, man. I figure that the kid bought it before half the homies had taken their shots. The rest of them were just beatin' and cuttin' a corpse. My shot was just for show."

Something stirred deep inside me. It rumbled and floated to the surface of my mind, like a whale rising from the depths of the ocean to breach. I put my beer bottle down on the floor. I needed to leave.

"Are you gonna be all right?" I asked Ten-Inch. "I need to hit the road."

Ten-Inch shrugged, "Yeah, man, I'm cool." Then he said, "Hey, you know that some people would say that by all rights, you should be the new tribal leader of the Northsiders." He took a swallow from his bottle. "Interested?"

"Nah, man," I said. "That's your job. I wouldn't be able to handle it."

Ten-Inch laughed. "Yeah, probably not. Well, I tried. I guess I'll just have to bust a few heads together until they respect me again. But, seriously, Sarge. If you ever need anything from me, just let me know."

I looked at him for a long moment. "Were you going to kill me tonight?"

"Fuckin' right I was," said Ten-Inch. "I woulda regretted it, but that's part of the deal." He smiled. "No hard feelings, I hope."

I laughed, "Fuck, man. No, no hard feelings on my end. Just do me a favor and let me know if you get the urge to try again. What about you? How do you like me now?"

"Ah, you're all right," Ten-Inch said with an easy tone. "Respect, man."

"Respect," I repeated. We bumped fists and I left.

***

As I drove away from Ten-Inch's place, wondering where I was going to sleep that night, I had a strong feeling that it was all coming together. I was about ninety percent sure that I knew who had killed Mila. Other pieces of the puzzle were falling into place, as well. I knew what I needed to do, but it was going to take a lot of quick preparation. If everything went like I hoped it would, it would all be over soon, one way or the other.

First things first. I was exhausted, but I didn't think that it would be safe for me to return to my own bed tonight. Graham and Stonehammer still had a net out for me. They knew about Crawford, so I couldn't go to him. They would have Lubank staked out, too. The police had ties to every hotel in the city, and I didn't relish the idea of trying to sleep in another cheap motel. Leena wasn't an option, and I didn't trust Atwater. I was getting to like his car, though, and his back seat was calling to me. In the end, I drove to an old quiet working-class residential neighborhood in Placid Point and searched along a street filled with parked cars until I found an empty parking place. I pulled in, took a look around, and climbed into the back seat, trusting that the car's tinted windows would keep me safe from prying eyes until morning. I covered myself with my trench coat and used my empty shoulder holster as a pillow. Within seconds, sleep knocked me out like a lead sap to the back of my skull.

Chapter Twenty-Four

"Okay, so here's my theory," said Kintay. "Don't laugh! Just hear me out and try to keep an open mind."

We were in Kintay's lab, seated on opposite sides of a work table. Kintay hadn't slept at all during the night, and he was hyped up on coffee and amphetamines.

"Okay," I said.

"So the stem cells aren't quite human, and they don't come from gnome, dwarf, troll, or anything else that I could test them against. And they were smuggled in to an abandoned pier at midnight in this rigged locked box, so it's obviously all very secretive and hush-hush, right? So we've got these mysterious stem cells, and there's a conspiracy of silence about them."

Kintay's eyes were wild. Bright red veins pulsed through the whites, and his pupils were tight, tiny pinholes in the middle of his bright robin's-egg irises. "So where do these secret, mysterious stem cells come from? So, okay, here it is." He paused to heighten the magnitude of his revelation. "Space aliens!" he declared.

I suppressed a chuckle. "Space aliens?"

"Don't laugh!" Kintay shouted. "Space aliens! And not just any space aliens—the progenitors of the human race!"

I didn't say anything, and Kintay interpreted my silence as encouragement.

"Hear me out!" he said. "These aliens are our distant ancestors. They colonized the earth long ago, and then more recently they came back to check up on our progress. That's why their stem cells are slightly different from ours, because over time we evolved differently here on earth than they did out there," he waved his hand in the general direction of the sky. "In space! You know, out wherever it is they live. And now they're back, and someone finds out about them. These stem cells are proof of their existence! And they were being sent to someone, I don't know why, but if the knowledge of their existence becomes known, well, who knows what kind of panic it might incite! I'm tellin' you, this stuff is dynamite!"

"Uh-huh," I said.

"You don't believe me," said Kintay. "I expected that. But it makes perfect sense!"

"Let me try another theory on for size," I said.

"Fine!" said Kintay, exasperated. "What?"

"Elves," I said.

"Elves!" Kintay exclaimed. "Don't be ridiculous! Elves don't exist!"

"Says the man who believes in space aliens," I said.

"Oh come on," said Kintay. "Elves? They're just characters in kids' stories and bad horror movies."

"And history books," I said. "We know that they existed until after the Great Rebellion. And then the Dragon Lords tried to exterminate them. But they didn't get them all."

Kintay hesitated. "You believe those stories?"

"It's all there in the history books," I said. "They taught us all about it in school, remember?"

"They taught us a lot of lies in school," Kintay protested. "I never believed half of it."

"But space aliens are cool with you," I said.

Kintay sighed. "Okay, okay. Let's just say—hypothetically—that these stem cells come from an elf. Why would they be so genetically close to human?"

"I don't know," I said. "Maybe elves and humans are genetically closer than humans and, let's say, gnomes."

Kintay considered my idea in silence for a few moments. Then he said, "Elves. Hunh! I have to admit that your theory is every bit as intriguing as my space aliens. And it would shake people up just as much! If you're right, then we are sitting on proof that these creatures from our worst nightmares really exist! In a lot of ways, that's even cooler than space aliens!"

"There's one other thing," I said. "I met an elf a few days ago."

Kintay stared at me with an amused grin on his face. "Bullshit!" he said.

"It's true," I said. "I met him at the abandoned pier the morning before this box was smuggled in." I hesitated. "It was a very strange experience."

"Ahhh!" Kintay said, waving a hand in dismissal, "Now you're just yanking my chain. If you'd rather believe in elves than space aliens, then fuck you." He sighed. "We're probably both full of shit. These cells are fuckin' frustrating! I can tell you for sure what these stem cells aren't. But I can't tell you what they are. If you wanna go with elves, then be my guest. I'm still holding out for space aliens, though."

"A more important question," I said, "is why would anyone want them?"

"Beyond proving that something we don't know about actually exists?" Kintay said. "Well, as it happens, these cells have some interesting genetic properties. I'm pretty sure that whatever creature these cells belong to, elf, space alien, or whatever, it has some unique characteristics."

"Like what?" I asked.

"Well, like I said, the creature would be very humanlike. But his senses would be very highly developed! He'd be able to see like a hawk, pick up scents like a bloodhound, and hear like a...like a...like whatever animal can hear really well. He'd also have a lot of brain power. So kind of an advanced human, like a super-human!"

"Okay," I said, "So how would this be useful to anyone?"

Kintay leaned over the work table. "For one thing," he said, "genes from these cells might have the potential to treat certain medical conditions. Even normal human stem cells can be used to treat specific forms of paralysis, for example. These 'super' stem cells might be able to do more along those lines. Or they might have some potential for treating cancer." He thought for another second, and said, "Here's a more interesting possibility. You could splice genes from these cells into a human embryo. Theoretically, the result would be a highly developed human. Better vision, hearing.... Maybe stronger, more resistant to disease.... More intelligent. That kind of thing."

I thought about what a man like Mayor Teague would want with cells that could be used in such a way. I doubted that he was motivated by something as altruistic as healing the lame or curing cancer. I thought about Kintay's second idea. Maybe Teague thought that he could generate an army of "super-soldiers," or that he could sell the stem cells to someone else with that idea. It sounded like something straight out of a comic book, and I suspected that Kintay and I were totally out of our league, not to mention out of our minds, but I had no doubt that these cells were taking us to realms of possibilities that I had never imagined.

An excited gleam appeared in Kintay's eyes. "But I'll tell you what *I* would do," he said. "I'd clone these cells and start churning out a designer drug! With these cells I could synthesize a hallucinogen that would give the user an *amazing* sense of clarity, like nothing he'd ever known before! He'd think that he was a fuckin' god! Imagine what people would pay to feel like that! All-knowing and all-powerful. Whoever produced a drug that could make a person experience that for a few hours would make billions!"

I didn't like where this was going. "Too bad I'm going to have to take the stuff with me when I go," I said.

Kintay leveled a stare at me. "Yeah, about that...."

Kintay reached into an open shelf on his side of the work table, but I knew exactly what was coming. Time seemed to slow to a crawl, and my focus sharpened. As Kintay's hand emerged from under the table, I was already moving to my feet. As his arm swung upwards, I reached down, grabbed his wrist with one hand, and the gat he was holding with my other. I jerked the gun back against his thumb, which loosened his grip and allowed me to take the gun away from him. I pointed the gun at him, and he froze.

"Sit down," I said.

Kintay's pent-up excitement vanished suddenly like air from a popped balloon. He sighed and plopped down into his seat, holding on to his thumb.

I put the gat into my coat pocket. "Sorry," I said.

"Oh, that's okay," said Kintay. "I don't know what I'd do with billions anyway. But can't you leave me with just a little something? For my time and effort? I worked on that stuff all night, you know."

"I'll owe you," I said. "When this is all over we'll see if we can come to some kind of fair arrangement."

"Fine!" he said, pouting. "I'll hold you to that."

"In the meantime," I said, "I'd like you to do one more thing for me."

"I haven't done enough?" he asked, depression in his voice.

"It's just a little thing," I said. "You still have the box that the cells came in, right?"

"Yeah."

"And where are the cells now?'

"They're in the clean room. Don't worry, they're safe."

"Do you have something that you could transport them in? Something besides the original box?"

"I've got a cooler I could pack them in," Kintay said. "That would keep them fresh for a day or two. After that, they'll have to be transferred into something more permanent."

"Is the battery in the box still good?" I asked.

"Sure," said Kintay. "Those things are good for about a month, and it's got another two weeks' worth of power, at least."

"Good," I said. "I want to put the box back together with some kind of substitute for the original stem cells. And then I want the box all locked up again."

"You're going to try to pass off a bogus package?" asked Kintay, his excitement beginning to grow again.

"That's the plan," I said. "But it's got to look real."

"Once the fake substance is tested, the jig will be up," said Kintay.

"That's okay," I said. "If everything goes right it won't get that far. I just need something that will pass a quick visual examination."

Kintay smiled, and the brightness returned to his eyes. "I've got just the thing," he said. "All I need is a couple of minutes of privacy. And access to my favorite porn site."

"Wait! What? You've gotta be shittin' me!"

"It's perfect!" said Kintay. "I'll mix up a solution that will look exactly like the original. Just give me five minutes, tops!"

***

A half hour later, I pulled into a storage lot and rented a five-by-five unit. I locked two metal boxes in the unit: the box that Graham had smuggled into the pier, and the box that Kintay had referred to as a "cooler." It was made of aluminum and was a little fancier than the coolers used for keeping beer cold at a family picnic, but it served the same basic function. The six plastic tubes of stem cells were stuffed into the cooler, and Kintay had assured me that the chemical freezer packs he had placed into the cooler with the tubes would keep the cells from spoiling for at least another two days. I didn't dwell on what was in the tubes now stored in the original box. I had to admit, though, that the viscous substance appeared to my layman's eyes to be identical to the original.

When I was back in the car, I worked a thread loose from the collar of my trench coat and squeezed the small storage unit key inside. I examined the results of my work and decided that the key would be safe there from all but the most thorough of searches. Satisfied, I started the car and headed for Lubank's office.

I found an empty parking space a few blocks from Lubank's office and put enough money in the meter to keep me from getting another ticket. A blanket of gray clouds hung low in the late morning sky, but the wind gusts were manageable and the air only moderately chilled. I put the collar up on my coat and put on my sunglasses and hat to hide my face. As I walked toward Lubank's office building, I studied the streets for signs of cops. A white van parked within sight of Lubank's building had police surveillance unit written all over it. I ducked into a neighboring building, pulled out my phone, and called Lubank's number.

"Robinson Lubank's," said Gracie's voice.

"Hey, gorgeous," I said. "The boss in?"

"If you think *he's* the boss, then you're off your rocker!" said Gracie. "How're you doing, handsome?"

"You know me," I said. "Getting by."

"I'm glad you called," said Gracie. "Robby wants to see you. Monday would be okay, but sooner is better. Where are you now?"

"Actually," I said, "I'm only a block away from you. But the police have your building under surveillance. Can you tell Rob that I'm here and get me in the back way?"

"Sure, sweetie," said Gracie. "Meet me around back in two minutes. And don't keep me waiting, baby!"

After we disconnected, I summoned Smokey. When the elemental arrived, I brought it just outside the building's entryway and pointed toward the van.

"You see that van there?" I asked, pointing.

"The metal moving box?" Smokey hissed.

"Yes, the big white one. I'm going into that building over there. If anyone comes out of that van and enters that building, come and tell me. Understand?"

"Smokey understands."

"And do you remember that troll that I had you follow?"

"Smokey remembers."

"If you see that troll around here, come and tell me immediately," I said.

"Smokey understands."

I left Smokey in the street and headed for the back of Lubank's building.

When I was in Lubank's office, he said, "Lord Alkwat's pecker! Th'fuck you been up to? You've got the freakin' police on my doorstep now?"

"Just a routine day for you, isn't it?" I said.

"Fuck you!" said Lubank. "Hey, I've got some papers for you to sign. Some protection for when you get arrested again. I figure that with you, it's inevitable. These papers make me your attorney of record and give me the power to intervene on your behalf and do stuff you're not smart enough to do for yourself. It's standard shit."

"Can I get an attorney to look it over?" I asked.

"Don't be a fuckin' wise guy!"

I skimmed through the paperwork and signed the appropriate spaces. Then I told Lubank about my meeting with Fulton, along with some of the other adventures I'd been having since we last saw each other.

"Holy fuck!" said Lubank. "You've been fighting gangsters? With your fists? What kind of barbarian are you? That explains your new bruises." He shook his head. "But Fulton? You're in deep, my man! Fulton is big trouble."

"Don't you have any leverage on him?" I asked. "Some blackmail or something?"

Lubank snorted. "Fulton has done a lot of things that a normal person would want to hide. But the bastard isn't ashamed of anything! Also," Lubank said with something that sounded like respect, "he's got more dirt on the people of this city than *I* do. Especially the people in power. I'd give my left nut to have a half hour with his computer files!"

"Are you saying that he's out of your league?" I said.

"Fuck you! Fuck you and the horse you rode in on!"

Just then, Smokey whisked into the room and hovered between the two of us. I could sense its excitement.

"Gaaaa!" Lubank bellowed. "Get that demon out of here!"

I ignored him. "What is it?" I asked Smokey.

"The troll is outside of the building," Smokey hissed.

"It's Stonehammer," I told Lubank. "He's coming up."

"Oh shit!" said Lubank. "Let me deal with him. You can hide in my library."

"Wait," I said. "Do you have anything on Stonehammer?"

"Plenty!" said Lubank. "But probably nothing that would stop him if he's determined."

"He's got a weakness," I said. "Do you know about his sister? He seems to care about her a lot. She lives on a ranch up north that his family has been running for generations. He writes her letters every month telling her that he's a good, clean cop who solves crimes like the good-guy cops in movies. She idolizes him. She doesn't know that he's nothing but a sadistic leg-breaker."

"That's great!" said Lubank. "I can use that! Now get into the library. And take your demon with you!"

He ushered me through a door in the back of his office to a room filled with books. In the center of the room was a table and some office chairs.

"And look," said Lubank before closing me in. "No matter what happens, stay right where you are. I've got this! You hear me? You stay there! Let me and Gracie handle this." He closed the door. I got next to it and focused my hearing.

I heard the door to the reception lounge open, followed by a deep rumbling cough. Gracie said, "May I help you?"

"Sure, doll-face," said the charming voice of Stonehammer. "Tell your boss that Detective Stonehammer is here to see him, and I don't plan on cooling my heels in his outer office."

Gracie called Lubank, and Lubank told her to send Stonehammer in.

"What the fuck are you doing here?" said Lubank after Stonehammer had entered his office and closed the door.

"That's not the way you talk to a police officer," Stonehammer admonished.

"Fuck you!" said Lubank. "What'd'you want? I'm busy!"

"Not too busy to help out in a police matter, I hope," Stonehammer growled. "I'm looking for your client, Alexander Southerland. He hasn't been home in a few days. He knows that the police would like to question him, and it occurred to me that his lawyer might be stashing him somewhere. So I'll tell you what. You give him up to me quick, and I won't hurt you much when I'm belting you around."

I tensed up, ready to help Lubank if Stonehammer got rough.

"Don't threaten me, you fuckin' ape. Graham released Southerland, and I know for a fact that he won't take him into custody again. Even if I knew where Southerland was—and I don't—I wouldn't give him up to Graham's Goon."

"Don't call me that, asshole!" growled Stonehammer. I heard the sound of flesh smacking flesh and nearly charged through the door. But I restrained myself, remembering that Lubank had told me to stay put no matter what. I waited to see what would happen next.

"You'll pay for that, you fuckin' pile of shit!" Lubank shouted. "I'll have your job for that! And then I'll sue you for everything else you've got! You cops may think that you own this city, but I've got a dozen judges in my pocket who will be more than happy to take your badge and lock you up in Q with the criminals you've helped put away. Believe me, they'd *love* to see you again!"

In the silence that followed, I could imagine the electric stare-down between the monstrous angry troll and the four-foot gnome with the ridiculous hairpiece.

It was Stonehammer who relented, "All right," he said. "No reason to get sore. Just stop trying to insult me and we'll get along fine."

"All right, then," said Lubank. "Like I said, I don't know where Southerland is if he isn't at home. What do you want him for?"

"He's got something Graham wants," Stonehammer said. "I think you know what I'm talking about. I'm thinking that it's something he might have left with his lawyer."

"Ohhh, the box!" said Lubank. "Well why didn't you say so to begin with?"

I wondered what Lubank was playing at.

"Do you got it?" Stonehammer asked.

"Maybe," said Lubank.

"It's worth a fortune, you know," said Stonehammer.

"Is it?"

"More than he probably told you," Stonehammer said.

"Is that right?"

"Seems to me," said Stonehammer, "that you and I might be able to make a deal. A *private* deal, if you get my drift."

"What are you saying?" asked Lubank.

"The way I see it," said Stonehammer, "Southerland has dragged some big trouble across your desk. Trouble you don't need. And Graham has got me running all over this city for a package that is going to make him rich, but which isn't going to do me any good at all. Doesn't seem right."

"Keep talking," said Lubank.

"Now, if I can get my hands on this box...." Stonehammer paused for effect. "Then I could sell it to the guy that Graham was going to sell it to, and we could split the profits, you and me. Graham don't have to even know about it, and as for Southerland...." There was another pause, and then Stonehammer said, "Fuck him. The dough you get from selling the box will be a hell of a lot more than what you'd ever get from representing Southerland. Hell, you could probably retire!"

"Interesting," said Lubank. "But what makes you think I know where the box is?"

"Come on," said Stonehammer. "You're a smart guy. You've probably got the box where you can get to it in a hurry. Maybe right here in your office. I'll bet you've been arranging for a buyer all along. Well, I know who was going to buy it from Graham. I'll give you his name, and you can make the deal.

You're probably better at negotiations than I am. More dough for us both!"

"But I already know that Fulton is the buyer," said Lubank. "So what do I need *you* for?"

I heard a growl rise up from Stonehammer's chest. "Give me the box," he shouted. "Or I'll punch your ticket for good and tear up this room looking for it!"

I had my hand on the door knob, but stopped just short of turning it. I heard Lubank shout, "Don't move, you fucking idiot! Before you do something that you'll regret, I've got something that I want you to see."

I heard some shuffling, and then I heard Stonehammer's voice from a speaker saying, "Now, if I can get my hands on this box...then I could sell it to the guy that Graham was going to sell it to, and we could split the profits, you and me. Graham don't have to even know about it, and as for Southerland...fuck him."

"That's right, detective," said Lubank. "I've been videocording this entire meeting. And look at this—three different views from three different cameras! Now watch this, this is cool. See? I can put all of the angles together into a three-hundred-sixty degree three-dimensional view! It's amazing what you can do with computer software these days."

There was a long pause. It was Lubank who broke it, "Now, Detective.... What's your boss going to think when he sees you offering to take his box and sell it to Fulton without cutting him in on the deal? Oh my goodness! I'll bet that he'll come unglued! I wouldn't want to be in your shoes trying to explain it to him."

Stonehammer laughed. It sounded forced to me. He said, "But Mr. Lubank. Can't you see that I was bullshitting you? I was just trying to get you to give me the box so that I could deliver it to Captain Graham. I wouldn't cheat him. He trusts me! And that's 'cause I've always come through for him. Show him your video! I don't give a shit, and neither will he."

When Lubank didn't say anything, Stonehammer continued. "Now, what I'm going to do is search your office. I'm not going to be nice about it. You'll be cleaning up the mess for months. And your precious computers will probably get obliterated in the process. But first, I'm going to break some of your fingers for trying to blackmail a cop. Nothing personal, but I can't have you thinking that you can fuckin' get away with something like that. I'm a fuckin' cop, and you need to show me the proper respect."

"One second," said Lubank. "You might want to look at this first."

I was getting anxious, but Lubank didn't sound concerned. Soon I heard the sound of smacking flesh coming through a speaker.

"That's you, in three-D," said Lubank. "Roughing me up a little earlier."

"So what?" said Stonehammer. "That's nothing compared to what I'm about to do to you now. Do you think Graham cares about that? He's seen me do much worse."

"I'm sure he has," said Lubank. "That's what you do for him, right? Rough people up? He's probably seen you kill some of the people that you've roughed up, hasn't he."

Stonehammer's chuckle sounded evil. "He doesn't stick around for most of the rough stuff. But, yeah, he's seen me ice a few guys. Like you say, that's what I do, and I'm good at it. But don't worry. I'll keep you alive long enough to wish I'd put you away for good."

"Tough-talkin' motherfucker, aren't you," said Lubank.

"Yeah," said Stonehammer. "And I back up every word."

"Gracie?" Lubank said.

"Yes, Robby?" Gracie's voice came from a speaker in Lubank's office.

"You know what to do, right?" said Lubank.

"Sure do, sweetie!"

"What the fuck?" said Stonehammer, mirroring my own thoughts.

"At the next sign of trouble from you," said Lubank, "Gracie will punch a button. When she does, my cool little three-D video will be sent to Graham."

"So what?" Stonehammer roared in disbelief. "I already told you that he won't give a flying fuck!"

"Maybe," said Lubank. "But another copy of my video will be sent to another interested party. Namely, your sister, up there on your family ranch. The one who believes that you're a good, honest, crime-solving detective, like she sees in the movies. The one who idolizes you, loves and respects you. I wonder if she'll continue to respect you when she hears you trying to make that deal with me. It didn't sound like the kind of thing an honest cop would do. It sounded kind of shady. More like a deal that the bad cops in the movies make. Well, I don't know. Maybe she'll buy your bullshit explanation. Love can be blind, they say. But I wonder what she'll think when she sees you roughing up a little old middle-aged gnome, half your size, and threatening him with more. I wonder how she'll react when she hears you confess that, far from being an intellectual crime-solver, you're nothing but a professional thug. A leg-breaker. What will she do when she hears from your own lips that you're a murderer? Think she'll still be proud of her big brother then? Think you'll still be her hero?" Lubank let it sink in. "Gracie is watching you right now," Lubank said after a pause. "One move. One threatening move. One threatening word from you! That's all it will take. Her finger is on the send button right now. All she has to do is twitch—even involuntarily!—and your sister will see you in action in high-def three-D. No—don't talk! Don't say another fucking word. Just turn around and walk out of here. And don't ever let me see you again. Gracie has already made a dozen copies of the video and stored them in places you'll never find. Anything suspicious happens to me, and those videos will be showing up all over the place. On social media, on your boss's computer, on the computers of a dozen judges, in media outlets all over town, and on telephones and computers of your sister and all of her friends. So bye-bye. Off you go now."

The next sound I heard was Lubank's door opening and Stonehammer's feet hitting the floor as he stomped out of the inner office, out of Gracie's reception area, and out the door into the hallway.

Chapter Twenty-Five

"Did you really have that video ready to send to Stonehammer's sister?" I asked. Lubank, Gracie, and I were in the inner office holding glasses of Lubank's smooth avalonian whiskey.

"Of course not!" said Lubank. "Until you told me, I didn't even know that Stonehammer *had* a sister! And all you told me was that she lived on a family ranch up north. I don't know her email address, her phone number—I don't even know her fuckin' name!" He took a sip of whiskey. "I'm going to have to get all that, though, and soon. Why don't I contract that job out to you? It will take care of a small, tiny fraction of what you're going to wind up owing me."

"Yeah, I'll get right on it," I said. "Soon as I can free some time up from my busy schedule." I raised my glass and took a mouthful of burning liquid gold from distant Avalon. I swirled it around in my mouth before swallowing it, and thought about what a contrast it was to Stonehammer's home-brewed firewater. Like the difference between a warm soapy shower and a cold acid bath. I thought about how Stonehammer was getting out of hand. He had sent his men after Crawford, and now he had tried to strongarm Lubank. He and Graham needed to be stopped. I put my glass down on the table and said to Lubank, "I'll get you your info, but I need you to do something for me first."

"Th'fuck you want now, you ingrate!"

"I want you to call Graham," I said. "Tell him that I want to make a deal."

"You're shittin' me!" said Lubank.

"Tell him that I want to meet him tonight, but not at the station." I thought a second. "Tell him that I want to meet him on the old Placid Point Pier, right where this all began. Let's make it at midnight, because why not? Tell him that I'm bringing the box, and that I'm willing to sell it to him for a fair price. You can negotiate it. It doesn't have to be a great deal, but it has to be for something that he'll be willing to wire directly to my account tonight. It's got to be tonight. That's important. I'll trust you with the particulars. After all, you've got my power of attorney, right?"

Lubank stared at me with an amused expression.

"Oh," I said. "Tell him that Stonehammer has to be there with him tonight. That's non-negotiable."

"How am I supposed to do that?" said Lubank.

"Tell him that I think Stonehammer's gone rogue. It's probably true. Stonehammer has been seriously fucking up lately, and he's in Graham's doghouse. Tell Graham what Stonehammer tried to do in here this morning. I doubt that he was acting with Graham's blessing. Be sure to mention that he tried to make a deal with you that would have aced Graham right out of the picture. Graham will love that! Anyway, tell Graham that I don't trust Stonehammer, and that I want him squarely in my sight when we do the deal tonight. If he's not there, then it's no deal."

"All right," said Lubank. "Anything else?"

"Yeah," I said. "I need a few things." I told him what I needed.

Afterwards, I made two phone calls. The first was to Leena. We had a good long talk. The second was to Ten-Inch. He was doing fine, he said, and he was willing to do what I wanted him to do. Eager, even, since it helped him with his own situation.

When I disconnected, I considered my plan, looking for holes. I found plenty, but what plan ever survives the beginning of the battle anyway? I'd just have to be prepared to improvise when necessary. After I thought that I had considered every angle, I grabbed up my coat, hat, and sunglasses and said my goodbyes to the Lubanks.

"Don't get your face messed up any more than it is already, handsome," said Gracie.

"You'll be getting my bill at the end of next week," said Lubank.

I kissed Gracie on the cheek, gave Lubank the finger, and left their office.

***

"That's Jaguar over there with his boys," said Ten-Inch. He was standing next to me in the parking lot at the old Placid Point Pier. "Looks like they're early."

"So are we," I said.

It was fifteen minutes short of midnight. Twenty Northsiders were lined up to the right of the empty parking lot behind Ten-Inch and me. Twenty members of the Claymore Cartel, along with their leader, Jaguar, piled out of three vans and meandered over to the left side of the lot. Stonehammer's silver sedan pulled into the lot, and the troll got out of the car from the driver's side. He hustled around the car like a servant and opened the passenger door. Graham got out, and the two of them walked over to join Jaguar. Graham and Jaguar exchanged a few words, and then the three of them came over to the center of the lot. I walked over with Ten-Inch and joined them.

I didn't pay much attention to Jaguar, noting only that he was younger than I expected, dark-haired and dark-eyed, radiated intensity, and appeared to be formidable. He also had purple wings tattooed under his eyes. Whatever.

Graham and I came face to face. We didn't shake hands. "Let's do our business at the end of the wharf," I said. "Your detective can come with you. The homeboy stays here." Jaguar tried to reduce me to tears with his most intimidating glare. I ignored him. He was Ten-Inch's problem.

"I'll need to search you," said Graham.

I held out my arms and Stonehammer conducted a rough, but thorough and efficient search. He returned my phone, which he had pulled out of my inside coat pocket, but I was otherwise unarmed.

I conducted my own search of both Stonehammer and Graham. Each of them carried a flashlight on his belt, but neither had weapons. All of this trust made me feel peachy. Well, the gangsters were armed. That's why the rest of us didn't need to be.

Graham asked me, "Are you coming alone then?"

In answer, I concentrated and summoned Badass, who appeared with a sudden whoosh a few seconds later. He took up a position next to me, twelve feet tall, looming over Stonehammer. The troll's eyes went wide, and then narrowed at me. Graham fell back a step.

"You want to search it?" I asked them.

"Hilarious," said Graham. "What are you planning on doing with that thing?"

"That's my bodyguard," I said. "Don't bother me and it won't bother you."

Graham hesitated and Stonehammer growled, but Graham nodded and said, "Fine. Let's go do this."

Graham, Stonehammer, Badass, and I left the gangsters behind in their battle lines and walked to the end of the pier. Heavy clouds rolled across the night sky, and the wind off the water was fierce. I had the collar of my trench coat turned up, and I had my hand on my fedora to keep it from blowing into the next county. I carried a locked box in my other hand. The box containing Kintay's contribution to his potential progeny.

Waves crashed against the end of the wooden wharf, and the wharf's pilings shuddered under the pressure of the angry Nihhonese Ocean. Pools of saltwater that had splashed onto the deck of the wharf indicated the severity of the turbulence. The elf's message had been on the money: we were in for a wild night on the west coast tonight.

After we reached the end of the wharf, Graham glanced toward the box secured in my arm. "That's it?" he asked.

"Take a look," I said, and I handed him the box.

Graham knelt to one knee, placed the box on the deck, and pulled a key out of his coat pocket. He put it in the keyhole on the right side of the box and gave it a quarter turn. He then gave the left keyhole a half turn. He went back to the right keyhole and gave it another quarter turn. Then he carefully opened the box. He unhooked his flashlight from his belt and used it to illuminate the contents. Then he looked up at me with a satisfied expression.

I reached down, pushed the box shut, and, before he could stop me, I pulled the box back into my arms. "Your turn," I said.

Graham frowned. "Give me the box, and I'll give you your money," he said.

"Uh-uh," I said. "That's not how this goes. You wire me my money. When I get confirmation that the dough is in my bank account, I give you the box. You've looked inside, so you know that it's legit. But no money, no deal."

Graham sighed, turned to Stonehammer, and said, "Go ahead."

Stonehammer hesitated for a second, and then pulled a tablet out from the inside of his coat. Shielding it from the moisture blowing off the water, he tapped at it with a stylus. He looked down at Graham, who nodded. The troll gave the tablet one last tap and put the tablet back inside his coat.

I held my phone in my hand. After about fifteen seconds, the phone buzzed and vibrated. I looked at the screen and saw that I had a notification from my bank. A couple of clicks later, I found that my bank account balance had increased from "living day-to-day" to "financially secure." I smiled and put my phone away.

"You guys have been great," I said. "Now there's just a couple more little details that we have to iron out."

Graham's eyes narrowed. Stonehammer tensed. A growl crawled up from his chest.

"Badass," I said. "If that troll takes one step toward me, do everything in your power to stop him."

The elemental's deep moaning howl rose above the wind: "Badass understands."

Stonehammer didn't move, but he continued to glower at me with his burning red eye.

"What are you trying to pull, Southerland," said Graham.

"Relax," I said. "We're all good. I have every intention of fulfilling my side of the deal. Like I said, I just need to take care of a couple of matters." I paused. "I had a meeting with Lawrence Fulton yesterday." Graham's eyes widened. "He offered to buy the box from me. Actually, he offered me a lot more money than you just paid me. A whole lot more. I'm guessing that it's the same agreement that he made with you." Graham looked a little confused. "But I'd rather deal with you, Graham. Even if I'm taking a big loss."

Graham continued to look confused. Stonehammer stopped growling. He looked confused, too.

I continued, "But Fulton offered me one more thing, and before I hand over this box, you're going to have to match it."

"What the fuck are you talking about, Southerland!" said Graham. "We had a deal! We've already paid you what your lawyer said you wanted. He never mentioned anything else."

"The money is fine," I said. "But Fulton offered me something else that I want: justice for Mila Waterfowl."

"What?" Graham exclaimed.

"It's simple," I said. "I need you to tell me who killed her. And I need the killer to pay. Fulton doesn't actually know who killed Mila. Not yet, anyway. But you do, don't you. Tell me who killed Mila, and you get the box. Otherwise, I take the box and return your money. That's the deal."

"This is an outrage!" said Graham, sputtering a little in the cold wet wind. "I don't know who killed that little twist!"

"Please, Graham, don't take me for an idiot. You know everything. You were there. Don't lie to me." I paused. Graham didn't speak, so I continued. "I had a talk with Quapo a couple of nights ago. You know who he is. He told me how you had him lure Mila out of my apartment and into his van, where you and the detective here were waiting for her. He told me how he dropped off the two of you and the girl in the adaro settlement and then drove off. Mila was killed there. I visited the crime scene with Kraken, Mila's adaro friend, and he confirmed that Mila had been there. He smelled her blood on the sidewalk. They can do that. So don't tell me," I said, "that you don't know what happened. It won't fly."

Graham and Stonehammer exchanged a glance. Stonehammer nodded. "Tell him," he rumbled.

Graham took a look at Badass before turning back to me. "Okay," he said. "I'll tell you, and then you give me the box and walk away, right? Yeah, we were there. The detective...interrogated the girl, but she wouldn't talk."

Graham paused and took another look at Stonehammer, who frowned at him. "Tell him!" said the troll.

Graham gathered himself. He rubbed his ungloved hands together and blew some warmth into them. He took a breath. When he was done stalling, or talking himself into something, he spoke. "All right. I didn't want to have to do this, but all right. I guess I should come clean." He made a point of looking straight into my eyes. "What you don't know," he said, "is that while we were questioning the girl, Leena showed up. I don't know exactly how she knew where we were. She followed us, I guess." He glanced again at Badass. "She controls water elementals, you know. All the adaro do. So maybe she used elementals to find us. Or maybe one of her adaro friends spotted us. They might have called her. She would have had time to find us. We, uh.... We took our time questioning the girl. Her sister, I mean. We were at it for a while...." He waved away whatever else he was going to say about that. "Anyway, Leena showed up. She wants the box as much as I do, you know. But she wasn't real happy about what we had been doing to find out its whereabouts. She told us to give her some privacy with her sister. She said that she could get the location from her."

A wave crashed against the end of the pier, and we all shielded ourselves from the splash. When it subsided, Graham continued. "So the detective and I went a little way off and let Leena have at it. After a minute or so...." he glanced up at Stonehammer, as if seeking verification. Then he turned back to me and caught my eyes again. "After a minute or so, we heard a shot. We ran over, and Leena was kneeling over the girl's body. Leena had a gun in her hand, and the girl had a hole in her head." He stopped.

"So you're telling me that it was Leena who killed her sister?" I asked.

"That's right," said Graham. "Leena killed her. She said that she got the location of the box from her, and then she shot her."

"Why would she do that to her own sister?" I asked.

Graham scowled. "Leena *hated* her sister. She told me that she had raised the girl like a daughter, but that the girl was nothing but an ungrateful bitch. The girl treated Leena like shit because of her...profession. She never showed her any respect. And she was running around with that gang. Selling and using illegal drugs, too, she said. I guess she'd just had it. Anyway, that's what happened. Satisfied? Now give me the box!"

I nodded. "Just one more thing," I said. "That elemental that tried to kill me at the crime scene. Was that Leena's doing?"

Graham nodded. "Yeah. She set you up. We planned that one together. Only the elemental wasn't going to kill you. She knew that you had the box, but we didn't know where you were hiding it! So she sent you to where she had killed her sister and arranged for the elemental to grab you. It was just going to incapacitate you until me and Stonehammer could get there. But by the time we got there you were with that big adaro." Graham hesitated. "Just out of curiosity, what happened there?"

"The elemental had me all right," I said. "The big adaro pulled me out of it."

Graham nodded. "Thought it must have been something like that. Anyway, when we got there and saw the two of you, we backed off and then followed you to Medusa's. Stonehammer grabbed you when you came out. You know the rest."

We sat in silence for a few moments. I listened to the wind and the crashing waves. Then I called out in a loud voice, "Did you get all that Leena?"

A saltwater puddle near the edge of the wharf expanded into a wide cylindrical water spout, about six feet tall. Leena, dripping wet, stepped out of the spout holding a twenty-five caliber pocket pistol in her hand. The pistol was pointed at Graham.

"You bastard!" Leena hissed. "You son of a bitch!"

"Leena, wait!" Graham held his hands in front of his face, as if they could stop bullets. "Don't shoot! Please!"

"You killed my sister!" Leena screamed. "And now you're trying to pin it on me!"

"No, baby!" Graham shouted. "It's not like that!"

"No? Really? Then why are you lying?" Leena aimed her pistol at Graham's chest.

"Please! Don't!" I didn't mean any of it!" Graham pointed at me. "I was just trying to throw him off track!"

"Then tell him the truth!" Leena shouted.

I became aware of the sound of gunshots from behind me. The standoff between the two gangs had come to an end.

"Okay! Okay!" Graham sputtered. "You weren't there. I lied about that."

"That's right," Leena said. "I was in the condo, clearing out my things. Because I was going to leave you! You put me behind bars like a common criminal, you asshole! You think I'd ever forget that? And then you came to me that morning and told me that Mr. Southerland had killed Mila. But it wasn't him, was it!" Leena raised the gun to point at Graham's head. "It was you! You killed my sister! And now--"

"Don't!" I shouted. "Graham didn't kill Mila!"

Leena's eyes never left Graham, but she didn't pull the trigger. "What?" she shouted.

"Mila was already dead," I said. "She died while Stonehammer was trying to beat the location of the box out of her. Graham shot her in the head after she was dead." Just like Quapo.

"That's ridiculous!" said Graham. "Why would I shoot someone who was already dead?'

"Because Stonehammer told you to," I said, watching Stonehammer. The troll hadn't moved since Leena had emerged from the elemental. He looked back and forth between Badass and me, calculating. I turned to Leena. "Stonehammer killed Mila," I told her. "He beat her to death during his so-called interrogation. And then he told Graham that he could pin it on you. He wanted you out of Graham's life, and he figured that this was his opportunity. He convinced Graham to shoot your sister with his pocket pistol." Leena was looking away from Graham and at me now. "He has a pistol that matches the one you're holding, doesn't he."

"Yes," said Leena. "He bought matching pistols and gave this one to me."

"Stonehammer wanted to frame you for the murder. He hates what you've done to Graham. He thinks that you've turned his captain into a pussy-whipped weakling. He wanted to get you out of the way and bring his old captain back. So he talked Graham into setting up a frame. And Graham agreed, because maybe he agrees with Stonehammer. Maybe he's tired of being under your thumb."

"No, that's bullshit! I couldn't go through with it, baby!" Graham said, trying to smile. "He's right about Stonehammer wanting me to frame you, but I couldn't do it! I pinned it on Southerland, instead. And it's not too late! We can still do it! He's the perfect fall guy. We'll take Southerland out of the picture, and Fulton will pay us a fortune for the box. All that dough, baby, for you and me!"

Shots continued to ring out from the parking lot. Leena kept the gun pointed at Graham. Stonehammer stared at Graham with disgust. None of us moved.

"It won't work," I said. "An autopsy will prove that Stonehammer beat Mila to death, and that she was dead before she was shot."

Graham laughed. "I had her body cremated, you fucking loser!" He shouted.

"You tried to," I said. "But at least a couple of your people work for Fulton. He has the body, and he'll be happy to find out how she died."

"That's a lie!" Graham shouted.

"No, it's the truth," I said. "Like I said, I met with him yesterday. He's got the body all right. Safe and sound, where you can't touch it."

Graham turned to Leena. "It doesn't matter, baby. We can still say that it was Southerland who beat her to death."

"I think an autopsy will show clearly enough that it was a troll who killed Mila," I said. Stonehammer's head shot up and he bared his teeth at me.

Leena continued to stare at Graham. She began to speak, measuring each word. "You were going to frame me," she said. "You tried to. Tonight. I heard you do it. You say that Stonehammer talked you into it, but you *let* him. Because you were *tired* of me!"

"No, baby! That's not how it is!" Graham went down on one knee and lifted his hands, pleading with Leena. "Please! Think of the money! Just you and me, baby. Please! Put the gun away!"

Stonehammer opened his mouth to say something, but closed it and shook his head. He sighed and glowered at Graham, his one good eye nearly hidden under his heavy brow. Something was happening there, and I decided to push it.

"Oh, I almost forgot," I said, taking out my phone. "You all might be interested in this" I held up my phone, screen out. "I've been recording this whole meeting on video. My lawyer provided me with three really nifty cameras, and I came out here earlier this evening and mounted them at the end of this pier." I pointed to where I had attached each of the cameras to the railings, one to either side of us, and one at the end of the wharf. "It's dark out here, but my lawyer assures me that these cameras are equipped with some state-of-the-art high-tech shit that allows them to shoot at night. The quality won't be great, he tells me, but it should be good enough. Hey, Stonehammer! You know how these cameras work, right? My lawyer says that you saw them in action earlier this morning. Some fancy software merges the images into a three-hundred-sixty degree three-dimensional video that looks almost like a hologram! See?" I held up my phone, though I doubted that anyone would be able to make anything out on the tiny screen, especially in the dark. I had no trouble seeing it, though. It was working just fine.

I glanced at Stonehammer. The rage that was building in him from watching his captain grovel in front of his mistress and listening to me explain the reality of his situation was causing his whole body to tremble. Veins were sticking out of his neck, and his eye was burning bright enough to cast the rest of us in a red glow. He was ready to explode. I gave him another nudge. "I'm broadcasting this meeting live to my lawyer right now, and, when we're all done, he'll send it to Fulton. Fulton is going to see and hear everything!"

The storm that had been building in Stonehammer reached its breaking point, and the troll could no longer contain it. "This is bullshit!" he bellowed, and I felt the whole pier shake. Probably from the waves. Not from the troll's rage. Probably. I hoped that I hadn't made a mistake.

Stonehammer squared his body at Graham. "You fuckin' cocksucker!" he thundered. "You little bitch! I gave you a chance to get out from under that fucking whore's spell, and you pussied out! You're hopeless! She's got your balls in her pocket, and you fuckin' love it! I'm done with you, you useless piece of shit!"

Before any of us could move, Stonehammer wrapped his massive hand around Graham's neck. Graham tried to scream, but his airway had been cut off. Leena turned the gun on Stonehammer and fired. The bullet tore through the troll's coat and hit him in the chest.

"You think that little peashooter can hurt me?" Stonehammer roared. He shook Graham hard by the neck. Graham's arms dropped, and his head lolled to one side. Leena fired again. Stonehammer threw Graham's body to the deck. Twisting his enormous body around faster than I thought he was capable of moving, he thrust out his arm and snatched Leena's gun away from her. He flung it over the railing with contempt.

Just then, something jolted me from behind. I nearly fell to my knees, but managed to stay on my feet. Looking down, I saw blood leaking out of my left shoulder. I turned to look back down the wharf and saw two of the Cartel gangsters aiming their rods at me.

"Badass!" I shouted. I pointed at the gunmen. "Attack those two! Don't allow anyone to approach from that direction!" Badass whooshed away.

When I turned back around, Stonehammer was smiling at me. He took one step toward me and ripped the box out of my arms. "I'll take this," he said. He lashed out with his free hand and aimed a backhanded fist at my head. The force of the blow would have broken my neck, but I saw it coming just soon enough to turn to the side and take most of the blow with my shoulder. Unfortunately, it was the shoulder that had been shot. I flew against the railing and struggled to keep myself from tumbling into the crashing waves. I heard a scream. I turned and saw Stonehammer towering over Leena, who was cringing on one knee, awaiting the worst. I was sprawled on the deck. My left arm was numb. There was nothing I could do.

Then I saw a burst of water rise over the far end of the pier. Kraken emerged from it and landed on his feet behind Stonehammer. "Mila!" he roared, his cry reverberating in the wind like a thunderclap. The troll turned, and Kraken wrapped his massive arms around him, crushing him into his chest. The adaro buried his teeth into Stonehammer's neck, and blood spurted onto his face. Stonehammer howled and tried to force a hand under Kraken's chin, but Kraken lifted Stonehammer off his feet. The adaro flexed his knees and launched himself backward, the troll still pressed against his body. The two of them crashed through the railing and into the churning waters. The box, still in Stonehammer's hand, went with them.

I pulled myself up and stumbled to the railing at the back of the wharf. I peered into the dark swirling waters. Neither Kraken nor Stonehammer were anywhere to be seen.

A piece of the deck in front of my foot ripped away as a bullet buried itself in the wood. I turned and looked back down the pier. Badass was halfway down the wharf whirling like a tornado. The elemental had ripped away part of the railing and was hurling chunks of jagged wooden debris at the crowd of gangsters. But Jaguar was stretched out on his stomach just beyond Badass and drawing a bead on me. I hit the deck, and a bullet flew past me over my head. Unarmed, I had no hope of getting off the pier in that direction. I stared down at the roiling water. There was no escape there, either. I was trapped.

Leena was calling my name. I looked up and saw her standing by the railing on the left side of the wharf. A water spout had risen out of the waves next to her. "Come with me!" she shouted at me. "It's your only chance!"

Leena was treacherous. She had fed me one lie after another. She had lured me into a trap and nearly killed me with an elemental. That much of Graham's story had been true. But she was my only way out. Could I trust her? Could I afford not to?

A bullet slammed into the back of my left leg. I looked up and saw that Jaguar, blood from a slashed forehead dripping over the wings tattooed to his face, had managed to make his way past Badass and was charging at me, gat in hand. He was no more than ten yards away.

"Hurry!" screamed Leena.

I reached out and grabbed her hand.

Epilogue

Three days later, Stonehammer's body washed up on a rocky stretch of shore a couple of miles south of the city. His obituary appeared in the newspaper two days after that. The detective was praised for his valor. It stated that he gave his life in the service of the city, helping to stop a vicious gang war at the old abandoned Placid Point Pier. He will be buried with honors next Sunday on the same day as his beloved commander, Captain Gerald "Gerry" Graham, who also died in the gang battle. May they both rest in peace.

***

The "gang battle" was an inconclusive bloodbath. Ten-Inch and Jaguar suffered only minor injuries, but they both lost so many of their followers that they were forced to come to a one-year agreement concerning the old pier. According to the agreement, each gang will have access to the disputed territory on alternate weeks. Ten-Inch gives the agreement about four months, which he says should be long enough for his tribe to recover and go back on the attack. "I need some time to rehab my arm," he told me. "I also need to take care of some internal matters. The battle didn't turn out too bad for me, actually. A couple of potential threats to my authority bought it during the fight. Just between the two of us, I might have helped one of them along. And besides, winter is coming. Winter is a bad time for a war. Spring is a time for renewal. We'll be ready to rumble by then."

***

I'm still cleaning up my office and apartment, but at least I was able to pay the rent on time. In fact, I paid six months' rent in advance. I felt a great weight fall from my shoulders when I put the check in the mail. I'd rather go another round with a troll than disappoint Mrs. Colby.

***

After taking the beastmobile to an auto detailer to clean the odor of gasoline out of the interior, I took it back to Atwater and tried to return it. But Atwater claimed that he could still smell the fumes and insisted that I buy the car from him. He actually offered me a nice deal, and I took it. I figured that if my apartment ever got trashed again, most of my belongings would fit in the car's cavernous trunk, and I could always sleep on the back seat. I took the car back to the detailer and had all of the decals removed. Then I had the exterior repainted a sort of innocuous brownish purple color that the detailer called "deep taupe." Whatever. The car is still a monster, but at least the color doesn't stand out. I kept the red interior, though. It seemed like too much trouble to change it.

I never did pick up my old sedan from the impound lot.

Atwater told me that Leena had come back to work for him. He said that she probably had about six or so years in her before she would be too old for the job, but he expected that he would lose her to another Graham long before then. "She'll find another wealthy and powerful mark in no time," Atwater told me. "She's ambitious, she's got a nose for dough, and she can spot a soft touch a mile away. There's no way that woman doesn't wind up in the lap of luxury, living the good life." Leena had saved my ass on the pier, whisking me away from the gunfire in her water elemental, and I wished her well. But I hoped that I would never see her again. A woman like Leena is only on your side when you're helping her, and any man in the same room with her, no matter how smart and tough he thinks he is, is in over his head.

***

Officer Littlecrow called to tell me that after Graham's death, Internal Affairs had searched his computer files and found details of enough corruption in the YCPD to keep his department busy for years. "At least eight high ranking officials in the department will be resigning within the month," he told me. "It's going to be a major shakeup. There's a guy coming up from Angel City to take Graham's spot. A troll who's been a lieutenant in vice for the past thirty-seven years."

"A troll?" I repeated. "From vice? Angel City?"

"I know," said Littlecrow. "I have a feeling that he's going to make you miss Graham."

"Hey," I said. "You never know. Maybe we'll wind up being good pals."

"Sure," said Littlecrow. "Why not?"

***

I had Lubank's raincoat cleaned and drove up to his office to return it to him. When she saw me walk in, Gracie put her cigarette in her ashtray and said, "Hi, sweetie! Have you come to sweep me off my feet and take me away from all this?"

"Yeah, baby," I said. "I'm rich enough to afford you now."

Gracie giggled. "You won't be so rich once Robby presents you with his bill. I'm typing it up right now, as a matter of fact."

"Hmm," I said. "We'll see about that! Is he in?"

He was, and Gracie sent me into the inner office.

"Th'fuck you want!" said Lubank when I walked in.

"I've got a hand-me-down raincoat for you," I said. "It's too small for me."

"Lord's balls!" said Lubank. "It's about fuckin' time! Come here and sit down. I talked to Fulton this morning."

"How's he doing?" I asked.

"He's pissed at you!" said Lubank.

"What's he so sore about?" I asked.

"What's he so sore about! I don't know. Maybe it has something to do with watching his precious elf cells get swept out to sea. You know, the ones he was gonna pay you a fuckin' fortune for. You think that might be it?"

I shrugged. "There's probably more where those came from."

"Oh, right! He can pick up a few at the corner store." Lubank pointed a finger at my chest. "You need to watch out for Fulton. He really is pissed at you. You promised that you would give that box to him. He says that you had a deal."

"I told him that I would think about it," I said.

"Yeah, well that's not the way he sees it," said Lubank. "He's a dangerous man, Southerland. You need to watch your step."

"He threatened to pin Mila's murder on me," I said. "But he can't do that now. That video clears me."

"He can take away your P.I. license," said Lubank.

"What would be the point? He knows that there's nothing I could give him now. He saw Stonehammer drag the box over the pier. I hear that he's dredging the water for the box, but his chances of finding it are about zero. The water that night was rougher than I've ever seen it. That box is deep in Davy Jones' Locker by now."

"He might do it out of spite," said Lubank. "Trust me. He doesn't like it when things don't go his way. He might be biding his time, but he won't forget. Watch your back! And call me if he gives you trouble. As long as you can pay my fees, of course."

I'd neglected to mention to Lubank that the stem cells weren't in that box anyway. We're associates, and even something like friends when it's convenient. But we have never been close enough for me to share all my secrets with him. Besides, he'd sell his own mother for the right price. The only person he'd never betray is Gracie, and that might be his only uncorrupted virtue.

***

The morning after Leena had rescued me from the pier, I returned with the cooler containing the stem cells. The sky was gray, but the winds had calmed, and the ocean waves, so turbulent the night before, now rippled beneath the wharf and lapped the shore, gentle as a puppy's tongue. I got out of the car, adjusted the brim of my fedora, and pulled my trench coat tight against the morning chill. My wounded shoulder ached in the cold, but I'd been lucky. The bullet had entered my back under my shoulder blade and passed on through, exiting through my upper pectoral muscle without hitting anything too important. I knew that the wounds would soon heal. They might not even leave a scar. I hoped that they would, though. My new healing powers threatened to make me believe that I was invincible, and I needed reminders that I wasn't. I'd seen soldiers enter a battle believing that they were immune from harm, only to find out the hard way how wrong they had been. Most of them were sent home in a box.

I limped toward the wharf. After Leena's elemental dropped us off at the shore, I had dragged myself to the car and driven myself to the emergency room, where they removed the bullet from my hamstring. It was a clean job, and the doctor was surprised to see that it was already on the mend. He attributed it to magic and didn't make a fuss when I checked myself out. I won't be running any marathons in the near future, but I probably wouldn't have done that anyway.

The wharf was littered with the aftermath left by a rampaging medium-sized air elemental. A section of railing on one side of the wharf was demolished, and the debris covered the bloodstained deck. I hadn't known for sure that he would be there, but my instincts told me that he would. The old fisherman stood at the end of the pier, leaning against a part of the railing that hadn't been torn apart when Kraken and Stonehammer crashed through it and plunged into the churning waters. His fishing pole lay against the railing next to him, and a bucket sat on the deck near his feet. He wore a raincoat with a hood, and he didn't turn around, but I knew that he knew I was approaching.

I came up next to him, set the cooler down on the deck, and put my elbows on the railing. We both watched the rippling gray water for about a minute. Without turning his head, the elf asked me in his remarkable voice, "Have you seen the ocean?"

I was confused. "The Nihhonese? It's right in front of us."

"This ocean is just a drop of water," said the elf. "As are you and I."

I knew what he meant then. "I've seen it in dreams," I said. "I was a drop, and I was the ocean."

"What did you think?"

I shrugged. "It was amazing," I said. "Like nothing I've ever felt. But it didn't pay my rent."

The elf turned his head slightly, and I thought I detected the hint of a smile. "I went more than six thousand years without speaking to a human," he said. "Ever since the Great Betrayal. In retrospect, that was a mistake."

I was surprised that I wasn't more affected by the fact that the creature standing next to me was more than a thousand years older than the Great Pyramids. I should have been staggered. But, somehow, I took the revelation in stride. "You seem to be in pretty good shape for someone your age," I said.

That got a good laugh from the elf. "Indeed, indeed," he said, between chuckles. "But I am old, even for one of my race. Only a few of us remember our war against the Dragon Lords, and even fewer still care."

We watched the waters together for another minute. Then I said, "You mentioned the Great Betrayal. Then it's true that humans first supported the elves in the Great Rebellion but then turned against them?"

I didn't think the elf was going to answer me at first, but then he sighed and said, "It's true. It was the elves who discovered the proto-humans in the rainforests of what is now called Ghana. We saw their potential and engineered them into an intelligent and sentient race. You humans became our children, in a sense. But humans have short lives. Individual humans spark into existence and then burn out in a flash. As a consequence, elves never took the time to get to know individual humans. It simply wasn't worth an emotional investment to associate with a creature who spent such a short time on the earth. We looked at humanity as a continuum, rather than as individual parts."

"An ocean, rather than drops of water," I said.

"Precisely," the elf agreed. "And our unwillingness to truly understand humans was our downfall. When the Dragon Lords emerged from Hell and mobilized the trolls, gnomes, dwarfs, and other Hell-spawned creatures, we went to war with them, the war you refer to as the Great Rebellion, which was the name given to the conflict by the winners. Humans fought at our side. Individually, humans aren't strong, but they breed far more rapidly than elves. Their strength was in their numbers, and we elves used those numbers to our advantage. At great cost to the individual humans, unfortunately. A generation of humans endured tremendous losses in the war, and the next generation of humans was far more reluctant to continue suffering those losses. But we elves turned a blind eye to their plight. We had a different perspective, more long-range. As long as *humanity* continued, we were unconcerned with the lives of individual humans. We saw humanity as a continually existing ocean, but humans saw themselves as individual drops of water."

"And so humanity switched sides?" I asked.

"And so humanity switched sides," The elf sighed. "In retrospect, who could blame them?" He stared over the ocean into the distance. "With the massive human armies on their side, the Dragon Lords could no longer be stopped. The genocide followed, and elves were nearly eliminated as a species. But a few of us survived. We went into hiding and concentrated on surviving. And we hated humanity for its betrayal." For the first time, the elf turned to look me in the face. "And most of us still do," he said. "Oh, indeed. Many of the surviving elves and their offspring have perpetrated much evil on humans, and humans are right to fear elves. Only I and a handful of other elves have forgiven humanity for their betrayal and come to understand them to some degree from their own perspective. It is difficult for elves who live for thousands of years to understand that short-lived humans are not responsible for the sins of ancestors who lived hundreds and hundreds of their generations before them. If you were to ever meet another elf, I would advise caution."

I nodded. "But I can trust you, right?"

He smiled, "Oh, I should hope so."

"What did you do to me?" I asked him. "You changed me somehow."

"Hmm? Oh, that. Just a bit of 'elf magic,' you might say. I stimulated some areas in your brain in order to make you a little more aware."

"Aware?" I asked. "I'm not sure that I understand what you mean. I can see at night now. And my vision in general has improved. So has my hearing."

"Yes, that's how your brain interprets your overall enhanced sense of awareness," the elf explained. "You are aware of your surroundings in a way that you've never been before, and your brain interprets this new sense of awareness as better vision, hearing, and other senses that you are more familiar with."

I considered this. It explained my fight with Ten-Inch, the way that I was able to anticipate his moves once I stopped thinking and started trusting my instincts. It also explained my new abilities with elementals, which stemmed from a greater awareness of their presence.

"What about my ability to heal?" I asked.

"That comes from your increased awareness of your body's operation," the elf said. "Your body is now better able to respond to damages inflicted upon it."

"Is this new awareness permanent?" I asked.

"Oh, indeed," said the elf.

"I suppose I should thank you," I said. "I have a feeling that I owe you more than that, though."

The elf looked down at the cooler. "You've repaid most of your debt by retrieving those stem cells," he said. "You've done me a great service."

"What's the story with that stuff?" I asked.

The elf looked out over the ocean again, eyes focused, as if he could see something beyond the horizon. "There is a compound on a small island off the coast of southern Huaxia. An official in Ao Qin's administration has been overseeing a project in this compound. His scientists have been genetically engineering human fetuses by splicing in elf genes. Their objective is to generate a human/elf hybrid, a creature with the strength and abilities of elves, but which would reproduce in great numbers like humans. I can only speculate on the purpose for such a project. Ao Qin is already the most powerful of the Dragon Lords, and my guess is that he wishes to build an army of these human/elf hybrids in order to subjugate the other Lords."

"So these stem cells were going to be used to splice elf genes into human fetuses?" I asked.

"I don't think so," said the elf. "I don't think that these stem cells come from an elf. I believe that they come from an experimental prototype of one of these human/elf hybrids."

I thought about the implications of what the elf was telling me. If these cells came from a successfully engineered hybrid, then it sounded as if the project was pretty far along. How soon would we be seeing hordes of laboratory-generated super-soldiers pouring out of the Huaxian Empire?

"How did these cells wind up in a smuggling boat?" I asked.

"I have some contacts in Huaxia," said the elf. "I received a report that these cells were coming secretly to Tolanica via Yerba City. My belief is that Ketz-Alkwat found out about the project and arranged to have these cell samples smuggled out of the compound. He may want the samples so that he can expose

Ao Qin's project. Or maybe he wants to try to duplicate the project for himself. I'm not sure."

"So Graham was working for Lord Ketz?"

The elf smiled. "Only indirectly. He was contracted by your Mayor Teague, who himself was contracted by someone higher up. Neither of them had any idea of what they were acquiring or its ultimate destination. They were working strictly for the 'dough,' as you would say."

I had suspected as much. "And what are *you* going to do with the cells?"

"I and some others will study them," said the elf. "We want to see how far the project has progressed. What we do after will depend on many things." He smiled at me. "Let's just say that a few of us are holding out hope that we can bring the reign of the Dragon Lords to an end someday."

I shook my head. "Well, good luck with that. I'm just a local private investigator. I'm not too concerned with who rules the world. One boss is as good as any other, as far as I'm concerned."

The elf picked up his pole and began to reel in his line. "There are great machinations at work in the world," he said. "Beyond your ability to imagine. Large gears turn smaller gears, which turn still smaller gears. Each little cog plays an essential role. Our association may be finished. Or I may return and ask you to attend to a small matter from time to time. I hope that you will consider any matter that I might bring to you."

"I'll always be willing to listen," I said. "I still think that I owe you."

The elf picked up the cooler in one hand and his empty bucket with the hand that already held the pole. He smiled at me and nodded.

The next thing I remember was gazing out over the ocean. I had the impression that only a few minutes had passed since I saw the elf holding his belongings and nodding his goodbye. I didn't remember the elf leaving, and for a confused second or two I wondered if our entire encounter had been a hallucination.

But the cooler was nowhere to be seen, so I assumed that our conversation had really happened.

    I stood at the end of the pier for another half hour, leaning against the railing and watching the waves roll in. The clouds began to break up, and the sun made its first appearance of the day. I wondered if I would ever see the elf again, hoping that I would. The world is filled with problems, large and small, most above my pay grade. Like I told the elf, I'm just a local P.I., trying to find a place to park the car and to keep from getting behind on the rent. I can't solve the big stuff, the kind of shit that involves Dragon Lords, and underground networks of seven-thousand-year-old elves, and grand schemes carried out by mad scientists in mysterious secret compounds. Maybe those problems can't be solved. But knowing that any small problems I have a hand in dealing with might turn some gears and have an impact on the world's bigger headaches, well, that gives me some hope. As purposes in life go, it's not much, but it will have to do.

The End

Books in this Series

Alexander Southerland, P.I.

Book One: *A Troll Walks into a Bar*

Book Two: *A Witch Steps into My Office*

Book Three (coming Spring 2021): *A Hag Rises from the Abyss*

THANK YOU!

Thank you for reading this book. If you enjoyed it, I hope that you will consider writing a review—even a short one—on Amazon, Goodreads, BookBub, or your favorite book site. Publishing is still driven by word of mouth, and every single voice helps. I'm working hard to bring Alex Southerland back, and knowing that readers might be interested in hearing more about his adventures in Yerba City will certainly speed up the process!

ABOUT THE AUTHOR

Dr. Douglas Lumsden is a former history professor and private school teacher. He lives in Monterey, California with his wife, Rita, and his cat, Cinderella.

More Alexander Southerland

As a bonus, please enjoy this preview of *A Witch Steps into My Office: A Noir Urban Fantasy Novel*, the second book in the Alexander Southerland, P.I. series. Enjoy!

A Witch Steps into My Office:
A Noir Urban Fantasy Novel

Chapter One

Yerba City was into its third morning of a rare heat wave when a witch stepped into my office.

"Mr. Southerland?" the witch asked from the open doorway.

I rose from my faux leather office chair. "Yes, ma'am. Please come in."

As the witch closed the door behind her and crossed the room to my desk, I took note of the colorful snake tattoos whose tails coiled around each of her moccasined feet and on up her gams before they disappeared under her chic apricot sun dress. She sat down in one of the chairs I provided for clients and crossed her legs, causing the hem of her dress to rise above her knees and expose another inch and a half of the two coiled serpents. I spent a few moments admiring the exquisite detail of the skin art. The snakes seemed to be shaded in darkness, with the scaled red, yellow, and black rings reflecting a pale glow, as if the creatures had been caught on camera crawling up the witch's body on a moon-lit night. It was remarkable work. I couldn't stop myself from wondering where the snakes' heads might be resting.

The witch waited for me to sit down and said, without preamble, "A man is going to die this afternoon at precisely 1:30 p.m. I will be the cause of his death. Do you mind if I smoke?"

"Go ahead." I indicated a clean ashtray on my desk. "Are you saying that you are going to kill him?"

The witch pulled a homemade cigarette and a lighter from her purse and shrugged. "I already have. He just hasn't died yet."

I waited while the witch lit her cigarette with the silver lighter. Silver, as in made of pure silver, not simply silver in color. I know the difference. She put the lighter away in her purse, drew in some smoke, and breathed blue-gray haze into the air above my desk. The haze drifted up toward a ceiling fan that, despite spinning at its highest setting, did precious little to disturb the warm dank air that hung in my office like a wet shroud.

The witch watched me and waited. I was struck by her lack of urgency.

I glanced at the clock on my desk. "It's 9:30."

The witch took another drag off her cig. I caught a whiff of something sweet blended in with the tobacco.

"Shouldn't we try to stop this man from dying?"

The witch shrugged. "There's nothing we can do, Mr. Southerland. If his death could be stopped, I would have already stopped it."

"And, to be clear, you are the cause of his impending death?"

She sighed, but didn't frown. "Yes. It's very unfortunate." She tapped her cigarette on the side of my ashtray, and a quarter-inch of spent ash dropped from the tip into the tray.

"Any reason I shouldn't be calling the cops about now?"

She stopped in the midst of raising her cigarette to her lips, and her eyebrows arched. "Whatever for?" she asked, mystified by my suggestion.

"I don't know. To have you arrested for murder?'

The witch's lips parted in a smile that reached the corners of her dark eyes. Her arched eyebrows relaxed. "Oh please, Mr. Southerland. Do you know who I am?"

I took a good look at the woman seated across the desk from me. She was a polished-up dame of indeterminate age. The silver streaks in her dark auburn hair, tied in a thick bun, said middle age, maybe mid-forties. But her smooth caramel face, free of all but the faintest of creases, suggested that the silver in her hair might be premature. Early thirties, then, one might conclude. Her nose was flat, her lips thin, her cheekbones high, and the irises of her eyes almost black, so that the pupils were difficult to distinguish. Not a face you would see gracing the cover of a glamor magazine, but an attractive face nonetheless. In a similar way, her body was more elegant than beautiful. She was neither thin nor stout, and I guessed that she was no more than five feet tall in bare feet. Besides the twin serpents winding their endless way up her legs to who knows where, colorful tattoos of flowers, spiders, and birds covered every visible inch of skin that was exposed by the sleeveless sun dress, including her arms and the backs of her hands. Only her face and the palms of her hands were free of ink. More than her appearance, though, it was the way she moved that caught my attention. She had swept into my office with an ephemeral grace, as if she were a mere projection of light, or a hologram. Or, perhaps, a bodiless spirit. I had a sudden urge to reach out and touch her shoulder just to ensure that it was substantial, but I resisted, proving once again that, reports to the contrary notwithstanding, I was still a gentleman.

I knew who she was all right. I had recognized her the moment that she stepped through the door. Everyone in Yerba City knew the infamous Citlali Cuapa. Dubbed the "Barbary Coast Bruja" by a long-dead newspaper columnist some fifty or sixty years ago, Madame Cuapa was the most powerful witch in western Tolanica, and she was much older—and infinitely more dangerous—than she appeared.

"Madame Cuapa, maybe we should start from the beginning."

"Of course." The witch placed her cigarette in a slot on my ashtray and let it smolder unattended. "Exactly one week ago, I placed a curse on a man named Donald Shipper. He's the general manager of Emerald Bay Mortgage, one of the many subsidiaries of Greater Olmec International. I, as you no doubt know, am the CEO of Greater Olmec, a holding company that was started by my father more than a hundred years ago. The curse is a powerful one. It will culminate in Shipper's death this afternoon at, as I said, precisely 1:30."

"I see," I nodded, more to show that I was listening than because I actually understood what she was telling me. "And why did you put the whammy on Mr. Shipper?"

The witch sighed, and this time her sigh was accompanied by a frown. "Now there's the problem. I don't know. I didn't wake up that morning knowing that I was going to do it, and afterwards I didn't know why I had done it. I hadn't been thinking about Shipper at all that morning. He's not a man who is often on my mind. I simply got out of bed, walked into my lab, put the necessary ingredients together, conducted the ritual—it's an unusually powerful one—and set the proper elements into motion. I was aware of what I was doing, but I had no idea why I was doing it, nor did I question what I was doing *while* I was doing it. It's a ritual that I haven't performed in decades, and one that I never thought I'd ever perform again. And yet it seemed as right and natural as drinking my morning coffee. It was only when I had finished the ritual that I thought to ask what had just happened. Very odd. And very, *very* unsettling."

"Uh-huh. And what did you do next?" I asked.

"I tried to reverse the spell, of course," answered the witch. "But my mind wouldn't respond to my desire. It was then that I realized I was under a compulsion."

"What do you mean?"

"I mean that I was forced in an unnatural way to curse Mr. Shipper, and I am unable to gather up the will to undo the curse." She reached for her cigarette, and for the first time I detected a trace of agitation in her demeanor, just the slightest break in her self-assurance. It passed in an instant. Her hand was steady as she smoked her cigarette, and her strange dark eyes were cool as she regarded me across my desk.

Meeting those eyes was a disorienting experience. At a shade over six-one and a solid two-ten, I was a giant compared to the woman seated across from me. Even in my shirt and tie, I was not what anyone would consider to be a picture of refinement and sophistication. My mug has been referred to by polite people as more rugged-looking than handsome, something I've learned to live with seeing as how I have little practical choice in the matter. As a private investigator, I've found that passing myself off as a tough guy can be good for business. It tends to make my clients feel like they've found the right man for the job, especially when the job borders on, or crosses over into, the shadier side of life. My life has not been pretty. I've seen action in the thick of the Dragon Lord's border war against the Qusco insurgents, where I killed enemy combatants and watched them kill my fellow grunts. I gained the respect of the baddest streetfighter in the City by taking him on in front of his gang in brutal hand-to-hand combat, rising out of a pool of my own blood to batter him into submission. I once went toe-to-toe in this very office with a murderous troll twice my size, and, although I was forced to take the run-out (he *was* a troll, after all), I gave as good as I got and left him bleeding before I scrammed out of there. By most accounts, I'm a dangerous individual. But Madame Citlali Cuapa, all five-feet nothing of her, showed no signs of tension or discomfort whatsoever as she sized me up with her coal black peepers. She sat in her flimsy sun dress, legs crossed, demure as a schoolgirl, and showed as much fear of me as a sated cat in the company of a canary. And yet, I knew that underneath her appearance of unshakeable serenity, this powerful lady was troubled. Something had happened to her—something unfathomable—and, for perhaps the first time in her storied life, she was faced with a problem that appeared to be beyond her incredible resources. So she had come to me, an ordinary private dick, for help. As unruffled as she appeared, I knew that she must be desperate.

"Madame Cuapa," I began. She waited. "I've read about you. They say that you are the preeminent practitioner of native Nahuatl magic in Yerba City."

Madame Cuapa's face remained impassive. "I would say in the entire west of Tolanica, at least. In fact, when it comes to the practice of brujería I have few rivals anywhere." She smiled. "The Barbary Coast Bruja, right? It's a well-earned title, believe me."

"And yet you say that you were forced, against your will, to conduct a ritual that is going to result in the death of this Mr. Shipper."

"That's right."

"And you are powerless to stop it."

"Also correct."

"How is this possible?" I asked.

Madame Cuapa took a quick puff from her cigarette and placed it in the ashtray. "I've come up with three possibilities. First, someone with an enormous amount of strength, perhaps more than my own, has overpowered my defenses. Second, someone unknown to me has uncovered a spell of compulsion against which I have no defense." She paused. I waited.

"Third," she continued at last. "Third, it's possible that I'm doing this to myself. It's possible...." She enunciated her words with care. "It's possible that I've lost control of my own mind." The witch's impassive expression hardened. "I *truly* hope that this is not the case. If it is, the consequences could be extremely dire."

"How dire?" I asked.

The witch took a final puff on her cigarette and crushed it out in the ashtray. "Are you familiar with the term, 'extinction event,' Mr. Southerland?"

I rolled this concept around for several long moments. She let me. The leaden air in the room was causing beads of sweat to trickle down my forehead and into my eyes. I took a handkerchief from the breast pocket of my suit and wiped my brow. I folded it and returned it, quite damp now, to my pocket. Madame Cuapa, in contrast, appeared to be as cool as a daisy in spring. No evidence of perspiration. Not even a glow. She was waiting for me to break the silence, so I did. "You're that powerful?"

The witch smiled with some amusement. "A television news host once tried to frighten his audience by declaring that I could destroy an entire battalion of soldiers with the wave of my hand. Sadly, that isn't true. But with my abilities and the resources at my disposal, I could, if I wanted to, set events into motion that would eventually wipe out whole populations and make the planet all but uninhabitable. It wouldn't be that hard, actually. Our governments control technology that could do the same thing." She shrugged. "Do you realize how precarious life is for thinking creatures? It's a fact that we live only at the sufferance of ruling authorities, both earthly and unearthly. There are many who encourage rebellion against the rule of the seven Dragon Lords, but it is only due to their firm guidance that many deadly forces—natural and unnatural—are safely contained, at least for now. There are enough storehouses of massively destructive weapons—nuclear bombs, chemical and bioweapons, cursed artifacts, and so forth—to bring about the permanent extinction of all life on this planet many times over. The Dragon Lords and their subordinate rulers stockpile these weapons and wave them at each other from time to time in order to show that crossing certain lines would cause mutually assured destruction, and this threat has so far produced a surprising geopolitical stability. But a ritual here, a few billion spent there, and it would be an easy matter for me to upset the applecart and, to mix my metaphors, send blood spilling everywhere. And then there is the matter of environmental conditions, which are about as balanced as a tightrope walker on a spider's thread in a windstorm. Do you realize that if the average temperature of the planet rose or fell by just a handful of degrees over an extended period of time all sentient life would be destroyed? Tipping that balance would be child's play for me. For that matter, even for hundreds, maybe thousands, of gifted fools who are less skilled than me. When you think about it, it's a miracle that we've lasted as long as we have."

The witch laid this all out for me in a calm, reasonable voice. These weren't the deluded ravings of a fanatic or some conspiracy nut with an internet blog. I knew that everything she was telling me was true, and that she knew that I knew the score. I guess at heart we all do. And yet, somehow we muddle along, ignoring and even denying the dangers, making the best of things while we still can. Rather than let myself get swept away by the big picture, I tried to keep myself focused on things that I could do something about.

"What you're telling me is that you'd like me to get to the bottom of your current dilemma before it gets out of hand. Specifically, you need me to find out who or what is causing you to perform dangerous rituals that you never intended to perform."

Madame Cuapa nodded. "Exactly, Mr. Southerland. I'll give you access to whatever information and whatever resources you need to do the job, and, of course, I'll pay you well. I'd like you to, as you say, get to the bottom of this as soon as possible. As you can probably imagine, I'm not comfortable with the idea of not being fully in control of my mind and actions."

Nicely understated. Not for the first time, I marveled at Madame Cuapa's show of calm. I could only imagine the inner turmoil that she was holding at bay behind those cool dark eyes.

"I understand." I wiped sweat off the corner of my lip and nodded at her. "But I still think we need to start by doing something about this Mr. Shipper. He's not dead yet, and we still have..." I glanced at the digital clock on my desk, "nearly four hours to keep it that way."

The witch shook her head. "No, Mr. Southerland. Shipper isn't the issue. His death is inevitable. The issue is finding the cause of the compulsion that has overwhelmed my will. You need to concentrate your time and attention on that."

I shifted in my chair and rubbed the stubble on my chin with the palm of my hand. "I'm sorry, Madame Cuapa. But I can't stand around and allow someone to die if there is any way at all that I can prevent it from happening."

"There isn't."

I continued, "Nor can I let his death go unpunished."

"You will."

I had nothing to say to that. This lady might be a big deal in her own world, but she had come to me, and, when it came to doing my job, I made the rules. I felt steam beginning to build in my head. It must have shown in my eyes, because Madame Cuapa uncrossed her tattooed gams and leaned forward an inch. "Mr. Southerland." Her voice was quiet, but her tone was hard. "I realize that you are feeling a little frustrated by all this. I'm aware of your capabilities, your career, and much else about you. I probably know things about you that even you are unaware of. About what kind of man you are, who you are inside. I'm a very perceptive person, not to mention a very well-informed one. I know that you are a man who believes strongly in justice, a rare thing in this unjust world. I know that until several months ago, you were a mediocre elementalist with an affinity for the spirits of air. I know that your mastery over air elementals increased suddenly at about the same time that you had a rare and secret meeting with an elf, a creature that most people believe to be extinct. Until this encounter, you were beneath my notice, but I've had an eye on you ever since. It's no accident that I came to *you* this morning rather than to someone else. But I hope that I haven't misjudged you. Believe me when I tell you that Mr. Shipper is an odious little man, loved by no one, not even by his wife and children. He's been a useful tool, but he's nobody special. The world will hardly notice his passing, and it might actually benefit in some ways by it. Yet if I thought for one second that you could prevent this fool's death, I'd encourage you to do so. But you can't. It isn't possible. Forget about Shipper. Move on."

In that moment, I formed a plan. My office was situated in an innocuous two-story free-standing rental located just outside of the more fashionable parts of downtown Yerba City. A staircase behind my desk crossed diagonally up my back wall and led to my living quarters on the second floor. A door on the side wall to the right of my desk and beneath the top of the staircase opened into a hallway that led out to an alley in the back of my building. From this hallway, I had access to a laundry room, which, after I bought a few free weights and hooked a heavy bag to the ceiling a few months earlier, had begun to double as a home workout center. My plan was to take a set of handcuffs out of my desk drawer, physically overpower and cuff the tiny dame sitting on the other side of my desk, brace her to a thick pipe in the laundry room, and then quickly find Mr. Shipper and prevent him from dying. After that, I would call the coppers, bring them back to my office, and give them the person who had tried to murder Shipper, albeit unwillingly, if Madame Cuapa's story was to be believed. After that, justice would be a matter for others to sort out, but my conscience would be clear.

I've had worse plans, but probably none that fell apart so fast. I never even got my desk drawer open. As I reached for it, I found myself falling headlong into a black pit. All semblance of light vanished in an instant. I felt myself plunging into nothingness, accelerating at an alarming rate. Within seconds I was falling too fast to survive the end of it. As I dropped faster and faster, I reached out in desperation for something to grab onto, knowing that even if I succeeded my arms would be ripped from their sockets. Finally, I curled into a ball and braced myself for an impact that I would never feel. My mind began to go black.

And then I was seated once again in my desk chair as if nothing had happened. The witch, legs crossed once again, sat composed with a hint of an amused smile on her plain, supernaturally youthful face.

"Satisfied, Mr. Southerland?" she asked me.

"I get it. I can't touch you."

"Well, not without my permission," she drawled, and I could swear that she was flirting with me. Just a little. I told myself that she was just enjoying her little show of dominance. That seemed more likely.

"Okay. But I still have to try to prevent Mr. Shipper's death. At least tell me where I can find him."

"Such a stubborn man. Oh very well." The witch sighed with a dramatic show of resignation. "But be quick about it. I need you to focus on solving my problem. He'll be at his office. It's not far from here, although the traffic is going to be miserable, and as for parking, well...." She waved her hand and snorted her dismissal. She gave me the address for Emerald Bay Mortgage, which was located in the upper floors of an office building on Market Street. "His weekly managers' meeting is scheduled for one o'clock this afternoon. The purpose of the meeting is to show the department managers who work for him that he has the authority to call such a meeting and to require them to attend. They'll file in by 1:10 or so, pour themselves drinks, light up cigarettes, and wait for Shipper to make his grand entrance at about 1:15. He'll make some small talk, and then at about 1:20, he'll bring the meeting to order. He'll yammer on about inconsequential matters that he's suddenly decided are important. And then, at 1:30 p.m., he'll die. You can look up his phone number online if you want to make an appointment. I doubt that you'll get to him that easily, but go ahead and do your best. You're a private eye: maybe you can come up with a clever disguise or some scam that will do the trick."

She was giving me the rib now, but I was thinking about the dozens of ways that I might be able to gain quick access to a self-important executive who was apparently an asshole and who had no logical reason to see me on short notice.

"I'm curious, though," Madame Cuapa continued. "If you manage to see him, what will you do? The ritual has been performed, and the curse has been unleashed. Nothing can stop

Shipper from dying at the appointed time. Believe me, if I can't stop it, neither can you."

I thought about this. "You said earlier that you tried to reverse the whammy, but couldn't summon the will to do so. Could somebody else reverse it?"

Madame Cuapa shook her head. "Sorry, but no. Naturally, I had the same idea. But the ritual involved using some of my own blood and a pact with a certain unearthly power. A particularly nasty one. The reversal would also require my blood, which the compulsion would not allow me to give up even if I wanted to, which I don't, and the pact can only be broken by an agreement by the original participants. The compulsion will not allow me to cooperate. Good question, though. You're sharp, I'll give you that."

I thought some more. "This unearthly power.... Could anyone else persuade him to act independently of you? Get him to retract his claws, or whatever is involved here? Maybe give him something that would make it worth his while?"

"Another good question! I think I like you!" Madame Cuapa, smiled. "Sadly, it's more complicated than that. The...spirit, let's call him...has already set in motion the forces that will result in Shipper's death. It's hard to explain, but time doesn't work the same for these unearthly powers as it does for us. The spirit's work is done, and he doesn't have to actually do anything further at this point."

"But could he prevent the death in some way?" I persisted.

"In theory, yes," Madame Cuapa agreed. "But the spirit would almost certainly require another death in Shipper's place. That's how these things generally work. And if someone has to die, well, better a lowlife like Shipper than pretty much anyone else."

"Would this spirit accept another form of compensation, other than someone's death?"

"Only something even more undesirable, I suspect." Madame Cuapa wrinkled her nose, as if she'd just sucked a lemon.

"Such as?"

"Such as my unending servitude. And I'm not willing to become his eternal slave."

I did some silent brainstorming, but the witch quickly interrupted my thoughts, as if she had been listening in. "Yes, you could try to seek the aid of another practitioner, get him or her to intercede with the spirit, or with another, more powerful spirit, and try to prevent the curse from taking effect. It won't work. Do you suppose that you were the first person I contacted for help? I've already consulted with my most trusted peers, and I'm sure that word of my troubles has spread to the rest of the witching world. There's nothing any of them can do, or would do if they were willing. No one with the power to help you will agree to do so. You can't imagine the risks in interfering with matters like this."

"And yet, you want me to get the dope on who or what is behind it all. Doesn't that carry some risk?"

"I'd be lying if I said otherwise," Madame Cuapa admitted. "But you seem like a capable fellow, and I'll help as much as I can." She hesitated. "Did I mention that I'll pay you well? Some of that will be what you might call 'hazard pay.'"

I took another look at my clock and pulled my phone from my breast pocket.

"All right," Madame Cuapa sighed. "You've got a conscience and you feel obligated to try to save Shipper's life. I suppose I have to let you." She stood. "Walk me out first. After you've failed to prevent Shipper's death, call me. I have an assistant outside who will give you my card and a retainer. You'll be wanting more information from me, and I'll give you whatever I can." She waited for me.

I put my phone back in my pocket and stood. I came around my desk, and the witch placed her hand on my arm as I walked her to my door. It was an oddly intimate gesture. I reminded myself that this wasn't some ordinary bit of fluff and couldn't help wondering whether she was syphoning away some of my life's energy, or something like that. I think that I might have trembled slightly at her touch, because she looked up at me from more than a foot below and gave me a wry smile. "Don't worry, big guy. I won't bite you. Not yet, at least."

We went outside. A beige luxury SUV that cost more dough than I earned in a typical year was waiting for Madame Cuapa in front of my building. I wondered how she had managed to secure such a prime parking spot on a weekday morning, but quickly dismissed the thought. I probably didn't want to know. Standing on the sidewalk in front of the SUV was a young jasper with a smirking grin and a thick mane of jet-black hair that fell below his shoulders. His eyes were hidden by a pair of cheaters with black rims and black lenses. A gold short-sleeved silk shirt, unbuttoned nearly to his waist, exposed a pair of tattooed biceps the size of bowling balls and a thick hairless chest that was nearly as broad as a troll's. One thumb was hooked in the pocket of a pair of skin-tight dark brown leather trousers that no sane person would wear on a day that was as hot as this one was shaping up to be unless he was trying to impress somebody special or the world at large. Gripped in his other hand was an iron chain. The chain was attached to an iron collar. The collar was around the neck of a creature that I had heard of, but never before seen. The beast stood on four massive legs, the top of its head even with the man's chest. Each of its paws was the size of my head. Yellow eyes glared at me from a fierce lion's face, surrounded by a spiky mane. Leathery black wings were folded against the big cat's powerful body, which was reddish brown with black tiger's stripes. The long segmented tail of the beast arched upwards over its back and was capped by a horned shell that narrowed to a pointed scorpion's barb. I stopped in my tracks and turned to the witch at my arm.

"Is that a manticore?" I asked.

"Magnificent, isn't he?" Madame Cuapa looked up at me. "Do what you must to help Mr. Shipper, but then find out why I am compelled to commit acts against my will." Her dark eyes flared. "It does not benefit the world for my mind to be outside of my conscious control."

I turned to gaze into the manticore's feral eyes and nodded.